AN ALL-NEW ORIGINAL NOVEL OF THE MARVEL UNIVERSE

DEVIN GRAYSON

MARVEL

AN ALL-NEW ORIGINAL NOVEL OF THE MARVEL UNIVERSE

DEVIN GRAYSON

MARVEL

DOCTOR STRANGE: THE FATE OF DREAMS PROSE NOVEL. Published by MARVEL WORLDWIDE, INC., a subsidiary of MARVEL ENTERTAINMENT, LLC. OFFICE OF PUBLICATION: 135 West 50th Street, New York, NY 10020. Copyright © 2016 MARVEL

ISBN 978-0-7851-9987-8

Printed in the U.S.A.

ALAN FINE, President, Marvel Entertainment; DAN BUCKLEY, President, TV, Publishing & Brand Management; JOE QUESADA, Chief Creative Officer; TOM BREVOORT, SVP of Publishing; DAVID BOGART, SVP of Business Affairs & Operations, Publishing & Partnership; C.B. CEBULSKI, VP of Brand Management & Development, Asia; DAVID GABRIEL, SVP of Sales & Marketing, Publishing; JEFF YOUNGQUIST, VP of Production & Special Projects; DAN CARR, Executive Director of Publishing Technology; ALEX MORALES, Director of Publishing Operations; SUSAN CRESPI, Production Manager; STAN LEE, Chairman Emeritus. For information regarding advertising in Marvel Comics or on Marvel.com, please contact Vit DeBellis, Integrated Sales Manager, at vdebellis@marvel.com. For Marvel subscription inquiries, please call 888-511-5480. **Manufactured between 8/12/2016 and 9/19/2016 by SHERIDAN, CHELSEA, MI, USA.**

First printing 2016
10 9 8 7 6 5 4 3 2 1

Cover art by Kevin Nowlan
Interior art by Chris Bachalo, Rafa Sandoval, Wayne Faucher, Mark Irwin, John Livesay, Jaime Mendoza, Victor Olazaba, Tim Townsend, and Al Vey

Special Thanks to
Jeff Christiansen, Mike Fichera, Kevin Garcia, Mike O'Sullivan, Roger Ott, and Marc Riemer

Joan Hilty, Editor
Design by Jay Bowen

VP, Production & Special Projects: Jeff Youngquist
Associate Editor: Sarah Brunstad
SVP Print, Sales & Marketing: David Gabriel
Editor in Chief: Axel Alonso
Chief Creative Officer: Joe Quesada
Publisher: Dan Buckley
Executive Producer: Alan Fine

For Arnold, with love.

Thanks for always believing.

AN ALL-NEW ORIGINAL NOVEL OF THE MARVEL UNIVERSE

DOCTOR STRANGE

THE FATE OF DREAMS

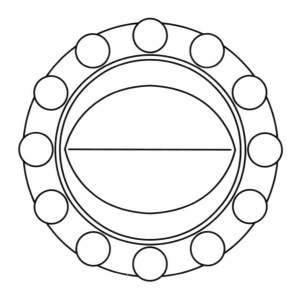

BOOK

1

PROLOGUE

JANE Bailey stood near the edge of a high, red cliff watching Alexander the Great's tank division maneuver into a defensive position. The sun was glaringly bright, the air thin and dry, and the young king himself stood so close Jane could have touched him. He was violently beautiful: tall and olive-skinned, his muscles taut under a bright white tunic. She admired the way his cropped hair had started to grow out into a crown of golden curls as she fiddled with the zipper of her anorak.

At the bottom of the cliff, flanking the tanks in front of an enormous wrought iron gate, stood soldiers wearing gleaming gold chest plates over blood-red tunics. There were rows and rows of them, shoulder to shoulder—a hundred deep, a thousand. Though most were furnished with long spears—the word *doru* came to Jane from somewhere far away—the fighters closest to the gates held a large battering ram. Alexander lifted a hand high above his head. From Jane's position, it blotted out the sun.

She turned away and found herself face-to-face with a woman who clearly wasn't human. The stranger was too large and too hazy; only her head, hands, and arms were distinctive, the rest of her streaming away like sand in hot trade winds. Her hair was a luminous cyan, her face ghostly and terrifying and yet theatrically beautiful—sharp and expressive. She had eyes as black as the universe and filled with the glimmer of distant stars.

"The Pathways have fallen!" the woman said triumphantly in a voice so loud Jane felt it rattle her teeth. "At last we are free to advance!"

Jane at first assumed the woman was speaking to her, but then realized that she had to be addressing Alexander's army. Glancing over her shoulder, she saw that the exclamation had also been heard by a severe 20-something man just behind her. He wore an oversized camouflage Army coat and had a peach-fuzz mustache, stubble on his jaw, and an HK416 slung over one shoulder. Though he was standing near Jane, he was clearly separated from Alexander both temporally and geographically. Jane stood between them: one foot on the hot, flat pavement of the young man's world; the other on Alexander's dusty plateau. Though it was also possible that she was in both places. Or neither.

The gunman turned and strode grimly toward a mall that had materialized a short distance away from him, and Jane began to worry for the people milling just outside it. At the same moment, Alexander dropped his hand with a shouted command, his green eyes sharp and avid as he looked out over his army.

"Open the gate!"

To Jane's right, the soldiers began to batter the gate. To her left, the man in the Army coat opened fire outside the mall. The sound was deafening: the clanging blows of the battering ram, the repeated explosion of gunpowder. Jane wanted to run but couldn't move, wanted to hide or close her eyes but could only watch as the gate crumpled and finally swung open, letting out a stampeding horde of the most horrific monsters she had ever seen. They were mutated amalgamations of childhood fears: giant skittering spiders with the torsos of dagger-clawed bugbears, marching skeletons with eyes of blazing fire, amorphous shadows of obliterating darkness, alien ghouls with gaping maws full of gleaming fangs…all of them swarming across the desert basin. Alexander's soldiers had dashed behind the tanks for protection, but the monsters ignored them. Even so, Jane felt sure the strange creatures would devour everything and anyone else in their path.

At the same time, to Jane's left, the people at the mall screamed and ran and dove behind trash cans and held each other in terror. The man in the Army coat continued advancing at a slow, steady pace, his gun ceaselessly hammering away. Tears streamed down Jane's face, but the woman with the blue hair wiped them away. "Do not cry," she said sweetly. "This is a glorious day. This is *my* day—my destiny!—and I will lead you from the shadows by my example, as I should have from the start!"

Jane turned away from the woman and found herself facing an old bearded man in a white wool toga and open-toed sandals. His eyes, perhaps once blue, had turned milky white with cortical cataracts. Jane knew she'd seen him before but couldn't remember where or when.

"Tell him it's you!" the man said urgently. He reached up and touched her face with dry, gentle hands, feeling across the shape of her features. "It is you, isn't it? You must be sure. You must have him bring you to Healing—only then will you know your path!"

It began to rain. The old man reached into his toga and pulled out a knife. Jane recognized it as the hunting knife her father had given her for her 19th birthday. She took it cautiously from his hand.

"It was science that eroded the Pathways, so don't be afraid to draw blood—but just a little cut. Only so he'll notice. Her name is Dr. Misra." He moved to go, thoroughly soaked, and then seemed to think better of it. He turned back to Jane and gently touched her arm.

"It won't hurt," he assured her. And then he smiled a beatific, toothless grin. "Tell me the same?"

"It won't hurt," Jane echoed back to him, even though she didn't understand.

The old blind man nodded and patted her arm. "I hope you're right. And I hope you understand...Doctor Strange."

Jane stared down at the knife, pausing only briefly over the mistaken name. Reality had been slipping away from her for months. When it had started, the effects had been simpler: confusion over whether a conversation had actually taken place, emotional hangovers from nightmares that had lasted all day. Later, she found herself grabbing her phone to search for the contact information of a person she knew intimately only to discover that they didn't exist. She lost objects in rooms she could no longer find and regularly performed feats she knew to be impossible. Finally, physics had stopped working altogether. People and places transformed before her eyes, and the continuity of time had utterly shattered. Resisting the chaos only seemed to make it worse, so Jane was doing her best to surrender to the turmoil. It was so confusing she barely had time to wonder whether she was going insane.

When she looked up again, she was standing on the orange carpet in the middle of the basement she used as a bedroom in her mother's Hudson Valley home. It smelled faintly of mold, but it was bigger than the tiny room upstairs she'd used as a girl, and it featured sliding glass doors that opened out into the woods behind the property. She was fully dressed, the hunting knife clutched in one hand. Glancing through the glass doors, she could see that it was light outside, late morning. Raindrops clung to the yellow leaves of the birch trees, just as inside they beaded and sparkled on her oversized green anorak.

She stood completely still for a moment—except for her hazel eyes, which roved the room restlessly until they landed on her phone. She walked over to it, touched the screen with a wet finger, and then absently dried off her hand on the front of her T-shirt.

"Google Dr. Misra," she said to the screen.

Three results came up: a pediatrician, an internist, and a neuroscientist. That part, at least, was easy.

Jane slipped the knife into a buckskin sheath, stuffed it and the phone into an already overfull backpack, and then slipped out the sliding glass doors, closing them behind her as quietly as she could.

CHAPTER 1

"I NEED you to dispel all doubt from your mind. *Believe* that I can bring you through this. Now, take my hand."

Doctor Stephen Strange, Sorcerer Supreme, addressed the figures in the mirror with calm authority. Instead of a reflection, the mahogany-framed rectangular glass showed three men—two uniformed police officers and one very distraught burglar—pressing their hands against the inside of the glass as they stared out imploringly at him. Behind Doctor Strange—just outside the glowing protection circle he'd drawn with arcane energy on the off-white laminate of the briefing-room floor—the burglar's partner, along with a historian from the Merchant's House Museum and most of the Sixth Precinct, watched and waited with bated breath.

Lt. Reynard Bacci took a sip from the mug of coffee in his hand and watched with narrowed eyes as Strange reached through the glass, grasped the burglar's arm, and carefully pulled the 173-pound man out of the three-inch-deep mirror. Behind Bacci, the thief's partner-in-crime exhaled with relief and moved to grab him, but a sharp look from Strange stopped him from stepping into the protection circle. The rescued burglar fell to his knees, babbling with fear and gratitude.

"Thank god! You gotta hurry! There's something in there with them, man, something that ain't happy to have visitors! Those cops're gonna get eaten if you don't get 'em out! Place's got skeletons, man—human skeletons!— in every corner! Something's in there, man, I'm telling you!"

A chorus of alarmed murmurs joined his terrified ranting as the room's occupants reacted to his news.

"You're all right now." Doctor Strange's words were reassuring, but his manner was brusque. "If I could please have another moment of quiet?"

"All right! All right!" The lieutenant waved his coffee cup over everyone's heads. "Pipe down and let the man work!" Turning back to Strange, the tall, gray-haired policeman spoke with obvious esteem. "You just tell me when I can cuff him."

"In a moment," Strange answered distractedly. He reached through the glass again and took the hand of one of the two policemen still inside. "I'd prefer they not leave the circle until I've cleansed them of spiritual residue."

"Sure thing, Doc."

Bacci had taken one look at the cursed mirror and gotten on the phone with Wong, Doctor Strange's assistant—and that was before officers Smith and Hoskin had managed to get themselves trapped inside of it along with the perp. It had all started earlier that afternoon when the perp's accomplice, Gabel, had come running into the precinct in a panic, carrying the mirror— which he had hastily covered up with his windbreaker—and hollering that his friend was trapped inside. He told the desk sergeant that he and his buddy had gotten the cockamamie idea to pull a B&E at the Merchant's House Museum, convinced they could get rich selling small antiques swiped from the National Historic Landmark. In addition to being ill-conceived—the Merchant's House Museum was a beloved city institution tended by a dedicated staff who would surely note missing items almost immediately—it was an oddly ambitious plan for two men whose collective experience with crime didn't extend past shoplifting candy bars. The job had gotten much, much weirder, though, when the one called McHale had "disappeared" into a mirror he'd found hidden away in a trunk on the third floor.

By the time Doctor Strange arrived, Officer Smith had been sucked into the mirror while trying to get McHale out, and Officer Hoskin had been similarly ensnared attempting to free his partner.

Bacci would have preferred to live in a world devoid of supernatural incident, but as it was, he was damn grateful to know the Master of Mystical Arts who lived at 177A Bleecker Street. Though the guy dressed oddly in a blue tunic, black boots, and a flamboyant red cloak, Bacci had always found him remarkably sane—and unfailingly effective. He was apparently some kind of big-shot sorcerer—head honcho of all magic users, if Bacci understood correctly—not to mention supreme defender of the entire planet or, as the doctor himself was more apt to put it, "the mortal realm." Whatever it was that he did, he always made himself available when anyone from the NYPD called him with something they couldn't get their head around, and he'd gotten them out of more than a few jams over the years.

The lieutenant, therefore, had complete confidence in Doctor Strange's ability to get everything back to normal. He leaned against the lectern, took another swig from his cup, and made a face. Damn stuff was getting cold. A gasp from the men around him made him look up again. Strange was holding Hoskin's arm and had him halfway out of the mirror, but a long, black tentacle reached out through the glass to wrap itself around the officer's chest, clearly attempting to pull him back in. A few of the cops pulled out their firearms in alarm. Bacci gestured coolly for them to lower their weapons.

"All right, boys, take it easy. The doc can handle this." Chin nodding in the direction of a particularly jumpy patrolman, Bacci thrust his mug at him.

"You, get me a refill. The rest of you, let the doctor work."

Doctor Strange only frowned and touched the large gold clasp that held his cloak in place. The amulet seemed to open like an eye, instantly bathing the mirror in a radiant, mystical glow. The tentacle unwound itself from around Officer Hoskin's chest and slipped back into the recesses of the mirror, allowing Strange to pull the man free.

"Don't leave the circle," Strange warned McHale and Hoskin over his shoulder as he reached through the mirror one final time to retrieve Officer Smith.

Hoskin nodded, but indicated his partner. "You gotta get him outta there! That thing's got his ankle!"

Doctor Strange's brow furrowed, but he didn't hesitate: He stepped into the mirror, appearing instantly next to Officer Smith on the other side of the looking glass. Bacci squinted again and tried to lean in closer, but couldn't quite make out what was happening. Strange had a hand out, bidding Smith to stand still, and both men had fixed their attention on something happening below the frame. There was a flash of yellow light—it appeared to Bacci to have come from the doctor's hand—and then Strange was helping Officer Smith climb out. As Smith emerged into the briefing room, the sorcerer turned to face something behind him in the mirror, his dark-red cloak obscuring Bacci's view.

Back in the briefing room, Hoskin clasped his friend's shoulder. "You okay, man?"

Smith's eyes were wide, but he nodded. "He sliced it offa me with some kinda laser beam that came outta his hand." He opened his mouth to say something else but was interrupted by the sound of shattering glass.

The mirror had exploded into a million glistening pieces.

The reactions were immediate: Several cops turned their guns toward the detonation as others pushed their fellow officers out of harm's way. Smith and Hoskin dove protectively over McHale as Bacci darted in front of the woman from the museum. He was trying to calculate who was in the blast zone when the mirror fragments froze. They hovered in midair for a full second before rushing back in toward their point of origin, then disappearing into a pinpoint of light from which a pillar of acrid, black smoke suddenly billowed up. Doctor Strange stepped calmly out of the smoke and waved it away. No sign of the mirror—not even a fragment—remained.

Bacci watched the sorcerer's eyes sweep over everyone in the room with something like regret. The radiant, mystical light was still pouring from the eye in Strange's amulet, and he somehow directed it outward with his hands, slowly and deliberately creating a concentric circle that expanded over every person in the briefing room. Without deciding to do so, Bacci took a deep breath as the light washed over him, feeling the adrenaline ebb as a comforting sense of serenity filled his body from head to toe. It seemed to have a similar effect on everyone it touched: Bacci watched the shoulders of his officers settling as they stood up a little straighter, several even sighing as the tension drained away.

The eye in the amulet closed then, and just like that, the light was gone. Strange made a precise gesture with his hand, and the protection circle he'd drawn on the floor faded from sight. He nodded to Bacci. "You may take them into custody now, if you wish." Bacci motioned to Hoskin and Smith, who helped the perps up off the floor and led them out of the room for processing as Strange spoke quietly with the museum historian.

"I apologize, Ms. Hazel, but I was not able to save the artifact. If it's of any comfort, I rather doubt it was an antique. It appeared to me to have been created fairly recently in an attempt to trap the entity within it."

Anne Hazel waved away the doctor's concern. Bacci imagined that, like him, she was caught up in the excitement of having spent a Friday afternoon witnessing such an unusual series of events. "No, it's all right. As I mentioned to the lieutenant, that absolutely wasn't an item belonging to the Tredwells—I'd never seen it before. I have no idea how it came to be in the house. Should we be concerned?"

Strange folded his hands into the recesses of his cloak. "The house has a reputation for being haunted, does it not? Perhaps someone hoped that you would know how to care for the dangerous item they'd created. In any case, no, please don't worry. I'll send one of my colleagues over to do a sweep and make sure no more dangerous objects are hidden in the building."

"Thank you, Doctor."

It seemed to Bacci that Hazel was rather taken with the mysterious sorcerer, and why not? If the cape didn't put you off, he was an attractive man—something of a throwback, the lieutenant mused, to Rat Pack elegance and *savoir faire*. Older than most of the capes-and-tights set you'd occasionally see around the city, Doctor Strange had an air of commanding maturity about him. He was quite obviously a man who had seen things, who knew things. Unfortunately for Hazel, he was also a man with places to be. Clearly determining the threat was over, Strange abruptly excused himself. Bacci followed, stopping to accept the refilled cup of coffee from his patrolman as he walked the doctor out.

"Thanks again for your help, Doc."

"Certainly."

"If there's ever anything we can do for you, you just call, you know?"

"Just be safe."

Bacci nodded, and then remembered that he'd wanted to ask the doctor about something else. "Oh, hey, real quick—I ain't been sleeping too well lately. It's gettin' real bad, messing with my concentration, you know? So I was just wondering. You know any hocus pocus for that?"

Doctor Strange stopped, turned, and looked pointedly at the cup of coffee clutched in the lieutenant's hand.

"Switch to decaf," he said dryly. As Bacci blinked down at the mug, Doctor Strange let himself out of the small brick building and disappeared into the pedestrian traffic of Greenwich Village.

STEPHEN hadn't made it two steps out of the police department before he felt an insistent pressure against the inside of his skull. Though the sensation was an unpleasant one, the presence that attended it was warm and familiar. He dropped the psychic shield—his usual precaution when he left home—and telepathically greeted his assistant, Wong. Though he probably would have looked distracted to anyone watching him, Stephen's lips did not move as he and his friend conversed over the distance of half a mile.

"Yes, Wong? Is all well? I'm leaving the police station now."

"Sorry to interrupt. I just wanted to let you know that we have a visitor."

Stephen stepped off the sidewalk onto a narrow parking ramp between two row houses and a six-story brick apartment building. "I'll be right there." Glancing at the garage entrance to make sure no one was watching, he opened a portal to his living room and stepped through.

Wong, as always, had directed the guest's attention toward the Richter painting, so Stephen was able to enter the room behind them without immediately frightening a stranger with a demonstration of dimensional transportation.

Rubbing his hands, which had started to ache, Stephen tried to hold back the assault of psychic information streaming off the woman standing beside his friend. Wong liked to introduce people as a formality, more for their sake than Stephen's. Stephen cleared his throat, and Wong turned, gently guiding the woman to do the same.

"This is Dr. Sharanya Misra of the Baxter Foundation," Wong began, with a decorous nod to his friend and employer. "Dr. Misra, this is Dr. Stephen Strange."

Stephen smiled, and the woman smiled back, but the pleasantry did not reach her eyes. She appeared to be in her late 20s, her shiny dark-brown hair pulled back from a square-shaped face in a sleek ponytail. Her dark-brown eyes were attentive, her lips pressed together with barely contained skepticism, and Stephen could feel tension and misgivings radiating off her slender frame in waves. Meeting her eyes as they flitted across his face, he was hit with a sharp vision of blood and viscera. She'd recently witnessed some kind of gruesome tragedy, which probably accounted for the tightness through her shoulders and back, not to mention the ten-foot-long Malebranchian psyche-leech burrowed between her shoulder blades. It was twice as thick as a flex duct, with black-spotted, purple-tinged skin and a large sucker mouth.

Casting a quick spell of divination with a barely noticeable flutter of two fingers, Stephen gleaned that she was 32, born in Queens to first-generation immigrants from Karnataka, lived alone, held a doctorate in Neurobiology and Behavior from Columbia, and was running a Baxter Foundation-funded metacognition study at the Ravencroft Institute for the Criminally Insane. She meditated and practiced yoga every morning, spoke Kannada and Hindi as well as English, was in excellent physical health, and had an inordinate fondness for kombucha.

"Welcome to the Sanctum Sanctorum," he said, pulling both hands back into his cloak at the precise moment most people would have thrust one out to shake. Though he had become comfortable enough with the scars that covered them to retire the gloves he had worn throughout the earlier years of his duties as Sorcerer Supreme, Stephen remained self-conscious about the extent to which his hands still trembled. "How might I be of service?"

Dr. Misra fiddled with a silver Ganesh charm bracelet fastened around her left wrist.

"I'm…not sure you *can* help, to be honest. I really shouldn't even be taking up your time, it's just that my mother…" She trailed off, the color in her cheeks rising as she eyed Stephen's nearly floor-length cloak. "She's really into psychics and everything, and I…to be honest, I'm not entirely clear on what you do. It's just…easier to humor her sometimes."

She said the word "psychics" with dismissive humor, and Stephen shared a look with Wong. He was now confident it would have made no difference had he emerged from the portal right in front of her. People were amazingly adept at explaining away the mystical; seeing a man step out of thin air was nothing to someone determined to negate the supernatural. Secret passageways. Mirrors. A trick of the light. Stephen knew from personal experience that once a person had made up their mind not to believe, they could willfully mistake a six-foot Berev'ha Dentii for an overfed hamster. He had been that person once himself.

"I could explore the circumstances surrounding your visit unaided," Stephen admitted, "but many people find such analyses invasive." He lowered his voice slightly, his bright-blue eyes dancing as he met Sharanya's gaze and sought to establish trust. "I know the first time my mind was read, I found it quite disorienting."

That wasn't technically accurate—the first time his mind had been read, he'd been too arrogant to notice—but it was true enough on an emotional level to be worth sharing. He studied the woman's aura as Wong picked up where he'd left off. She was surrounded by a strong field of rich, deep blue, tinged with gray around the edges, reinforcing Stephen's sense of a normally strong and balanced individual coping with a temporary darkness.

"What is it your mother thinks you need help with?" Wong prompted. He had an easy way with guests that Stephen had grown to rely on.

Sharanya winced and dropped her gaze. "There was an…incident at my work. A lot of people died. Quite violently." Her voice had lowered to a hush, and Stephen caught himself leaning forward to better hear her.

"Through supernatural means?" he asked, one eyebrow jutting up in curiosity.

"What?" Sharanya looked up at him with confusion before belatedly comprehending his question and shaking her head. "Oh. No. No, nothing like that. They murdered each other. My research subjects." She spoke haltingly, the psychic trauma of the experience still reverberating within her. But something just beneath that had caught Stephen's attention: a burning need she carried to understand what had occurred. He could tell it wasn't enough for her to know *what* had happened—Sharanya's mind was caught on the why of it, turning the question over again and again, like a tumbler polishing a small stone.

Stephen waited until she looked up at him. "Why don't you start at the beginning?"

Sharanya hesitated, her eyes darting toward the pocket doors of the living room. "Like I said, I'm sure there's nothing you can do. There's nothing for anyone to do; the police have finished their investigation and everyone involved is…"

Dead. In Sharanya's sudden silence, Stephen heard the word as clearly as if she had shouted it. Wong shifted his weight slightly as he stood beside her, gently bringing her attention back to the living. She continued, her speech becoming more and more rapid, as if she was suddenly in a hurry to get the story over with.

"I'm working on a study of metacognition in lucid dreaming at Ravencroft. We have a full Oneirology department and study all kinds of dreams: problem-solving, healing, prophecy, epic, lucid… Anyway, we're looking specifically at how dreaming interacts with behavior—how the dreams of the most violent criminally insane differ from other offenders, for example—and ways we can use dream therapy to guide them away from acting out their psychoses. We have a sleep lab at the Institute, and eight days ago 12 research subjects woke up and…attacked each other. And didn't stop. No one could stop them, there were people there that night who tried, but they…they just kept going until everyone was dead."

Stephen nodded. That explained the psyche-leech; the giant, wormlike psychic parasites were very partial to survivor's guilt. He'd have to remove it before she left the house.

"Twelve people, all snapping at once. I mean, these were violent offenders, but they knew each other—they'd been participating in this study together for months without incident. On the security-feed playback it looked like they all woke up from nightmares at the same time and just…" She stopped to rub her forehead, and Stephen could tell there was something she still wasn't saying. He looked at Wong, who caught his gaze. Stephen knew what he was thinking; the same thought had crossed his mind. Nightmare, a demon who ruled the Dream Dimension realm that bore his name, was one of Stephen's oldest and most dangerous enemies. It was certainly possible that he had had a hand in the events Sharanya was describing. It did not seem possible, though, that Sharanya could have surmised as much.

Though horrific, her story was surprisingly devoid of supernatural danger from a common perspective. Normally people didn't find their way to the Sanctum until they woke up compulsively vomiting flies, their head twisted around 180 degrees. It was true that Sharanya was hosting the psyche-leech, but *she* didn't know that. Her brain wasn't being used as a dimensional breach for an invading demonic army, or as a relay post for paranormal splinter cells. No one was making entire buildings disappear just by walking into them or being harassed by corvids screaming at them in Esperanto. There wasn't even a psychic sinkhole. Stephen had already made up his mind to do everything in his power to help her, but other than removing the psyche-leech—and perhaps initating a chat with Nightmare—he wasn't yet sure what that might be.

Seeming to notice Stephen's distraction, Wong began to question Sharanya about her mother, giving Stephen time to gently probe her mind. As Sharanya clarified how her mother had heard of Doctor Strange's work—apparently he'd helped her grocer's niece with a possession—Stephen closed his eyes and psychically touched her mind with his own, quietly sifting through her memories of the event.

His eyes flew open a second later. Sharanya winced and touched her temple.

"They called my name?" Stephen asked, his tone hard.

"Yes, but how would that even…? It doesn't make sense!" Sharanya was stammering, thrown off by Stephen having uncovered the part of her memory she'd been reluctant to share. Stephen turned to Wong to explain.

"When they woke up, all of her research subjects screamed 'Doctor Strange!' Seconds later, they attacked each other."

"How do you know that?" Sharanya seemed to be oscillating between curiosity and consternation, her eyes wide and her fists clenched. She turned to Wong, desperate to articulate a version of reality that made sense to her. "Maybe they were just calling for me or one of the other doctors and saying that they felt strange. I mean, yes, it's true, they all said it the same way: 'doctor strange!' But they could have been referring to anything, right?"

Wong smiled at her enigmatically. "Simpler explanations are generally better than more complex ones. Even when you don't understand them."

Sharanya shook her head at Wong. "So he's reading my mind, and you're quoting Occam's razor to me. You're right, I don't understand any of this."

"My work frequently intersects with other realms," Stephen said, by way of explanation. "It's possible that these individuals were made to speak with the voice of an alien entity intent on getting my attention. That's potentially a good sign, as it implies a willingness to cooperate." As he spoke, Stephen pulled his hands free of his cloak and discreetly drew a sedation ward across the back of the psyche-leech with the index finger of his left hand. To those inexperienced in magic, it would read as a distracted hand twitch. "My guess is that what you've experienced is an echo of a larger imbalance in a neighboring dimension."

And are there many of those?" Sharanya asked, her voice pitched somewhere between derision and wonder. "Neighboring dimensions?"

Stephen met her eyes, wondering how much she really wanted to know. There were thousands of them—aggressive and predatory and ever-expanding. The reality she existed in was such a small, fragile thing that it had already been completely wiped out and replaced at least once that he knew of.

He was the only one alive who remembered.

"There are," he acknowledged. "And I suspect the answers you seek lie within one of them. If you'll allow me to investigate on your behalf, I'll be sure to contact you as soon as I have more information."

Pretending to adjust the position of an artifact on the mantel as an excuse to move out of his guest's line of vision, Stephen maneuvered himself behind the psyche-leech and placed a booted foot firmly on its tail. He wasn't usually shy about tending to his business in front of the general public, but he did take pains to pace himself, mindful of not causing undue distress. Most people were happier remaining oblivious to the spiritual organisms swarming their mortal frames.

"What, um…what would something like that cost me?" Sharanya asked apprehensively, craning her neck around to follow him with her eyes.

"We can't know that until we better understand the forces with which we may be dealing," Stephen replied distractedly. The psyche-leech had become aware of his presence and was burrowing further into Sharanya's back.

Wong rushed in to clarify. "There's no monetary cost associated with the doctor's assistance."

Sharanya brightened considerably at that and turned back to Stephen.

"So, is there anything else you need from me at this point, or…?"

"I'd like to put a ward of protection on you before you go, but don't let that alarm you. It's not an indication that I'm anticipating threats to your safety."

Stephen threw the ward up hastily as the scientist watched him over her shoulder. When he was done, he gestured for Wong to escort her out of the room.

"If you'll follow me, please, Dr. Misra?"

Sharanya looked startled as Wong began moving toward the living room doors. She started to turn all the way around to face Stephen—the leech turning with her, trying to slip out of his grasp—until Wong stopped her with a gentle touch to her elbow. "Oh, uh, bye," she said to Stephen over her shoulder. "Thanks for your…help. It was nice meeting you."

Stephen nodded in acknowledgment, but didn't so much as look toward her. He was busy quietly wrapping tendrils of energy around the psyche-leech's cylindrical frame. It was a simple enough matter to separate it from its host.

Doing so without causing harm to either, though—that took concentration.

CHAPTER II

SHARANYA didn't believe in magic, but the protection ward made her nervous. Doctor Strange had waved his hands at her so casually it was disconcerting. Shouldn't he have made a bigger show of it, had something glow or sparkle or smoke? She couldn't make sense of him. Nothing about Doctor Strange had in any way aligned with her expectations.

Most of the psychics and fortune tellers Sharanya had met through her mother's insistence had been solicitous and extroverted. Though seemingly compassionate, there had been something quiet and reserved about Doctor Strange. He felt more like a scientist than a mystic to Sharanya, right down to the distracted preoccupation with…whatever it was that preoccupied him. Sharanya realized she had no idea. She'd understood very little of what he'd said, and even less of what he'd done. And yet she did feel better for having spoken with him, almost as if she'd hired a private detective to clean up the darkest, most frightening corners of her life.

She stopped to glance at the pocket doors the majordomo—or whatever he was—had drawn closed as they exited the magician's living room. As soon as they shut, a ruckus erupted from the room—crashes and bangs, and the magician's voice, chanting. "Is everything okay in there?" she asked.

"He'll be fine," Wong replied. He seemed completely confident in his statement, so Sharanya decided to let it go, her attention darting to an unfamiliar shape toward the back of the entry hall. There was something hugely unsettling about this house.

She was about to ask Wong whether he saw it, too, when she felt an abrupt tug on her upper back. Glancing over her shoulder, she discerned nothing out of the ordinary, but wished she could touch her shoulder blades. Her whole back felt weird suddenly, as if a layer of clothing had been ripped away from it, leaving the skin exposed. She shuddered involuntarily, but then had to admit that she was unexpectedly feeling much better. Following Wong out into the slanted sunlight of late afternoon in the Village, she rolled her shoulders experimentally and was amazed by the increased range of motion.

"Please don't hesitate to come see us again," Wong said. Sharanya nodded to him and then bent her neck to each side, hearing it crack. It really did feel like a hundred pounds had been lifted from her shoulders, but she was loath to credit a 15-minute visit to some quack's house on Bleecker Street.

"I'll leave you my number," she told the majordomo as she fished for a business card in her purse, wanting to be polite. "So he'll be able to find me if, you know, anything comes up."

Wong smiled placidly as he stood on the steps of the white, three-story mid-Atlantic Colonial, lifting his face to the light spring breeze. "I'm sure that won't be a problem."

"I know I've got a card in here somewhere… Ah! Here we go!" She handed him her business card, which he accepted graciously as she continued speaking. "I think my mother may be a little confused about the kind of magic he does. Which, honestly…I suppose I am, too. Neighboring dimensions, did he say? Is that some kind of Reiki work?"

Wong clasped his hands behind his back and continued to smile. "It's a little more far-reaching than that."

Sharanya nodded as she closed her purse. "More like astrology then? That explains it. My mom must want him to do her chart. She's obsessed; calls me every morning to read my horoscope to me. Anyway, speaking of my mother, I promised I'd call her when I was leaving here, so...thanks again for seeing me."

"It was our pleasure."

Sharanya turned to wave one last time as she started up Bleecker Street toward Macdougal, already putting in her earbuds and speed-dialing her mother. As she hurried down the tree-lined street, past the old brick mid-rise apartments and early 19th-century row houses with their wood and cast-iron storefronts, she was thinking she could still make it back to the Foundation in time to review some study notes.

Her mother's voice filled her ears. "Sharanya? Is that you? What took you so long?"

"I'm sorry, Mom. I'm leaving now."

"Are you going home?"

"No, I'm going by the office."

"But it's almost five already! Will anyone be there?"

"There's always security in the building, Mom, I told you that." Sharanya looked up into the branches of a Callery pear, sunlight filtering through the soft green leaves down across her upturned face. She had always been fond of the little tangle of streets that made up Greenwich Village—the seemingly endless succession of shops, cafes, bars, and restaurants. It felt safe there somehow—contained.

"Well?" her mother was asking. "How did it go?"

Sharanya sighed. "It was fine. But to be honest, Mom, it was also pretty much a waste of time." She glanced at the pulled-down steel roller door of a closed shop across the street. "Though he did put a ward of protection on me," she added with a smirk, thinking her mother might be impressed with such a detail. "I could probably walk through Hell's Kitchen right now unscathed."

On the other end of the phone, her mother's voice rose with panic. "Hell's Kitchen? Don't you dare! Sharanya, don't make me send your brother to come get you."

Sharanya rolled her shoulders and her eyes simultaneously. "Mom, it's full of young professionals these days, I was just teasing you."

"Well, that visit will help you, you'll see. Even just that you talked to him."

Sharanya was tempted to mention the sudden relief in her back, but didn't know how to explain it. Her mother would just worry about what had been wrong in the first place. "If it makes *you* feel better that I did it, I guess that's enough."

"You should not dismiss what you do not understand, Sharanya. But never mind. Tell me everything. Is he really a doctor?"

"Mom, *I'm* really a doctor. I have *no idea* what he is."

"No, no, I don't mean a Ph.D. Mr. Jayaraman's niece, Amiya, said he was a surgeon. She heard it from her husband's grandfather. You didn't ask? Men like it when you show interest in their accomplishments, Sharanya. And a surgeon would be a very good match for you."

Sharanya crossed Macdougal and, deciding she needed some caffeine, pushed through the heavy swing-door of the chain coffee bar on the corner. "Mom! He was introduced as 'Doctor.' What was I supposed to do? Demand to see a medical license? I thought you wanted me to go there to ask about the murders, not get engaged. You want me to go back?"

"Do not take that tone with me. It is not my fault that you are not yet married."

Sharanya groaned as she got in line behind a young man in a red T-shirt carrying a laptop messenger bag. Usually the rich scent of freshly ground coffee beans and the gleam of polished wooden floors elevated her mood, but her mother was sorely trying her patience. "It isn't anyone's *fault*, Mom."

"He wasn't attractive?"

"For the love of—! He looked like a pale-skinned, blue-eyed version of Kunal Kapoor, okay? But what does that have to *do* with anything?!"

Sharanya started as a guy in a gray suit muscled past her and the young man, shouting at the barista over both their heads.

"Double macchiato to go!"

"Oh, with the mustache and the soulful eyes? I loved him in *Rang De Basanti*!"

The man in front of Sharanya turned to make eye contact with her, indicating his surprise at the other man's rudeness. Sharanya shrugged to convey that she was equally shocked and then tried to answer her mom as the young man in the T-shirt turned to address the line cutter. "Hey, there's a line here, pal…"

"Did I mention he was wearing a cape? Inside. Like a super hero or something. And he had an assistant who looked like some kind of monk. Asian, I think, and bald, but with a really nice smile."

"I don't stand in lines," the man in the gray suit sneered. "I have places to be."

The young man turned to Sharanya again, aghast. He looked like he couldn't decide whether to be outraged or amused. "Did he really just say that?"

"Hold on a second, Mom, something's happening…"

"What is it, Sharanya? Are you okay?"

Sharanya pressed the mute on her headset and addressed the line-cutter with an authoritative air of censure in her voice. "Excuse me, sir, but you can't just cut in line like that. We've been waiting."

The man had reached the barista and was pounding his fist against the counter in time with his words. "Double! Macchiato! To go! *NOW*."

The barista, who had two nose piercings and bright pink hair, looked like she was seconds away from bursting into tears. "Sir, you *need* to get in line!"

"Whoa! *Hey!*" The young man in the red T-shirt was surging forward suddenly, grabbing the back of the line-cutter's gray jacket. Sharanya froze as she realized the line-cutter had reached across the counter and grabbed the barista's upper arms. He was shaking her violently.

Sharanya flashed back to the horrifying night at the prison when she had unlocked the sleep-lab doors. Her first thought had been that her subjects had been attacked by some kind of wild animal—blood was spattered and smeared across the entire room, covering the cots and the flowered cotton sheets and almost every inch of the linoleum floors. Dr. Conde had been strangled with an interface cable. An orderly had been beaten with a respiration monitor; one of the study subjects repeatedly stabbed with a 25g hypodermic needle. The rest had beaten each other to death with their fists. Sharanya couldn't imagine an actual nightmare being any more frightening or grisly.

"Sharanya? Sharanya, what's happening? Are you still there?"

What *was* happening? Sharanya looked up, blinking. Reality had abandoned her. Not 10 feet in front of her, the young man in the red T-shirt was wrestling furiously with the man in the gray suit. The barista had jumped up onto the counter and was screaming that she quit, that she had always been too good for this place. Sharanya's still raw nerves were poised to panic, but she was distracted by the startling beauty of the shimmering barrier that had coalesced into place around her, shielding her from harm.

CHAPTER III

"STEPHEN?"

"Over here, Wong."

Stephen closed the basement door and sealed it shut with a quick barrier spell as Wong entered the library.

"The Malebranchian psyche-leech?" Wong asked.

Stephen nodded. "I coaxed it into the game room. It should be able to feed on the residual ghosts down there without causing them any harm. Did Dr. Misra notice the extraction?"

"She looked a little more comfortable, but none the wiser. Gave me her card so you'd be able to find her."

Stephen knew Wong found such underestimations of the Sorcerer Supreme's power amusing, but his own focus was elsewhere. He stared off into space, thinking for the millionth time about the problem of preparing humanity for more active inclusion in the universe they truly inhabited. The world was so much bigger, so much more complex and aggressively threatening than most people knew; Stephen often found himself wishing there were better ways to share the more wondrous, inspiring facets of magic with the general population while continuing to shield them from the terrors that lurked in the shadows.

As it was, he endeavored to drip-feed knowledge of the paranormal to them, hoping to slowly raise the consciousness of the general population at a speed they could tolerate.

"I've been thinking about her sleep-study subjects calling for me from their dreams. It's intriguing. Obviously anything touching on the Dream Dimension brings Nightmare to mind, but if he's up to something, why court my attention?"

Wong nodded. "I had the same thought. You'd expect the opposite— some kind of smokescreen or deliberate attempt to distract you. I take it all's well at the police station?"

Stephen smoothed down his mustache. "Yes. Though I do wonder how someone ended up needing to stash an Abthalavuun in the first place."

Wong's forehead wrinkled. "A...?"

Stephen waved dismissively. "An Abthalavuun. Pet of the Old Ones. Small, tentacled soul devourer with a taste for human flesh."

"Charming."

"In any case, I was going to look in on a few more dimensional portals, make sure everything's the way I left it."

Wong smiled indulgently. "No. You were going to the Bar with No Doors."

Stephen's brow furrowed. "Didn't we just do that?"

"Four months ago, yes. I'm afraid it's time again." Wong was referring to a semiannual meeting of magic wielders, and although Stephen understood the importance of fostering community among those who drew on arcane powers, he found the gatherings taxing. Telling himself he could use it as an opportunity to share information about the matter at hand, he nodded.

"Right. Thank you, Wong." He started toward the front vestibule, but then turned back to his friend. "Keep an eye on Dr. Misra, will you? I can't put my finger on it, but she seems to have caught the attention of something."

"Certainly, Doctor."

Slipping back out into the amiable bustle of Greenwich Village, Stephen turned left on Bleecker and then again onto Sullivan. He didn't notice the sinking sun or the faint spring draft, distracted by the variegated mystical energies and interdimensional bacteria swarming over the pulsing auras of the people he passed. Paranormal entities moved in and out of his peripheral vision, some working hard to hide from him, ducking into shadows shimmering with psychic imprints, others stuck in emotional time loops, insensitive to his attention. The citizenry of New York went noisily about their business, largely unaware of their attendant ghosts or the spiritual burdens they lugged behind them. But Stephen knew something was off. In addition to the shorter-than-usual tempers around him—an argument over cab fare at the corner seemed likely to escalate into a fist fight, and there were cops outside the local tea-and-spice shop apprehending a teenage boy who was shouting something about needing poppy seed for a Hoodoo spell—he could feel danger bearing down on reality like the barometric-pressure drop of an approaching storm.

Crossing just past the intersection, he dodged a bicyclist and turned his back to the black awning of a small palm-and-tarot-reading storefront tucked between a deli and a bar, reminding himself to stop in one day. Once safely across the street, he glanced around to make sure no one was watching him—not that it probably mattered in New York—and then walked through the brick wall of a four-story apartment building.

It was one of many entrances to the Bar with No Doors, a small tiki lounge with sticky floors hidden in the bowels of the city and accessible only to magic users. Warmly lit by the glow of hanging lanterns in jewel-toned hues, and lushly decorated with tropical foliage and magical relics from around the globe, the bar was tended by Chondu the Mystic, a self-proclaimed master of the mystic arts of yoga so advanced he didn't need a body, preferring to appear as a head in a jar. Stephen had days when he thought he could see the appeal.

It was less crowded than he had expected it to be. There was a skinny, bald young man he didn't recognize sitting on a stool at the bar, but otherwise, only the Scarlet Witch, Doctor Voodoo, and Satana were in attendance.

"Do any of you have poppy seed on you, by any chance?" he asked as he moved toward the thatch-covered booth in the back where his colleagues were gathered. A giant glass bowl of fuchsia liquid—decorated with orchid flowers, fresh mint leaves, and orange slices—sat on the table between them, three oversized straws climbing out of the miasma. Seeing him, the Scarlet Witch smiled, Satana sat up a little straighter, and Doctor Voodoo bowed his head in a quick nod of respect.

"I just changed purses, sorry." Wanda, the Scarlet Witch, was a blue-eyed, auburn-haired beauty dressed from head to toe in her signature red. She specialized in an ancient form of eldritch hex magic that allowed her to manipulate probability fields. Stephen was one of the few people on Earth who understood how it worked. "And clearly we're gonna have to reschedule this—everyone's just crazed right now. We got rainchecks from Hellstorm and Magik, and I can't even reach Topaz or Jennifer Kale. Are you free the first Monday in April?"

Stephen slid in next to Satana, who scooted over, leaving him beneath the watchful gaze of a carved wooden tiki called Kanaloa. Satana, a literal succubus from Hell, was dressed almost exclusively in black, perhaps to contrast with her almost transparently pale skin. Her black hair was streaked with red highlights, and she often wore the wickedest smirk Stephen had ever seen.

"April should work," he told Scarlet Witch. "With the usual caveats."

Doctor Voodoo sighed. "Assuming you're still alive by then, and in a reasonably humanoid and/or corporeal form, and that this particular plane of existence has not been compromised beyond access, and/or in the absence of imminent doom. Yes, yes, we know." Jericho had dark skin and short black hair with a white streak down the center. He wore a large red cape, similar in size and color to Stephen's cloak, and was a disciple of the Loa. Like Stephen, he'd led a civilian life before becoming fully immersed in magic, though as a psychologist rather than a surgeon.

Stephen accepted the straw Satana pushed toward him and took a small sip from the communal tiki bowl. "I like to be clear."

Satana snorted. "You'd think the Sorcerer Supreme could commit to a weeknight. Can't you use your amulet to look into the future or something? You know, '*expecting an invasion of Muspelheim fire demons Monday, let's try for Thursday...*' kinda thing?"

"It's the All-Seeing Eye of Agamotto, Satana, not a PDA." Stephen heard the stool scrape back from the bar behind him and saw a flash of movement in the corner of his eye. The magical undercurrent in the room went flat suddenly, as if pulled away by a riptide; Stephen felt the void like an absence of air. He threw up a simple barrier spell in front of the table just in time to deflect a surge of dark energy that came rushing toward him like a laser blast.

"Was that a paralysis spell?" Satana asked incredulously, sensing the magic behind Stephen's barricade.

The stranger from the bar now stood in front of their table, sneering; a set of runic tattoos glowed bright blue across his forehead. He was thin and wiry, with a clean-shaven head and a five o'clock shadow across his long jaw.

"*You're* the Sorcerer Supreme?" he demanded, glaring at Stephen. Strange motioned for his colleagues to remain seated and looked the aggressive interloper up and down with more confusion than anger.

"For this realm, yes, on my better days. Also known as Doctor Strange. And you would be?"

"Oh, please say 'your worst nightmare,'" Scarlet Witch urged, bright-eyed.

"I was hoping for 'your successor,'" Satana added drolly.

"I'm the guy who's gonna kick your ass," replied the stranger.

Doctor Voodoo sighed and indicated the women. "Theirs were better."

"I'm afraid I'm here on business and don't have time to…duel with you," Stephen countered evenly. "Not to mention that magical dueling is both strictly forbidden in the bar and a bad idea in general."

The young man only gritted his teeth and raised his fists in a boxing stance. Power began to radiate around his hands, glowing the same electric blue as his tattoos, and then he shadowboxed two fast, hard jabs into the air in front of him. In response, two massive blasts of magical power punched against Stephen's barrier. Though his expression remained impassive, Stephen could feel the blockade shudder. The young man might have been an unknown, but his magic was not lightweight.

"Okay, I'm gonna call him the Scrappy Southpaw," Satana said.

"No, no." The Scarlet Witch shook her head. "He led with his right, and I think that was the Dual-Limb Squall of Shaggoth. How about the Capricious Cue Ball?"

Doctor Voodoo grunted. "I just want to know what he's drinking. Taking on Doctor Strange? That's 190-proof-level courage. Which, incidentally, is also known as stupidity."

Stephen rose to his feet, instinctively moving in front of his friends, and frowned at the newcomer.

"Let's do this: If you want to tell your associates that you threw down with the Sorcerer Supreme, I won't contradict you. But this isn't a good way to make a first impression, and I'm only going to give you one more chance to withdraw."

Undeterred, the young man expanded his chest, stepped forward on one bent leg and opened his mouth as if to roar. A hazy, black vortex filled with flashing blue phosphorescent light swirled to life on the back of his tongue. He inhaled through it as it grew, raked the air around him with his fingernails, and sucked away Stephen's barricade—along with half the ambient spiritual energy and illumination in the room. The runic tattoos on his forehead pulsed with energy—as did his eyes, which had taken on the same cerulean hue.

"Okay, what the actual Hell?!" Satana bound to her feet, all traces of humor gone from her face. Doctor Voodoo also slowly rose. Stephen's hands clenched into fists at his sides as his frown deepened, but his voice remained composed when he spoke again.

"You're unschooled. And dangerous. Even *I* wouldn't be arrogant enough to open and attempt to control a singularity on the mortal plane. If you persist, someone's going to get hurt."

"And spoiler alert, newbie," Satana hissed, gesturing toward Stephen. "It won't be him."

The interloper swallowed Stephen's barrier whole, then grinned darkly, blue energy crackling through his teeth.

"I'm taking you down, old man. Such is my destiny, and there's nothing you can do to stop it."

Clapping his glowing hands together and then pulling them apart again, Stephen's adversary began to collect a sizzling, writhing ball of dark energy between his palms. Just as he pushed his hands forward to send it flying toward the Sorcerer Supreme, Stephen dropped his center slightly and pivoted toward his attacker, stepping in close as he gently grabbed the spell-caster's wrist with one hand and pushed his elbow out with the other. The spell seemed to implode, absorbed back through the caster's skin as Stephen turned his hips, threw his attacker to the ground, and pinned him there. He let go of the caster's wrist as the young man convulsed, the spell reemerging as some kind of mystical electrified net that surrounded and bound him in what appeared to be a painful, shuddering paralysis.

"What spell was that?" asked Doctor Voodoo, looking down at the young man almost sympathetically.

"No spell," Stephen answered calmly as he adjusted his cloak. "That was aikido."

"Is something wrong with your powers?" Satana asked, eyeing the straw she'd shared with him as though she feared it might be contagious.

Stephen examined the young magic user on the floor. "Not at all. I'm just setting a good example." He unconsciously began to ball and flex his hands, then turned to peer straight into Satana's red eyes. "Mundane solutions for mundane problems. Physical interventions are often more predictable than magical ones."

Doctor Voodoo nodded thoughtfully. "Also a good way not to lose touch with your humanity, I suppose."

Stephen noticed Satana's slight scowl. "Humanity" was something of which she was technically devoid. He caught and held her gaze until the corners of her mouth lifted in the hint of a smile. Scarlet Witch took another sip from the Scorpion Bowl.

"What do you think got into him? I mean, talk about bravado. Even *I'd* think twice about challenging you, Stephen, and *I'm* an Avenger."

Satana turned to Scarlet Witch, confused. "I thought Strange was an Avenger, too?"

"Yeah, but I was an Avenger *first*."

Doctor Voodoo reclaimed his seat, apparently satisfied that the interloper wasn't getting back up any time soon.

"'Such is my destiny'? You don't hear that turn of phrase every day. And yet he's not alone. In his bravado, I mean. Been seeing a lot of it lately."

Scarlet Witch nodded as Stephen slid back in next to Satana. "That's true. The last week or so has been insane. Heavy-casualty accidents are *way* up, and the crime rate is at an all-time high—everything from murders all the way down to jaywalking. You wanna talk bravado, Stilt-Man tried to rob the Federal Reserve yesterday. *Stilt Man*."

Satana raised her eyebrows at Wanda. "Do I even wanna know?"

The Scarlet Witch shook her head. "You absolutely do not." She sighed and rubbed her forehead with one gloved hand. "God, I wish I'd slept better last night. Such weird dreams. And then we got a call at dawn from Luke Cage—he and Iron Fist needed backup. And not for big stuff, either, just to control the sheer volume of crazy. It's like every aggro d-bag in the known universe had a big bowl of Wheaties for breakfast this morning and decided to be all that he can be."

Jericho leaned back in his seat, directing his comment to Stephen. "Did you know someone took a shot at T'Challa yesterday?"

"The Black Panther?"

"Yes. And not a super villain, either—just some racist from the suburbs. We're still talking correlation rather than causality, but there's definitely a sense of group dynamics at play here."

Stephen's hands had begun to tremble, so he slipped them under the table and turned his attention back to the prone form on the floor in front of the booth. Opening his third eye, he attempted to get a read on the young man. His name was Nicholas Volkov, he was 22, and he lived with his parents on the Upper East Side. Aside from the runic tattoos and a few magic items in his possession, his power seemed to be largely mutation-based and fairly new to him, and yet there was something…else there. Stephen couldn't place it, but it teased his senses like an elusive scent or a moment of *déjà vu*.

"Getting anything?" Doctor Voodoo asked, following the line of his gaze.

"Not really," Stephen admitted. "Nothing that explains anything, anyway. His blood alcohol level's only point oh two; he doesn't appear to be mind-controlled or possessed. He's just…ambitious." Out of habit, he examined the young man's brain functions, shaping a divination spell into an approximation of an MRI with a quick, precise gesture of his left hand. "There's a surprising amount of activity in his visual cortex, considering that he's unconscious…"

"That just means he's dreaming." Jericho's somber attention was on the communal drink. "I'm telling you, there's something in the water. Not everything stems from magic, you know."

"Actually," Stephen said quietly. He was looking at the table, where a billion tiny lives twinkled in and out of existence as cells grew and divided and multiplied and died. "Everything does."

FOR A little while, Jane hadn't been sure she was going to make it into the city. Metro-North service was interrupted around Scarborough, and the driver of the Megabus she boarded afterwards decided he was going to drive to California instead of Manhattan, because he'd "always been meant to be in the pictures." Jane found herself wandering around Glenwood for a short time, but then managed to cut through a copse of trees in Sprague Brook Park and come out through the Bug Carousel at the Bronx Zoo. Seeing a taxi rush by on Southern Boulevard one second, she looked up a second later to discover she'd somehow made it all the way to Grand Central Terminal. She couldn't remember how she'd gotten there, though, and was pretty sure she didn't have enough money to have taken a cab.

The 35-story Baxter Building was located at 42nd Street and Madison Avenue, less than a block from Grand Central. It housed Parker Industries as well as the Baxter Foundation, and although its architecture was unremarkable, it was known for having high security. Jane watched the building from outside a commercial bank across the street, wondering how she'd get in. Behind her, agitated people standing in line for the ATM suddenly swarmed inside the bank as rumors of a stock-market crash reached Midtown. Someone fired a gun in the money exchange across the street from the bank. Jane drifted toward the Baxter Building in the ensuing chaos. She found the screams, honks, and distant sirens oddly comforting. It was as if the external world had finally caught up to the chaos inside her head.

The building's glass doors slid open as she approached, and she realized that the lobby was open to the public. A security desk was set up just to the right of the entryway, though, and card-operated electronic turnstiles secured the elevator bank. Eyeing the guard, Jane couldn't decide whether to be afraid. Was this going to be one of those liquid days when he would turn out to be someone she knew, or a gargoyle, or she'd suddenly find herself making out with him in the building's maintenance closet? Or was it going to be the kind of day when he'd stop her and make her sit in a small, airless room while they waited for her father to come pick her up?

He looked up as she approached, but his eyes quickly darted past her, scanning the lobby. She continued moving toward the turnstiles, convinced that she could feel the building breathing. Every intake of breath rooted it firmly in the real world; every exhale became a dream.

She had just made it past the guard when her attention was drawn to a huge painting on the wall. It was typical corporate art: innocuous abstracted Cubism with beiges, browns, and olive greens in overlapping squares of various sizes. As Jane stared, patterns of stairs began to emerge. She walked slowly up to it, transfixed. After a quick glance over her shoulder confirmed that no one was watching her, Jane stepped into the painting.

Some of the steps were large, the squares hard to climb over, but Jane persisted, moving through the thick paint with the determination to ascend.

Stopping to catch her breath, it seemed for a moment that she was in an elevator, standing behind a few other people, unnoticed. But then she climbed out of a mirror onto the third floor and roamed labyrinthine hallways until she found a row of offices in an area marked "Biology Complex."

She stopped to fish her knife out of her backpack, trying to remember what she was there to do. There were name plaques along the wall, but the letters swam and swayed. The light in the hallway was starting to die; one of the plaques began bleeding. Jane watched the blood run down the wall, read the name, and remembered.

It was science that eroded the pathways, so she didn't need to be afraid to draw blood. Just a little cut.

Only so he'd notice.

CHAPTER IV

STEPHEN thought about the conversation he'd had in the bar as he made the brief walk home, rubbing his aching hands. Integrated into his life as it was, magic had ceased to be an isolated element within the framework of the universe—everything was about magic the same way everything was about life or the cycles of nature. Magic was just there, indelibly part of the structure of things, a component of existence without which existence itself could not be. Once you'd seen it, it couldn't be concealed.

And yet it existed beyond the realm of human thinking, much like quantum science or alien life; most people rarely, if ever, thought about it, and the few who studied and understood it did so at the risk of permanently estranging themselves from mundane reality. Though Stephen understood all the ways in which the individual was a construct, there was a part of him that felt increasingly at risk of total absorption into some greater force, *the* greater force, a kind of transcendence that would subsume and ultimately obliterate his sentience and his ego. Maybe it was another stage of the enlightenment the Ancient One had guided him through during his initial arcane training. His goal then had been a state of perfect union with the universe. Had the Ancient One known that Stephen would one day find himself obligated to resist that very union if he hoped to continue serving as the Sorcerer Supreme? They'd discussed what it meant to consciously defend the Earth, but Stephen had never asked whether it was possible to do so unconsciously. He knew he had to surrender to magic in order to use it as an instrument to manifest his will, but didn't he also have to resist it in order to *have* a will to manifest? Such contradictions defined his life.

As he had sent Wong to trail Dr. Misra for the evening, his assistant was not there to greet him when he returned to the Sanctum Sanctorum. Not that the place was quiet—the Sanctum never was, not really. Balanced over inter-secting ley lines, riddled with interdimensional portals, haunted, hallowed, and bursting with occult relics, the place in which Stephen resided was really an entity in its own right—a nexus of magical, spiritual, and paranormal gateways. He had protected it from external magical invasion with a spell that drew from the property's own power, and had learned to navigate the labyrinthine hallways and volatile doorways with relative calm, but it was not the sort of place in which one ever truly let down their guard. Even so, Stephen felt fondness for it. The Sanctum was the only thing he had in the way of a home.

He headed upstairs to his meditation chamber and carefully prepared for astral projection. As the Sorcerer Supreme, he was capable of physically traversing all realms and dimensions, but could travel greater distances more quickly in astral form. He took a moment to purify himself in incandescent white light, created a circle of protection, and called upon the Vishanti for guidance. Finally, he lit a tether-candle and sat cross-legged in the center of a large rug. Exhaling, he closed his eyes and entered a deep state of relaxation, concentrating on the frequency at which the known universe was vibrating. Opening his astral eyes, he gazed back at his physical form as it sat in deep meditation across the candle from him. Everything appeared to be in order.

Traveling out of body, Stephen immediately saw more of what his fellow magic users had discussed in the bar. There was a palpable restlessness that seemed to be growing, a sudden impatience with the banality and insignificance of day-to-day life that was leading people to attempt spectacularly ill-advised power grabs—from incidents of personal and professional overreach, to violent crimes, even mass murder. He witnessed purse-snatchings, newsstand grab-and-runs, and three road-rage fistfights within a four-block radius. The subway stations were all closed in response to some kind of threat. It looked very much like humanity had fallen under the influence of some malevolent spirit, but Stephen couldn't detect its manifestation, or even the means by which it had tethered itself to so many mortal souls. The disturbance did not appear to be demonic in nature, nor extraterrestrial. And if it was interdimensional, then it had to be from a dimension Stephen didn't know, because none of the conduits with which he was familiar were open.

Unless...

...Unless it was internally generated. It was one of the first lessons he'd learned in medical school: Damage to an organism wasn't always created by external forces—some of the worst disorders stemmed from malfunctions within the body's own systems.

Floating in astral form above the fountain at the circular center of Washington Square Park, Stephen thought back over the day: Dr. Misra's story about mass murder in an asylum sleep lab; the subjects waking from nightmares calling his name; the overactive visual cortex of the young man who'd attacked him...they all pointed to the Dream Dimension. And because the Dream Dimension was so organically connected to sentient mortal reality, individuals influenced by their dreams wouldn't register as being possessed, controlled, or in any way tethered to an alien realm.

In fact, the Dream Dimension was so intrinsically linked with humanity that most people assumed they personally created it every night from scratch. Even those who pictured it as a physical place usually thought of it as being located, however improbably, within their own brains—a concomitant plane of existence. And this wasn't entirely inaccurate. A sleeping being traversed no physical space to reach the Dream Dimension. To get there when awake, though…The Dimension was its own habitat with its own rules and perils. And chief among the latter was one of Doctor Strange's most ancient and dangerous adversaries: Nightmare.

With a knot of foreboding in his stomach, Stephen made his way to a mystical gateway that led to Hypnagogia, the state between wakefulness and dreaming. To actually enter the dimension, it was safest to conjure it much as any dreamer would: by visualizing the point he wished to enter. It was a notoriously difficult dimension to map because it existed in a constant state of flux and re-creation, shaped by protective Pathways that separated the realms. Stephen was of the mind that the Pathways also held the dimension together. There was a distinct sovereign ruling each independent dream realm, but the Pathways existed as neutral territory, a place where dreamers could safely enter the dimension and travel between realms. He'd often wondered over the lack of a sentient guardian for them; he didn't even know what had created and sustained them over the years.

To Stephen, the Pathways had always looked like giant glass tubes, all but invisible until the light hit them just right, the walls solid to dreamers but permeable to the dream figments and realm inhabitants that slipped in and out of them to guide the unconscious sleepers into their individual dreams. These figments took on every conceivable shape, from people to objects to small animals; sometimes they were even snatches of song or a landscape that unfurled to meet the dreamer who would know it.

Stephen assumed a floating lotus position under the arch of the gateway and visualized the Realm of Signal Dreaming. Devoted to problem-solving and decision-making, it seemed like a good place to start. Though he hadn't been there in a long time, he recalled it opening up to either side of the central Pathway, all blue skies and rolling green hills—the kind of landscape Stephen might have drawn as a child in Nebraska, sunny and safe. He couldn't remember what the greater realm felt or looked like from there, but the Pathway leading up to it was very familiar to him and simple enough to conjure in his mind's eye.

Which is why, the moment he stepped foot onto the Pathway, he immediately turned to check his entry point. The pale blue sky was thick with clouds—colossal, dark peaks of gray speared by forks of lightning and crashing together with booming claps of thunder. The once soft, rolling hills were now a flat, scorched hellscape, punctuated by one giant mountain—Stephen understood immediately that it was Olympus—shooting up through the clouds and towering over the strangely circuitous Pathways. The membrane that made up the walls of the Pathways seemed unusually thin and elastic, swelling and shrinking around him indecisively. A few confused dreamers wandered through the tube, peering at equally aimless guides they did not seem to recognize. Stephen shivered involuntarily and pulled his cloak closer around himself as an icy wind blew through him, seeming to want to push him back into the gateway through which he'd entered.

He had just touched the Amulet of Agamotto, intending to open the Eye, when a somnavore dropped in front of him with a predacious roar. Creatures from the Nightmare Realm, somnavores generally formed from the fears of their prey, many of them combinations of phobias, such as the arachnid centaur werewolf facing Stephen. A hirsute, muscular human torso was perched on top of eight giant spider legs and crowned with the head of a slavering dire wolf with glowing dark-green eyes. Though normal dreamers were immune to physical harm in astral form, the rules were always different for Stephen, who paid for the power to influence the realms he visited with his own vulnerability to their physical laws. He raised his hands, palms pulsing with arcane energy, and prepared to defend himself.

The creature leapt with a growl that Stephen felt at the base of his spine. He blasted a pulse of pure force at its torso, but was thrown off when it landed behind him and tore a guide figment to shreds in front of a terrified dreamer. Frowning, Stephen carefully watched its interaction with the dreamer, relieved to see that although the somnavore did its best to panic and intimidate her, it did not seem able to cause corporeal harm. As Stephen muttered the first few words of a binding spell, the creature turned to glare at him over its shoulder, then suddenly lunged. Stephen finished the incantation, twisting his left hand into the apotropaic Karana mudra he used to channel mystical energies and blasting the spell toward the creature's legs.

Carried by its own momentum, the somnavore fell forward as its feet grouped up beneath it, drawn tightly together by magical rope as Stephen clenched his left hand into a fist. The beast clawed at Stephen's left arm with its human hands, drawing blood, and snapped at him with its canine jaw before the bottom of its muzzle hit the ground. Stephen fired a gravitational blast at its skull, just to make sure it stayed down, and was momentarily horrified as its fur and flesh and bone slid away to reveal an enormous brain. As Stephen stared at it, the brain brutally ruptured, as though cut into by a scalpel held by a surgeon with violently shaking hands.

Stephen's eyebrow raised. It was odd to find a somnavore from Nightmare's realm this far past his appointed domain; odder still to find it capable of personalized dream-weaving in the middle of the Pathways. Normally, Stephen thought to himself wryly, one had to actually be within Nightmare's realm for that kind of attention.

The beating wings of a flock of birds in flight overhead drew his attention upwards. Clearly fleeing some encroaching danger, they were flying both within and outside the boundaries of the Pathway, the flock separated in a way Stephen had never seen before. He turned around in time to see the Pathway walls distend as dozens more somnavores of varied shapes and forms permeated the thinning membrane. They came through in waves like rabid predators, giving chase to the gentler dream figments. The creatures easily overtook and eviscerated the guides, leaving a trail of carnage in their wake. Within seconds, the bloodied, ashen figments rose again, nightmare zombies of their former selves. They glowed a mottled dark green, thoroughly corrupted by the forces of the invading realm.

Stephen inhaled and squared his shoulders as they came for him in an onslaught, both surprised and relieved that Nightmare wasn't leading their attack. Wary of pushing them forcibly back through the already fragile membrane of the Pathways, even to return them to their realm, Stephen quickly dismissed the idea of a banishment spell and thought through his options. Summoning spells were out for the same reason: It didn't seem wise to bring interdimensional entities into the Pathways while the domain was so chaotic. Elemental attacks could exacerbate the membrane's fragile state, and although effective in the short term, a binding spell large enough to shackle the volume of creatures moving toward him could compromise the mobility of dreamers and dream figments trying to pass safely through the zone. He needed to neutralize the somanvores as a threat while leaving them more or less where they were. It was a complicated magical maneuver—but fortunately, Stephen was very good at his job.

"By Agamotto, the All-Seeing
for whom danger is reborn!
With aspects far more gentle
Let these creatures be transformed!"

As a surge of arcane energy crested inside him, Stephen expertly held it. He mentally gathered up every thread of it, twisting the spell into the transmogrification he needed before releasing it through his hands across the attacking somnavores. The magic crashed over them in a wave of flame-colored light, interfering neither with their momentum nor their intent. Several hundred somnavores leapt at the Sorcerer Supreme, their sharp claws aimed for his thick red cloak. Many of them even hooked it.

But by the time they got to him, each and every one of them had been transformed into a tiny, mewling kitten.

CHAPTER V

SHARANYA coughed into her elbow and glanced up at the sage stick to see how much longer it would burn. After the incident in the coffee shop, which she had escaped unharmed, her mother had pleaded with her to purchase one from a small shop on Christopher Street on her way to the Baxter Building and light it in her office to "clear the space." It hadn't seemed worth it to explain for the umpteenth time that her workplace was psychically sound; the murders had all occurred at Ravencroft. It was easier just to go along with the little ritual—and besides, it gave her something to discuss with her mother other than her bewildering sense of having been sheltered from danger by a glittering shield of pure light.

Sharanya knew that her mother would attribute the experience to Doctor Strange's protection ward, but of course that was nonsense. On her way to her office, Sharanya had decided that it had most likely been a hallucinatory manifestation of post-traumatic stress. The incident at the prison had certainly been upsetting enough to trigger temporary PTSD, and perhaps her mind had felt the need to create the sensation of being physically shielded.

In any case, the smudge stick did smell better than the industrial cleaning agent the Baxter Foundation used. Sharanya flicked on a desk lamp to counter the gathering darkness of evening and turned back to her notes.

She was going over the reported dreams of every subject who'd woken up calling Doctor Strange's name, trying to find commonalities among them, but had so far been frustrated in her efforts. Other than all being nightmares, which she had already noted, they didn't seem to have much in common. The polysomnography readings varied within expected parameters, and the reported subject matter ranged widely, as it always had. All the most common themes were there, and none of them were significantly dominant: being chased, falling, physical aggression, interpersonal conflicts, missing events, losing teeth, paralysis, failure and helplessness, animal attacks, insects and vermin, health concerns, death, murder, family, natural disasters, the disappearance of loved ones, war, monsters, Armageddon… Sharanya had already sorted them by the Hall/Van de Castle System of Quantitative Dream Content Analysis, and then again by Schredl's Nightmare Topics, and was busy highlighting mentions of specific sensory experience when she heard her office door open.

Looking up, Sharanya saw a girl standing in the doorway. Though it was a little late for such a visit, Sharanya assumed that she was a student there to inquire after internship possibilities. Her hair was dyed black and looked tangled despite the shoulder-length bob that should have been easy enough to smooth down. Her frame was slight but athletic, and the size of her hazel eyes was amplified by the dark circles beneath them. In addition to the ubiquitous university-student uniform of jeans, sneakers, and a graphic T-shirt, she wore an oversized green anorak with a faux-fur collar; she even had the prerequisite overstuffed backpack slung over one shoulder.

Sharanya was mustering a smile of greeting when she saw the glint of a knife in the girl's left hand. She jumped up behind her desk and grabbed her phone.

"I'm calling the police right now!" she warned, her hands shaking as she unlocked the touch screen. The girl was unfazed. She ran at Sharanya with a wide, fixed stare, her lips pulling back from two rows of perfectly straight, white teeth.

Sharanya froze in terror, and the phone slipped from her hand before she could dial the second "1" of "911." Once again her vision was distorted by a strangely lovely shimmering, and she had the sense of being shielded even as she watched her phone fall. Just before it clattered noisily to the desk, another form materialized between her and the girl.

There was a blur of motion as the person who had so gracefully interposed themselves between Sharanya and her attacker disarmed the girl with a fluid movement, and then a familiar voice quietly uttered a single command: "sleep." The girl fell backwards, the knife spinning on the linoleum as the other figure caught her inches from the floor.

"Wong?" Sharanya squeaked.

Wong bowed his head in acknowledgment, hoisting the unconscious girl into his arms. Sharanya pressed a hand against her chest and tried to slow her breathing, but realized she was still fighting off hysteria when she saw the girl's knife float off the floor and slide neatly into Wong's belt.

"Are you all right, Dr. Misra?"

Sharanya swallowed. "Y-yes. I think so." She let out a long shuddering exhale. "But…who is that? And where did you come from?"

"Doctor Strange asked me to keep an eye on you," Wong replied, as if that in any way answered her questions. Sharanya looked around the office, confounded. Though it would have been possible for someone to hide under the desk, she had been sitting at it—and Wong had come from the direction of her filing cabinets, which were pushed up against the east wall. "As for the young woman, I do not know, but I would like for the doctor to have a look at her." He hesitated, his head tipping slightly to one side. "I am sorry she was able to get so close to you. I'm afraid I didn't see her coming until she was already at the door."

"This—this is crazy…" Sharanya protested, sinking shakily back into her seat. She was about to ask Wong whether he wanted her to call security, but he had turned to face the far wall and appeared to be having a conversation with thin air.

"Doctor! You're bleeding! Are you all right...? Ah... I'm sorry to interrupt, then, but Dr. Misra was just attacked... No, the ward held, and I have the situation under control... Not that I can see, I'm afraid... Very well. We'll be there shortly."

Wong turned back to Sharanya with a reassuring smile, as if he'd just made a phone call rather than chatted with a wall.

"The doctor would like for us to meet him back at the Sanctum. He left his physical form there and would prefer to retrieve it before proceeding any further. This is going to feel peculiar, but please don't panic."

Sharanya unscrewed the top of her aluminum water bottle and took a long swallow before answering. Obviously she wasn't going to go anywhere with this man—that would be insane. She couldn't let him take the girl, either—she was clearly unstable and in need of a medical evaluation. Sharanya was trying to think of the best way to explain this to Wong when she was distracted by a sudden anomaly in her field of vision. For a moment it looked as though Wong and the girl were shimmering out of existence. Or perhaps it was the entire room that was fading...

Sharanya felt a nauseating drop in her stomach and closed her eyes. When she opened them again, the white linoleum of her office floor had been replaced by a wool Persian rug.

WONG teleported into the meditation room with Dr. Misra and the sleep-spelled girl just as Stephen opened his eyes and blew out a tether-candle. Sharanya looked like she was on the verge of being ill—a common response to one's first experience with teleportation—but managed to keep the contents of her stomach in check.

After arranging the unconscious girl on a pile of meditation cushions, Wong stepped inside Stephen's protection circle to squint at his wound. Though there was no physical damage to either Doctor Strange's sleeve or forearm, Wong could sense the psychic gash he'd picked up in the Dream Dimension Pathway.

"Somnavore?" he asked.

"Indeed," Stephen answered. "They were running wild through the Pathways—whole packs of them. I think we can safely identify our culprit now." Stephen nodded at Sharanya before glancing toward the unconscious girl. "Dr. Misra, welcome back. Have you ever seen this young lady before?"

Sharanya shook her head, apparently too overwhelmed to speak. Wong realized he should have better prepared her for the teleportation and wondered whether Stephen would mind-wipe her before sending her home. He watched her eyes dart around the large attic, taking in the artifacts and architecture. Despite boasting a few impressively large pieces, such as a four-foot-tall bronze incense urn and a 12-foot-high sitting Shakyamuni Buddha, the meditation room was one of the least cluttered spaces in the Sanctum Sanctorum and therefore one of the most normal-looking. It featured thick, Arabian carpets that, although luxurious, were not out of the realm of the expected in a grand old house, and jewel-toned meditation cushions one could find in any ashram or New Age center.

The room's defining feature, though, was the Anomaly Rue, also known as the Window of the Worlds: a large, circular rose window crossed by four swooping lines denoting the Seal of the Vishanti. It was a stunning feature that never failed to absorb the attention of guests, even those unaware of its power to repel mystical assailants. Wong found it strikingly beautiful in the morning, when shafts of sunlight poured through it, but knew that Stephen tended to be more drawn to it in the dark, when it framed a billion sparkling stars against the deep-blue velvet of the evening sky. Every time he noticed Stephen looking through the Rue, Wong couldn't help wondering what he saw. Though technically a human mortal, the Sorcerer Supreme was more powerful than many gods, wiser than most philosophers, and, Wong knew, more dedicated than most of the super heroes he fought alongside.

Stephen rose, stretching before he crossed the room to crouch by the unconscious girl's side.

"The Mists of Morpheus?" he asked his assistant.

Wong nodded.

"She should be at the hospital," Sharanya said quietly, apparently finding her voice as she watched Stephen. "She needs help."

"I'll help her," Stephen assured her. He rose to his full height, made a sharp, precise gesture with his right hand, and watched dispassionately as the girl levitated four feet off the floor and followed the movement of his hand until he paused, stopping her in the center of the glowing-white protection circle he'd created beneath the Anomaly Rue.

Wong turned his attention back to Sharanya, watching the scientist struggle with her skepticism. Super heroes, invading aliens, interdimensional beings hurtling through the fabric of space and time—none of it seemed to make people more comfortable with magic. Even nonbelievers understood, somewhere deep in their psyches, that magic was innate—rooted in existence as they knew it, springing from the soil of reality—and tangible if only they reached for it. Scientists like Dr. Misra, though often dismissive of the trappings of mysticism, saw the universe at its most unfathomable every day. Mitosis, expanding symmetry, the 50 billion galaxies of the known universe—even those who declined to define them as magical could feel their power.

Stephen seemed to be putting on a bit of a show for her, though whether this was to convince her of the veracity of his powers or to impress her personally was hard to say. Though it hadn't always been so—Wong could still remember the almost aloof self-containment Stephen had displayed before meeting the woman who would become his wife—the last decade or so had seen the Sorcerer Supreme develop into something of a ladies' man. A string of unfocused relationships had gradually given way to what seemed to Wong to be an increasingly spontaneous series of one-night stands; yet all were handled with decorum and a casual warmth Stephen's partners clearly found disarming. Wong was therefore unsurprised to see Stephen calling on the power of Agamotto and opening his third eye with more pageantry than strictly necessary, but he did note that Stephen seemed almost impatient—he was skipping over smaller divination spells and going straight for the most invasive insights. By the time he was floating, crosslegged, by the girl, his fingertips pressed against her forehead, Wong had realized Stephen intended to let his own consciousness into her mind to interview her directly, and decided he needed to shepherd Sharanya out of the meditation room. It was impossible to harm someone with a standard divination spell, but slipping into someone else's mind was potentially perilous.

"Let's let him work in quiet," Wong whispered, pulling the door shut behind them. "Perhaps I could fix us some tea?"

Dr. Misra looked uncomfortable as she saw the artifacts lining the dark hallway outside the meditation room, but she didn't protest. She had to be feeling completely out of her depth. Wong smiled reassuringly as he began to lead her down the narrow, winding staircase. "If you'll follow me, please? You may hold on to the rail, but please be mindful not to touch anything else. And I suggest keeping your eyes forward at all times."

"I suppose the house is haunted?" Dr. Misra asked thinly before pulling her hand off the rail as if it had just touched—or been touched by—something unpleasant. Wong continued his descent, knowing it was best to get her into the kitchen as quickly as possible. Provided, of course, that once there he could keep her out of the refrigerator, which was a literal doorway to Hell.

"It is," he answered. "And also frequently full of unusual guests, as well as alive in its own right." He paused and waited on the second-floor landing until she had safely cleared the stairway, which had a tendency to rearrange itself in impromptu homages to Escher. "The Sanctum Sanctorum is home to the most extensive collection of occult artifacts and mystic phenomena in this dimension…quite probably in any dimension. As such it can be a bit impish, with a sense of humor verging toward the cosmic in scale. It's best to just go about one's business as directly as possible. I'd ask that you refrain from touching, opening, rubbing, reading, praying to, tasting, or conversing with anything not explicitly approved by the doctor or myself."

"And you live here?" Dr. Misra's voice was hushed and hollow, as if everything she said was carefully articulated in an effort to keep from screaming. "You and Doctor Strange?" Facing the bedroom hallway, she gasped suddenly and threw herself back against the wall. "Something just…*looked* at me! From back there!"

"Pay it no mind, Dr. Misra. We're continuing this way…" Wong gestured down the next flight of stairs, pleased to note that they were, indeed, currently slanting downward.

"But it wasn't…I mean…*human* or…or any animal I've ever seen. It… was very small. And it looked right at me."

"Possibly a homunculus. I wouldn't worry. Just stay close to me, please." Wong started down the second stairway. "And to answer your question, yes, I reside here, as does Doctor Strange." Wong looked up to find Sharanya carefully watching the Persian-wool-and-silk stair runner as she followed him down, desperately clinging to something that looked normal.

"And you're his assistant?" she persisted.

"That's correct."

"But you know…*magic*…too?"

The question was delivered as a statement; Sharanya seemed to be trying to talk herself into believing the things she was saying, the word "magic" uttered with such great effort Wong had to press his lips together to keep from laughing.

"Not nearly as much as Stephen. He instructs me in the mystic arts, and I instruct him in martial arts. I also cook, clean, curate, schedule, guard, buttle, and sometimes do a bit of healing."

Sharanya finally dared to look up again as she stepped onto the first floor, meeting Wong's eyes with a slight wince. "My mother wanted to know if Doctor Strange is a medical doctor?"

Giving her a moment to orient herself, Wong smiled before ushering her gently away from the banister. "Not anymore, but he used to be the head of neurosurgery at New York Hospital."

Sharanya's eyes lit up with interest; Wong could tell she was pleased to learn something that made sense to her. "Really? When was that?"

He sighed, preparing himself to watch her face fall. "Several decades ago. This way, please…"

CHAPTER VI

STEPHEN realized it had been some time since he'd wandered around inside someone's mind, but even so, this one seemed unmanageably alien. It took him several moments to comprehend that some of it literally *was* alien, and longer still to locate the girl in question. She seemed lost within the landscape of her own thoughts, a territory far too large for her to navigate safely. It was beyond anything a human mind could construct.

"So," he said when he finally found her sitting on a windy hill of purple Allium, hugging her knees to her chest. "You're an Inhuman."

She glared up at him. *"You're* inhuman!"

Stephen sat down next to her. "No, Miss Jane Beatrix Bailey of Poughkeepsie. *An* Inhuman. Terrigen Mist, cocoon, sudden strange new powers… Sound at all familiar?"

She looked away from him with a slight twitch of her mouth. "That's happened to other people?"

"Indeed it has. Hundreds, I believe. I can imagine it's very unsettling, but let me assure you that it is not, in and of itself, a bad thing—nor in any way the result of anything you might have done."

Stephen followed her gaze out to the unfamiliar vista, noting a cliff in the distance. "What is it, then?" Jane asked, turning back to him, her hazel eyes wide with worry.

"What is an Inhuman?" As he considered how to explain her genetics, Stephen was reminded of medical consultations from his past. Amazing how many he'd gotten through without evidencing the slightest trace of empathy. A very small smile played across his lips as he silently thanked the luck and desperate obstinacy that had brought him to the Ancient One all those years ago. It was something he caught himself doing with a pleasing degree of regularity. "My understanding is that you have some alien DNA in you, from a race called the Kree. But you're essentially human—an evolutionarily accelerated human. There's a community I can help you get in touch with, but first, Jane, I'm going to ask you the obvious question. Why did you attack Dr. Misra?"

"Who?"

"Dark-haired dream scientist, about five foot seven, works for the Baxter Foundation...? You went after her with a knife."

Jane's brows furrowed, and she looked down at her knees.

"Just a little cut. Only so you'd notice. And help. We have to get to Healing. But I think I was too early, maybe?"

Stephen shook his head, understanding neither her answer nor the question that followed. He looked up to survey the view again and found that the landscape had shifted beneath them, bringing them right to the edge of the cliff he'd noticed before. It was unusual for someone to be able to surprise him with a change like that—he could hear Jane's every thought, feel each shift in the tempo of her heartbeat. Every mind he'd ever been inside—surgically or magically—had been unique in some way, but Jane's was disorienting, even for him.

"What did you want me to heal, Jane?"

"What?" Jane blinked at him and shook her head. "No, not you." She covered her face in her hands with a small groan. "Too many doctors..."

Stephen got to his feet, his cloak flapping in the wind behind him as he peered over the edge of the cliff. A battalion of men in gold armor and red tunics stood in phalanx formation at the bottom of the cliff; they seemed to be silently awaiting orders, though Stephen couldn't determine from whom.

"What did you want me to notice?" he asked, trying again.

Jane chewed on her thumbnail, her features tightening in confusion. "It was science that...exploded... No, that's not right." She squeezed her eyes shut for a moment, as if trying very hard to remember something, and then opened them again and looked back up at Stephen. "He did say it won't hurt."

"Who did?"

"The blind man."

It seemed clear that talking to her wasn't going to yield any comprehensible information, so Stephen turned his attention to a magically assisted check-up of the girl's mental health. There were no chemical imbalances beyond what one normally found in adolescence, no brain defects or injuries. He was about to look for genetic markers when the sky darkened above them so dramatically they both looked up.

"It's gonna rain again," Jane said miserably. She got up, moved closer, and gripped Stephen's forearm. Stephen glanced down at the hands clutching the sleeve of his tunic, startled by how protective the small gesture made him feel. "Maybe blood."

The weather had indeed turned ominous: A biting wind forced the large purple flowers covering the hill nearly horizontal with the grass and made Jane shiver.

"I thought I had my coat," she said quietly, more to herself than to Stephen. Reluctantly, she withdrew her hands from his sleeve to rub her bare arms. Lightning ripped through the sky, casting long, eerie shadows across the hill even though there were no objects there to create them.

Stephen glowered, annoyed with his own confusion. Raising his arms above his head to draw the shape of a parabolic arc with the first two fingers of each hand, he conjured a one-room cottage. Instantly, they were inside the small, dark space, standing by a lit hearth, cozy and warm even as rain began to pelt against the structure's exterior. There was a hand-carved table behind them, complete with twig-and-twine chairs; a little cupboard against one wall; and a small, simple bed in one corner. It looked like something out of a fairy tale; though Stephen had created the structure, he knew the girl was unconsciously responsible for the interior decorating. He absently massaged his left hand as he turned to her.

"Jane, are you aware that you're drifting in and out of dreams?"

The girl looked up at him with obvious distress clouding her dark eyes, her lips pressed tightly together. Thunder clapped directly above them, shaking the cabin as though with actual hands. The frightening sensation reminded Stephen to finish checking for insanity. Sending his senses outward, he found and followed the thread of the girl's consciousness. Although frayed, it was still creating an uninterrupted line across her mindscape. That, at least, was good news.

He was about to reassure her that everything was under control when he felt a drop of water splash onto the back of his neck. Turning his attention upward, he saw that the roof was swarming with sharp-teethed somnavores shaped like small baboons. They were eagerly gnawing away at the edifice, making short work of the ceiling beams. He looked at Jane to see whether they were under her control, but she seemed paralyzed by fear, unmoving even as the roof caved in. Stephen threw an energy field over her and then spun around as tusks exploded through the back wall. Wild creatures the size of buffalo began boring through the cottage from every side. As they tore open holes in the walls with their tusks, Stephen saw dozens of them outside in the rain, their eyes blazing as they worked together to dismantle the structure.

Stephen placed a hand on Jane's shoulder, squeezing reassuringly when he felt her trembling. "Just stay calm," he instructed, raising his voice to be heard above the din of the wood-eating creatures, the growling of the larger beasts, and the rain.

As he began mentally crafting a banishment spell, two of the cabin walls collapsed altogether, and Jane screamed as mole-like monsters with long whiskers and sharp claws began burrowing up through the floor. The buffalo-creatures began a slow, menacing advance as Stephen started his incantation. He'd drive them out of Jane's mind and into the Dream Dimension, thereby clearing the girl's head long enough to center her.

"Thou denizens of Nightmare
whom this mind doth overwhelm
Let the Wondrous Winds of Watoomb
blow you back into your realm!"

A squall of iridescent wind gusted across the hill, through the cabin and the rain, and scattered the somanavores like sand. The bedcovers swirled and flew, mingling with ashes from the hearth, and then there was nothing but Jane and Stephen in the rain on the hill, standing in the remnants of the ruined cabin, of which less than a full wall remained.

Exhaling in the relative quiet, Stephen turned to face Jane. "This is all in your head, Jane. I won't say thoughts can't hurt, but you're in no real danger here."

She shivered, hugging herself tightly. Stephen remembered the large, hooded green coat she was wearing back at the Sanctum and conjured it from memory. "I'm always in danger," she said as he helped her slip back into it. "And I'm always dreaming."

Stephen had no doubt she believed what she was saying. "We're going to fix that," he assured her. She looked at him with relief—but then her gaze wandered over his shoulder, and her eyes widened with horror. Turning, Stephen followed the direction of her stare. All of the somnavores he had banished were swarming up over the cliff, streaming back toward them in a raucous stampede.

It should have been impossible. He'd banished them back to the Dream Dimension. Even if the girl's unconscious was stuck on them, they shouldn't have been able to return so quickly.

Stephen was wondering whether he should have tried banishing them with a different spell—the Conjurer's Cone, perhaps—when Jane decided to run. She bolted from the crumbling cottage out onto the rain-soaked hill. Stephen let her go, knowing that though it was certainly possible to disappear into one's mind, it was not possible to hide from someone inside with you. He would simply follow her thread of consciousness back to her when he was ready, in the meantime using her absence as an excuse to perform greater and more violent feats of magic without fear of damaging her psyche.

But as her fleeing form disappeared over the slope of a neighboring hill and the somnavores bore down upon him, Stephen realized that the girl's consciousness was gone. It had vanished entirely from inside her own head— which should not, under any circumstances apart from coma or death, have been possible.

Unable to find the sound of Jane's heartbeat or even a glow of life force to indicate her presence, Stephen released his hold on her mind and returned to his corporeal body with an impatient snap, leaving the somnavores in her head to fight among themselves. He was determined to check her vitals back at the Sanctum—but when he opened his eyes, he found the fingers he had pressed against her forehead suspended in midair.

He was floating in his protective circle alone, Jane's body nowhere to be seen.

The good news was that he no longer harbored any doubts about who was to blame for her plight.

SHARANYA held the Bizen ware teacup in both hands, feeling the warmth seep through the reddish-brown clay. The night after the murders, she had tried to comfort herself with the thought that she would likely never face anything so frightening again, but at least those events hadn't made her question her own sanity. There had been no men floating in midair, no magical protection shields, no mystic martial artists or spontaneous teleportation. Sitting in Doctor Strange's weird little kitchen on Bleecker Street, sipping the oolong Wong had served her as he prepared a tray to bring upstairs, Sharanya was slowly starting to feel calm again. Until, that is, she saw Doctor Strange's apparition opening and closing the cabinets around her with a distracted squint. The figure looked just like him and moved completely naturally, but was colorless and transparent. She recoiled instinctively, but Wong looked up with his usual tranquility.

"Looking for something, Doctor?"

The apparition spoke in a voice that—despite sounding thin, as if it were coming to them from across some great distance—belonged unmistakably to Stephen Strange.

"Jane. Have you seen her?"

"The girl? No." Wong stopped what he was doing to lean thoughtfully against the stove. "You didn't have the Crimson Bands of Cyttorak on her?"

The apparition of Doctor Strange sighed in annoyance, braced itself in front of the refrigerator, rapidly pulled open the door, and then slammed it shut even more quickly. "It didn't occur to me that she might physically slip away within the confines of her own mind."

"Did you check the whole attic?" Wong asked, taking a sip of tea.

"I'm looking there now," said the apparition, while glancing under the small kitchen table at which Sharanya sat. Sharanya stood up hurriedly, not wanting to find out what it would feel like to be touched by such a thing.

"We'll be right up," Wong promised. He lifted the tray he'd been preparing and smiled at Sharanya. "Shall we?"

"He lost the girl?" Sharanya asked as she nervously fidgeted with her bracelet. "Here? In the house?" Though it seemed clear that both Doctor Strange and Wong put genuine effort into making their visitors feel safe, Sharanya could think of no place she'd more dread to be lost.

"Not necessarily," Wong was backing out of the swinging door of the kitchen, his hands full with the tray, and Sharanya hurried to follow him back up the stairs to the meditation room. "She may be in another dimension."

Sharanya wasn't sure whether that would be better. She wasn't even sure what it meant. She put on an extra turn of speed at the second-floor landing, remembering with a shudder the strange creature she'd glimpsed there, and tried not to touch the banisters.

Wong moved more quickly on the way up than he had on the way down, but if he was worried, that was the only external sign of it—and he was likely responding to the stairs rearranging themselves twice on the way. Sharanya swallowed and alternated between looking down at the steps and focusing on Wong's back, watching the muscles there expand and contract with his breath, which she tried to match.

She stopped breathing altogether, though, when Wong dropped the tea tray upon crossing the threshold into the meditation room. She tensed, waiting for the pot to shatter and send hot tea splashing across the floor. Without even looking at them, Strange made a quick hand gesture in their direction, and the falling objects stopped in midair.

The magician...*wizard*...Sharanya wasn't sure *what* to call him...had levitated into the air again, his cloak floating dramatically around him as he concentrated on a large gash in the air. It sizzled with energy, orbited by an oval of glowing red hieroglyphs. It looked to Sharanya as though Strange had ripped open the space-time continuum itself.

Wong gaped at his employer in obvious astonishment. "Doctor! What are you doing?!"

"I've had enough of these games, Wong. I'm summoning Nightmare."

Sharanya felt her heart rate double as she noted the distress in the major-domo's voice.

"Summoning him *here*? Stephen, is that wise?"

A third eye snapped open in the center of Doctor Strange's forehead as he peered into the crackling void he'd created and began what Sharanya felt sure was an incantation, his tone hypnotically commanding.

"Let the Vapours of Valtorr divide,

in the name of the All-Seeing

reveal my ancient enemy,

in whose realm all lay dreaming!"

Apparently finding what he was looking for, Strange thrust his right arm elbow-deep into the gash as he answered his assistant through clenched teeth.

"Jane, it turns out, is a living conduit to the Dream Dimension—*that's* how she disappeared. Her consciousness is directly attached to it; she literally ran from this realm into that one without ever leaving her head. I'm sure Nightmare thinks he can use her to lead an invading army right back this way. But I'm putting a stop to it now."

Sharanya's brow furrowed. Dreams and nightmares were something she knew a good deal about, but she was completely unable to follow what Strange was saying.

"I'm sorry, *where* is the girl now?" she asked.

Wong spoke at the same time. "But how do you know this isn't what he wants?"

Strange wasn't listening to either of them. With one arm still plunged into the breach, he looked up at the large circular window that dominated the room and resoundingly intoned another incantation. If Sharanya hadn't already been scared, Wong flinging his arms out protectively in front of her would have done it.

> "Let the Vapours of Valtorr divide,
>
> And hasten my decree.
>
> Nightmare of the Everinnye
>
> I summon thee to me!"

With a savage grunt, Strange pulled an entity through the laceration he'd made in the air and flung him onto the rug in the center of the circle of protection.

The creature was humanoid, but easily nine feet tall with spiky dark hair and an unsettling green tint to his flesh. He had the pointy ears and long gnarled fingers of a goblin, and a demonic gleam in his overly large, red-tinged eyes.

Sharanya retreated in terror, but then paused as the initial shock faded. On closer inspection, the entity appeared gaunt and weak, as though starved of food and light.

"Stephen," it rasped, not even bothering to rise. "Thank Shuma-Gorath you finally got my message..."

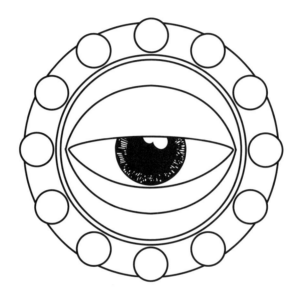

BOOK
II

PROLOGUE

JANE ran blindly down the hill in the rain. Something moved swiftly above her; looking up, she saw a golden eagle gliding through the storm, its wingspan casting a dark shadow across the wet grass. She ran faster to follow it, racing across a small valley and up a short hill, puffing small breaths of steam into the cold, damp air. As she stopped, panting, at the top of the hill, the rain slowed and finally died away, shafts of sunlight breaking through the clouds to illuminate the stone ruins of a shrine. The air smelled like ozone and wet earth. Jane inhaled deeply and began to feel calmer.

Squinting up into the brightening sky, she saw a second eagle gliding toward the other, coming from the opposite direction. They met at the center of the sun, directly over the remains of a circular stone temple. Only three Doric columns stood intact, together holding up the fragment of a three-tiered cornice a few feet out from a crumbling stacked-stone wall. Though she'd never seen it before, Jane suddenly understood that she was standing at the Oracle at Delphi. She stepped carefully into the center of the Tholos, where the eagles had met overhead. But as she searched the sky for them, shielding her eyes from the sun's blinding glare, she found no evidence of either bird.

"They called it the *omphalos*," said a thin male voice behind her. Jane spun to see an old bearded blind man sitting on one of the low square stones that had once been part of the temple wall. He was leaning on a long, gnarled walking stick. She felt almost certain she knew him. "Belly button of the world."

"We've met before, right?" Jane asked, tucking a stray strand of dyed-black hair behind one ear.

The old man smiled.

"Yes, Jane. I'm Praedivinus, remember?" He gestured broadly around them. "And this is my dominion: Realm of Prophetic Dreams."

Jane looked around doubtfully. "I thought it was Greece."

"So it is," Praedivinus agreed with an absent nod. "At least for the moment." He was squinting up at the sky, as Jane had, addressing himself to the sun as much as to her.

Jane crouched in front of him, hugging her knees. "Why are we here?"

Praedivinus rubbed his brow. "It's hard enough to understand the answer to a 'what' question, my dear. There's really almost no hope for a 'why.'"

Jane sighed and fixed him with an exasperated stare. "Okay. *What* am I doing here?"

Praedivinus used his stick to struggle to his feet. "Becoming," he answered with a soft smile. "There is a healer, and a bridge…and a remedy." He winked at her and then opened his arms wide. As if in response, the ground in front of them split with a deafening crack and fell away, leaving nothing in its place. The Earth had divided in two and dropped half of itself into oblivion.

Jane gasped and cowered under the Tholos cornice, astonished by how quickly half of everything had disappeared—half the planet, half the people, half the seas and sky. It looked as though she could take a single step forward and jump off the jagged edge of a flat world into the waiting galaxy, stars sprinkled throughout the endless black of space. She looked over her shoulder for Praedivinus but saw no one; gathering her courage, she crawled to the jagged side of the halved sphere that was once Earth to peer over the edge.

Though the sight was dizzying, Jane's heart leapt with hope. Below her, spinning slowly in space, was Earth. She was somewhere else, and maybe her peril didn't signal the end of everything. Maybe reality marched on without her.

Looking closer, she saw billions of tiny iridescent lights twinkling across the planet's surface, connected to one another by silvery cords as thin as spiderwebs. Tears sprang into her eyes as she realized what they signified: every light a human life, all connected, spinning together, thinking, breathing, evolving, dreaming...

She dragged the back of her hand across her cheek and caught her breath. Maybe it was all right to be dying, or going crazy, or whatever the hell was happening to her, as long as all of that down there continued.

No sooner had she had the thought than some of the lights began to sputter, their soft golden glow dulling and darkening as the threads between them fluttered and fell away like streamers.

"No, please...!"

Jane reached out into the cold darkness of space, but Earth was too far away. She couldn't touch it, couldn't reach anything that mattered. She screamed but knew they couldn't hear her.

She couldn't even hear herself.

CHAPTER VII

STEPHEN had to admit that his old nemesis looked terrible.

Though unimaginably powerful in his own dimension, Nightmare was less so in the realm of waking reality. This was part of why Stephen preferred summoning him away from his native realm, as dangerous as it was to have him walking the Earth. The extradimensional demonic entity was not to be underestimated anywhere, though. He was shrewd, strong, cruel, and ambitious in all places and at all times, consistently retaining the ability to overwhelm anyone who was afraid of anything. Stephen had learned the hard way that it was almost impossible to exist completely without fear, something that Nightmare knew instinctively. He was the living embodiment of terror, and could use anything as a weapon—from someone's thoughts, to the very air around them.

Regional diminishment in powers, in any case, could not account for the Fear Lord's ragged appearance. After settling Sharanya a safe distance back, Wong had pushed a chair into the middle of the protection circle—now functioning as a restraining circle—and Nightmare had slumped into it wearily.

"Your message?" Stephen eyed the demon as he questioned him. Nightmare looked as though he was starving, but how could that be true of a creature who fed on fear, something that was never in short supply, and least of all during the kind of chaos Stephen had witnessed in the past week? "You're the one who had dreamers calling my name?"

One corner of Nightmare's lips pulled away in a dangerous snarl, but he remained otherwise impassive. "I would have sent you a text, but it's so dreadfully hard to get a decent data plan in the Dream Dimension. I take it those gentlemen did manage to pass my message on, though?"

Stephen spoke through clenched teeth. "Moments before they beat each other to death, yes."

Nightmare's eyes widened with interest—or pleasure. "Oops. My bad. I suppose they may have picked up on some…residual aggression toward you on my part." He turned his glowing eyes on the Sorcerer Supreme and grinned slowly.

Stephen looked at Sharanya. She was hyperventilating slightly, no doubt trying to reconcile what the creature had just said with her own understanding of what had happened at her lab. Wong put a hand on her shoulder reassuringly. "Why were you trying to reach me?" Stephen asked Nightmare, turning back toward him.

Nightmare's grin disappeared, and he answered with obvious impatience in a voice that Stephen had always found unsettlingly urbane. "Because the Dream Dimension is a war zone, Stephen. And I'm one of its casualties."

The demon sounded genuinely riled. Out of the corner of his eye, Stephen saw Sharanya stir. Though clearly terrified by Nightmare's presence, she seemed to be working up to asking a question. He shot a warning glance to Wong, who tightened his grip on her shoulder. Though Stephen expected to make use of her insights later, he did not want her calling undo attention to herself in Nightmare's presence.

"A war zone? Who's fighting?"

Nightmare shook his head, his tone contemptuous. "You haven't been sleeping much, Stephen, have you?"

That was true, but not unusual. Stephen had never slept much—both because he was too busy, and because he routinely had such horrifying nightmares he was concerned that more than one dream cycle a night might damage his sanity. Many of these were of Nightmare's personal doing: Stephen had clashed with the dream demon before, saving the waking world numerous times from his attempted invasions. Having come to know Stephen very well over the years, Nightmare had tailored a series of vivid night terrors to every one of the sorcerer's fears and doubts he had uncovered. For years Stephen had endured these nightly attempts to break him, and the Sovereign of Nightmares had yet to find a significant crack in Stephen's armor. Stephen's belief in the work he did—in the entities he served and the universe he defended—was absolute. As time went on, Nightmare seemed to have grown bored with the exercise, or perhaps he realized that Stephen's work caused enough mental agony of its own accord. He left Stephen to torment himself; in turn, Stephen accepted the nightmares—whether of Nightmare's making or his own—as one of the many burdens attendant to the mantle of Sorcerer Supreme.

Nightmare glared at him. "The Pathways are collapsing. No one seems to know what started it, but it appears that one of my fellow Dream Sovereigns is taking advantage of the crisis and attacking other realms, no doubt intent on conquering the whole dimension."

Stephen narrowed his eyes. "That sounds very much like something *you* might try."

"And yet here I am, asking for your help! Do you honestly believe I would do that if I had any other option?" Nightmare's distress appeared to be sincere. "With the Pathways compromised, any one of us can push into another's territory almost undeterred. The Dimension becomes essentially defenseless against external threats—and internally, entire realms can be subsumed."

"The Pathways?" Wong shot Strange an apologetic look as Sharanya, ignoring his warning, suddenly stood and addressed Nightmare directly. "What are those?" She slowly moved closer to the binding circle, but froze mid-step the moment Nightmare's attention cut back to her.

"They're the entry points to the dimension and the literal paths between the realms; they keep the realms separate and safe within the dimension," Nightmare explained, his head canted slightly to one side as he studied her with hard, glittering eyes. "Without them, or sometimes in spite of them, realms can pollute one another even to the point of absorption. Warning dreams, for example, once existed in a space of their own, but have now been absorbed into my realm. Prophetic Dreams and the power of their sovereign, Praedivinus, have weakened as science has eroded people's faith in prophetic dreaming, so that realm has shrunk." His red-tinged eyes flashed back to Strange. "I can feel it happening to mine—another realm pushing in, trying to swallow it whole. In response, my denizens have begun frantically challenging me for control. It's not unheard of for one or two Horrors to test me from time to time, but now it's as if the Dream Dimension's entire population has become poisoned with implacable ambition. They're actively trying to drive me out. And the longer I'm here, the longer my realm stands undefended!"

Remembering the wound he'd received earlier, Stephen crossed his arms. "If you're so concerned with the integrity of the Pathways, why do you have your somnavores rabidly swarming them?"

"That's not my fault, Stephen. They're hungry. As the realm gets smaller, they're forced to go hunting for prey."

Stephen gestured to Nightmare's ragged condition. "And I suppose the same could be said of you?"

Nightmare grimaced. "Yes. I'm starving. My realm is shrinking every day. What few dreamers I do capture all seem to be intrepid zealots, too megalomaniacal to fear anything other than failure. Dreams of which I torture them with, to be sure, but it's not enough to sustain me."

"I'm sorry..." Sharanya interrupted again, this time holding the demon's gaze when he turned to meet her eyes. "You said your realm is...shrinking? What does that *mean*?"

The Everinnye demon rose—slowly unfolding to his full, intimidating height—and smiled darkly at Sharanya. She shrank away from him; Stephen knew all too well the feeling of deep, panicked aversion that had to be turning her stomach to lead as Nightmare's shadow fell across her form.

Stephen's breathing quickened. "Take one step closer to her and I'll destroy your realm myself," he said quietly.

The room darkened. Nightmare flew at Sharanya with his teeth bared, moving so fast Stephen didn't have time to figure out how he'd broken free of the binding circle. Stephen sucked in a breath of alarm and hurled an immobility spell at the demon's streaking form. Black, fizzing energy streamed too late from his palms: He heard the unmistakable crack of Dr. Misra's neck breaking.

"Doctor?"

Wong's worried voice reached Stephen the same instant he remembered the protection ward he'd thrown over Sharanya earlier that day. He was panting with exertion, trying to calm his breathing, when the room as it truly was came back into view. Sharanya was standing next to Wong, blinking at him, and Nightmare stood exactly where Stephen had left him in the binding circle, sniggering nastily.

"Clearly it's been too long since our last encounter, Stephen. So unlike you to show your hand in such a manner. But thank you for the snack. I feel better already."

As Stephen flexed his jaw and drew a rune of protection on his own forehead with his index finger to keep the Fear Lord out, Nightmare turned his attention back to Sharanya.

"Little Sharanya Misra." The demon smiled almost charmingly at the neuroscientist, his voice disconcertingly human in contrast to his appearance. "It's been years since you've visited my realm. How lovely to see you again."

Sharanya recoiled slightly under the intensity of his gaze but did not look away. "We've…met?" she asked, her voice muted with confusion.

Nightmare continued to smile chillingly at Sharanya as he addressed the Sorcerer Supreme. "I doubt she'll forget this time. Unless you intend to mind-wipe her, Stephen."

Stephen glowered at him. "Never mind her. Where's the girl?"

"What girl? What are you talking about? Aren't you going to help me?"

Denial. Dissension. Deflection. Stephen knew that all of these were typical of Nightmare. Nothing the demon said could be trusted. With a flick of two fingers, he cast a small spell to illuminate falsehoods. "Jane Bailey. The Inhuman. You can't tell me you don't know her—you were practically broadcasting through her dreams."

Nightmare's eyes narrowed, and he rolled his shoulders in agitation. "That girl? Is she the one behind all of this?"

"Doubtful." Stephen moved closer. "How do you know her?"

Nightmare looked annoyed by the line of questioning. "The same way I know everyone, Stephen. Bad dreams." Stephen's spell indicated that Nightmare was telling the truth. The demon continued. "Am I really the only dream sovereign who's attempted to make contact? I would have thought every one of them would have been frantically trying to reach you. Though if I'd known you were simply going to tear me out of the Dream Dimension altogether, I would have thought twice about it. Without me there to protect it, the Nightmare Realm will be in ruins by nightfall!"

Stephen had already made up his mind to investigate, stop the power threatening the Dream Dimension, and save the whole of it—Nightmare's realm included—but he couldn't resist needling his enemy. "No more nightmares, no more you... I must confess, I'm not seeing a downside."

"Well, not so fast." Sharanya spoke up suddenly. Nightmare walked slowly up to her in response, his toes just within the boundary of the circle Strange had cast. Sharanya froze. They were close enough to touch, and although Stephen knew his binding circle should prevent that, he was fairly certain Sharanya didn't. If she was banking on the demon proving to be some sort of holographic trick close up, though, she was in for a rude surprise. She swallowed and continued. "Nightmares are unpleasant, but they serve a function. We need them." As Sharanya spoke, she peered up at Nightmare's face more frequently and for steadily longer increments of time. Stephen guessed that she was forcing herself to do so, trying to normalize him by including the dream lord in the conversation most connected to her area of expertise. He wished her luck. "Working through that kind of anxiety when you're asleep is part of what keeps it from dominating your thoughts when you're awake."

Stephen had begun to rub his hands, but stopped abruptly when he realized Nightmare was watching him, noting the absentminded gesture. He crossed his arms and shoved his hands into the recesses of his cloak.

"Say something's bothering you, sitting in your mind as an active anxiety, causing tension." As Sharanya continued, her eyes drifted nervously back to Nightmare. "When you sleep, your dream turns it into a narrative, a story that your brain then moves—literally, via chemicals—into your memory. Memories are easier to deal with than active stress because we understand them as having happened in the past—they're something, in other words, we've already survived." Her gaze collided with Nightmare's then, and she sucked in a quick breath of alarm before looking away and resuming her explanation. "That's any bad dream, really. Technically, a nightmare is specifically a bad dream you wake up from actively stressed…"

Stephen nodded, one hand finding its way back out of the folds of his cloak to pinch the bridge of his nose. He understood the functional necessity of bad dreams—but also knew how pernicious Nightmare could be. It was intriguing to imagine a presence in the Dream Dimension that could temper the demon's aggression, but Stephen tucked the thought away to reconsider once he had more information about the nature and intent of this potentially exploitable threat. In the meantime, he had to focus on finding Jane. "I'm aware of all that. But there's still a girl missing who was in this room mere moments ago."

Nightmare lifted one shoulder in a defensive half-shrug. "I'm afraid there's nothing I can do to help with that, Stephen. I can't imagine why you think I know anything about where she is."

Stephen noted the first faint red glow of his lie-detecting cantrip, indicating that Nightmare was not being completely honest. His hands balled into fists; with an almost indecipherable wince of pain, he released them. "Perhaps because your somnavores chased her into the Dream Dimension."

"She's in the Dream Dimension? Physically?" The demon lifted a single eyebrow. "How is that possible?"

"I'm not entirely sure yet." Stephen turned to Sharanya. "Dr. Misra, if dreams did exist in a physical space, and that space was being encroached upon, what would that mean for humanity's experience of dreaming? Could it, for example, influence behavior?"

Still standing practically toe-to-toe with Nightmare, Sharanya turned her head toward Stephen. It looked as if the movement cost her effort, a deliberate attempt not to fear something that was clearly terrifying. "If a type of dream became less frequent or ceased to exist, you mean?"

Stephen thought for a moment before answering. "Let's assume the opposite. What if a specific type of dream began to dominate everyone's experience in their sleep?"

Sharanya nodded. "I suppose it's possible. If all nightmares became subordinate to, for example, erotic dreams, then eventually, yes, you might see changes in courtship. Or if all anyone ever had were pleasant, happy dreams, you might see a slow erosion of mental health as stressors built up, or possibly for some people a decrease in drive and ambition." Stephen watched as Sharanya finally allowed herself to take a step back from the binding circle. "This is all theoretical, though. Obviously, I can't speak to direct causalities."

"What if this Inhuman girl you're looking for is just a conduit?" Nightmare thoughtfully pressed a finger to his lips. "You said you sensed an immortal channeling through her, but I'm quite certain it wasn't me. What if it was...Dormammu?"

Nightmare infused the name with so much menace Stephen found himself turning toward him. "It wasn't Dormammu, but your commitment to trying to scare me is admirable." Stephen gazed up at the Anomaly Rue. "The information we need isn't here. It's there, in the Dream Dimension. Wong, do you still have the knife Jane used to threaten Dr. Misra? I want to put a psychometry spell on it so that I can use it to locate her once inside."

"Yes, Doctor." Wong pulled the hunting knife out of his belt and carefully handed it to Stephen. The Sorcerer Supreme opened his third eye to examine the object, looking for psychic traces of its owner. It was a solid hunting knife, designed to allow for interchangeable blades. Weighing six ounces, it had a thermoplastic handle and a nearly four-inch, stainless-steel drop-point blade. More significantly, it had been a gift from Jane's father on her 19th birthday. She associated it with the upstate camping trips they took together every summer, making it exactly one of the two things Stephen needed.

He placed it on his altar to enchant and turned to the other.

"If not nightmares, Dr. Misra, do you have any thoughts as to what kind of dreams might cause an increase in violent crime?"

Sharanya began fiddling with the elephant charm at her wrist again as she answered. Stephen assumed it was an unconscious effort to quiet her nerves. "That's more or less what I'm looking at in my research. Or rather, the opposite—what kind of dreams might help decrease instances of violence in psychotic populations. But..." Her eyes dropped to the floor, "...that's assuming that all of that happens within the brain."

She gestured toward Nightmare without looking at him. "I couldn't even begin to tell you how it might fit into..." She trailed off, unable to put Nightmare and the dimension he represented into words. When she looked up at Stephen again, he recognized the burning curiosity in her eyes. "I thought I had my hands full trying to determine how the right and left hemispheres communicate, but if dreams occur in another realm entirely...one we travel to without leaving our bodies...I... How would that even *work*?"

Stephen thought about how far brain science had come since he'd first studied it—and how far it still had to go. "You want answers," he said, allowing a slight smile to lessen the intensity of his gaze. "There are none I can express to you with words. But I can bring you directly to the experience."

Sharanya looked confused for a second, and then she balked. "Wait—you mean go with you? To another dimension?"

"You go there every night, Dr. Misra. Though, admittedly, not like this." As Sharanya continued to gape up at him, Stephen's smile broadened. "Come with me, and you'll get answers you never dreamed of..."

CHAPTER VIII

"HOW ARE you not trying to talk me out of this?!" Sitting on a pile of meditation cushions against the east wall listening to her mother's encouragement, Sharanya was beginning to wonder why she'd bothered calling home. "I don't think you understand what's happening here, Mom. I'm about to go to sleep in a strange man's attic with another man 'watching over my body' so that we can access the Dream Dimension, find a girl who tried to kill me, and walk a demon home! Oh, and probably stop a war, too, while we're at it!"

Strange had finished enchanting Jane's blade and was busy preparing a magical conduit to the Dream Dimension. Sharanya shuddered as she recalled Jane brandishing the hunting knife at her. And yet ever since she'd seen the young woman lying unconscious on the rug with the sorcerer hovering over her, she'd found it difficult to feel fear or anger toward her. Though Sharanya was still having trouble with the idea that Jane Bailey had somehow disappeared into an entirely separate dimension, it was clear enough that she was lost and in need of help. If saving her was on the agenda, then one part of what Sharanya had agreed to do, at least, seemed valid.

"You have to go out and try new things if you ever hope to meet anyone, Sharanya. Do not tell me you think the head of neurosurgery at New York

Hospital isn't worth a few hours of your Friday night."

"That's not—he doesn't do that anymore. Forget I told you that part. It's completely irrelevant." She took a sip of the new tea Wong had given her and wrinkled her nose. The oolong had been replaced with a special medicinal brew meant to aid her sleep and enhance her dreams. It had none of the graceful grass notes she'd enjoyed before, tasting instead of soil and must.

"It is not irrelevant. It speaks to his character and his earning potential. People trust this man, yes?"

Sharanya glanced at Doctor Strange. Framed by the circle of the unusual window that dominated the room's western wall, he muttered strange words and made dramatic gestures while wearing the calmly rational expression of a scientist. It seemed to Sharanya that he spoke like a scientist, too, which had the dangerous effect of making her feel like he made sense, even when the things he said were so clearly impossible. Worse, when his bright blue eyes looked directly into hers, Sharanya had the unsettling sense that she'd do almost anything he asked of her.

She went to put the teacup down on a nearby coffee table, but it was covered—as was almost every surface of the room—in books. Curious, she examined the ones closest to her. The book on top had something to do with quantum tunneling; beneath it was one on twin primes, as well as a quadratic equations workbook.

Sharanya looked back up at Strange and then dropped her voice. "Mom, I think he does math. For *fun*. There's a book here on twin primes. Do you know how much of a math nerd you need to be to study twin primes?"

"Go and enjoy yourself, Sharanya, and call me the minute you get home. I have to go now. Your brother's on the other line…"

"Yeah, okay, good night, Mom. Love you." Sharanya hung up and pulled the Bluetooth out of her ear. "Really hope to see you again someday."

She forced herself to take another sip of the tea, thinking how much she'd prefer to have a glass of wine. Strange was making an inverted sign of the horns with his hands and murmuring something in a language she didn't understand. Nightmare was watching, too, with avid interest, and Sharanya caught herself wondering whether he knew magic, as well—and if so, was it the same magic Strange knew? She shook her head and peered suspiciously into her cup. She was quite sure she'd woken up that morning as someone who knew better than to drink a strange beverage offered to her by a strange man in a strange house, but it had been a very long and very peculiar day.

When she looked up, Strange was crouching beside her, looking completely sane except for his long red cape.

"Normally we would enter the Dream Dimension through the Pathways," he explained calmly, wearing an expression that made it clear that he expected to be taken seriously. "But that's not an option right now. Instead, I'm going to open a portal into one of the dream realms with which I'm familiar. When you arrive there, you're going to be in a dream, and we probably won't be together. It can be a little disorienting at first, but remember—dreamers are very powerful in the Dream Dimension. You should find the realm quite receptive to your thoughts." He looked directly into Sharanya's eyes then; although his gaze was compassionate, she found herself looking away. There was something intense about him, and she was already feeling a little unanchored by the tea. "I'll come find you as soon as I can. Just focus on your breathing and wait. Wong will protect your physical form here; you won't be in any true danger."

Sharanya blinked up at him again as a new thought occurred to her. "But you will be? In danger, I mean?"

Strange looked unconcerned. Sharanya got the distinct impression that he risked his life often and with little fear. Increasingly muddled by the dreaming tea, she couldn't decide whether that was reassuring. "Nightmare and I are going in physically—so yes, technically we'll be vulnerable to corporeal harm, as will Jane until we can get her body safely back to this plane. But let me worry about that part."

Sharanya was surprised by how willing she felt to do just that. Maybe it was because he accepted responsibility so readily. Or maybe it was the tea. "What if Nightmare finds me before you do?" she asked through a yawn. Though the thought was alarming, Sharanya noted her own panic with drowsy detachment.

"It will take him a while to regain his strength," Strange answered. "And we won't start in his realm. Just remember that you've survived every nightmare you've ever had."

He reached out suddenly and touched the exact center of her forehead with one finger, drawing what felt like an oval before pressing the heel of his palm against it. It was the first time she'd really looked at his hands. They were horrifically damaged—stiff and scarred. And as he touched her, sending a small jolt of energy through her flesh like a pinpoint of electrical current, they began tremoring.

"Wong says you were a brain surgeon once," she blurted suddenly, feeling like she ought to know more about the man in whose attic she was about to sleep. "Is that true?"

"That was another lifetime ago." He was about to get up, but seemed to think better of it, steepling his hands as he explained. "I should probably clarify—I don't mean that literally. It was a long time ago, and I was a different man then." Sharanya watched him intently, trying to ignore the feeling of Nightmare's eyes on her back. "I can see that you're struggling with all of this," Strange acknowledged. "Think of magic as an extension of science; go beneath the molecules and the atoms, and there it is, holding everything together. It's the why, the triumph of collective interdependencies over classifying dissimilarities.

It's life wanting to exist, and finding a way to thrive, in an indifferent universe." He took her hand, calmly balling it into a fist as he covered it with one of his own. It seemed to Sharanya that the scars were from operations—maybe dozens of them. "Reality," he said, with his hand covering the whole of her fist. Next, he lightly tapped her thumb. "Science." And then he tapped her pinky. "Magic. All the same components—we're just untangling the problem from the opposite end."

His confidence seemed absolute, and when he rose again she could think of no objections worth uttering, as crazy as the whole plan still seemed to her. She settled carefully into the cushions, trying not to worry about the lightness in her limbs or the tingling in her head as she lay down.

Feeling pleasantly lethargic, Sharanya watched the luminous energy from Strange's spell cast colorful patterns across the ceiling of the Sanctum attic as he opened a portal through time and space, his incantation the most peculiar lullaby she had ever heard.

"Arise, you sulfurous mists,

to dissolve three-dimensional seams.

Open a door to the Realm Unreal,

Uncloak the Dimension of Dreams!"

CHAPTER IX

STEPHEN stepped through the shimmering portal and instantly sank into the rippling softness of a thick, white, eiderdown quilt. Though he could have resisted, he let it settle over him, smiling as the illusion, fetched from his memories but not of his doing, coalesced around him.

If he hadn't recognized the cool feel of the Frette sheets against his skin, then the chandelier above his head and the gold-gilded crown molding would have cinched it. The room was dark, lit only by the glow of low flames crackling in an open-hearth fireplace. It was his favorite hotel room at the Plaza—or would have been, if not for the chimerical enhancements. The circular bed, the floor-to-ceiling windows, the profusion of orchids—he was dimly aware that those details were borrowed from other rooms in other places, creating a new room altogether, but one in which every detail was reassuringly familiar. His hotel room—the one that existed only in his mind.

And in the Dream Dimension.

Feeling a warm, soft hand on his arm, Stephen remembered why he couldn't properly call himself a practitioner of Zen. So much of the philosophy depended on letting go—of yearning, of attachment, of desire—for perfectly good reasons that had everything to do with equilibrium and nothing to do with self-denial. But Stephen wanted. He had always wanted. In his earlier life, he had hungered for prestige, the eldest son of a farming family in Nebraska intent on some imagined better life in which no one could ever look down on him. He had raced through medical school and the cascading deaths of his family members with singleminded focus, increasingly convinced that success would validate the emotional sacrifices he was making to get there. It was circular logic, but it had been effective. He had become a world-famous brain surgeon—head of his department, top of his game—but also an aloof, arrogant, cold, and narcissistic son of a bitch by anyone's standards. The hunger, of course, had never abated, though he had become unsure about how to feed it. More money? More prestige? More lives saved? He'd reached the pinnacle of his career and still felt empty.

He would have gone on like that, though, if not for the car crash. He'd run off the road, plunging headlights-first off the side of an embankment. They'd told him he was lucky to be alive—but where other doctors saw a miracle, Stephen saw only a malicious twist of fate. The accident destroyed both of his hands, the ulnar and median nerves severed. His career as a surgeon was over. He would never hold a scalpel again.

There were things he could have done to adjust, but he did none of them. Instead, he fell into drinking and despair. His only thought was to get back what he'd lost, and to that end he'd chased obsessively after a cure. He took experimental pharmaceuticals, demanded operations, endured painful and expensive procedures—to no avail. By the time he was ready to admit that Western medicine—his creed—had failed him, he was broke and drunk and drifting aimlessly.

It was in that state that he first heard whispers about other kinds of remedies—supernaturalistic health-treatment methods, mystical cures. Convinced he had nothing left to lose, he had followed the most compelling rumor to Tibet.

There was so much chance in it. He laughed sometimes over how hard he'd made the universe work to get him where it needed him to be. The car crash, the hand damage, the overheard stories about a magical being who could cure any ill—Stephen knew his fate had once rested on nothing but sheer luck and his own obstinate nature. And yet, in his pursuit of a lost status quo, he had stumbled across a rebirth. The all-consuming need to put everything back the way it had been before the accident fell away from him like a bad dream. A new life emerged, one full of magic and compassion and awe. Under the Ancient One's fond tutelage, he'd realigned himself mentally, morally, and spiritually while training to be a sorcerer. He'd replaced arrogance with humility, materialistic greed with selfless service, misanthropy with true empathy. His careless way with his fellow human beings grew into a protectiveness so keen, their collective need would have felt unbearable had he not also developed the power to aid them. The hunger for prestige was replaced by a hunger for knowledge, and the world that opened up before him was so vast, he knew he could feed that appetite for the span of five lifetimes and still have a million things left to learn.

"You're forgetting something," a lyrical, feminine voice whispered into his ear. "You're forgetting the other thing you learned to want."

Stephen turned to examine the beauty lying beside him. The woman to his left had flowing blonde hair, creamy skin, and eyes as deep and blue as a mermaid lagoon, her bee-stung lips flushed and gently parted.

"What's that?" he asked lightly, hooking an arm around her shoulders. Her flesh was smooth beneath his fingertips.

"Oh, I forgot," she teased. "It's a secret you like to keep from yourself. But I'm going to tell, Stephen Strange."

Gently, she took hold of his hand, slipping her fingers between his. She paused, frowning playfully, and looked pointedly at his wedding band.

Stephen startled, pulling his hand back. He couldn't remember when he'd put it on. More upsettingly, he couldn't remember when he'd taken it off. It was a magical ring, but only half complete, a single band that he and his wife wore simultaneously.

"You still call her that? Your 'wife'?" The blonde smiled mockingly as she walked her fingernails up his chest, and Stephen realized he was in bed with the sovereign of the Realm of Erotic Dreams. "Well, look who turned out to be an incurable romantic after all…"

He knew what she meant by "after all." Romance had not been part of his life before his metamorphosis. He'd had neither the time nor patience for it, shunning intimacy so effortlessly he occasionally wondered whether he wasn't missing the drive that should have pushed him toward it altogether. Other people were messy. They needed things. They died. He wanted none of it.

And if he were being honest with himself, that disconnect continued, albeit in a less egotistical way, after his transformation. There had been so much to learn, so much to let go of and experience and master. The Ancient One and Wong became his only true friends; he thought of everyone else as being either in need of his protection or his opposition. No one got close, not truly. At least, initially. At least until—

"Are you keeping count, Stephen?" Erotica giggled, gesturing out past the bed, where the room suddenly filled with beautiful women he knew—by some definition of the word. Occasionally one would catch his eye and share a secret smile. There was Wanda again. Morgana. Linda. A student of magic whose name he couldn't remember. Well, more than a few students of magic whose names he couldn't remember. "Because I feel like I missed some."

Stephen cleared his throat and started to sit up. "Lovely to see you, as always, Erotica, but I'm here on business and really must excuse myself…"

"Stephen Strange!" She took a playful swat at his shoulder. "One might think you're more afraid of your good dreams than your bad ones." Before he could speak, she had straddled him and was gripping the headboard, wearing a predatory smile. He sucked in a shaky breath.

"You…don't seem to want me to leave," he acknowledged, letting one hand gently caress the small of her back. "But I have work to do here—"

"Oh, I know. More work than you realize, Stephen." She bent down toward him, her hair falling like a curtain around his face, her lips mere inches above his own. "It'd be easier if you'd stop by more often, but I suppose Nightmare keeps you busy."

Stephen held her gaze and slowly filled his chest with air, regaining control of his breathing. "Where is he, Erotica? We came through the portal together, and you know as well as I that it wouldn't do for me to lose him here."

The Dream Sovereign's expression took on a sad, petulant quality, but her voice remained seductively sweet. "And why would you do that? Why would you bring him here? As pleased as I am to have you here physically, actually in the flesh, I can't help wondering why you're so intent on destroying this part of yourself?"

Uncertainty crept into Stephen's tone as he put his hands on her upper arms and moved her carefully back. "Destroying this…?" He sat up. "I don't know what you're talking about, Erotica, but I'm here to help." Moonlight flooded the windows, illuminating the room with streams of silvery blue. Stephen began looking around for his clothes, spying them, finally, on a chaise across from the fireplace. He tried to move Erotica off his lap, but she shifted her weight and pressed her mouth against his ear.

"Nightmare's here," she whispered. "You needn't worry over him. And you needn't worry over me, either, because at the moment he's too weak to hurt me. I would have sent him far away, but I assumed you had him with you for a reason."

Stephen tried to stay on point. "Nightmare's assisting me with the problem in the Pathways. They're riddled with somnavores, as I'm sure you've noticed, and either indicative of or supporting a larger problem here in the dimension."

Erotica gazed imploringly at Stephen. "Of course I've noticed," she said. "Larger realms are swelling and consuming smaller ones whole. Every time that happens, the Pathways separating them are also subsumed. And so it becomes cyclical: Weak or absent Pathways lead to expanding realms; the expanding realms destroy more Pathways. Without them there are no boundaries, no divisions. Do you really want to see a merging of erotic dreams and nightmares? Just stay with me, Stephen. The realm will be safe as long as you're here." She leaned forward long enough to bite his lower lip and then rocked back again, dropping her voice. "And I promise I'll keep you very entertained…"

Stephen kept his eyes on Erotica, trying to maintain his focus. "It's not Nightmare, though," he said. "It's happening to his realm, too." Finally forcing himself to admit that he'd recovered from the initial fog of delirium that always clouded his thinking in this realm—and knowing he would sink right back under it if he didn't leave the bed—Stephen teleported himself over to the fireplace, careful to arrive there fully dressed. "I have to figure out who's behind it, and the answer's buried somewhere inside the psyche of a very confused girl…"

"A girl?" Erotica got out of the bed slowly, her skin gleaming in the moonlit dark. "What possible use could you have for a girl when I'm here?"

"She's lost, and scared, and potentially connected to the problem with the Pathways." Stephen graced Erotica with a modest smile and a bow. "I promise I'll visit again, but now I have to go."

He didn't see her cross the room, but Erotica was standing in front of him suddenly, her hypnotic blue eyes flashing into his as she drew a heart with her finger across the front of his tunic. "You're going make me pull out the big guns, aren't you?"

The room dissolved suddenly, leaving Stephen momentarily unsure of his location. He looked up in an effort to orient himself, only to see the stars spinning overhead. When they stopped, he was sitting on the roof of the Sanctum Sanctorum in the dark of predawn. Erotica sat beside him, her head on his shoulder, his cloak wrapped around her as they huddled together for warmth. Stephen swallowed. He knew this memory.

"Don't—" he warned huskily.

"Don't what?" Erotica's neck seemed to lengthen and her curves became more voluptuous. Under the moonlight, her hair took on a silvery quality, shimmering soft white. Stephen's throat constricted. Before he could stop himself, his hand went up to brush it back. He was longing to see Clea's face with such intensity that it somehow failed to surprise him when he did. She lifted her head to smile at him, her wide blue eyes full of wonder, and Stephen lost his breath. The expressive brow, the small upturned nose, the delicate lips...he knew them all so well.

"Don't look directly at it," he heard himself say, from the distance of a great many years. "It's bright enough to hurt your eyes."

"How old are you here?" It was Erotica again, kneeling on the roof behind him, naked and apparently unseen by Clea. Stephen ignored her. The planet was rotating slowly toward the sun, and Clea had turned to witness her first sunrise on Earth with an awe as warm and wide as the star she was watching. Stephen couldn't take his eyes off her. "Late 30s? Already 40? And you'd honest-to-god never been in love before."

Clea grabbed his arm and squeezed it. "Oh, Stephen! It does this every morning?"

He laughed, enchanted by her delight. "It does."

One of Clea's hands flew to her mouth then; her fingertips pressed against her lips as she continued watching the sun come up over New York City. After a moment, radiant in the first golden rays of daylight, she turned to Stephen and met his eyes.

He knew it wasn't real, but he caught Clea's hand just the same, drawing it to his heart before reaching up with his free hand to pull her closer. Tangling his fingers into her hair as he locked his lips against hers, he was overawed by the scent of her skin, the taste of her mouth as it opened to his.

Just one. Just to remember.

It had always been magical when they kissed.

CHAPTER X

SHARANYA opened her eyes and found herself lying barefoot on a comfortable bed in a clean hotel room. The sun outside the large windows was high and felt pleasantly warm on her face.

Sitting up, she stretched and smiled, delighted by the peaceful stillness. Noticing a sliding-glass door at the far end of the windows, she stood, padded over to it, and pulled it open. The air outside was fresh and cool with just a hint of brine, and, peeking over the narrow cement balcony, she saw that she was at least 20 floors above a tranquil ocean view. It reminded her of a photo she'd seen of a hotel in San Diego while researching a conference she had eventually decided she couldn't afford to attend. Had she gone after all, and somehow forgotten the plane ride? Considering how serene she felt, it was strangely difficult to think clearly.

She started as she heard the sound of a card key in the door. Stepping back into the room, she closed the sliding door behind her and stared in confusion at the man who walked in. He was undeniably handsome: tall and broad-shouldered with thick dark hair, intelligent brown eyes, and an endearingly lopsided smile. He was even Indian—her mother would love him. Sharanya felt sure that she knew him, and that he belonged there, but had no idea what his name was.

"So these are the only ones they had in your size. I tried to convince myself they were 'charcoal'…" He pulled a pair of black flip-flops out of the bag, still attached to one another by a plastic tag-fastener, and grimaced apologetically. For a second, his confidence almost won her over. He was so sincere, intimate—even armed with an in-joke about how much she hated wearing black. Longing to touch him, she was suddenly aware of the laughing conversation she'd had with him before he'd run down to the lobby gift shop for her. She had sent him to fetch waterproof shoes so they could take a romantic stroll down the beach. The whole discussion played out as though it were happening right that second. She could see the love-making they were planning on engaging in later that evening, too. And she was still standing in the room, looking at him. Time was no longer even pretending to move linearly.

Cheeks flushed, Sharanya let herself move closer. As he dangled the flip-flops from his right hand, she tentatively touched the sinewy muscles of his left forearm, melting when he smiled in response. Standing toe-to-toe with him, the chemistry was overwhelming. He was absolutely perfect. How was she not able to remember who he was? He dropped the shoes and slipped a large, warm hand behind her head, gently lifting her hair off the back of her neck as he pulled her closer. Sharanya closed her eyes and shivered with pleasure as he leaned in to kiss her.

"That's strange," he said suddenly. She opened her eyes; he was peering over her shoulder at the open suitcase she'd left sitting out on the small metal luggage rack by the television. "Did you pack a hunting knife?"

Sharanya's breath caught in her throat. She did have a knife. No—she'd *seen* a knife. She'd seen a knife somewhere recently, but couldn't remember why the thought of it troubled her.

"Strange," she repeated; a sense of urgency was building in her chest. She took a step back and away from him, feeling like she was missing something important. "That is strange. That's strange, and I need to go…"

"Shar, no, the conference doesn't even start until tomorrow morning. You don't have to go anywhere."

With less alarm than the situation seemed to warrant, Sharanya realized she'd been completely mistaken. It was a woman in the room with her. She had the same shiny dark hair as the man, but much longer, and golden eyes that glittered with mischief when she pushed her sunglasses up to the top of her head. The chemistry was just as strong. The woman smiled, dimples softening an otherwise rakish grin, and once again Sharanya felt convinced she knew her, even without being able to remember how they'd come to be there. The woman kicked the thongs under the bed with a spirited snort of disgust.

"You're right, though, these are hideous. So plain-Jane. Go barefoot. I'll rub your feet when we get back…" She cocked her head to one side and then suddenly pulled Sharanya close again. "Unless you'd rather I rub them now…?"

"Oh, umm…" Sharanya was stuck on the phrase "plain-Jane," but felt her knees go weak as the woman playfully pushed her onto the bed before seating herself at the footboard.

"Come on, let me see those feet."

Sharanya obeyed, languorously sliding her feet onto the woman's lap and closing her eyes. She swallowed, tingling with pleasure, as the soft, sure hands worked their way from the arches of her feet up her calves. She even sighed as someone sat down on the bed behind her and began to rub her shoulders.

"Ah, massages," said the man who had purchased the shoes. He was working on her shoulders while the woman with the sunglasses rubbed her feet. "Always the pathway to a woman's heart."

Sharanya's eyes flew open, and she jumped off the bed. Both her would-be lovers stared at her, apparently unconcerned with one another's presence in the room.

"No, no, no," Sharanya stammered, flustered. "I'm sorry. I have to go. I have to."

"Seriously?" The woman got up off the bed, crossed her arms over her chest, and rolled her eyes. "You doctors just absolutely can't do work/life balance, can you?"

Still seated on the bed, the man agreed. "It's possible to have a relationship *and* a career, you know. You can even have more than one of both. But you have to be open to it."

Sharanya blinked rapidly, stung. Maybe it was just because she hadn't met the right person yet. It annoyed her that some of her family had decided she was a lesbian the moment her 30th birthday had passed without an engagement. She liked women, it was true. But she also liked men. And yet even with that seeming advantage when it came to dating, she was alone—and less unhappy about it than everyone else seemed to think she ought to be.

"There's no rush," she said defensively. "I have a lot going on at work right now, and—"

The woman threw her hands up. "I give up. The compartmentalization is insane. You're just as bad as Strange."

Strange! Doctor Stephen Strange! With a rush of relief, Sharanya felt it all come back to her: the study, the attack, the Sanctum, the journey to the Dream Dimension. Strange had warned her about the disorientation. She glanced nervously at a bedside clock, wondering how much time she'd wasted, but couldn't read it.

"You're both absolutely lovely." Moving quickly to the door, Sharanya spoke rapidly to the bewildered dream figments. "If either of you *are* real, please come find me—when I'm, you know, awake." After one last look at each of her suitors, she backed out of the room into the hotel hallway.

The door swung shut behind her with a firm click, and Sharanya realized she didn't have a key. She didn't even have her shoes. The excitement of re-membering what was happening died out as quickly as it had sparked. She looked up and down the long hallway in dismay, feeling increasingly pan-icked, the scrollwork on the patterned carpet runner undulating endlessly to either side of her. She had no idea how to find Doctor Strange.

She went up and down the hall, listening at a few of the doors, but couldn't make out Strange's voice in the collection of groans and sighs and laughter that seemed to emanate from every one of them. Remembering the view from the balcony in her room, she began to despair. She wasn't even sure she could find *that* room again. The hotel was huge and filled with dreamers with whom she probably wasn't meant to interact. She could wander the halls forever, be forced to subsist on ice and vending-machine snacks. And what if everything Strange had said about the Dream Dimension was true? What if it was at war, or collapsing in on itself? How would she ever get out? Would she end up locked in her mind as her body slowly decayed on the third floor of the Sanctum Sanctorum? Or would mental and physical death be instantaneous, wiping her out of existence altogether—like the girl, Jane, who had vanished into thin air?

The hallway lights sputtered and then went out, plunging Sharanya into darkness. She spun, searching for the faint glow of an exit sign, and found her path blocked by a warm, solid form. Holding her breath, she moved to one side. It moved with her. Red eyes flashed in the dark. White fangs gleamed. Sharanya screamed.

The lights flickered and then came up again, revealing Nightmare in the middle of the hallway. He smiled at her darkly. "Was it as good for you as it was for me?"

Sharanya caught her breath, a hand on her heart. She had the disconcert-ing sensation of being both horrified to find herself alone with the demon and relieved to have located a member of her party. Nightmare appeared somewhat more energetic than he had in Strange's attic, though whether that was due to being back in the Dream Dimension or having just frightened her, Sharanya wasn't sure.

"Have you seen the doctor?" she asked tersely.

Nightmare glared first up and then down the hall. "Stephen's in here somewhere, most likely with the realm's sovereign, Erotica. She adores him." He went to the door closest to him and rattled the handle. It was clear he couldn't get in, and Sharanya wondered whether he'd been in the hall the whole time, unable to access any of the rooms. "It's mystifying, I know, but she's somewhat less fond of me."

Sharanya eyed the doors closest to her, wishing they were numbered as they would have been in a normal hotel. The math books she'd seen on Strange's coffee table made her think she could have started looking for him by knocking on the rooms marked by primes—but no such luck. "That's good, right? He's enlisting her aid?"

Nightmare leered nastily. "If that's what they're calling it these days." He looked up suddenly, narrowing his eyes at Sharanya, and she felt her stomach flip. He still terrified her. "Though, come to think of it, it's probably the other way around. I'd imagine she's begging him for his protection right about now." Nightmare took a step closer to Sharanya, smiling down at her in his discomforting, unfriendly way. "Quite the knight in shining armor, really, our Stephen. You'd throw yourself at his feet in a frenzy of gratitude if you knew how many times he had stood, unyielding, between you and unspeakable horrors." Sharanya said nothing, and the demon continued, seeming to warm to his theme. "Day in and day out, the Sorcerer Supreme is the watcher on the wall, a single man tirelessly holding back the annihilation of everything you hold dear." He peered sideways at Sharanya. "And quite a dashing figure he cuts there, wouldn't you say? What with that…jaunty?…facial hair and… hm…*taut* physique…"

Sharanya, aghast, peered up at Nightmare. "What is wrong with you? Why are you talking that way?"

Nightmare squinted at something over Sharanya's shoulder and then turned his attention back to her. She tried to locate what might have caught his eye but saw nothing beyond the rows and rows of indistinguishable doors.

"You don't find him attractive?"

Sharanya blinked. "Have you been talking to my mother?"

"Just imagine what he could do with all that magic in the bedroom."

"I don't understand—is this leading up to you trying to scare me again?"

"It's not a frightening thought, is it? *Imagine* it."

Sharanya shrugged, but her mind was already running with the suggestion. Truthfully, it wasn't difficult to think of Strange amorously—but the demon had the important details all wrong. It wasn't the mustache or the physique; it was the intensity and the calm self-assurance. He seemed like a man who knew his place in the universe—and probably yours, too. And then there were his hands. Though it surprised her, Sharanya found the damage alluring. There was vulnerability in his scars that elicited a tender, sympathetic response from her. Whatever else he might be, those hands made him human.

Just as her cheeks were beginning to color, Nightmare smirked with satisfaction and gestured to something behind her: a door to a roof-access stairwell. It had not been there seconds before, Sharanya was sure. She gaped at Nightmare, confused.

"You're a dreamer," he explained impatiently. "And we're in the realm of Erotic Dreams… Do you still not understand?" He pushed open the heavy metal door and gestured for her to go first.

Sharanya stepped into the stairwell, the concrete floors and ascending metal stairway cold beneath her stockinged feet. She glanced at Nightmare over her shoulder. "Are you telling me I just conjured him?"

Nightmare let the stairwell door close behind him and began following her up to the roof. "Well, Denak knows *I* wasn't going to do it."

Watching her feet as she climbed the stairs, Sharanya tried visualizing a warm, comfortable pair of shoes. The Dream Dimension obliged her so readily that she smiled, wondering what she ought to conjure next as she pushed open the second heavy door that led out to the building's roof.

SENSATION crashed through Stephen like white-water rapids. For a full minute he was lost in it—the exquisite shock of unguarded intimacy, the warmth of her soft body as she trembled in his arms. It was the first time they kissed.

Or, Stephen supposed with growing anger, the second time they kissed for the first time. Because this wasn't really happening. It wasn't really Clea. He wasn't really sitting on the roof of the Sanctum, and this wasn't really fair. Hearing an access door creak open, he abruptly pulled away from Erotica. Two silhouetted figures made their way out onto the roof, one of them unmistakable even in the dark.

"Oh, a little role-play, how delightful!" Nightmare drew closer to the couple with a mocking sneer, stepping in front of Sharanya. "And yet how sadly predictable, Stephen. You could have recreated that foursome—ooh, or remember that masked Halloween ball? But no—you spend an evening in the Realm of Erotic Dreams chastely smooching your wife."

Still cloaked in Clea's illusion, Erotica jumped up to glare at Nightmare. Stephen bristled as he got to his feet after her.

"Take that face off," he said darkly to Erotica's back. "Immediately." Nightmare's presence amplified his urgency. Stephen had no intention of being subject to another bad dream about Clea's death. It was one of

Nightmare's favorite scenarios with which to torture him.

When Erotica transformed back, he let out a long, slow breath. Even a naked goddess was less distracting to him than the fully clothed Clea. Standing just behind Nightmare, Sharanya watched Erotica with fascination before turning shining eyes on the Sorcerer Supreme. Stephen nodded to her, and she smiled back with what Stephen assumed to be relief.

"Come no farther!" Facing Nightmare, Erotica flung out a hand, suspending the Fear Lord a few inches above the rooftop. She was livid as she turned back to Stephen. "I want him out of here! He is not welcome in this realm!"

Nightmare scoffed, seemingly unconcerned with his predicament as he hung limply in the air.

"Oh, Erotica. I'd watch that tone if I were you. Has any human ever visited here without dragging in a shadow of fear and shame behind them? Can you not smell the stench of mortality hanging over their frantic dreams of copulation? You don't exist without me, and it would be embarrassingly simple to sweep this realm up into mine."

"And yet that is so very much *not* why we're here," Stephen cut in tightly, putting himself between the two sovereigns as he pushed down Erotica's arm. Nightmare descended to the roof, Erotica glaring at him wildly over Stephen's shoulder, flashing her teeth in the dark.

"You're weak," she taunted, trying to surge toward her enemy as Strange held her physically in check. It was dangerous to touch her. He could feel her warmth seeping through him, banishing the fear and darkness that emanated from Nightmare like a scent. "Look how weak you are! You think you could subsume me just by destroying the Pathways between our realms? You think death eclipses life?" She stopped struggling, and Stephen let go of her, watching as she calmed herself. "What makes you so sure," she hissed at Nightmare, "that your realm isn't dependent on *mine?*"

Nightmare only smiled menacingly in response, giving Stephen another chance to interrupt their argument.

"We have to leave now," he said. "You can pick this up some other time."

"Leave?" Erotica grabbed Stephen's arm, looking up at him pleadingly. "Just send *him* away! I already told you I need you here to protect the realm with me."

Stephen gently but firmly pulled his arm away from her and moved to stand between Nightmare and Sharanya. "You'll be all right. Just continue to keep the realm sealed off. Pull as far back from the Pathways as you can until I restore them."

"And what if you can't restore them?"

Stephen was already striding toward the door that led back down into the building. "I find it best serves my purpose to assume success," he answered.

He had just pulled open the entrance to the stairwell when the handle flew out of his hand and the heavy metal door swung itself shut. He heard the sound of a bolt mechanism on the other side and turned back to Erotica with a challenging stare.

"Clea dreams," Erotica said softly, the moment she captured Stephen's gaze. In contrast to her voice, her eyes were hard. "Stay, and I'll bring her to you."

Stephen felt himself start to lose his temper, which was not something he often did. Keeping it in check, he walked slowly back to Erotica, feeling Sharanya and Nightmare's eyes on him as he passed them.

"Erotica, I cannot protect your realm without protecting the dimension as a whole. Until I can reverse the Pathway erosion, there isn't anything I can do—from here or any other dream realm—to influence what does or does not survive. You explained that to me yourself just moments ago."

Erotica continued to stare at him rapaciously. "You protect Earth. Sometimes at the expense of other neighboring dimensions."

Stephen heard the accusation in her words, but he wasn't in the mood for a philosophical debate. Erotica wasn't entirely wrong: There *was* a hierarchy at play in his defense of sentient life. But there was no reasonable compromise here: He couldn't focus on protecting a small enclave when he was capable of saving the larger system. "If you don't let us go, I'm going to have to create my own exit. And that has the potential of doing immediate and serious damage to your realm."

"Why not just flatten it now, Stephen?" Nightmare interjected cheerfully. "Perhaps it could create a kind of firebreak between some of the more important realms and the Pathways. I mean, really, what's here that's so important? Gender-integration tips disguised as mystery lovers? Nocturnal emissions?"

Animosity flashed in Erotica's eyes, and Stephen could tell that the restrained voice she used next indicated a far greater level of rage. "Perhaps you're right," she said quietly. "Perhaps it is time you go."

She thrust her hand, palm out, toward Nightmare. A red blast of force sent him sailing off the side of the building.

Stephen didn't hesitate. Snatching Sharanya up as he passed her, he ran for the ledge and dove after Nightmare. Sharanya screamed as they fell, clutching Stephen's waist so hard it was a struggle to breathe. They were so high up that all Stephen could see was Nightmare plummeting several feet ahead of them toward a cloud bank that obscured the ground. Wind rushed past his face, and Stephen had to concentrate to keep the Cloak of Levitation from slowing his descent. With one arm around Sharanya, who had closed her eyes and buried her face against his chest, he freed his other hand to reach out toward Nightmare, catching him, finally, in a band of light. Only then did Stephen allow the cloak to billow out around him and reduce the speed of their fall.

Stephen fought to reorient himself as they broke through the cloud bank, but another layer of clouds blocked the ground. He waited until they plummeted down through that one—and a third appeared. They were caught in a loop, plunging through the same altocumulus stratiformis again and again.

With a sigh, Stephen released his hold on Nightmare, needing one hand free again to channel energy through a Karana mudra. Releasing a strong blast of arcane force into the cloud bank, Stephen punched through the barrier; he caught Nightmare again as they dropped out of the Realm of Erotic Dreams.

There was a flash of darkness, an obliteration of light so profound it made Stephen fear he'd passed out, and then an unpleasant pressure against his abdomen, as if his ribs were being compressed. He felt he was falling too quickly again, but then the cloak caught him; he descended gently down onto a valley of yellow sand, releasing Sharanya and Nightmare the second his boots touched ground.

Glancing up, he had to shield his eyes from the flat glare of a low sun. They were in a desert, with nothing but sand and scrub for miles, the sky above them a dull, dirty white.

Sharanya took a shaky breath as Nightmare turned to him with a smirk.

"Never a dull moment, Stephen. That much I'll give you."

CHAPTER XI

"WHERE are we?" Sharanya asked. She was looking around at the expanse of dry, eroded dirt punctuated by small bursts of scrub brush. The air smelled dusty and hot, with faint traces of a distant wildfire.

"This is what's left of the Pathways," Stephen answered solemnly. "It's worse than I anticipated. The whole membrane has been burned away." He saw Sharanya's eyes widen with interest as he pulled out Jane's knife.

"Wait," she said, sounding confused. "How did you get that? I just saw it—it was in my suitcase."

"Your suitcase?" Stephen raised an eyebrow but kept his gaze fixed on the object in his hand. A stream of soft, glimmering purple light emanated from the knife's tip and trailed westward. It appeared the psychometry spell he'd prepared in the Sanctum was working—presumably the light trail would lead him to Jane.

Nightmare smiled darkly at Sharanya. "You don't have anything with you. Technically, you're not physically here, remember? You're just a dreamer."

Sharanya nodded slowly. "Of course. The weirdness of dreams. That must have been my unconscious trying to give me clues." She crossed her arms. "This place is going to take some getting used to."

"Don't get too comfortable." There was a hint of disparagement in Nightmare's voice as he picked imaginary lint off his leggings. "'This place' may not be here much longer."

Sharanya turned to Stephen. "Can you fix it?"

Stephen shook his head. "Not easily. The Pathways grew slowly and were made up of organic material from throughout the realms. I can probably come up with a healing spell of some kind to help them spontaneously reconstruct, but it would need to be anchored in a talisman—something with a strong connection to this dimension. The damage here is going to take a very specific type of energy to repair."

Looking at the knife again, Stephen began tracking the pale trail of light across the wilderness, trusting the others to follow. Sharanya, he knew, would want to stay close to him, and even if Nightmare decided to try to make a break for it, there didn't seem to be anywhere for him to go.

"May I ask you a question?" Sharanya was eyeing Stephen's cloak but looked up and met his eyes when he nodded. "I noticed when you...recite your spells that they tend to rhyme. Is that necessary, or...?"

"Or just something we do for show?"

Sharanya allowed for a slight smile. "Exactly. It's just that it seems a little..." She trailed off, maybe hoping Stephen would provide an adjective. When he said nothing, she continued. "I don't know...theatrical?"

Stephen nodded. "Theatrical. Yes, that's correct. The magical arts have a long literary tradition. Words are powerful. So powerful, in fact, that when we first started writing them down, we 'spelled' them." A corner of Stephen's mouth curved up as Sharanya inhaled sharply. "Spells have to be crafted, and using rhyming or alliteration is one way of channeling power and intent through them." He glanced at Sharanya then and offered a soft shrug. "It can also make them easier to memorize."

Sharanya opened her mouth to reply but was interrupted as the ground began to shake violently beneath her. Stephen spun and saw a giant fissure splitting the earth behind them. It started somewhere past the horizon line, and was approaching them with apparent purpose and tremendous speed. Stephen barely had time to throw himself in front of Sharanya before a giant wormlike creature erupted out of the ground directly in front of them, spreading a pair of jagged brown mandibles to expose the triple jaw and circular teeth of a leech. A baleful green light emitted from its horrific maw, and it screamed, an ear-splitting shriek Stephen felt all the way down his spine. The monster was easily 50 feet tall with the circumference of a stave silo.

Hurriedly stashing Jane's hunting knife into the recesses of his cloak, Stephen channeled the energy of a binding spell through his hands. As he cast it in the direction of the creature's cavernous maw, the spell wove into a giant muzzle, shielding his party against the beast's teeth.

"One of yours?" he asked Nightmare as the colossal worm smashed its own head into the ground in a furious attempt to free its jaws. Sharanya was effectively paralyzed, standing still in the sand in open-mouthed terror.

"Yes," Nightmare admitted. "But—"

Glancing at Nightmare, Stephen did a double take. The demon had his back to the worm and was staring in entirely the opposite direction. Turning to follow his sight line, Stephen saw another monster bearing down on them. As large as a jet plane, it was shaped something like a boar, with huge, sharp tusks and a head covered in hundreds of dark-green, glowing eyes. Instead of legs, it galloped toward them on twelve thick tentacles, snorting smoke and slavering as it came. The muzzled worm, meanwhile, now reared threateningly over the oblivious Nightmare.

Gritting his teeth, Stephen reeled toward the massive boar and fell to one knee in the sand, hands extended in front of him in the Karana mudra. As the boar-beast ran at him, Strange levitated it into the air and flung it over his head, hurling it at the annelid a split second before the enormous worm could pound Nightmare into the ground. Slammed by the flying boar, the annelid fell backwards against the crack it had riven in the ground. Strange simultaneously spun around and ascended above both immense creatures, making a clawing gesture with his hands. In response, the earth ripped farther apart beneath them. Levitating 20 feet or so above the terrain, Strange shot them both with a blast of fire-colored force, knocking them into the trench he'd created.

> "By the Hoary Host of Hoggoth,
> And the Moons of Munnopor
> Now shall these beasts of Nightmare
> Be absent ever more!"

The ground shuddered again and closed over the monsters as Strange descended. The sound was deafening. When his boots touched down, the soft sand had transformed into dry, hard-packed earth and had taken on a sickly gray hue. The sorcerer exhaled and wiped a small trickle of blood from his nose. Looking up, he found Nightmare watching him attentively.

"My, but aren't we flamboyant today?"

Stephen ignored the mockery in Nightmare's voice. "Why can't you control your own creatures?"

"Obviously they've been turned against me." Nightmare sighed. "I did try to warn you about that, Stephen."

"Turned against you?" Stephen smoothed down his mustache. "By someone else, you mean?"

"By one of my minions, I assume."

Stephen studied his ancient adversary's face. Nightmare appeared genuinely shaken by the attack. Walking over to Sharanya, Stephen placed a scarred hand lightly on the neuroscientist's shoulder. "It's over. You can look now."

Sharanya's eyes fluttered open, and she blinked back tears.

"I'm sorry," she said quietly. "I'm not proving to be much help."

Stephen pulled the hunting knife out as he dismissed her apology. "Don't be concerned. Those weren't your average dream figments."

He began walking again, following the purple light trailing from the tip of the hunting knife. Sharanya shadowed him. "Do people really dream these creatures? I suppose I've been luckier in my sleep than I realized."

"Have you?" Nightmare had caught up to Sharanya and leaned in toward her ear as he walked beside her, speaking quietly, intimately, his footsteps making no sound as they moved across the sand. Sharanya's eyes widened. "Don't tell me you've forgotten your very own personal rakshasi? That crazy, matted hair and those burning red eyes that scared you so? Her ghastly, fanged mouth, and the long, poisonous, clawing fingernails she'd brandish at you? Didn't she track the scent of your flesh through the night, able to find you, it seemed, in any dream? Didn't she lurk behind every corner, thirsting insatiably for your blood, which you knew she'd drink straight from your hollowed-out skull? Don't you remember how scared you were, Sharanya? That leaden feeling in the pit of your stomach when you realized *there was nothing you could do* to escape her?"

"All right." Strange spoke without looking up from the spelled hunting knife, still following its glow. "That's enough."

"Forgive me." Nightmare apologized without looking the least bit sorry. "I was merely trying to draw a parallel. Those creatures you just stopped are normally in the care of Intimidāre, one of my more powerful minions. And, perhaps not incidentally, one of the first to try to take over my realm."

Sharanya glared at the dream demon.

"And what did he come at *you* with, I wonder? What intimidates the personification of nightmares?" She gestured toward Strange. "Is it him?"

Nightmare sneered bitterly in response and didn't look as though he intended to reply. Stephen was beginning to wonder about the answer himself when he caught sight of a faint gleam in the distance. The trail from Jane's knife led straight to it. Without slowing his pace, Stephen touched the Eye of Agamotto, releasing a beam of powerful mystical light and opening his third eye.

"Realm of Prophetic Dreams dead ahead," he reported. "Jane's in there."

Nightmare squinted into the distance, careful to remain behind Strange and the light emanating from his amulet. "It hasn't been closed off?" He sounded surprised.

Stephen continued toward it, unsure of how long they'd be walking before they breached the realm's borders. "It doesn't appear to have been, no. The sovereign may have pulled back to his palace, though."

"Or maybe he doesn't need to defend his land." Nightmare was becoming increasingly agitated. "Maybe he's the one behind all this."

Sharanya matched her stride to Stephen's. "He's the sovereign of prophecy, right?" She tucked an errant strand of hair behind her ear. "Maybe it's just that he already knows what's gonna happen."

Stephen exchanged a tense look with Nightmare, confident they were both thinking the same thing. If what Sharanya said was true—and it sounded probable—what had the prophetic sovereign seen? Was he waiting, undefended, for inescapable defeat? Or did he know that he alone had nothing to fear from the events unfolding in the Dream Dimension?

Stephen was still pondering the question when the energy around him shifted and the ambient light began to dim. His next step led him into a cool, still darkness.

He was entering the Realm of Prophetic Dreams.

CHAPTER XII

STEPHEN was surprised by how hard the smell of his mother's pine farm-house table hit him. Along with cow manure and the lake, it was probably the dominant smell of his childhood. How many hours had he spent sitting at it, reading tattered books he'd borrowed from his one-room schoolhouse? Growing up in Lincoln's Hamilton County, he had spent solidly three-quarters of the day out of doors—doing chores, exploring, or, after the drought ended, swimming in the lake that touched his family's property. But there was something about the illusion of security in the dining room that had appealed to him, even when food had been scarce. With his chair scooted in as far as it would go and his back to the dusty windows, the table served as a physical boundary between him and the rest of the family. It was a place where he could be separate from the flow of the household while still a witness to it. Sheltered, but also vigilant.

Though Eugene Strange would pass through the room in sullen silence, Stephen's mother, Beverley, spoke constantly. Her chattering voice was as firmly affixed in his memory as her face. She talked about Jesus, whom it was clear to Stephen she loved more than either him or his father; she talked about other relatives, particularly her older sister; and she talked about Dr. Boynton, especially after Stephen's young brother, Victor, was born. Victor had been a colicky baby, and Dr. Boynton's advice was solicited frequently.

Beverley was talking about the doctor now as she paced with the baby over one shoulder—what a miracle worker he was, how blessed they were to have him nearby and willing to consult free of charge, how she honestly didn't know what she would have done without him. Stephen was the eldest of three, his brother Victor nearly nine years his junior. His sister, Donna, came between them, two years younger than Stephen and six-and-a-half years older than Victor. "You wouldn't think it would work so well, just a warm water bottle on his tummy, but I did exactly what Dr. Boynton said—and, hand to God, the baby just quieted right down. He also told me to have him sitting up when I fed him, and didn't that just do the trick? Honestly, that man is a miracle worker. I say a prayer of gratitude for him every night. Every single night."

Stephen couldn't quite make out the pages of the book he was reading, but had the sense of being deeply absorbed in it nonetheless. Though it created conflict with his father, who believed that his eldest son needed to spend more time with the inerrant Word of God, Stephen had taken pleasure in reading anything that wasn't the King James Bible. His mother's words drifted toward him, only half-heard as he studied the well-worn pages in front of him.

"I tried to give him something, I did, but he said there weren't no charge for advice, and none for babies, neither. That man is a saint, pure and true. He has saved us I don't know how many times."

"This is when you decided to become a doctor."

Stephen startled, remembering that he was no longer a nine-year-old boy. He was amazed by how easily he'd been transported back to that time and place—almost as if someone had worked an intricate spell on him—but of course it was only a dream. As if to underscore that point, Jane Bailey was suddenly sitting next to him at the table. Her hair was disheveled, and there were deep circles under her eyes, but she appeared essentially unharmed.

"Jane! I've been looking for you."

"I know," she answered. "You're close now."

"Close? Aren't you right here?"

Jane scrunched up her face as if that were the silliest thing she'd ever heard. "Right. Like I'm in your father's farmhouse in Nebraska. As if."

"Where are you, then?" Stephen remembered the hunting knife and pulled it out.

"I'm with Praedivinus. He's trying to help me. I wanted to show you something, though."

She pointed to Stephen's left. Turning, he saw a young woman seated at the end of the table, intently watching his mother, Beverley.

"Jessica Clifton," Stephen said. "Her folks raised chickens. We got eggs from them when we could."

Jane nodded, but seemed to be waiting for him to say something else. Stephen shrugged, placing the knife carefully on the table between them before flicking it to make it spin.

"My mom liked her, she visited often."

Jane turned to watch Beverley pace as she bounced the baby. "And this is the summer before Jessica struck out for the West Coast. She wanted to be a veterinarian but wasn't sure she could handle all the school it would take. Your mom thought she could." Jane stared at Stephen for a moment and then looked back at Jessica Clifton. "And you barely even realized she was here," she said quietly, after a moment.

Stephen's attention was on the knife, which continued to rotate rapidly like a game spinner. It didn't appear to be slowing down. Jane placed a hand on his arm.

"You don't get it. This is your *whole life* right here, or the first half, anyway. You heard your mom praising a doctor and decided she would be proud of you, talk about *you* that way, if you became one, too. You wanted to be like Dr. Boynton, or like Jesus with his healing super-powers. You were convinced that's what she was trying to tell you, but look..." Jane turned her attention back to Jessica Clifton's somber face. "*She wasn't even talking to you.*"

Stephen allowed for a quick, tight smile. "Great theory, but you're wrong. This isn't when I decided to become a doctor. It was when my sister got hurt and let me help her—easily three years after this."

Jane shook her head. "That's when the idea made it up to your *conscious* brain. *This* is where it was born." She stopped and scratched her nose. "Weird, right? That so much of your life was shaped by an overheard conversation you weren't even part of?"

Stephen sighed. The knife was still spinning. "Point taken. Being a surgeon turned out to be wrong for me on several levels, but that's all in the past. How is any of this prophetic?"

Jane was expressionless as she met his gaze. "There are many different kinds of prophecy dreams. This one's a warning."

Stephen was about to ask what it was a warning about, but Jane vanished just as quickly as she had appeared. Or rather, she simply wasn't there anymore, and of course never had been, because, as she'd noted, what would Jane Bailey be doing in Eugene Strange's dining room in Nebraska?

Stephen stood up quickly but saw no hint of her presence. The knife continued to spin. Was the Realm of Prophecy immune to psychometry, or was the spinning an indication that he was actually in close proximity to Jane? Deciding he might have better luck outside, he snatched the knife up and kept his eyes averted from the dream image of his mother and baby brother as he headed for the kitchen door.

Stephen hadn't seen the farm in decades. He'd sold the property to a divorced single mother from his hometown years ago. Though his childhood had not been an entirely unhappy one, it had been difficult. Stephen was convinced, however, that he had escaped the destiny it would have prescribed. Stopping just inside the screen door that led from the kitchen out toward the barn, he considered the assumption. The work ethic. The connection to the land. The supposition that social interactions should be framed in civility. That was pretty much all he had left of Nebraska. The rest he'd either deliberately eradicated from his life—his Midwestern accent, his reflexive closed-mindedness, his father's religion—or lost.

Of the losses, it was the people that had hit him hardest. He'd lost his sister, mother, father, and brother in rapid succession over a seven-year period, starting with Donna's death on his 19th birthday. His brother's death was last, and less than 10 years later came the car crash that nearly ended Stephen's own life. Now, as Earth's Sorcerer Supreme, he regularly battled interdimensional villains and the darkest forces of the occult, risking his life multiple times a day. What could a dream about his mother's influence on his initial choice of career possibly be warning him about?

Stephen let himself out the kitchen door and stepped onto an ice floe on one of Saturn's rings. Behind him stood a blind man in a white hooded tunic and sandals, holding a gnarled, wooden walking stick. They both had their backs to the planet, staring out into the galaxy. Earth was a tiny dot in the distance. Stephen turned and offered the man a hand.

"Doctor Strange, Sorcerer Supreme. You must be Praedivinus. I'm sorry we haven't met before—I get most of my prophetic visions from Agamotto."

"Oh, but we have," the man replied with a smile. He reached out to take the hand Stephen had offered, but instead of shaking it, turned it palm up in his own and ran his fingertips across the surgical scars. His hands were warm and dry, with skin made papery thin by age. "Met, that is. I've known you since you were a child."

"And I suppose I've been ignoring your warnings for just as long?" Stephen meant it as a joke, but immediately recognized that it was probably true. He'd never paid much attention to his dreams, not even after learning their true point of origin. "In any case, you'll have to excuse me again. I'm trying to locate a young woman..."

"Jane, yes." Praedivinus let go of Stephen's hand and gestured toward a door that appeared before them, set against space. "She's right through there."

"Thank you." Stephen took a step toward the door but was stopped by Praedivinus' stick, which the old man brought down suddenly just in front of his knees.

"You're not prepared."

"Prepared?" Stephen wondered whether it was a bad sign about the way he spent his days that he immediately thought of four different spells he could use to get past the old man—a blind old man who represented prophecy and knowledge, no less. He tried to make himself still, to listen and be open.

"To pay the price."

Stephen sighed. "You've been talking to my friend Monako, haven't you? Believe me, I've heard the lectures: Magic has a price, a life for a life, the universe must remain in balance, the bill is coming due...I promise you, I understand my job and will do what must be done."

"Will you?" The ice beneath Stephen's boots transformed into a rocky field of dark, springy grass in a valley covered by fog. He took a step forward and found himself at a stone altar, upon which lay a lamb. He recoiled, surprised.

"You have a reputation for being cryptic, Praedivinus, but at the moment I'm not seeing it. This is worse than Monako drowning his rabbits."

He was answered by Monako himself. "What's that?"

Stephen found himself on his knees on the black-and-white-tiled floor of a bathroom he didn't recognize, holding a struggling white rabbit over a full bathtub. The room was dim, but there was enough light coming in from the hallway to see by. He could hear Monako, Prince of Magic, coughing from the next room. A fellow magic-user, Monako was obsessed with the cost of the arcane, insisting that every spell had its price. He "paid his bill," as he put it, by drowning a rabbit every time he saved a life.

"Best to just get it over with quick, Stephen. Otherwise you and the rabbit psych each other out."

The water had a strange saline scent to it. Stephen thought about fudging it. He could cast an illusion, make Praedivinus think he'd done what he was asking, and then get on with the business of saving Jane and the Dream Dimension—and, by extension, reality. As if reading his thoughts, Monako appeared in the bathroom door behind him, a thin old man with hair and eyes nearly as black as the top hat he never seemed to take off. One of his eyes was obscured under a makeshift eyepatch, but it did nothing to lessen the sensation of the man's gaze boring into Stephen's back.

"If you're ready to cheat on a dream rabbit, god help us all. But by all means, take your time, Sorcerer Supreme. It's just the fate of mankind hanging in the balance—day at the races for you."

The rabbit kicked and twisted, and Stephen's impaired hands weren't strong enough to hold it. It slipped from his grasp, plummeting into the bathwater. Stephen sucked in his breath and plunged his hands into the water, but couldn't find it. He jumped to his feet to get a better view and saw that the tub had turned into some kind of scrying pool.

"Don't just look," Monako said from close behind him. "You have to really get in there if you want to understand." Stephen felt a deft shove at the small of his back and was suddenly tumbling headfirst into the tub.

Though it became immediately apparent that he was no longer in a bath-tub, Stephen was having trouble orienting himself, unsure of which way was up. He was about to do his best to articulate an underwater-breathing spell while already underwater when he saw two shafts of light penetrate the darkness. Swimming toward them, he realized he was moving through someone's consciousness, the twin shafts of light their open eyes. Trapped behind them, Stephen was a mere observer to another man's actions.

Howard Kolswolski of Queens, age 47, was feeling confident. Otto was out sick for the fourth day in a row, and someone had to operate the crane. So Howard had convinced—charmed, really—the overwrought shift manager into letting him take charge of moving one load of I-beams to the secondary roof supply. Talking to the manager had felt just as it had in the dream: He was assertive and eloquent, spinning a tale that probably would have worked even if the manager hadn't looked like he was half asleep. And it wasn't as if the poor guy could prove that what Howard said was false in any way. After all, Otto and Howard ate lunch together all the time; it was completely plausible that Otto might've taken the time to show Howard how to operate the crane on one of those occasions. Technically, of course, anyone behind the controls had to be certified, but rules were for people who couldn't think outside the box, right? It was a risk Howard was willing to take. Stepping in, getting the job done, saving the day—this was his big chance to show them all what he was really made of. This was his destiny.

Now, sitting in the crane for the first time, Howard was struggling to perform the task he had described as being as easy as plucking a fuzzy toy bear out of an arcade claw game on the boardwalk. Getting a grip on the load had been pretty simple—god knows he'd watched Otto do that part enough times—but as he had rotated the crane into position, he must have moved the controls too quickly, causing the load of I-beams to sway and spin. His attempts to right the error became increasingly clumsy, causing the load to swing wide, out over the crevice between buildings, where it dangled above the busy street below.

Everything slowed as Howard saw the first I-beam start to slip out of the pallet toward the gridlocked cars stuck in early morning traffic. Trying not to panic, he reached for the rotation brake, confident that he could cause enough of a jolt to swing the load in the opposite direction, scooping the loose I-beam back onto the pallet. Pulling the hand crank hard, he was horrified to hear the familiar ka-chunk of the crane's hook block disconnecting from the load cable. He stared at his hand on the cable release in horror, and watched as the entire pallet of I-beams dropped and plummeted earthward...

Trapped, tiny and insignificant, behind Howard's eyes, Stephen tried to wrestle his focus toward the falling load, but Howard's vision seemed to be failing. Or perhaps it was Stephen's vision that was becoming obscured. He blinked and squinted in vain as the image dissolved into a whirlpool of light, and the next thing Stephen knew, he was swimming up into another consciousness.

Raymond Foster of Reno, age 22, lined up the sights of his Glock 19 to target one of the nervous patrons of the Nevada Regional Bank while his older brother, Garvin, intimidated the teller, screaming at her to fill the duffel bags full of money. Paco stoically watched the doors for approaching cops, a pair of Berettas in hand. All three had pantyhose pulled over their heads to mask their appearances.

Raymond was nervous and tired...mostly tired. The idea of a broad-daylight bank robbery still seemed risky to him. He'd said as much to his brother, but Garvin had exuded confidence, claiming that the fact that no one expected a robbery in the middle of the day was precisely what made the plan so perfect.

"Security's lax, people just wanna get in and out of there fast as they can—bet the cameras ain't even recording!"

He kept insisting that it was his destiny—that he was completely sure it would work, and that the robbery would be remembered for decades to come. He said it had all come to him in a dream. Raymond wanted to believe him, but personally he thought dreams were maybe less reliable than getting an idea from a TV show or the Internet or something. Plus, they weren't proper bank robbers—had never taken on anything bigger than a convenience store. Seemed like there ought to be something in between those two things, though he couldn't quite think what it might be. He hadn't had the resolve to resist Garvin, anyway, probably because he hadn't had a solid night of shut-eye in a week. He slept, but it was a fitful, hollow experience, devoid of dreams, and he awoke feeling more tired than he'd been when he'd collapsed in bed the evening before.

That was probably why he hadn't seen the old security guard taking position across from Garvin, service pistol drawn.

"Hands where I can see 'em, boy!" the guard yelled at Garvin.

Raymond's brother spun with his weapon drawn and leveled it at the guard. "Be smart, old man! Drop the gun!"

Raymond was moving his own weapon to cover his brother when out of the corner of his eye he saw one of the bank patrons jump up from the floor, draw a gun from the holster at her belt, and fire in one smooth motion. The bullet tore into Garvin with enough force to slam him back against the counter.

The security guard, probably acting on instinct, spun and fired his weapon in the direction of the shot, hitting the woman as the man standing next to her drew his own sidearm from an ankle holster. Raymond shook off his shock just in time to dive toward a desk for cover as the man fired off a few shots. Paco's guns were roaring with return fire as he screamed Garvin's name.

Watching from behind Raymond's eyes, Strange tried to fire off an immobility spell, but only managed to freeze the water still surrounding him. He pounded against the ice in frustration—and to his surprise, it cracked in front of him and fell away to reveal a monitor view of Earth.

Imperator Kt'Dvarn, commander of the dreadnought Kaldaharn, *age 122, surveyed the blue-green planet on the main monitor, still surprised zir orders had led zim to such a backwater galaxy. It was a small planet to require the might of the entire armada, but word had come down from high command, and it no longer seemed prudent to disobey. Gone were the days when each Imperator ruled as zie saw fit. Now, even questioning an Imperial command could be a death sentence. As much as zie valued zir independence, it wasn't worth losing zir life over, so zie was resolved to follow zir orders first and zir conscience second.*

Rumors abounded concerning the Emperor's new Astrologer—some sort of dream interpreter, Kt'Dvarn had heard, and apparently now zir chief advisor. It sounded as if the Empeir had become obsessed with zir place in history—all zir speeches were suddenly about zir destiny and the destiny of the empire as a whole.

It all sounded a little over the top to Kt'Dvarn, but all zie knew for sure were zir orders and how desperately zie needed zir job. If the Empeir needed to destroy other planets to feel important, Kt'Dvarn was in no position to argue.

Zie reviewed the planet's entry in the library computer as zie sipped a cup of hot spourma. It was resource-rich and had at least one major life-form that could easily be adapted for slave labor—potentially dozens. With all the possibilities evident from even such a cursory search, it seemed a waste to just destroy it.

"We are in position, Commander," zir helmsman reported. A quick check of the monitors confirmed that the armada was in attack formation.

"Send word to the fleet," Kt'Dvarn sighed. "Ready the Inbiotors."

"Relaying orders, Imperator."

Kt'Dvarn double-checked zir orders and squared zir shoulders. "Relay decimation code and fire at will."

Strange's consciousness pulled back from the massive vessel and saw hundreds like it spread out in orbit around his homeworld. Huge cannons on each of the ships glowed hot before spewing forth beams of red energy that slammed into the Earth's surface. It took less than two seconds for the planet to explode in a fiery eruption of meteoroids.

Stephen struggled to act, trying to think of a spell formidable enough to reverse the destruction unfolding in front of him. He closed his eyes to concentrate and felt as much as saw a shift of light across his eyelids.

In the space of a heartbeat, he understood that he was on his knees in front of Monako's bathtub again, the old man having grabbed him by the back of his head to yank him out of water.

"That's tomorrow, Stephen, *tomorrow*. Prophecy, remember? Want to see some more?"

"I don't understand." Stephen reeled around to face the crazy old magician. "Are they just suffering from lack of sleep? Is there some kind of nightmare theme running through this? Pride? Hubris?"

Monako's lip curled up in disgust. "They're infected, you damn quack. What kind of doctor are you? You can't see that?!"

Stephen looked back, the tub once again a scrying pool filled with the images of the people and beings whose realities he'd inhabited. Monako was right—all of their auras glowed with a dark-green stain, a black-speckled, golden glint around the edges.

"Infected? By a dream? By a *prophecy* dream?"

"There are different kinds of prophecy dreams," Monako replied coolly. "This one's a warning."

The old magician had moved to the side of the tub, which had begun to overflow with blood, and was carefully rolling up one sleeve. As the tub roiled, blood splashed over the side, soaking his shoes. He bent over sideways to reach into the churning liquid, finally straightening as he yanked out the rabbit's unmoving, blood-soaked form with a grunt.

"Wanna try that again?" he asked, tossing the dripping animal to Stephen, who caught it and was horrified to see its eyes moving in its small, wet head. "If you don't do it with *intention*, it doesn't count. You'd best *remember* that."

Stephen felt himself losing control. What the hell did lambs and rabbits have to do with saving the Dream Dimension? He thrust the animal back at Monako.

"You think I can't do what has to be done? Demons of Denak, Monako!

Do you have *any idea* what kind of madness I deal with daily? The magical attacks from the farthest corners of the netherworld, the full-scale invasions from dimensions that, thanks to my efforts, you *still* don't know exist—why, the sheer volume of psychic corruption alone…"

Stephen stopped, realizing he was unaccompanied. He was standing in the middle of a field in Nebraska, and everything was dead—not a bird gliding in the sky, not a car moving on the highway, not a single insect buzzing, every blade of grass yellow and withered. It reminded him of the dust storms of his early childhood—only worse. The silence made his chest hurt.

Catching a flash of movement out of the corner of his eye, he turned to see the lamb standing unsteadily on the ground beside him, its small white head bent to sniff at the dead grass. Stephen winced as it looked up at him with black button eyes and bleated for food. It took a small step toward him. Stephen stepped back—and lost his footing, slipping down the slanted, desiccated bank of a waterless lake.

He lay on his back on the dried, cracked lake bed for a moment, breathing heavily as he stared up at the sky. He was about to get up when a torrent of water crashed down onto him, pouring out boundlessly from some unknown source, pinning him flat against the mud as it rushed to fill the lake around him.

Stephen clenched his jaw, supposing he should be thankful it wasn't blood.

CHAPTER XIII

WHEN the shadow fell across her, Jane was floating near the edge of a lake, fully clothed, staring up at the sky with wide, fixed eyes. She stood up on a weed bed in the hip-deep water and shielded her eyes from the glare of the sun. The creature that stood considering her was tall with a pointy, pale face, spiky black hair, and strange, glowing eyes. He was dressed all in green and looked as out of place in the woodland clearing as she felt.

"I like your cape," she said.

Nightmare glanced behind him at the dark, frayed hem of his mantle before resuming his scan of the horizon. He seemed to be searching for something—or someone. "You must be Jane," he said. "Please don't...*go* anywhere. My—" He stopped and sneered, as if a word had just died a fetid death on his tongue. "There's someone looking for you." Scowling, he turned back to her. "I don't suppose you've seen him? One of your species, big red cloak, mustachioed frown...total stick-in-the-mud, absolutely *no* sense of humor..."

Jane smiled. "You mean the sorcerer?"

Nightmare looked on the verge of rolling his eyes. "Yes, that's the one." He turned his attention to the water with a suspicious glare. "What are you doing out there? I don't have to come and get you, do I?"

Jane looked around at the water. She wasn't entirely sure. "Didn't they say that if you could float, you were a witch?"

Nightmare narrowed his eyes. "You're not a witch, Jane. Witches have made a choice to enter into a pact with an external source of power. You're just…unlucky."

Jane was struck by the pronouncement, her gaze dropping as her mouth contorted into something like a pout. As she thought about it, though, she began to appreciate the truth of his words. Unlucky. She pressed her lips together before taking in a slow, shaky breath. "What are you?" she asked Nightmare.

The demon stared at her impassively. "I'm Nightmare."

Jane nodded, her attention wandering to a large red dragonfly that alit on a bulrush blade to her left. "I guess you saw it, too, then?"

Nightmare stepped closer to the water's edge. "Saw what?"

The dragonfly flew up over the water. Jane followed its progress, and then shook her head. "You're right," she said quietly. "It doesn't matter."

Nightmare didn't appear to be sure what he was right about, but watched as she grabbed both sides of the fur-lined hood of her anorak. Squeezing her eyes tightly shut and pressing her lips together, she pulled it up quickly, and a torrent of water poured out over her head. She kept her eyes closed as the water ran down her face, and then slowly opened one eye to peek out at him. Nightmare's head tilted to one side in utter bewilderment, his eyes wide. Jane opened her other eye and smiled shyly. One side of the demon's mouth slid up uncertainly, his expression otherwise unchanged, and Jane laughed as she began to slog out of the water to join him on the bank.

When she slipped in the mud before reaching his side, Nightmare held out a hand to steady her, which she accepted. His skin was cool and clammy. The moment she was safely on the bank, he let her hand go, and Jane guessed he wasn't used to touching people. She shoved her wet bangs off her forehead.

"Did the world end yet? It's really hard to tell in here."

Nightmare scrutinized her for a moment, and then shifted his jaw as he looked away to survey the clearing. "No. Not yet. Is that what Praedivinus has been showing you, Jane? The end of the world?"

"I guess." She shrugged off her coat and began to wring it out. "The end of mine, anyway. But I don't actually think that's *her* plan."

Nightmare watched her struggle with the waterlogged anorak for a moment; then, seemingly on an impulse, he waved his hand across it. "Whose plan?"

Jane was surprised to find her coat suddenly dry. She shook it out and, increasingly used to an utter lack of continuity in her experience of time, pulled it back on with a shrug. "Do you like graves?"

"I do, actually."

"Me, too. Come on." She grabbed Nightmare's hand in her own and started tugging him away from the lake.

They climbed a small hill covered in tall green weeds and knee-high black-eyed Susans toward a modest but large farmstead. Jane scrambled over a length of wooden fencing, waited for Nightmare to follow suit, and then led him back behind a barn where a neat row of graves had been dug in the shade of the building. They were all marked with simple wooden crosses onto which names had been burnt: Eugene Strange, Beverly Strange, Donna Strange, Victor Strange…

Jane crouched down and touched the cool dirt of Donna Strange's grave. "It looks so peaceful," she said quietly.

"Not for Stephen." Nightmare smiled slightly and cracked his knuckles. "And I assure you, the real graves aren't this close to the farmstead. Perhaps this has prophetic meaning for him somehow."

"Is this a prophecy, then, or are all these people already dead?" Jane asked.

Nightmare looked pleased to have a direct answer to a direct question.

"They're already dead. Have been for quite some time." He pointed to the grave of Victor Strange and smiled ominously. "That one died twice."

Jane nodded slowly, unfazed. "Like he was a vampire or something?"

Nightmare turned sharply back to her, failing to hide his surprise that she'd guessed such a thing. "That's correct, yes."

Jane looked up at him, her eyes wide and sad. "We aren't yet, though, right?"

"Vampires?"

"Dead."

Nightmare shook his head. "Jane, dear, the dead don't dream."

"This is a dream, then?"

Nightmare raised one sharp eyebrow as he regarded the young Inhuman. "Not precisely. But I assumed you thought it was. I had guessed that that was why you didn't seem to be afraid of me."

He offered her a hand, and she took it, letting him help her back up to her feet.

"I don't need to be afraid of you," she said flatly, brushing her hands off on the back of her jeans.

Nightmare cocked his head to one side and began following her as she started back toward the lake. "You don't believe me capable of harming you?"

Jane glanced at him over her shoulder as she continued walking. "Oh, I'm sure you could. It just doesn't matter."

Nightmare looked completely perplexed. "It doesn't matter if you get hurt?"

Jane turned around, walking backwards, her arms spread wide. "Not really. Because of how unlucky I am. I didn't think of this until you said it, but it's almost like a super-power." She dropped her arms back to her sides and turned around to face the lake again, her back straight and her head high.

"You don't really have to be afraid of anything when you're gonna die. Dead trumps hurt every time."

Nightmare stopped. Jane listened as she continued walking and smiled when she heard the leaves crunching beneath his footsteps behind her again. "I think you're the first person in three or four centuries who hasn't been afraid of me," he commented to her back. His voice sounded almost amused.

Jane looked up at the trees as she answered him, her hands in her pockets. "It's nice to have a friend, isn't it?" She snuck another glance at him and crinkled her nose in pleasure. The demon had folded his arms across his chest and was tapping one long finger against his chin as he walked, apparently giving her question careful consideration.

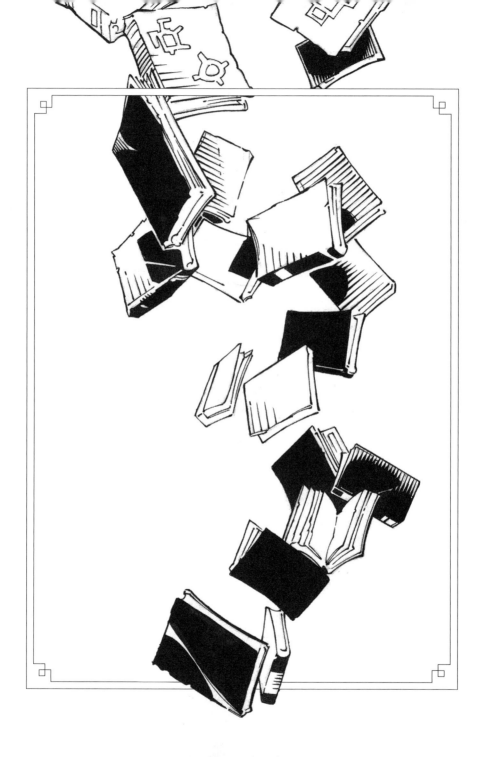

CHAPTER XIV

SHARANYA felt a force against the small of her back, as if someone had given her a brisk shove. She stumbled forward onto the bank of a river, the Badlands of the Pathways nowhere in sight. A platform rose from a wide, flat plain of sand behind her, upon which towered an ancient walled city of kiln-fired mudbricks. The city gates were open. As a deep-blue twilight gathered, torch flames flickered within brightly painted terracotta cones embedded into the front of ornately carved buildings, lending the walls a coppery glow. Slender minarets rose from either side of a resplendent temple, and an early but elaborate irrigation system ran through houses, fields, date groves, and sheep pens. Sharanya didn't notice how empty the city looked until she heard a commanding, orotund voice behind her.

"From the Great Above she opened her ear to the Great Below…"

She turned to see a woman standing on the bank of the river and sucked in her breath, recognizing her. Though not tall, the woman stood slender and erect, her graceful arms adorned with gold bracelets but otherwise bare. A draped wool garment dyed deep claret and trimmed with intricate, handprinted geometric patterns complimented the warmth of her bronze skin, just as a wreath of wild grape leaves contrasted with her smooth, shinning black hair. She balanced a flat-bottomed terracotta pitcher on one elegant shoulder; her intelligent, topaz-colored eyes, lined with kohl and glittering in the torchlight, penetrated Sharanya.

"Geshtin-anna?" the scientist asked, stunned.

"From the Great Above the goddess opened her ear to the Great Below..." the woman intoned.

Geshtin-anna was a Mesopotamian goddess who, as one half of the Sumerian myth of seasons, spent six months of every year in the underworld. Her beloved brother, Dumuzi, dwelled there during the cold half of the year, making Geshtin-anna the harbinger of autumn—and, by extension, harvest and wine. But she was known to Sharanya primarily as the first person in history to have written down and analyzed dreams, having famously helped her brother with a series of prophetic nightmares.

"From the Great Above Inanna opened her ear to the Great Below..."

Sharanya recognized the words to be from the Sumerian poem "The Descent of Inanna," but somehow she knew that they were intended for her. Momentarily awed to find herself in the presence of a goddess, Sharanya reminded herself that she'd spent the last few hours with a sorcerer and a demon. She began to think through what she remembered of the poem, which was mostly about Geshtin-anna's sister-in-law, Inanna, visiting the underworld and dying within it, but then ultimately escaping it when other people—specifically, Geshtin-anna and her brother—paid the price for her release. Sharanya began to grow nervous.

"I—I don't understand. Is this prophecy? From ancient Mesopotamia? How would that even work?"

Sharanya paused, waiting to see whether the goddess would answer, but Geshtin-anna said nothing more, only stared at her with inquisitive, glittering eyes. Finally, she crouched down. Sharanya held her breath, watching as Geshtin-anna cupped one hand around a small cluster of mushrooms. Sharanya sank down into a crouch to join her, lowering her voice.

"Mushrooms? In dream symbolism, they often indicate poison—or more likely a poisonous situation, something potentially harmful. Or sometimes they represent an altered state of consciousness, either of which would make sense for me right now, I suppose."

Sharanya stared at the mushrooms for a moment longer, then turned her attention back to the goddess. As beautiful as she was, it was difficult for Sharanya to imagine Geshtin-anna's presence prophesizing anything positive, unless perhaps some form of rebirth. Despite his sister's warnings about his dreams, Dumuzi had been slain as she had predicted. Like Inanna, though, he had eventually been resurrected.

"Maybe it's just that everything's changing," Sharanya said aloud, to herself as much as to Geshtin-anna. "A metaphorical rebirth—a need for me to integrate this new understanding of the world into my life and work...?" Remembering that Geshtin-anna's name meant "date wine of heaven," Sharanya smiled wryly. "Or maybe I just need a drink."

"We have a selection of complimentary liquor and wine available for your enjoyment. Would you like to see a menu?"

Sharanya blinked. She felt dizzy suddenly, weightless. She was on an airplane—Air India, by the looks of it—seated between a man and woman she didn't know, a flight attendant leaning over her with a pleasant smile. Though there was nothing sinister about the experience, Sharanya began to feel anxious. If she ate or drank, would she be trapped in the Dream Dimension forever?

"I believe you're thinking of fairies," the man in the aisle seat next to her said with a gentle smile. Sharanya realized it was Wong, Doctor Strange's assistant.

"Where am I?" Sharanya asked him. Of all the questions colliding in her brain, it was one of the less urgent, but also the only one she could manage to articulate.

"You're between two worlds," Wong answered, his smile broadening. "And I suggest you try to get comfortable."

The flight attendant had vanished, so Sharanya settled back in her seat and turned to gaze past the woman to her right to get a look out the window. The sky was bright blue, a bank of clouds below them. They were probably somewhere over the Norwegian Sea. Forcing herself to think clinically, Sharanya began trying to deconstruct the dream the way she would for one of her test subjects or clients.

Wong's words could be taken literally. She was between Earth and Heaven, between departure and arrival, between America and India, between her family's homeland and its adoptive country. They also had figurative implications: Sharanya was sitting between a man and woman, perched between dreaming and wakefulness, and—if she were honest with herself—moving from a state of intellectual skepticism into one of intuitive wonder. Airplanes in dreams sometimes symbolized an overcoming of obstacles, or ascension to a higher plane of existence. Sometimes they urged the dreamer to look at a problem with greater perspective. Sometimes they were just symbols of adventure or escape.

She snuck another peek at Wong. "Are you really here?" The moment she asked the question, she knew how he'd answer.

"Really where?"

He wasn't, of course. Why had she pulled him into her dream, this man she'd met just hours ago? Was it his nice smile, or his preternatural calm? Was it an indication of her longing to be reunited with her body, or at least reassured as to its safety? Sharanya rubbed her temples and wished she had her neti pot. Airplanes always made her congested. Though she wasn't truly on an airplane, was she? Not physically. Physically, she was still in the Sanctum

Sanctorum. And mentally, she was in the Realm of Prophetic Dreaming. The most important thing for her to do was find Doctor Strange.

"Excuse me." Sharanya stood. Though she was fairly sure she'd been in her business attire only a moment before, she found she was wearing her favorite pink-and-orange sari, which made it hard to move gracefully past Wong to reach the aisle. "The weirdness of dreams," she mumbled with an apologetic smile.

No one stopped her as she wandered through Economy Class and then through Executive Class and up into First Class, searching the seats. The faces of her fellow travelers were mostly indistinct or unknown to her. There was no sign of Doctor Strange, who she figured probably didn't use airplanes, anyway. Nor did she see Jane or Nightmare.

Filled with an anxious despondency, Sharanya let herself into one of the small bathrooms and shut the door behind her. The dream was so vivid, so detailed and real, she was finding it difficult not to be afraid. What if it was true that dreaming was just the frontal cortex running through a haphazard series of moods and images—just neurons firing randomly? That theory held that it wasn't until one woke up that the brain arranged the images into a narrative, in which case... What if she *didn't* wake up? What if the plane was really taking her away, farther into the Dream Dimension? What if the others didn't know how to find her?

Sharanya took a deep breath and cleared her mind. She was grasping, getting caught up in conjecture. Yes, she was in an unusual situation, but she was also within her field of expertise, and she was not alone. Everything would be all right. Everything *was* all right. Here, in the present, she was on her feet, and all was well. She had everything she needed.

She blew her nose, adjusted her sari, and then reached down to pull up an ankle strap on her shoe. A slow smile broke across her face. The shoes! She'd created them in the Realm of Erotic Dreams…with her mind. And if what

Nightmare had said was true, that was also how she'd found Doctor Strange on the roof. She only had to concentrate—to imagine and move toward him.

Feeling much calmer, Sharanya unlatched and opened the bathroom door, thinking that she'd return to her seat and meditate, holding a picture of Stephen in her mind until she got a clue about where to look for him. But instead of the plane's interior, the door opened onto the back porch of a Midwestern farmhouse. She took a careful step forward, hearing a screen door bang shut behind her. There was solid earth beneath her feet. A few grasshoppers flew overhead; she saw no evidence of an airplane as she squinted up toward the sun. A gentle breeze brought with it the smell of a nearby lake, and Sharanya turned away from a large barn to her right and began walking toward the water. Halfway there, she noticed that she was again wearing her work clothes.

The lake was large and calm and seemed to anchor the landscape, which otherwise consisted of so much sky and such wide fields that Sharanya could easily have felt lost. She sat down at the water's edge on a large, flat rock under a birch tree and was about to begin the meditation she'd planned when a disturbance in the water caught her attention. First, there were just a few bubbles, and then the surface became agitated. Sharanya noticed a dark-red stain spreading out from the center of the commotion. For a moment she was afraid it was blood, but then it looked almost as if a large blanket had floated up from the depths of the lake. Finally, Stephen Strange surfaced, soaking wet, spluttering and gasping. The Cloak of Levitation floated around him, as if unwilling to remain submerged.

"Fangs of Farallah, Monako!"

Sharanya beamed, relieved to see him. "Did you swim here, Doctor? I took a plane."

Turning toward Sharanya, Strange took two strong strokes toward the shore and then stopped, looking around with an expression Sharanya couldn't read. Seeming to think better of the swim, he levitated out of the water, his red cloak billowing behind him as he flew the rest of the way across the lake to her side.

As Strange landed beside her, adjusting his cape, Sharanya plucked a small flower growing near the rock. She wanted to practice her dream-weaving. Four small lavender petals fanned out from a round red center, and Sharanya wondered whether she could change their color.

"Have you ever been to Nebraska, Dr. Misra?" Strange was asking.

Sharanya shook her head. "Other than India, I've never been outside of New York. Is that where we are?"

"No." Strange looked around slowly. "But yes. I suppose this landscape has been taken from my memory. This is where I grew up."

Sharanya looked up at him, surprised. "On a farm? I wouldn't have guessed that. You seem so...urbane."

It looked to Sharanya as though he tried to smile but couldn't quite manage it. His shoulders were tense. "A carefully cultivated image, I assure you. At least initially." He'd turned to peer out at the lake again, so Sharanya returned her attention to the flower she held, concentrating on the petals. She was trying to turn them white, but the flower seemed to shrivel slightly in her hand. After a second, the light purple deepened to black.

A shadow fell over her. Sharanya looked up to find Nightmare standing directly behind her, staring over her shoulder at the flower and smiling darkly. She dropped it and was about to scold him when she saw Jane standing beside him.

Sharanya felt her throat tighten and the blood in her temples pulse. She thought it said a lot about her day that a young, distracted woman a solid two inches shorter than her caused her at least as much anxiety, if not more, than a sorcerer, a haunted house, a demon, a goddess, and skyscraper-sized monsters. Of course, the young woman in question had, earlier that day, brandished a hunting knife as long as Sharanya's forearm and tried to kill her. But Sharanya couldn't help seeing Jane as she had been in the Sanctum Sanctorum: small, pale, unconscious, and almost unbearably vulnerable. She was desperately in need of help, that much was clear.

Acting both from an impulse toward compassion and a desire to neutralize any lingering animosity, Sharanya stood and very deliberately extended a hand to the young woman.

"Hi, Jane," she said warmly as Strange and Nightmare acknowledged one another with tight nods. "I'm Sharanya."

STEPHEN noticed Jane glance at him before turning back to Dr. Misra and tentatively taking the offered hand, shaking it with slumped shoulders and a shy aversion of her eyes.

It wasn't Jane's relationship with Sharanya that concerned him, though. Now that he had Jane in front of him, Stephen was intent on finding the entity that was exercising so much undue influence on the young woman.

As Dr. Misra distracted Jane with introductions, Stephen activated the Eye of Agamotto, bathing Jane in its aureate light. He was thinking about the dark-green energy Monako had just shown him, expecting to see it clinging to Jane's aura. What he actually saw was even more disquieting.

The dark-green stain was there, and it trailed from deep within Jane's soul off to some unknown point of origin in the distance—but it wasn't the only sign of some external force having its hooks in her. A bright-blue line wended off northward, and a vivid-red stream led back toward the Realm of Erotic Dreams. A reedy silver thread wove its way across the Nebraska farmlands just under the dark-green trail, and a hot-white light pulsed over her third-eye chakra. There was even a thick, jagged black beam coursing back and forth between her and Nightmare.

Other than the black stream leading to Nightmare, which was robust no doubt due to the sovereign's proximity, the green one pulsed most strongly, winding off toward the west—very much like the trail he'd initially created between Jane and her hunting knife. Stephen closed the Eye and started to move westward.

Sharanya made a small sound of surprise. "Wait…I know dreams are weird, but did your broach just…open its eye?"

"This way," Stephen said, gesturing in the direction the trail had indicated.

He thought he heard Sharanya sigh and was fairly sure her frustration was aimed at him. She was distracted, though, by Nightmare, who came up behind the women and looped an arm casually around Jane's shoulders.

"You'll have to forgive our sorcerer friend," he said in a conspiratorial tone still quite loud enough for Stephen to hear. "This lake brings up bad memories for him. His sister drowned in it when she was only 17. I'm quite sure it was a defining tragedy, and considering how many catastrophes there have been in his life, well…that's saying something, really."

Stephen stopped in his tracks. He'd recognized the lake within two seconds of swimming up to its surface, but had been trying not to think about it. His hands started to ball into fists, but then a spasm of pain made him release them. The incident with his sister was well in his past, but Nightmare was right. It had marked the beginning of a dark period of his life, and being in those waters again had left him tense and queasy.

"Don't do that," he heard Jane say to Nightmare. "It's not nice."

"Jane." The demon's tone was both intimate and scolding. "I am, by definition, *not nice*."

Stephen composed himself, smoothing out his mustache as he continued walking. He looked over his shoulder just long enough to see Jane taking Nightmare's hand in her own. Nightmare looked surprised, glancing down at the hand clutching his in complete and obvious confusion, but he did not pull away.

"I know you all thought I was the one behind all the craziness back in the waking world," Nightmare said after a moment. "But hopefully you've changed your minds about that. It seems, in any case, that we're pressing on with the intention of exploring other options, so let's entertain one." He paused.

"Go on," Stephen prompted darkly without turning around to face him.

Nightmare obliged him. "I can see into your mortal realm, as well, and what I've noticed is bravado. People are taking foolish risks, utterly convinced they'll get away with whatever they're attempting. It's as if their common sense has been completely erased."

Sharanya caught up to Stephen and synched her steps with his as Nightmare continued. "If one is *sure* that one knows what's going to happen, risks don't feel as dangerous as they otherwise might. And what kind of dreams offer such insights and premonitions? Prophecy dreams. Leading me to wonder: Isn't it possible that we're facing off against the ruler of *this* realm?"

Stephen narrowed his eyes, thinking back to the nightmarish quality of his own experience moving through the realm. "Very possible," he acknowledged, glancing at the lake as they continued to travel along its south bank. "In any case, we'll know as soon as we get to the end of this trail."

Sharanya hugged herself as she continued walking next to Stephen, her head slightly bent in thought. "I'm not so sure about that theory. It seems to me these dreams have been trying to assist us."

"That's also possible," Stephen admitted, more quietly.

Sharanya indicated the luminous trail. "What is that, by the way? What did you do to her?"

Stephen gave Sharanya a sideways look, wondering how much skepticism she'd shed since he'd first met her that afternoon.

"Jane's directly connected to the sovereigns of this dimension," he explained. "I suspect it has something to do with her powers as an Inhuman, but that's a bit beyond my purview. What I do know, from divination spells and an investigation into her consciousness, is that one of them—at least one of them, as it now appears—is exerting influence on her, and may be using her as a conduit to amplify that influence in the waking world. Jane can pass back and forth between both dimensions, although—" He glanced over his shoulder at the young woman. "—it doesn't appear that she has much control over it." He turned his attention back to Sharanya, assuming she would contradict him if something he said fell outside the logic of contemporary metacognitive science. "For the people having these nightmares, or prophecy dreams—or whatever they turn out to be—the experience is so persuasive that it's influencing their behavior in their waking lives. In a very dangerous way, obviously." He added the last comment tersely, his attention back on the energy trail.

"And why would a dream sovereign do such a thing?" Sharanya asked. "It seems to be doing as much harm here as it is back home. Couldn't it eventually lead to...I don't know...anarchy? Is that something a...dream...would want?"

Stephen could tell she was struggling with the personification of dream typologies. Truthfully, he wasn't sure about the motivation yet himself. He looked out at the lake again. Someone seemed to be going to a great deal of effort to challenge him emotionally. "I have it on reasonably good authority that, unabated, the situation could lead to the end of the world as we know it. But as for why, you need only look a few feet behind you. I know he's terrifying even now, but Nightmare is diminished at the moment. He's indicated that this is because his realm has been isolated, and he's starving. The dream principalities feed off of the energy they elicit from us in the dreams they control, so even if Nightmare's not being entirely honest—which is always a strong possibility—it does point to the real battle being here, in this dimension. Some kind of turf war, essentially." He exhaled, blowing out his cheeks. "You'd be amazed how often it comes down to some kind of turf war."

"So we're just...collateral damage?" Sharanya pressed a hand against her stomach, looking unwell.

"I don't know yet. But I won't let it come to that." Stephen met her eyes and offered a small, rueful smile. He could tell that she was on the brink of belief, trying to reconcile the world he'd introduced her to with the one she'd known before meeting him. She hadn't yet made the connection between science and magic, and was still holding out a sliver of hope that he would explain away the Dream Dimension and all its contents, returning her to a life she could still comprehend.

He empathized with her confusion. It was a difficult thing to accept the coexistence of mundane reality and magic. He had been lucky: The Ancient One had confronted him with empirical evidence, and the implications of a larger universe had appealed to him. By the time he had found magic, he'd been ready to accept it.

But magic came to find Sharanya, and Stephen suspected that she was still wondering whether it was something from which she could run and hide.

CHAPTER XV

AS HE continued following the lambent green trail that connected Jane to the sovereign he sought, Stephen tried not to take the fact that it ran alongside the lake personally. It was no surprise to find the mutable landscape taking its cues from his unconscious: Of everyone in his party, it was reasonable to assume that his will and vision were strongest. His concern was over his concentration. Though he tried to resist the sensation, he felt like he was drowning, his focus sinking and getting tangled up in the submergent aquatic vegetation at the bottom of the lake.

Though Stephen and his sister had grown up in the middle of an historic drought—record temperatures and dry, dust-filled winds blowing visible heat across the empty corn fields—by the time they were teenagers, summers in Hamilton County had normalized. The corn was growing again, the grasshoppers had been vanquished, and the lake behind their family's property was once more full. With their bodies seeming to hold the memory of childhood heat and scarcity, both Stephen and Donna were drawn almost inexorably to that glistening, cool water, frequently putting off their chores to swim before the rest of the household was up and moving. They would tease each other about how cold the water was, but loved feeling the shock of it in their bones.

She was 17; it was her last summer at home before starting college in the fall. He was already enrolled in pre-med at New York College but was home on a visit; it was the morning of his 19th birthday. They were both preoccupied with the meaning of everything, looking for signifiers of their rapidly approaching adulthoods in the tall grasses and the bracing water and even in the wide, bright sky as they floated on their backs in the lake following wisps of altostratus across the boundless blue.

As Stephen remembered it, she was there one minute—and then she simply wasn't. There had been no flailing, no struggle, no shouts for help... She was a few feet away, floating on her back just as he was floating on his, watching a few thin clouds drift by. At some point he had dropped his feet, raised his head to look around, and been unable to locate her. The surface of the lake was undisturbed.

The panic built slowly. She was healthy, a strong swimmer, and in her own backyard. And she was his teenaged sister; it wasn't as if she always told him where she was going or what she was doing. He didn't start to worry until he saw her towel still on the south bank. Then, finally, hot embers of doubt stirred to life in his stomach and sent stinging sparks of dread up the back of his neck. It was cornflower blue, her towel, worn almost transparently thin, frayed, and even ripped in one corner. But she'd loved it since she was eleven, would not have left it behind even if she hadn't bothered to dry off.

Stephen spun in the water two, three, four times, shouting her name before finally thinking to dive. The water was deep and dark and filled with life. Bass, panfish, catfish, and northern pike had all been spotted swimming through the pondweed. Stephen couldn't even make it to the bottom before being forced to turn around and swim up to the surface to suck in another huge breath. He dove again, wanting to comb the entire lake, the instinct to do so fighting with the dawning realization that he needed to leave the water and go for help.

Things had accelerated quickly then. His mother had come out—one hand on her hip, the other shielding her eyes from the sun—to fetch them for breakfast. Stephen had heard the screen door slam as she'd run back into the house screaming for his father, and dove again. He continued diving, over and over, until, in the end, he found her, pale and still except for her hair, which wafted on the currents like the serpentine stems of the watermilfoil in which she'd become entangled.

He couldn't even remember her last words. They'd been chatting all morning—silly, meaningless banter filled with long, comfortable silences. The doctor had said she'd probably suffered from a cramp, and Stephen had snapped at him, growling about how she hadn't even had breakfast yet. A cramp? The utter banality of it infuriated and haunted him—what could he have done? And yet he blamed himself—how could he not? He was the doctor of the family, the one who had promised to keep them all healthy and safe.

Even now, so many years later, as the Sorcerer Supreme, with all his power…it seemed totally possible that that kind of accident could happen again. A *cramp*? He could drain the lake, levitate her out of it, unknot her muscles, give her gills, tether her to shore, reverse time, restart her heart…*if he noticed.*

One minute she was there. And then she simply wasn't.

"Stephen, it's not your fault."

Stephen stopped, glancing at Sharanya to see whether she could see Donna, too. It appeared that she could. His sister stood directly in front of him, not three feet away, dripping wet but fully clothed and eternally 17.

"It had to happen," she said kindly, reassuringly. Water slopped from her mouth as she spoke, and the sunlight reflected off the crown of her shiny, long brown hair was like a halo. "It was destiny."

The rest of the party had caught up to them; behind him, Stephen could feel Jane maneuvering to get a better look. Nightmare's shadow fell first across Stephen and then the apparition of Donna, instantly decomposing one side of her face so that her beautiful smile slid into a rigid skeletal grin. Before Stephen could say anything, the demon seemed to realize his transgression and stepped back.

"It was part of you becoming who you are," Donna continued gently.

Stephen felt a wave of rage crest within him. The harder the Realm of Prophetic Dreams worked to convince him not to resist what was meant to be, the more determined Stephen became to reshape the future. Sacrifices were sometimes necessary, it was true. He was completely prepared to give up his own life should it one day come to that—had gambled on it many times. He knew from experience that should he fall, someone else would take on the mantle of Sorcerer Supreme; it had happened before. Earth would not go unprotected. But his sister's death had been accidental, meaningless. He'd known this with absolute certainty when it happened, and with all he'd learned since, nothing had changed his mind on that score. People did not die so that other people could suffer and grow. The universe didn't work that way.

Looking at his sister, he wanted to tell her no. He wanted to explain about the car accident and his hubris, about the meditation and the mystical training and how hard he'd worked to unlearn all his bad habits, to master the knowledge that now shaped his life. Her death was not a checkmark in a column of events that had led to him becoming the Sorcerer Supreme, not a necessary sacrifice made to attract or appease his fate; he would entertain no such thought. He almost told her he was sorry for not visiting her, wherever she was, because surely he could have figured out how to, being what he was, who he was. There were so many things he wanted to tell her, but instead he squared his shoulders and began to recite an incantation.

"Awaken, Agamotto!
Open wide your all-seeing eye!
Let the Winds of Watoomb blow away
The illusion of this lie!"

Stephen felt the third eye at the center of his forehead open as a cone of lucent, aureate light poured from the amulet fastened to the front of his cloak. Donna's figure shimmered and then blasted apart, leaving an indistinct spectral form: a diaphanous, faceless being in the shape of a gangly man.

"What are you?" Stephen demanded, upper lip curling away from his teeth. "Speak."

The apparition shied away from Agamotto's light, flitting just beyond its glare without the use of legs, even though it appeared to have them.

"That's one of Praedivinus' minions, Stephen," Nightmare murmured from behind him. "I don't think it can speak without borrowing someone's voice."

"Apparition dreams," Sharanya added, barely above a whisper. "They're a common subset of prophecy dreams." She paused, glancing at Stephen with concern. "Who was she?"

Stephen started to answer but felt Jane's hands touch his right arm through his cloak. She was trying to get past him, to get closer to the apparition. Stephen shifted toward Sharanya, blocking her progress. Something wasn't right, and he didn't want the Dream Dimension underling noticing Jane until he figured out what it was.

"Stephen, think of all the good you've done," the apparition said in Donna's voice, though without reclaiming her form or even bothering with the illusion of a mouth. "It's not always about one life, until it is. You know that. You know that there's no creation without destruction."

Nightmare, still standing a short distance behind Stephen with his arms folded over his chest, stepped forward again, ignoring the gruesome effect his shadow had on the apparition as it once more turned skeletal. "This is what I'm talking about, Stephen. This is Praedivinus trying to poison your mind. His whole realm is trying to convince you to kill me."

The apparition flickered again, looking as though it might blink out altogether, and then a man in his mid-60s stood in its place. He was looking at Stephen sternly, even though his hunched posture suggested he was weak and in pain. "Obey the will, son. Do not let yourself be consumed by the sin of pride. This family is counting on you—don't you let us down."

Stephen's hands balled into fists again, this time staying clenched despite the pain. First his dead sister, and now his dead father? If the wretched thing planned on dragging every corpse out of his past, they were all going to be standing there for quite some time. Glancing at the sparkling trail still leading from Jane to some unknown point within the realm, Stephen decided he was done with threshold guardians. Shaping Agamotto's brilliant cone of light with his hands, he balled it up into a concentrated knot of pure mystical power and hurled it back out at the apparition while thundering out another incantation:

"By mighty Omnipotent Oshtur!

By Valtorr and Denak!

Those false of name, from whence you came

You now are ordered *back*!"

The specter that had assumed his father's shape tried to shield itself from the ensuing prismatic blast of light, but Stephen smiled grimly as he watched it explode into a million small pieces instead. He was about to turn to address his companions when he noticed the fragments hovering strangely in the air, glittering a baleful dark green as they slowly spun, suspended in place. It reminded him, for a moment, of the spell he'd used to halt the blast wave of exploding glass at the police department—but as he watched, horrified, every shard burst into life as a new apparition. Donna returned, as did Eugene, his father. Even his mother, Beverly, was there, and his brother, Victor. And behind them stood every entity he'd ever failed to save, every enemy he'd slain, every person he'd ever heard had passed on, every creature he'd ever helped dispatch. There were hundreds of them, thousands, shoulder to shoulder, row upon row, an entire army between him and a grassy hill in the distance. Though there were faces he didn't recognize, the gasp from Sharanya told him that she was seeing her dead, as well.

Nightmare leaned over the Sorcerer Supreme's shoulder to smirk into his ear. "Careful with those 'whence' spells, Stephen. The dead belong to the living. They're ineradicably tethered to the people who remember them."

Sharanya recoiled, her eyes wide. "These aren't really ghosts, though, right? I mean, aren't they just…dreams?"

Before Stephen could answer, Jane let out a joyous cry and ran up to embrace an older man with soft white hair and kind brown eyes who was standing near the vanguard of the revenant army.

"Grandpa!"

Stephen reached out to stop her. "Jane—"

"It's okay—it's Grandpa Fred!"

Jane was on her tiptoes, her arms thrown around the tall, thin man's neck, her head against one of his bony shoulders. "I missed you so much!"

As the revenant looked down at Jane, Stephen spun toward them and cast the Eye of Agamotto upon the old man's pleasant face. A ghastly zombie visage was revealed in its light. Grandpa Fred opened his mouth, showing two rows of perfect white teeth, and was about to bite into the top of his granddaughter's skull when Stephen sprang forward to wrench Jane back.

"That's *not* your grandfather."

Seeing the apparition revealed in the glow of Stephen's amulet, Jane deflated. Nightmare moved up and placed a hand on her shoulder. "Sorry. *That* might be my fault." He gazed out over the army of the dead and shook his head. "Prophetic nightmares. I suppose I'll have to remember that one…"

As though on cue, the revenants began to advance. Turning to Sharanya, Stephen was all business. "By now you should have some sense of how to manipulate the environment with your thoughts, and I need you to use those powers to keep the others safe."

Sharanya pressed her lips together in determination. "I can do that. It's just like being in a lucid dream."

Stephen gave a single nod. "You *are* in a lucid dream, but one you won't be able to wake up from on your own because of the sorcery I used to get you here. Nightmare and I, by contrast, are not dreaming. And Jane...Jane is unique. Her full capabilities are still unknown to me."

With no more time to explain, Stephen blasted several bright-yellow bolts of energy from the palms of his hands into the oncoming horde. He watched with narrowed eyes as one of them hit the midsection of the giant worm he'd destroyed earlier that day, causing the apparition to vanish in a puff of blue smoke. Perfect. They were vulnerable to magic, and he was in the mood to cut loose.

Calling on the Chains of Krakkan, Stephen conjured a thick band of them in front of the first row of revenants, magically pulling the heavy links tight across the chests of the vanguard to drag them forcibly across the grass. Once he had them in a tighter clump, he called down lightning on the dream ghosts, letting hot arcs of white electricity rain on them indiscriminately, thinning the herd.

While the lightning cracked, filling the air with the scent of ozone, Stephen knelt on one knee in the prairie grass to place his left hand flat against the earth.

"Foul Demons of Denak,

Heed my word now spoken!

Tear the fabric of this realm

And split this earth wide open!"

Stephen pushed intent and energy from his scarred palm into the ground, and the earth began to tremor and rumble. A chasm cracked open under the back leg of the apparition army, swallowing up an impressive swath of undead. As he pulled up his hand, Stephen noticed that the ground beneath it had withered and dried up, almost as if Nightmare's shadow had fallen across it. Glancing over his shoulder, he saw that Nightmare appeared to be waiting out the fight, standing quietly off to one side several yards back. Jane danced around him excitedly, imitating Stephen's moves with enthusiasm. Sharanya had apparently dreamed up the *Ashta Dikpalakas*—the Hindu guardians of the eight directions. Eight small deities stood in a row, defensively dividing their small group from Stephen's battlefield. Though he didn't have as much time to study them as he would have liked, Stephen noticed that one of them was mounted on a lion and another rode an elephant.

Rising to his full height, Stephen blasted shots of pure will at the remainder of the apparitions, pushing them back into the gulf behind them. He shot another energy bolt at the revenant of Jane's grandfather, knocking him back into the rift with an apologetic wince—then heard a high-pitched war cry behind him. He spun in time to see Jane charge an errant cluster of apparitions with a branch she'd snatched from the ground, driving them back into the chasm with rage and excitement.

Stephen transformed her stick into a war hammer without hesitation and waded into the fray beside her, blasting any apparition that tried to flank her. He was unleashing the Flames of Faltine on a group of aliens to Jane's right when a demon in his peripheral vision exploded into a burst of dark-blue powder.

He turned to see the entire battlefield detonate in a riot of jewel-toned hues, every apparition—including the guardians Sharanya had dreamed into being—bursting into a salvo of pigment-saturated rice flour. Sharanya was smiling modestly from the sidelines as the skirmish transformed into the Hindu festival of spring, *Holi*, the green grass striped in blankets of chalky color. Next to Stephen, Jane dropped her weapon, laughing and spinning as clouds of pink, orange, and yellow powder settled over her.

Stephen turned to Sharanya. "I think you have better dreams than I do."

Sharanya blushed, her smile widening. "I'm sorry I didn't think of it earlier." She glanced at Jane and then back at Stephen. "I hope it's okay that Jane joined you. She asked if it would be all right, and I told her it would be." She dropped her voice even though Jane was watching her and could clearly still hear. "I thought it might be good for her to blow off a little steam."

Jane grinned at Sharanya as Stephen nodded. Though he was concerned that Jane's connection to the Dream Dimension made her vulnerable to physical and spiritual harm within its borders, she was clearly better off for the brief engagement. With a flick of his hand, he conjured the Winds of Watoomb to blow the colored powder into the chasm.

"If you're serious about cleaning up after yourself, Stephen, don't stop there." Nightmare crouched to examine another dead patch of grass. Stephen looked around with concern. His magic seemed to have taken a disconcerting toll on the landscape. In between the haphazard regions of colored grass, patches of the Nebraska farmland had been eaten away, drained of all detail and color—holes of flat, gray clay. It was as though Stephen's magic had worn away the paint of his dream memories, leaving only the realm's exposed bones. He turned to gaze at the chasm he'd made and quietly spoke another incantation.

"By the power of the Vishanti

And the Vapors of Valtorr

Mend what we have riven

And this soil now restore!"

There was a deep, rumbling sound, and the earth shuddered once again. The two sides of the gulf heaved toward one another and closed over the colorful remains of the apparition army, leaving an ugly clay seam running across the landscape like a badly sutured scar. The enemy was vanquished, but Stephen still sensed danger in the air. It felt like ice-cold rain running down the back of his neck. He crouched down and examined a patch of blasted earth, considering it for a moment before turning to study Jane.

She had been frolicking on what was left of the grass, keyed up from aiding him in battle, but stopped suddenly to bend down and peer at one of the holes in the turf. After poking at the gray clay with her finger, she rose and looked at Stephen quizzically, as if she'd known he'd been watching her. "Aw," she said, sounding distressed. "It's dead."

Stephen wasn't sure "dead" was the word he'd use, but he couldn't disagree. The blasted patches where his spells had landed were devoid of mystical energy, which troubled him. Normally, any magical casting would leave behind residual energy. Considering the force with which he'd been hurling spells, he would have expected the affected areas on the battlefield to be crackling with arcane energy. Jane was right, though. They were lifeless.

Not so, though, the dark-green energy trail that connected Jane to whatever lay at the realm's center. It continued to sparkle vibrantly, wending westward, emanating unbroken from the center of her chest. It was time to move on.

"This way." Gesturing for the others to follow, Stephen started up a patchy hill that was half meadow brome and half clay, his back to the lake that had caused him so much grief.

"Did you see me?" Jane was asking Nightmare excitedly. "I was all like, *bam*!"

Stephen peered over his shoulder. Though Nightmare's expression remained impassive, Stephen thought he could see a sparkle in the demon's eyes as he answered her. "You were epic, my dear."

Stephen turned his attention back to the hill in front of him, wondering whether Nightmare's unexpected affection for Jane was contributing to his current tractability. He was pondering her connection to the Dream Dimension when Sharanya caught up and fell into step beside him.

"May I ask you a question?" Despite the escalating dangers, Sharanya seemed to be finding her footing. Her eyes were brighter than they'd been when Stephen had first met her, and she seemed increasingly energetic. "What I just did—turning all those...*things*...into *Holi* powder—I understand it in terms of what's possible in a dream, but find myself wondering: Is that what *you're* doing? Only awake?"

Stephen thought for a moment before answering. "I know it would be more comfortable for you if I said yes, and there are a few components in common—such as imagination and intent—but...no. Dream-weaving may seem magical, but what you're doing—even what Nightmare does, for that matter—it isn't technically magic."

Sharanya appeared a bit flustered. "Oh, I didn't mean—that is, of course, I'm well aware that I could never do what you do."

Stephen returned his focus to the lambent green trail winding up and over the hill. "That isn't true, either. Anyone can learn magic. Some people will have more natural aptitude for it than others, but don't buy into 'chosen one' elitism. With enough training and application, anyone can learn anything."

"I think I just discovered your super-power, Doctor Strange." Sharanya's face was lit with a sudden insight. "Surgeon...sorcerer... You, sir, are an excellent student."

Stephen allowed for a half-smile as they crested the hill together, and then he stopped, staring out at the view. Across the wide, grassy plain rose a huge Cistercian monastery—and the trail emanating from Jane led straight into it.

Sharanya cocked her head to one side, squinting. "What is that?"

"It's a dream palace," said Nightmare, joining them at the top of the hill. "No doubt the work of Praedivinus. Construct of the construct, seat of power, that kind of thing. Surely you remember mine, Stephen?" He flashed his teeth at the Sorcerer Supreme.

Stephen sighed and started down the hill toward the field below.

"Where are you going?" There was a hint of panic in Nightmare's voice. Stephen stopped, turning around to stare at him. "You can't fight Praedivinus in *there*," Nightmare continued. "That's where he's at his most powerful. Dreams, magic, reality...inside that place, they're all woven together—in ways you might find very unpleasant."

"I don't see that I have much of a choice."

Jane reassuringly placed her hand, still splashed with orange *Holi* powder, on Nightmare's arm. "Don't worry. We can take him."

Nightmare snorted. "Let me explain this to all of you one more time. The realms are separated for a reason. It's not good for *anyone* when realm sovereigns go head-to-head." The demon turned to Stephen with a sneer. "The energy invested within each of us by our individual realms, by the dreamers, is a potent, indestructible force that will always seek to be contained within a powerful vessel. If one of us is...*dispatched*...then that energy has to go somewhere, preferably into another sovereign." Nightmare shifted, his shadow falling over Stephen as he glared at him, chin nodding toward the dream palace with contempt. "I don't care *what* that old bat has foreseen, I'm too weak for this kind of battle right now, and I have no intention of being absorbed into *this*." He waved to indicate everything around them, his sneer deepening into a snarl.

Exasperated, Stephen turned to fully face him. "One of your fellow sovereigns is trying to take over the dimension. He or she is inside that palace. It may be Praedivinus, or it may be that Praedivinus has fallen and the entity you're so worried about has *already* taken over this realm. Maybe they're working together. Maybe Praedivinus is in danger as we speak. There's no way to know from out here. You asked for help uncovering and neutralizing the threat to the Dream Dimension, and I intend to honor that request now. As you yourself have noted, I'm probably the only one who can."

Nightmare folded his arms in front of his chest, planting his boots in the grass stubbornly. "I'm not ready to face another Dream Sovereign."

Stephen sighed. As gratifying as it was to see Nightmare so afraid of something, he was impatient to identify the cause of the demon's dread. "I understand you're still in a weakened state, but I can't very well leave you here. You'll have to trust me to protect you."

"I'll stay with him." Jane stepped in front of Nightmare as she volunteered, shielding him with her body as if she thought Stephen was worried *for* the demon instead of about him.

Stephen's eyebrows arched up in surprise. "Oh, well…"

"And I'll stay with her." Sharanya locked her gaze with Stephen's, clearly wanting to help. "I'll make a *Holika* pyre or something; we'll be fine."

"A pyre?" Jane's curiosity was piqued.

"The *Holi* celebration—where the colored powder comes from—starts with a bonfire," Sharanya explained. "It's called *Holika Dahan*. We use the fire to symbolically burn away our internal evil. We'll be doing things out of order—the fire always comes before *Rangwali Holi*, the festival of color—but of course that's not uncommon in dreams."

Stephen glanced back up at Nightmare, who was obviously unhappy with the plan, but then caught the look on Jane's face. She was surveying the valley, pale and wild-eyed again, as she'd been when he'd first found her. Following her gaze, Stephen turned around and blinked.

Praedivinus' Cistercian dream palace loomed above them, gleaming in the sunlight. It had moved itself all the way across the grassy plain, as if in an effort to get closer to them.

Jane took a step backwards. "She's here," she squeaked.

Stephen wasn't sure who she meant, but he intended to find out.

CHAPTER XVI

PRAEDIVINUS was waiting for Stephen inside a large stone transept filled with light. High arched ceilings left room for rows of gothic windows set into the pale-yellow façade in groups of three, each topped by high rose windows that reminded Stephen of the Anomaly Rue. Six thick columns supported the vault, the only ornamentation being the architecture itself. The air was still and cool, alive with the mineral scent of ancient stones.

The sovereign of the Realm of Prophecy looked old, frail, and disappointed as he hobbled toward Stephen on his walking stick.

"Soon thou wilt realize how deeply she hath affected thee."

Stephen looked around for any indication of a trap. "Donna? Yes, of course, it was horrible. But I grieved, I meditated, I stopped blaming myself, and I let go—"

Praedivinus shook his head at him, pointing his walking stick like a long finger. "Not your sister, foolish sorcerer! Would your sister have you tearing through the realms like Bia in a glade of unicorn? The world has no need of your hippopotami, Stephen! 'Mundane solutions for mundane problems'?' Were those not your words?"

Stephen glared down at his own aching hands. He understood less than half of what the old man said. Perhaps his use of magic had been excessive, but so too had been the forces brought to bear against him. "I like to think I'm reasonably intelligent, Praedivinus, but I'm unaware of any mundane solution to being attacked by an army of zombie dream apparitions, much less an entire planet out of its mind with prophetic visions they've gleaned from dreams. So why don't you just explain to me what it is you're trying to accomplish here, and I'll see if I can figure out a way to help you before you drive every dreamer in the known universe insane."

"Help me?! You've torn holes in the fabric of my realm, Stephen. I've never been weaker! Look at me!" Praedivinus gestured to his frail form with a shaky hand. "Do you understand nothing? Flinging magic around an unprotected realm like bird seed! Well, now the vultures have landed, Sorcerer, and I am out of time!" Stephen shook his head as the old man began to mutter, tapping his walking stick against the stone floor in agitation. "The healer, the bridge, the remedy… Have to *prepare* you… Must accept your role…"

Stephen forced himself to exhale, reminding himself that his work often relied on diplomacy as much as arcana. "The magical arrows led me here, Praedivinus, to you. I understand that you mean no harm, but the dreams you've been sending out pose a threat to reality. If you need help, I will do everything in my power to provide it. But I need you to release your hold on the dreamers, and on Jane, and stop doing…whatever the Faltine Flames it is you think you're doing. Then I will take myself and my magic out of this dimension and leave you in peace."

"Leave? You must *not* leave! I am trying to set you on the path!"

"Then perhaps you could do so a tad less cryptically." Stephen crossed his arms impatiently. "I don't know who Bia is, and I've never seen a unicorn."

"Well of course you haven't!" Praedivinus snapped. "Bia was a daughter of Pallas and Styx, and she destroyed all of the unicorns—turned them into hippos. Like you with your magic, turning castles into straw huts."

Stephen pinched the bridge of his nose. "You couldn't have just said 'bull in a china shop'? This is why no one understands you, Praedivinus. Your allusions need updating."

Praedivinus deflated slightly, making his already slight frame look weaker. "It is true. I am old, and your kind too literal. Perhaps that is why things are fated as they are. As for you, Sorcerer Supreme, one can learn only that which one is truly willing to receive. And, alas, there is almost no more time for dreaming." Praedivinus moved closer, his white eyes locked onto Stephen's. "I am sorry. I have tried. But the snake is coiled to strike, and there is no other way."

The energy in the room shifted. Stephen reacted instantly, sending his senses out in search of the disturbance. Before he could divine the source, Praedivinus' walking stick transformed into Jane's hunting knife, the blade glinting in the sunlight that streamed through the large windows. The sovereign of the Realm of Prophecy Dreams darted forward with surprising agility and slashed at Stephen's arm, cutting through his sleeve and the flesh of his right triceps—precisely where the somnavores had scratched him earlier. The Sorcerer Supreme's bright-red blood dripped onto the smooth stone floor of the transept.

"What in the name of Oshtur—?!" Stephen reflexively clapped his left hand over the wound, and almost as quickly brought his right hand up to blast back at his attacker.

"Stop!" Praedivinus dropped the dagger, which instantly transformed back into his walking stick. "No more arcane magic! I cannot say it more clearly: You aid the enemy with every spell!" He waved a hand angrily, and Stephen found his own hands bound by a glowing white light. As he opened his mouth to protest, Praedivinus made a quick gesture, as if grabbing something out of thin air. Stephen didn't have to try to speak to know he had no voice. He pressed his lips together in annoyance, knowing this dream all too well. He'd always hated it. "Physician, heal thyself!" Praedivinus commanded with obvious frustration. "I wound thee only that thou might seek help. The healer and the bridge and the remedy must be united in the Realm of Healing Dreams—that is as far as I can see now. I cannot tell you why. But I can tell you that Healing is through the northern woods. Remember that. You must go there. The remedy must be prepared."

Stephen's eyes widened, comprehension beginning to dawn. Praedivinus had clearly told Jane much the same thing. He was not the rogue dream sovereign—he had only been trying to prepare them for that confrontation. And for some reason, he was intent on getting them to the Realm of Healing Dreams. Stephen wondered whether perhaps Jane was ill in some way he didn't know about. Surely the Healing Sovereign wasn't the one poisoning humanity's dreams?

Praedivinus stopped, winded—the small display of dream-weaving had obviously cost him dearly. Reaching down to the stone floor for his walking stick, he froze. The stick had transformed into an asp, its bright-yellow eyes flashing as its small black tongue darted out to scent Praedivinus' hand. The light in the room shifted, taking on a dappled-green hue—almost as if they were suddenly under water.

The space behind Praedivinus began to fill with color and shape until suddenly a woman was there hovering in midair, though to call her a woman was perhaps reductive: She was easily three times the size of a normal human, and her flowing blue hair and billowing robes filled the narrow transept. Stephen was struck by her radiance. She was at once familiar and alien, alluring and re-pellent. Her pupil-less eyes showed nothing but a vast universe—deep, velvety black, and filled with distant stars—and her lips curled in a predatory smile. Be-fore Praedivinus could straighten, she reached out and clasped one hand on the back of his neck, holding him still like a lioness with her teeth in the scruff of a cub, his face and hand dangerously close to the asp. When the woman spoke, her voice reverberated through Stephen's entire body, melodious but insistent, so warm with approval it seemed capable of setting off spontaneous efflorescence.

"Stephen," she said intimately, yet at a volume that shook the windows. "You've done so well, as I knew you would. You have always been so dedicated in the pursuit of your dreams. I knew you would be the perfect champion for me here."

The hairs on the back of Stephen's neck stood up, and his wounded arm throbbed. Praedivinus remained paralyzed in the newcomer's clutch.

Still unable to speak, Stephen could only fix the newcomer with a quizzical stare.

The woman's head tilted at a peculiar angle, as if in a pantomime of disbelief, and her smile dissolved. "Stephen, it's *me. Numinous.*"

SHARANYA could feel Nightmare smirking every time she walked past him. She was hauling armloads of kindling from the woods that bordered the northern foothills up to the top of the hill overlooking Praedivinus' dream palace, and it appeared to be taking all of the demon's restraint not to mock her. Sharanya wasn't surprised that he didn't offer to help, nor that Jane did so only twice before wandering off to sit near him. She just disliked the amusement in his eyes, the look that so clearly indicated he believed himself to be watching something hysterically foolish. What was so comical about building a fire, especially one that represented the burning away of evil?

It wasn't until she'd made five trips and arranged the wood into a perfect little cone in the center of the stone pit she'd dream-weaved into existence that it hit her. She'd been spending dream exertion hauling dream wood up a dream hill when she could have just dreamed it all into being in the first place.

Sharanya sighed, closed her eyes, and visualized her pyre burning. Opening her eyes again, she was pleased to see a cheerful fire. Though it didn't give off much warmth, she smiled as it crackled, the humor of her efforts reaching her. In any case, the joke was on Nightmare. She had started explaining the *Holi* festival to Jane, but hadn't gotten around to the story of the bonfire, *Holika Dahan*, which translated to "Holika's Death." Should Nightmare decide to join her, Sharanya would be happy to tell him all about the burning of the demoness and the triumph of good over evil. She only hoped Stephen could see the blaze from wherever he was inside the palace.

She wished him comfort as he defended all of them—all the realm, all reality—but was no longer sure how she felt about Stephen Strange, the man. At some point during the adventure, she had stopped thinking of him as an actual person with dead relatives and other people who cared about him and the normal, attendant baggage of everyday life—probably around the time she had given up on calling him a magician and started referring to him as a sorcerer. A sorcerer was a magic creature, unknowable. He was their guide, and the catalyst of her new reality. If something finally did explain away all the weirdness, he would be one of the casualties of that explanation, disappearing into myth along with Nightmare and somnavores and the Dream Dimension as a whole.

But something about the deeply personal nature of what he'd faced at the lake had reminded her that he was human after all—and it was a terrifying insight. He was proof that the utterly unpredictable world through which she now walked and the ordinary one she had known before coexisted side by side. He embodied that truth, carried the weight of it on his shoulders. Strange was that coexistence. And although Sharanya could already tell that he was a willing participant in that duality, something about the knowledge of it made her sad for him. Or maybe for everyone *but* him—everyone, like herself, who lived on one side or the other.

CHAPTER XVII

NUMINOUS? Stephen had a vague memory of hearing about a benevolent cosmic entity with a similar name, but was fairly certain it bore no relation to the creature in front of him now. Whoever she was, this Numinous was radiating power—she reminded Stephen of Nightmare when he was at full strength, and he would have guessed that she was a dream sovereign except that Praedivinus looked so small and helpless in her grasp it was hard to believe that they were cut from the same cloth.

Praedivinus, in fact, seemed to be weakening. Stephen opened his mouth to ask Numinous whether she was hurting him before remembering that he couldn't speak.

The stars in Numinous' eyes twinkled, and her smile returned.

"Oh, Stephen." She laughed, though not without compassion. "Did he take your voice? As formidable a sorcerer as you are, you never did learn to control your dreams, did you?" She let go of Praedivinus and floated through him like a ghost. His shape was eclipsed by hers as she filled Stephen's vision. Pressing her lips against Stephen's forehead, she restored his voice, her kiss an icy, tingling thing that sent shivers through his spine.

Stephen swallowed and then spoke. "Numinous, I need you to let go of the dream sovereign." He made the statement as unequivocally as he could, even trying to look directly into the entity's eyes, but found the effort dizzying.

Numinous cradled Stephen's face in both larger-than-life hands, and the ties that bound his wrists slipped away. He rubbed them absently, watching her in wonder, and then brought up a hand to cover his still bleeding cut. Though far from the most astonishing thing he'd seen, there was something hypnotically familiar about Numinous that he was still trying to place.

"*I* am the dream sovereign, Stephen. The only one that matters. I thought you understood that." As she stared at him, her expression slowly darkened with doubt. "Isn't that why you weakened his realm for me?"

Stephen frowned in confusion. "Weakened his—? What do you mean, 'weakened'?"

A flash of rage set the beauty of her face ablaze with danger, and Numinous withdrew, stopping just behind Praedivinus again and then attenuating down to his size. Though Numinous no longer held him, Praedivinus was still hunched over the poisonous snake, one hand out. Stephen couldn't tell whether he was afraid to move, or incapable of it.

"You want me to list your glorious deeds?" It seemed to Stephen that Numinous' voice had grown a little harder. "Very well. The most stunning was your recent summoning and subsequent annihilation of that ghostly army. An entire magical battle across the fields of Prophecy! Such a rousing, inspired way to bring the realm to its knees!"

Stephen shook his head. "No, you're—you don't understand. The 'whence' spell that summoned them was an accident, and everything after meant only to protect my companions."

Numinous ignored his protest, continuing with rising enthusiasm. "And the way you kept using unrestrained magic in the Pathways… They were wearing away so slowly when I first noticed their decay, but I immediately saw the possibility in their eradication. There was nothing I could do to hurry it along, though. But you, with your distaste for messes, burning them away so cleanly... It was beautiful!" A small moan escaped Praedivinus' lips. Numinous watched him with a soft smile as she continued addressing Stephen. "And then calling to me with that divination spell, following my life force here... Forgive me for hiding behind Praedivinus, my dear special one. I always intended to reveal myself to you. I just didn't want you to feel that I didn't trust you to succeed on your own. I pick my champions with full faith in their abilities." She bent down closer to Praedivinus and ran the back of her hand down his cheek. "And this one...I knew he had to be one of the first to go. He does so love spoiling surprises."

Stephen stiffened. Could what she was saying be true? He was there to help! How could his magic be hastening the disintegration of the very thing he'd come to save? He hadn't wanted to believe it, but he'd seen the signs himself, and Numinous' gloating was starting to align with Praedivinus' warning. He'd been impatient and careless ever since his first venture into the damaged Dream Dimension Pathways. Though it seemed counterintuitive to cast a divination spell in the face of her accusations, he had to know. Opening the Eye of Agamotto, Stephen thrust his shaking hands into the amulet's brilliant light. And there it was, the mottled dark-green stain, moving through him like an infection. He looked up as the light spread across Numinous. She was burning with the sickness, leaking it, generating more and more...

"You chose this," she said, welcoming his examining gaze. "Again and again." Stephen thought he saw a comet blaze across the night sky of her eyes. "How many times have you rejected the word of prophecy in favor of mastering your own destiny?" She pulled up Praedivinus then, allowing him to finally straighten his back, and tenderly tidied his robe around him as if tending to a child, the asp appearing once again as his walking stick. "You rejected your family's religion, you rejected the shallow stagnation of the life you created for yourself, you rejected the limitations that should have been imposed upon you as a mortal man. And even now, that is what you do every time you cast a spell, is it not? Reject what is? What was said to be? Reshape the very world?"

Stephen closed the Eye, cautious about making things worse with yet more magic, and stared at Praedivinus. Except for his breath visibly expanding and contracting his skinny chest, he remained frozen with dread. "Look how weak he is," Numinous cooed, following Stephen's gaze. "You've bested him at every turn, Stephen." She grasped Praedivinus' chin between her thumb and forefinger, and smiled at him coldly. "It's too bad you've been condemned to talk in riddles, old man. It hasn't served you. You would have been better off with a power like mine. I inspire my dreamers to feel good about their chances; give them vision to see a better version of themselves and the confidence to achieve it. Not all of them are skilled, it's true, but at least they try! No one in my thrall could be patient with your nonsense about the preordained—they shape their own destinies!"

Praedivinus found his voice then, trembling as he spoke. "Not inspiration...blind ambition..."

Numinous made a gentle shushing sound as she patted him like a pet. "No one has heeded your warnings, you blind old relic, but look how beautifully they've championed my cause." Her eyes darted to Stephen, and she spoke in familiar tones. "I think I shall have you rule by my side, brave sorcerer. We can take over this dimension, you and I. Though we won't need Prophecy anymore, of course—we'll do something much better with this realm: free humankind from the shackles of forewarned fate." Continuing to hold Praedivinus' chin in one hand and gently stroke his head with the other, Numinous turned her attention back to the sovereign of prophetic dreams. "Can you see me, old man?" she asked him with what sounded like genuine curiosity. "Surely you saw me coming. Surely you saw all of this."

Praedivinus exhaled and closed his eyes with an expression of resignation. Stephen felt a surge of worry for him less than a second before Numinous wrenched the old man's head to one side, snapping his neck. The dream sovereign dropped to the cold stone floor, lifeless. Stephen inhaled sharply and raised his hands, his palms crackling with energy. Numinous turned to smile at him sweetly.

"What did you do?!" he asked, horrified.

"I gave you back your choice," Numinous replied. Her voice remained gentle and warm.

Gritting his teeth, Stephen blasted her with the Sapphire Bands of Storaan, but they shot right through her, wrapping instead around the transept columns. Her already black eyes darkened as all the affection drained from her expression. She raised one hand into the air and then clenched it; as if in response, the bands tightened around the columns, cutting right through the stone. The monastery shuddered and began to collapse around them. Numinous flew at Stephen then, grabbing the sorcerer by the shoulders and shaking him; in her rage, she grew until her visage filled his vision, and he could hear nothing but her voice and the falling stones of the disintegrating building.

"Still you don't remember!? I came to you after the accident…led you to Tibet! You were an aloof, shallow narcissist, terrified of death and your own defenselessness in the face of it, trying to hold it back with scalpels and denial! But *now* look at you! *Sorcerer Supreme*! You had a vision, Stephen—you saw yourself take another path. That was no *prophecy* dream that led you there! And those nightmares of never being able to use your hands again…they were just your fear transforming itself into impetus. You were spurred by *me*! By an *epic dream*!"

She released him, catching her breath and quieting herself, and then glanced over her shoulder at Praedivinus' body before turning back to Stephen.

As the ceiling began to crumble above her, she reached out and gently touched the sorcerer's lacerated arm.

"That was my gift to you, Stephen—that dream." She pulled back her hand and examined the way his blood glistened on her fingertips. "And now you are going to help me with mine."

WATCHING Sharanya from a short distance away, Jane paused from absently pulling seeds off the sandreed stalks and turned to Nightmare, wrinkling her nose. "Can you do that? Build a pyre or start a fire or something?"

The demon snorted derisively. "Jane, I'm the sovereign of Nightmare. I created my entire realm."

Jane scattered the seeds in her hand and pulled another stalk. "Then why haven't you shared your dreams with me? You know, in my head. Like the others do."

Nightmare shot a sideways glance at her. "Your life is enough of a nightmare already. You don't need mine."

The girl was silent for a moment, studying the stalk in her hand, and then spoke quietly. "I wouldn't mind. If you wanted to, I mean."

Nightmare watched an oil beetle slowly make its way across the field. "Careful what you wish for, Jane. I'm quite formidable."

Jane looked back up at the demon with playful skepticism. Her mocking visage was somewhat undercut by a large swath of hot-pink Holi powder that ran across her forehead and left cheek. "Well, you *say* that, but I've never seen you *do* anything."

Nightmare examined his clawlike fingernails impassively. "I've been recovering. When we started this little adventure, I was rather debilitated."

"And now?" Jane smiled as the demon cracked his knuckles.

"Now? Now I've had time to drink up the delicious fear of your companions, and I'm starting to feel much better."

Jane waved his claim away dismissively. "Doctor Strange isn't afraid of anything."

Nightmare looked up and narrowed his eyes. "Jane, dear, the man could end the world with an errant thought. You don't think that causes him some disquiet?" The sky darkened—first just a lessening of the light, but then a dramatic obliteration of the sun as thick, dark clouds rolled rapidly in. Sharanya looked up, dismayed, as a bolt of lightning licked the sky, followed almost instantly by a deep growl of thunder. Jane grinned, turning her face up to the deluge as the rain began to fall.

Tracing the storm to its creator, Sharanya flashed a censuring scowl in Nightmare's direction before turning back to her increasingly threatened fire. Jane laughed, lying down flat on her back in the grass to watch the raindrops' plummeting descent.

There was another loud rumble, and the ground shuddered beneath them.

Sharanya glared at Nightmare. "Okay, that's enough. No need to show off!"

Nightmare pushed himself off the tree he'd been leaning against, moving toward the edge of the hill. "That wasn't me."

Turning to face the monastery, Sharanya inhaled sharply. Jane jumped up, wiping off her wet hands on the sides of her coat as she followed Nightmare to the edge of the hill. She stood between the demon and the neuroscientist as they all gazed down at the dream palace.

The roof was coming down, large square stones crumbling off the side. The entire monastery was collapsing in on itself.

Sharanya's eyes were wide with worry. "Doctor Strange is still in there."

Nightmare's dark eyes glinted as he watched the dream palace fall. "Don't worry about Stephen. I promise you the Sorcerer Supreme is more than capable of taking care of himself."

NUMINOUS was right.

All Stephen had to do was close his eyes and he could still see every detail of it, as if he'd only just awoken. It was the most vivid dream he'd ever had, and yet he hadn't thought of it in ages. It had become buried under time and nightmares, absorbed into a larger ongoing practice, sparking a transformation that was both a *fait accompli* and such an ever-evolving part of his life as to seem beyond a point of origin.

The dream started in water—the cold, dark water into which his car had plunged, headlights first, the night he lost the surgical use of his hands. Fear. Hubris. Isolation. And it ended in pure light: an awed, warm, incandescent sense of connection and well-being he could only describe as enlightenment. Acceptance. Awakening. Absorption into something so much larger than himself it defied quantification.

In between the two states there had been the climb, a literal struggle up an icy mountain face that foreshadowed an internal ascension from the depths of ego to the summit of *vimutti*—a transcendent release of all that came before.

The dream had changed everything, giving him the courage to spend the last of his money, hope, and dignity on a one-way plane ticket to Tibet, where he'd eventually met his teacher and changed his life. That dream had burned within him as he boarded the plane, kept him warm as he scaled Labuche Kang, renewed his determination and focus during the first four or five hundred times his mind had wandered during meditation. If Numinous truly was responsible, she had once given him a gift of astonishing inspiration and clarity.

What by the Ruby Rings of Raggadorr had happened?

Numinous' voice shattered the glass of the transept windows as she continued to grow, filling Stephen's vision and threatening to send him adrift in the universe of her eyes.

"You may be my best creation yet, Stephen, but you were not the first."

Though Stephen felt sure it had been sunny when he'd entered the dream palace, rain pelted down through the ruptures in the monastery roof and the newly empty window frames. "All the great men and women of history—I nurtured their dreams, cradled and inflamed their ambitions. They conquered continents for me, woke to write in words of fire, fashioned inventions that changed the course of history!"

Stephen saw a silver emanation rising slowly from Praedivinus' corpse, like a heat mirage shimmering off a sun-beat blacktop. Was the dream sovereign's body desiccating? The building continued to cave in around them—yet Stephen realized the falling ceiling slabs never came anywhere close to hitting Numinous, large as she was, nor Stephen, nor even Praedivinus' lifeless body. Though her voice remained warm, Stephen was therefore inclined to suspect that it was more an act of containment than protectiveness when Numinous clasped him in one of her giant hands and placed the other over Praedivinus' corpse as she knelt in the monastery like a child trying to squeeze into a dollhouse.

"And then something changed," she continued, her expression betraying confusion. "There were so many more of you, so fast, and the images in your head…they were no longer imagined, they were real, and they were *dreadful*. Oh, Nightmare loved it, and Erotica…her job became so easy. But I had to sift through them all, Stephen, all those flickering images, and try to find a spark of inspiration. The once soft glow of prominence became a glare revealing the shadows under everyone. And once no one could stand under the scrutiny of renown unblemished, everyone seemed to feel they belonged beneath that light—no matter how ugly or empty!"

Stephen gritted his teeth and held back the waves of energy he so desperately wanted to release. Magic was always a dangerous force to attempt to control—positively treacherous once the element of doubt had been introduced. And now he was more than doubting himself, he knew. He'd been poisoned by reckless ambition, uncharacteristically careless—forgoing ritualistic safeguards and using increasingly aggressive spells—ever since the somnavore had scratched him in the Pathways.

"There were still great people, but more powerful even than their drive was the drive of others to destroy them, to tear them down. And soon it was those intent on destruction who began to fixate, who kept steady images in their heads. They dreamt of killing strangers, of murder and dismemberment, anarchy, kidnapping, rape, torture, strangulations… The world developed a thirst for notoriety over renown…bind, torture, kill…pentagrams and decapitations, and finally the guns, Stephen…so many guns!"

Stephen forbid himself from struggling in the grasp of the giantess and did his best to address her with calm authority. "The world has always been a violent place, Numinous. You should know that better than most. But if you saw these changes occurring, then why not inspire others to fight against such forces, as you did with me?"

Numinous shook her head sadly. "I did try. But those who visit my realm now have a strange sickness upon them. They want so desperately to be remembered and yet dream of nothing more inspired than dispensing death at six thousand rounds per minute. That is not an epic dream, Stephen, that is a nightmare! Yet they come to my realm all the same. Would you have me turn them away? Could I, were I so inclined?"

While she talked, Stephen turned his attention back to Praedivinus. He was worried that Numinous was imbibing the other dream sovereign's spiritual energy, but he didn't know how to stop her. She continued her oration, glancing at Stephen from time to time as if they were having a confidential tête-à-tête in a quiet, secluded location instead of shouting amid the tumbling stonework of a falling monastery.

"I kept thinking it would lead somewhere. All that desperate longing to end a handful of strangers and themselves…it had to mean something! They burned with such anger and loneliness and incompetence, their dreams so toxic and dull they were starting to erode my very realm."

Unbidden, Stephen's hands began to glow, instinctively summoning the energy it would take to force open her giant hand. He had to remind himself over and over again that he couldn't release it. In addition to harming the realm, it was possible that his magic was feeding Numinous' power. She gazed down at him again as if reading his thoughts.

"Yes, it makes me angry, too. Go ahead, Sorcerer Supreme, strike out with your black arts, help me destroy all that is here! It took me too long to realize, but they are beyond hope, your people, their dismal dreams of no consequence. We must start over. I have my own dream now! My own destiny! I will rule all of this, the entire Dream Dimension, and use it to inspire gods!"

Numinous inhaled deeply, and Stephen thought he saw her draw in the final wisps of misty silver emanations from Praedivinus just as the last of the monastery came crashing down around them, leaving them exposed to the elements. He peered up at the hill for his companions a second before Numinous did. They were all there—Nightmare, Jane, and Sharanya—gaping at the colossal Numinous as she unfolded from the ruins of Praedivinus' dream palace, smiling in triumph, her eyes closed as she tilted her face up to the rain. When she opened her eyes again, Stephen saw that they were clouded over by a white film identical to Praedivinus' cataracts. She looked around for a moment as if awed by her new prophetic vision, and then her sightless eyes fell upon Nightmare. Stephen saw the demon tense, and realized that he might have to defend his longtime foe—without the use of magic. Then Numinous recoiled suddenly, as though she were the one afraid for her life. The giant dream sovereign gasped, shaking her head as her vision seemed to clear and her eyes returned to their customary inky blackness.

At that same moment, on top of the hill, Jane screamed, dropping to her knees in the wet grass with her palms pressed over her eyes. Numinous turned and fled, tearing through the landscape like a tornado. Back on the hill, Jane fell unconscious at Nightmare's feet.

It was difficult to see clearly through the rain and the smoke of Sharanya's dying fire, but Stephen thought he saw Nightmare wince with worry and banish the clouds with an angry swipe of his hand before kneeling in the grass beside Jane. And then, as Stephen watched, the demon pulled his cape over Jane, shielding her from the last straggling drops of rain.

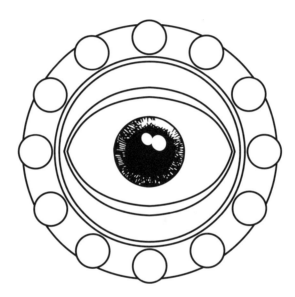

BOOK
III

PROLOGUE

JANE opened her eyes to find herself in complete darkness. She blinked several times, but could discern no difference between having her eyes open and having them closed. Something like sharp little pebbles pierced her bare feet, and she crouched down to touch the rough gravel. Trying to orient herself, Jane had to take several deep breaths before she felt brave enough to move forward, hands out in front of her. She didn't think to start counting her steps until she'd already taken four or five; she made it three more before her hands found a rough stone wall. Still feeling through the dark, she shuffled sideways until she came to a corner and sat back down, huddling into it, hoping she was safe and that her eyes would adjust. There were no sounds save for her own ragged breathing and the rasping of the sharp gravel when she shifted against it, and the room smelled faintly of urine. She assumed she was in a cell of some kind, because she couldn't imagine where else she could be.

She had no sense of time but didn't think she'd been in the corner long before she forced herself to continue exploring. She followed the wall around to another corner, and then to another, this one unpleasantly cold and damp under her feet. The next corner was dry again. She had to go around the whole room twice to convince herself it was a square. Once she knew where all the corners were, she let go of the wall and inched carefully out toward the center of the room, crossing it in 15 small strides. She found no furniture, no indications of a door or window—nothing to inspire even the slightest bit of hope. She was pretty sure there was someone she should call out for, but she couldn't remember who. And when she tried to scream for help, her voice came out as a hoarse, breathless whisper.

She had folded herself back into one of the corners when she heard a quiet bleating sound.

"Hello?" Jane jumped to her feet as she called out the greeting, but there was no answer. She was about to sit back down when she heard the sound again, closer and with obvious distress.

"Baaa!"

It sounded low to the ground, so Jane got down on her hands and knees and crawled toward the center of the small cell, making soothing clucking sounds with her tongue and calling out in a voice barely above a whisper. "Hello? Is someone there? Hello?"

"Baaaaaa!"

Jane's arm brushed against something soft and slightly oily. She jumped back, then reached carefully toward it.

"Baaa!"

Jane quickly identified the form of a lamb. It didn't protest as she ran her hands across it in the dark, perhaps too scared to move. With tears in her eyes, Jane pulled it into her arms and hugged it tightly. The small animal was clearly distressed, and Jane was desperate to soothe it. Somehow her own plight no longer mattered; she wanted only for her lamb to be content.

"It's okay," she told it gently, rocking it in her lap. "You lost your flock, didn't you, poor thing? And you're cold and hungry, and it's so dark!" The lamb continued to bleat intermittently, and Jane found herself becoming increasingly distraught, unable to bear the thought of the small, helpless creature being hungry and scared.

Slowly, the light began to change, as though the sun was rising somewhere far away. Jane realized with a shiver that she was sitting on a damp, grassy hill in a cold, pre-dawn wind. She wrapped her anorak around the lamb, taking comfort in her growing ability to make out its features. She kissed its small dark eyes and its round black nose, and stroked its tiny pink ears.

It wriggled out of her arms to reach the grass as color began to spread through the sky. Jane looked over her shoulder to see the sun glinting behind the hills; when she turned back, the lamb was running up an incline toward Stonehenge.

Jane ran after it, up into the monument, searching through the circle of standing bluestones. With a terrible twisting fear in her gut, she saw something fleecy and white lying on one of the horizontal stone slabs in the middle. She wanted to turn away, or close her eyes, but it filled her vision, vivid and close, until all she could see was the sacrificed lamb staring at her with sightless, dead eyes, its small tongue hanging out of its sweet little mouth, its belly split open, entrails splayed.

Jane took a step toward it, a sob rising in her throat, and stopped as she felt something slip from her hands. Looking down, she saw her hunting knife drop to the grass.

Like her hands, it was slick with hot, red blood.

CHAPTER XVIII

"WHY ISN'T she waking up?"

Nightmare hovered over Jane with an expression on his face that Sharanya would have called "concerned" on anyone else. It seemed that he and the girl were becoming friends. Was that even possible? Well, if there was one thing Sharanya had come to understand while traveling with Doctor Strange, it was that nothing was truly outside the realm of possibility.

Strange had flown up out of the ruins of Praedivinus' dream palace to rejoin them once Numinous fled, his red cloak billowing around him as it carried him to the top of the cliff. Now he crouched beside Jane, taking her pulse, which Sharanya found slightly disconcerting. She'd gotten comfortable enough with the doctor's magical talents to find his use of Western medical procedures startling. But he'd admitted to having once been a surgeon, and after seeing the man levitate, pull a demon out of thin air, fight giant monsters and zombie hordes, and emerge from the center of a lake in the middle of a dream version of Nebraska to have a chat with his dead sister, there was no longer much Sharanya found hard to believe about him.

And seeing him administer to Jane was much easier to make sense of than the sky, which for a moment had seemed to take on sunset hues but now appeared to be filling with fire. Sharanya blinked up at it nervously and then quickly dropped her gaze as the ground began to tremor beneath them.

"She will," Strange assured Nightmare. He looked down at the hillside as it continued to shake violently, and Sharanya realized the grass was disappearing—not so much dying out as fading from existence, replaced by black shale and granite. "Her vitals are normal." He stood, and the shuddering stopped. Sharanya couldn't contain her questions any longer.

"Was that an earthquake? What happened in there? Who was that giant woman? Did you see Praedivinus?"

Strange was peering over the side of the cliff, down toward where Praedivinus' dream palace lay in ruins. His troubled expression made Sharanya follow his gaze out across the valley. In the distance, where the dream palace had been before it moved itself to the base of the cliff, an army could be seen marching in on foot and horses. Olive-skinned men in golden armor and blood-red tunics carried spears as they advanced across the land. They numbered in the thousands.

"We can't stay here," Strange insisted, turning to meet Sharanya's eyes but ignoring her questions. "It isn't safe. Numinous' army is solidifying her control of this realm. We need to head into the woods."

He'd barely even finished the first sentence when Nightmare lifted Jane up in his arms and started moving toward the tree line. "Due north," Strange commanded, striding after him. Sharanya followed them down the side of the hill she'd descended and climbed repeatedly to get the wood for her pyre. It seemed steeper now, and treacherous without the grass there to cushion her steps. Another earthquake shook the land, and Sharanya almost lost her footing—it felt as though the hill itself were jutting up under her. Looking around, she saw that it was transforming into a mountain range.

"Praedivinus is dead," Strange informed her as they skidded the last few feet down the hillside. Dust and gravel slid treacherously beneath their shoes. They stepped into a stand of birch, and Sharanya braced a palm against the white bark of a tree's thin trunk, grateful for the opportunity to correct her balance. "That woman you saw was Numinous, sovereign of the Realm of Epic Dreams. She's the one sending out dangerous dreams and attempting to take over this dimension."

The woods seemed disconcertingly full of the scent of smoke, dry leaves crunching underfoot as the hazy light from the orange-tinted sky flecked like flames on the detritus.

"Epic dreams?" Sharanya was surprised. "People usually love those. They're rare, but so vivid and unforgettable, and often so inspiring."

"She lost her way—discomfited, it seems, by the Information Age. She mentioned images several times—the shift, I suppose, in the nature of the content in our heads."

Sharanya eyed Nightmare, who walked a few feet ahead carrying Jane. "Oh my god, yes. Television and the Internet have been affecting brain chemistry in ways we don't yet fully understand. That's something I've been looking at in my studies, as well."

"That was part of it, but she seemed to be alluding to a larger sociological shift."

Sharanya shook her head slowly as she walked, eyes wide with wonder. "I can't even imagine what it must be like to be a dream sovereign. Think about the explosion in population, the shifts in cultural trends, the events that shape epochs…"

Jane must have stirred, because Nightmare stopped suddenly to prop her, seated, against the trunk of a sturdy pine. He crouched beside her, his red eyes narrowed. Sharanya wasn't positive, but she thought she saw him smile when the girl finally opened her eyes with a gasp.

"Jane?"

For a moment it seemed that Jane's eyes were clouded over with white cataracts, but then she blinked and her vision cleared, her hazel eyes slowly focusing on Nightmare as he stooped over her. She looked puzzled for a moment—and then she screamed.

Nightmare's face fell, but he got up quickly and moved away from her. Strange glanced sharply at Nightmare and was about to go to Jane, but Sharanya beat him to it, kneeling in the pine needles beside the girl and smoothing her dark hair off her sweaty forehead.

"It's okay, Jane." Sharanya was about to add something comforting—*you're safe, you're with friends, you're going to be all right*—but realized that none of it was necessarily true. They weren't safe, Jane had known none of them for more than a few hours, and Sharanya had no idea what was really wrong with her, much less what lay in store. No wonder Jane looked so terrified.

Sharanya settled herself down on the leaves beside her and tried to meet her eyes. "How are you feeling?"

Jane shuddered and wrapped her arms around herself. "I'm okay," she said after a moment, looking around with only mild confusion. "Where are we?"

Strange had approached and spoke quietly as he gazed down at her. "We're somewhere in the outskirts of Prophecy, or maybe in what's left of the Pathways, heading toward the entry to the Realm of Healing Dreams."

"Where's Nightmare?"

Sharanya indicated the copse to which the demon had withdrawn. "He's right over there. You don't remember screaming at him just now?"

Jane's brow furrowed, and she started to get up, letting Sharanya help her back to her feet. Brushing dead leaves off the back of her jeans, she went straight to Nightmare. Sharanya hung back but tried to overhear what the girl was saying.

"I'm sorry," she told him. "That wasn't me. I think that was Numinous and I think she's afraid of you and I think I saw her in your realm."

Strange came to stand beside Sharanya then, nodding at Jane as the breeze played with the edges of his cloak. "Is she all right?"

Sharanya was about to answer when she noticed blood soaking through the Sorcerer Supreme's shirt sleeve. "Are you hurt?"

Strange started to pass his left hand over the injury, and then hesitated. "It's a clean incision—I'll be fine."

"What's wrong?" Sharanya asked. "Can't you can heal yourself?"

Strange crossed his arms over his chest. "I'll take care of it when we get home. I need to be careful about using magic here."

"But isn't magic—"

"Stephen, we have to get to my realm immediately." Sharanya was interrupted by Nightmare, who approached urgently with Jane close behind him. "Jane thinks Numinous is heading there next, and without me to protect it, it's entirely defenseless."

"I understand," Strange replied evenly, "but we're going through the Realm of Healing Dreams first."

Nightmare threw his hands up. "We don't have time for that."

Sharanya cut in. "I think it's a good idea. He's bleeding; she's passing out for reasons we don't understand..." She indicated Strange and then Jane in turn.

Jane snapped her fingers as if just remembering something. "No, no, that's right! Praedivinus said so. That was why I was supposed to..." She trailed off suddenly, glancing shyly up at Sharanya from under her side-swept bangs.

"Supposed to what, Jane?" Sharanya asked.

Jane made a sound and gesture as if she was cutting Sharanya's arm with a knife. Sharanya blinked at her, astonished, but Jane smiled suddenly, noticing Strange's wound.

"But now I don't have to, because *he's* hurt!"

Nightmare snarled, growing more impatient by the second. "We're detouring to get the the Sorcerer Supreme a Band-Aid? Your timing's off, Jane. You struck too early the first time, and now it's too late." The demon squinted up at the sky and let out a brief, shrill whistle. The sound made Sharanya nervous, though she couldn't say why.

"Wait a minute, Nightmare." Strange squared his shoulders, and Sharanya was suddenly reminded of the animosity between him and the demon who ruled the Nightmare Realm. They'd struck an uneasy truce in the face of a greater mutual threat, but Sharanya sensed for the first time how tenuous the alliance truly was. "You're still not strong enough to go up against Numinous alone—"

"And yet it appears that's exactly what I'm going to have to do."

Sharanya wasn't sure which came first, the darkening of the sky or the sound of beating wings. Looking up, she saw a coal-black horse with burning-red eyes and wings like a bat's soar out from between the trees. As it drew close, she instinctively recoiled—the beast was so large, and so swift, and Nightmare was on its back so fast that she felt a whole new peak of visceral fear. Once astride the great creature, Nightmare reached a hand down to Jane, but the girl hesitated, clearly torn.

"Don't be afraid, Jane. This is Dreamstalker; he won't harm you."

Jane glanced up at the demon, met the horse's eyes and then stared glumly down at her sneakers.

"I have to go to Healing," she whispered. "I promised."

Nightmare's expression was stony as he urged his winged horse up. Jane remained on the ground, her shoulders drooped in misery. Strange's hands glowed with power as he raised them to stop Nightmare, but the demon rounded on him. Dreamstalker reared with a snort in midair, its ears pinned back against its head. Suddenly, the demon terrified Sharanya. It was becoming more difficult by the second to believe that he was the same reserved creature who had been traveling so quietly with them, obeying the sorcerer and befriending the girl.

"Really, Stephen? You're going to fight me now? Here? Didn't you just finish tussling with a dream sovereign?" He and the horse both started to grow, the horse's dark, leathery wings kicking up dried leaves as they beat against the air. "And didn't you *lose?*"

Stephen glared angrily up at Nightmare and his horse, but he said nothing. Nightmare and the steed rose to the tree line and hovered there.

"Go lick your wounds in the Realm of Healing Dreams if you must," Nightmare called down. "But the war's not over!" He lowered his gaze one last time—Sharanya felt sure he was waiting to see whether Jane would look up at him—and then turned the horse and flew off in the opposite direction.

Sharanya swallowed her fear and turned sympathetically to Jane, who kept her gaze firmly focused on the forest floor. "Everything will be all right," she said softly, deciding that bolstering Jane's confidence was more important than being completely truthful. "Don't worry."

"He isn't strong enough, yet," Jane mumbled sullenly. "Not to face *her.*"

"He'll derive strength from his realm," Strange countered. He did not make it sound like a good thing.

Sharanya hesitated and then turned to Strange. "Do you know how to get where we're going?"

Strange nodded. "We're very close." He resumed walking north through the woods, which began to thin. The trees were increasingly bare, and the leaves beneath their feet looked moldy and decayed. Above them, the sky was still filled with fire.

"When we go through, into Healing, are we going to be separated again?" Sharanya asked anxiously.

"I've been thinking about that." Strange kept walking as he spoke, his voice carrying commandingly through the dying trees. "I was going to cast a binding spell to help us stay together before we entered, but…that's not minor magic."

Sharanya nodded slowly, her lips pursed together in thought. "And you were saying something about that a minute ago. About needing to be careful. With magic." Strange entered a clearing that had burned and stopped, regarding the scorched trunks and smoldering detritus soberly. The air was pungent with wood smoke, and a persistent crackling sound pulled Sharanya's attention toward hints of creeping fire still scattered throughout the brush, the bright orange of the low flames startling against the black of the charred forest floor. Sharanya waited until the sorcerer's gaze swept back toward her. "Magic, as in what you used to get us here, and how you protect us, and yourself? Magic, as in how you intend to heal the Pathways, and get us home? That magic? That's the magic you can't use anymore?" Sharanya realized her voice sounded more confrontational than she had intended and tried to soften it, but she was scared, and an audible tension remained. "Isn't that kind of a problem?"

"I can use it," Strange clarified evenly, starting across the burned clearing. If he was aware of the edge in her tone, he didn't show it. "But it appears that I must remain cautious. As you yourself have seen, my spells seem to be having a destructive effect on the environment."

Sharanya noted the straightness of his back and the confident angle of his chin. "You don't seem to be quite as worried about that as I think I might be in your position."

"You are in my position," he said with a slight smile. "You're an investigative scientist in a world of symbolism, both uniquely suited and completely unprepared to address the issues at hand."

Sharanya thought about that for a moment. "Uniquely suited how?"

"I keep telling you," Strange said in a voice as calm as hers had been sharp. He began walking again, and Sharanya and Jane followed suit. "You're dreaming now, which puts you in complete harmony with this dimension. Jane and I are—at the moment, at least—intruders, subject to different laws."

Sharanya was quiet for another moment and then slowly nodded her head. "Okay. Then *I'll* do it. I'll get us back together after we get separated. I've been practicing my lucid dreaming and should be able to manage that much, at least." She followed Strange as he stepped carefully over a burning log and felt as much as saw the light around her shift. The blackened woods opened up into a lovely glade, a cloudless blue sky suddenly visible above a large circle of wildflowers and soft, new grass. Shafts of unfiltered yellow light streamed down into the center of it, looking so warm and inviting that Sharanya wasn't surprised to see Jane's face brighten as she lifted her head to take it all in.

"Very well," Strange agreed. "We'll count on you to help us regroup."

Sharanya was pleased to have Strange place his trust in her. But when he put his hand gently on Jane's shoulder, she shook him off.

He tucked his hands into his cape and spoke quietly to her back.

"It seems quite likely that we'll encounter the realm sovereign. If you see them before I'm with you again, try to encourage them to reunite us. Make sure they know that I'm here to help, and that you're working with me."

Jane glared at him over her shoulder. "Don't be nice to me," she said tensely. "It's only gonna make it harder."

Sharanya and Stephen shared a questioning glance before stepping into the glade, instantly entering the Realm of Healing Dreams.

CHAPTER XIX

STEPHEN discovered he was sitting in the quarter lotus position, apparently at the edge of a small pond in a forest glade. Quickly, he ran through the seven points of meditation posture: seated, spine elongated, hands in the Dhyana mudra, relaxed shoulders, chin tucked, jaw unlocked with tongue against roof of mouth, gaze rested and fixed... He inhaled deeply, catching the scent of damp soil and pine, and felt the warmth of the sun against his back—though he knew instinctively it was not Earth's sun. Part of him wanted to leave the meditation to figure out where he was and how he had gotten there, but another part of him recognized how much he'd needed this very thing. He acknowledged the desire to leave and let it go, following his breath back to his center.

"Sensory cortex active. Re-stimulating frontal lobe."

Stephen's mind jumped to the confrontation with Praedivinus and Numinous. He kept coming back to Praedivinus' claim that his use of magic was hurting the Dream Dimension somehow—aiding the enemy, he'd said. But Stephen had used magic in the Dream Dimension before—many times, in fact, while fighting Nightmare. And although it was true that Numinous seemed to be absorbing power beyond what one would normally associate with a dream sovereign, it was both obvious and logical to Stephen that the power in question correlated to the other sovereigns and realms she'd conquered. He'd watched her almost literally absorb Praedivinus, after all. Arguably, even if a dream sovereign could somehow ingest or wield arcana, it would be of little use to them…unless, perhaps, they meant to use it within the waking world, which was not at all what Numinous had claimed to be interested in doing.

"Vital signs stable. Tox screen negative. W.B.C. elevated at twelve thousand per microliter."

Stephen thought back to his first excursion into the damaged Pathways earlier that day—that had to be when he'd become infected by Numinous' dream. Had that infection tainted his magic? In the past, the power of Stephen's magic and Nightmare's dream-weaving seemed largely balanced, countering each other with predictable results. If Nightmare threw a dream blade, Stephen could block it with an arcane-energy shield. Conversely, if Stephen attempted to capture Nightmare with a binding spell, Nightmare might use dream-weaving to create an illusion that would allow him to escape, or make an attempt to break Stephen's concentration by scaring him. That seemed to still be true, and yet never before in any of that had the dream realms themselves been harmed. He tried to let the thoughts go again, but became aware of a throaty, muffled voice somewhere behind him. He exhaled and set aside the meditation.

"Such a gift, is it not? The reminder that it is enough to simply be."

Stephen looked over his shoulder and saw a tall Kree woman smiling reservedly at him. She was dressed in the white lab coat of a doctor, her skin a deep cerulean blue, her head a clean-shaven, elegant oval. Warm, amber-colored eyes were fringed by long lashes, and Stephen noticed she had extremely thin, graceful wrists. She was holding a small electronic device Stephen assumed was a PDA of some kind—perhaps a mobile storage system for patient files.

He stood and immediately realized that he wasn't in a forest glade at all, but rather in a small tropical atrium set in the center of what appeared to be a large, futuristic building. The pond he'd been staring into, the moss he'd been sitting on, the deep-green fronds surrounding him, and the magenta-winged butterflies flitting about—they were all tucked inside a transparent dome with a balmy climate-control system complete with atmospheric humidity. The woman stood on the other side of the translucent encasement, which explained the slight muffling of her voice.

"I'm Men-Dar," she said with an air of impatient efficiency Stephen associated with those in the medical profession, "sovereign of the Realm of Healing Dreams." Her attention dropped down to her PDA. "Though of course we've met before, Doctor."

As Stephen began looking for a way out of the atrium, Men-Dar opened a horizontal panel over the enclosure, prompting Stephen to reorient himself once again. It turned out that he wasn't standing up, wasn't in an atrium at all, but was actually lying prone in some kind of diagnostic chamber. Men-Dar was helping him out, detaching bio readers from his head. "Please allow me to welcome you to the Kree homeworld. This is Hala—or, at least, your subconscious perception of it."

Stephen nodded in acknowledgment as he sat up. A unobtrusive, motorized whir sounded as the pod mechanically transformed into an exam table, the top and outer edges contracting neatly below the table surface.

"Have you seen my traveling companions?" he asked. "I came in with another doctor and a young Inhuman."

"Yes, they're here. I met Dr. Misra, and she informed me of your arrival. I'm on my way to collect Miss Bailey now and will bring you all together shortly. But first, I need to finish my exam." She lifted his right hand in her own, and Stephen had to exhale to keep himself from pulling it back. "How are your hands feeling?" she asked.

Stephen forced himself to look at them. They were covered in surgical scars and felt alien to him, like relics from someone else's life. And they hurt—always. In addition to the constant dull aching and occasional flare-ups of burning nerve pain, thinking about his hands always seemed to bring up some deeply buried biological memory of having been under surgical anesthesia—the nausea and bitter aftertaste—as well as a stab of shame concerning the man he used to be.

"They're fine," he said, more brusquely than he meant to. "Or rather, they're unchanged, but I'm fine." He paused, realizing he didn't definitively know whether that was true. "Was that my white blood cell count you noted? I was scratched by a somnavore earlier, and I suspect I've been infected with whatever it is that Numinous emits through her dreams."

Men-Dar flashed a penlight across his field of vision. "Ambition?"

Stephen scoffed. "Ambition? No. No, I'm very familiar with ambition. This is something else."

Men-Dar's expression remained impassive as she continued her exam. "Does it hurt to cast?"

Stephen shook his head as she leaned in even closer to peer into his right eye with an ophthalmoscope. "Only if I'm really overdoing it. Generally, casting is the one time my hands *don't* hurt."

Men-Dar straightened up and indicated his wounded arm. "Let me take a look."

Glancing at his lacerated triceps as he rolled up his sleeve for her, Stephen suddenly remembered that the wound had been inflicted *twice*—first by the somnavore, and then by Praedivinus wielding Jane's knife.

The dream sovereign began examining the gash, carefully moving long, blue fingers around the muscles of his upper arm. "Epic dreams aren't normally toxic, Doctor, as I'm sure you know. They're inspirational. But this does appear to be infected."

Stephen nodded. "As do Numinous' dreams. Ambition has mutated into blind ambition. Inspiration is now zealotry. And it will only get worse if I don't stop her." He looked around the exam room. "Do you have anything for the infection?"

Men-Dar produced a clear glass bottle containing a light-blue liquid from under the exam table. "I'm afraid not. You'll fight it off eventually. In the meantime, you should be careful not to spread the contamination."

Stephen fixed her with a quizzical stare. "You mean cover my mouth when I cast?"

Using a cotton pad, Men-Dar dabbed the solution carefully over Stephen's cut. It burned slightly, and Stephen assumed it was some kind of antiseptic. "Doctor, are you under the impression that *you're* my patient?" Men-Dar asked, her eyes never leaving the wound she was working on. She pulled out something that looked like another penlight and held the wrist of his injured arm with her free hand, immobilizing it.

"No," Stephen admitted. "I assumed you needed to see Jane."

"You're here on a consult," Men-Dar clarified. With the small device held an inch above the top of his laceration, she pushed a button on it with her thumb. It released a thin, white stream of light that she began to guide down the length of the wound, painlessly cauterizing it.

"And our patient is—?"

Men-Dar stopped what she was doing long enough to meet his eyes. "This is the patient, Doctor. The Dream Dimension."

Stephen arched an eyebrow as she went back to sealing the cut. "Presenting symptoms?"

"The Pathways are down, Doctor—fully ruptured. Think of them as a buffer, a kind of membrane that protects the realms from one another and allows this dimension safe intercourse with all the other dimensions that necessarily pass in and out of it as their denizens dream. Without that protective barrier, the realms are vulnerable to internal threats such as hostile takeovers and indistinct merging, as well as external threats. A primal energy like magic…when you discharge a spell here, it now goes careening through the entire dimension—with potentially disastrous results."

Stephen blinked at the dream sovereign. "You…you want me to use protection?"

Having reached the bottom of the laceration, Men-Dar clicked off her cauterizer. Only the faintest scar remained where the wound had been. "That's right. Turn your attention to healing the Pathways, employ dream-weaving, and resist the impulse to let Numinous' influence push you toward bombastic displays of power."

Stephen's mind raced through the types of magic he'd been using. He was an interdisciplinary practitioner—syncretistic, even—who tended to lean heavily on black magic, Eastern mysticism, and interdimensional arcana. He was proficient in more forms than he had time to consider, but dream-weaving—the magic inherent to the Dream Dimension—was one of the very few at which he was *not* adept. And that was mostly because, as he'd explained to Sharanya, dream-weaving—while potent in a very magical way—did not constitute true magic.

He also knew that he hadn't properly considered the effect Numinous' infection was having on his personality, and saw immediately that Men-Dar had a point. He'd been less vigilant ever since his first visit into the Pathways—impatient and overblown. Spell-casting always had consequences, he knew that. Though elemental magic was sometimes less disruptive than disciplines like blood magic or conjuring, its innocuousness was based on the harmony of the elements with their environment. That concept didn't exist in any predictable way in the Dream Dimension. It reminded him of an argument he'd once had with Hellstorm about necromancy. To Stephen, the idea that reanimating the dead was one of the most wildly unnatural and irresponsible uses of magic imaginable was so obvious as to be unworthy of debate. But Daimon had spent over an hour arguing that death, as an inevitable component of the natural life cycle, made necromancy a simple matter of bestowal or even augmentation—and therefore a lesser evil than regeneration, which went against the concept of entropy. The Ancient One had made a similar case for omniscience once, claiming that true enlightenment and omniscience were inseparable, making omniscient vision a more natural state than the lack of it. But none of the arts or arguments Stephen knew applied to the Dream Dimension, which existed within an independent and highly variable set of physics.

He was simply going to have to be very careful, very controlled. Enchanted objects and self-contained cantrips directed at himself likely wouldn't impact the environment. But large spells that interacted with the realm were clearly problematic. He'd have to direct the actions of those traveling with him and root his own work in protective rituals. He'd use proper incantations, call on reliable higher powers, and watch for ways to work in sealings and cast-offs. He would do no harm. He would be—as Clea had once playfully accused him—as cautious as a white-magic neophyte stumbling into a Black Mass.

Until it was time to heal the Pathways, of course. That was, unavoidably, a consequential spell.

He regarded Men-Dar as he began to roll his sleeve back down. "I have some ideas about the Pathway regeneration, but I'm missing an essential component. I don't suppose there's any way you could supply me with an object made up of organic realm material? Specifically, I'm looking for something from the Dream Dimension with the strength and resilience to have a great deal of energy channeled through it."

Men-Dar turned her back to him as she began to look at the data she'd collected on him via her diagnostic pod. "I'll see what I can do."

Stephen nodded. It had just occurred to him that as a technologically advanced society known for their innovative work with genetics, the Kree might have useful information about Jane—they had, after all, created the Inhumans. "Also, is there a central patient database here? With your permission, I'd like to pull the charts for the Inhuman I came in with."

Men-Dar turned back to him and folded her arms across her chest. "Certainly, Doctor. But there is something I need to discuss with you, physician to patient, after all."

Stephen got up off the exam table feeling certain she was going to say something more about his hands. Maybe she was going to scold him for not spending more time engaging his unconscious in the task of working through his physical limitations. Or perhaps the Kree had developed medical protocols they had yet to share with Earth. If, like Erotica, Men-Dar wanted to keep Stephen in her realm for protection, she might offer to heal his hands. Glancing down at them again, he wondered both whether it was possible and how much he cared. He certainly had no plans to perform surgery ever again. Though a lessening of discomfort would obviously be agreeable, the constant aching was, in some small way, an anchor to his humility. He'd accepted them for what they were, which made the pain much easier to bear.

She waited until he looked at her again.

"I need to know," she said evenly, "what you're doing about your heart."

Stephen's head jerked back. "My heart?"

"It's broken," Men-Dar informed him without a hint of irony, studying her PDA. "And the one-night stands aren't working."

Stephen felt as disoriented as if Men-Dar had opened another chamber to reveal that they were once again not where they seemed to be. Hearing the diagnosis stated out loud, he immediately recognized the futility of denying it, but couldn't imagine a single thing that either he or she could do about it.

"I'll…take that under advisement," he muttered, staring at the white tiled floor. He could hear the impatience in his own voice as he quickly changed the subject. "Patient records?"

Men-Dar hesitated only a second before moving swiftly past Stephen and starting down the hall. "Right this way, Doctor."

THE BARS on the windows weren't a good sign. But the room in which Jane found herself smelled too antiseptic to be a prison, and the floors were too shiny. It looked like every rec room of every psych hospital she'd ever seen in a movie or TV show, except this one had a better color scheme—glossy white and a pleasing, Maya blue—and was more futuristic…or really, retro-futuristic, like a vision of the future from the 1950s.

The good news was that it was Art Therapy time. Jane was pleased; she had always liked to sketch and had a talent for visual arts. The instructions— explained serenely by a nurse with bubblegum-pink skin who Jane hadn't seen since—were to carefully visualize and share a picture of her "safe place." Jane hadn't felt particularly safe anywhere for quite some time, but found herself painting a wide dirt road through the woods. Tall pines, profuse oaks, and flowering butternut trees lined either side of the trail, meeting overhead to form a leafy canopy. The sky was a rich, warm blue, and Jane felt she'd done a particularly good job with the sunlight dappling through the foliage.

She was adding small patches of Blue Star Creeper when a tall, blue-skinned woman with a PDA and a long, white lab coat came and sat down on a couch near her. There was an air of practiced efficiency about her, but her eyes—a bright amber—struck Jane as being kind. Jane assumed she was a doctor.

"That's beautiful, Jane," she said, looking at the painting. "Is that the Pathways?"

Jane looked back at her painting, uncertain. It was certainly *a* pathway. "The ones that science killed? I guess it could be."

The doctor was watching her with an intensity Jane found uncomfortable. "Do you understand what they were, Jane, and how they fell?"

Jane shrugged, still working on details of the small flowers. "Sort of."

The doctor sat back on the blue couch, crossing her long legs. "They were beautiful when they were healthy. Every dreamer saw them a little bit differently, but always enjoyed being within them. Have you ever had a moment in a dream where you felt completely at peace—safe and tranquil?" She didn't wait for Jane to answer, which was good, because Jane had not had that feeling for ages. "That's the Pathways: the breath between one adventure and the next, the possibility of striking out in a new direction, the benevolent guardian of the realms."

"They were alive?" Jane asked. She realized as soon as she said it that she'd meant "sentient"—they had to have been alive, otherwise how could they have died?

The doctor nodded. "Indeed they were. And they eroded slowly, over a long period of time. No one really knows why. Praedivinus and Numinous seemed to believe it had something to do with the intrusion of science into dreaming, but I'm not so sure. Examining and understanding things don't harm them. Perhaps, like some of us, they simply needed to evolve." She looked at the painting again and then put her hands on her knees as she sat forward. "How are you feeling this evening?"

"I fought a ghost army," Jane answered. She was feeling shy until a thought about the woman's identity occurred to her. She turned and peered at her with interest. "Are you the realm sovereign?"

The woman smiled. "I am. I'm Men-Dar."

Jane dipped her brush in a small jar of water by her easel. "You need to see the sorcerer," she informed her, excited to finally carry out Praedivinus' instructions. "Doctor Strange. Though Nightmare calls him 'Stephen.'"

"I'm speaking with him now," Men-Dar assured Jane. "But I also wanted to see you. May I ask what you're doing on this floor?"

"Painting?" Jane shrugged and dried off the brush.

Men-Dar tapped her PDA thoughtfully. "You don't believe you're mentally ill, do you?"

Jane put down the brush and bit a paint-splattered fingernail. She was *sure* she was mentally ill, but perceived that Men-Dar didn't want her to believe that. Jane felt strangely reluctant to disappoint her. Still, if the sovereign was a doctor, surely she could tell. "I'm here so you can heal me," Jane said finally, hoping she was displaying what her father liked to call "a positive attitude."

"Heal you from what?" It appeared to Jane that her answer hadn't gone over as well as she'd hoped: Men-Dar looked somewhat irritated. "Didn't Doctor Strange explain to you that you're an Inhuman?"

Jane glanced back at her painting. "Yeah. Why?"

Men-Dar leaned forward, attempting to make eye contact. "Do you understand what that means?"

"Not really," Jane admitted. "Something about key DNA and...powers...?"

"Kree. Kree DNA. I'm a Kree, Jane. We're your progenitors." Men-Dar checked something on her PDA and then turned her attention back to Jane. "Not me personally, of course, but my race."

Jane understood that the news was being shared in an effort to make her feel better, but wasn't sure it was helping. "So I'm some kind of genetic experiment?"

Men-Dar shook her head. "Not an experiment. We're some of the best genetic engineers in the galaxy, light years ahead of humans. You were *designed*, Jane. And although I can see that it's been uncomfortable for you, you have to understand: You're not sick, and you're not adrift without purpose, as so many of your fellow Earthlings tend to be. You have a function, a place in the universe."

"A place in the universe?" Skeptical, Jane crossed her arms over her chest. "Where?"

Men-Dar rose. "Here, Jane. In the Dream Dimension." She squeezed Jane's shoulder, then abruptly started toward the door. Jane hurried after her. "Though certainly not on this floor. Let me take you to your friends."

Jane brightened, following Men-Dar out of the room. "Is Nightmare here?"

Men-Dar's shoulders tensed, but she kept her tone neutral. "He's not allowed here. It would be highly counterproductive to the healing processes of my patients."

Jane deflated again, and quietly followed Men-Dar to a tubular, partly transparent elevator. It opened the moment Men-Dar stood in front of it, and she gestured Jane inside. Jane entered, turned to face the door, put herself against the clear back wall, and dropped her eyes as Men-Dar addressed the elevator panel. "Third floor."

"What's on the third floor?" Jane asked quietly.

"That's our metaphorical department," Men-Dar answered, glancing at her PDA as the elevator began its descent. "For people who don't approach physical issues literally."

Jane gave a slight nod without looking up and waited until the doors opened again to ask the question that had begun forming in the back of her mind. "What is it, then?"

Men-Dar reached out to keep the elevator doors from closing. "I'm sorry, what?"

Jane raised her head and met the sovereign's eyes. "You said I have a function. What is it?"

Men-Dar hurried Jane out of the elevator. "Praedivinus didn't tell you?" She began leading Jane down a long hallway full of doors to an exam room that, like all the others, had no numbers distinguishing it.

Jane stopped in front of the door, trying to remember everything Praedivinus had said. "He said I had to be with him in the end—not 'him' Praedivinus, but 'him' someone else. Doctor Strange, I think." With a swallow, Jane remembered the stones of Praedivinus' palace tumbling down as Numinous emerged from the ruins. "He said it wouldn't hurt," she said more quietly. "And then he asked me to say it back to him, so I did." She looked up at Men-Dar with distress darkening her rounded eyes. "But I don't actually know if it did or not."

Men-Dar was quiet for a moment, her head slightly bowed. "I'm sorry. The sorcerer did inform you that Praedivinus died, then?"

"No," Jane sighed. "I saw it. In a vision. I have a lot of those."

Men-Dar opened the door to the exam room. Though Jane could see the physical limits of the room from the hallway—like where it ended, and how the door to the next room was just a few feet away—the door opened onto a cheerful yellow-and-green walking bridge stretched across a wide river. The banks on either side were formed out of a bright-orange, loamy soil that led to a profusion of leafy green trees, from low brush to high palms. Sharanya stood at the center of the bridge, facing the water as she balanced on one foot. She had her left leg raised behind her, her left arm extending back so that her hand rested lightly on the sole of her elevated foot. Her right arm was stretched out above her head, as if she were reaching for the sky.

Jane ran to meet her, excited by the unusual pose. Men-Dar pulled the hallway door closed behind them, obliterating all visual evidence of the hospital. Jane was halfway across the bridge before she realized that the realm sovereign had never answered her question about her purpose.

"Yoga, right?" Jane asked breathlessly when she reached Sharanya.

Sharanya, glistening with perspiration, slowly lowered her arms and leg, turning to smile at Jane. "Jane! Oh good, she found you!" She relaxed her posture. "Yes, yoga. That pose is called Natarajasana. Maybe I can teach it to you someday."

Jane was peering over the side of the bridge. "Is this your subconscious metaphor for your health?"

Sharanya looked surprised. "Is it? I didn't even think of that."

"The bridge represents your internal sense of balance in this dream," Men-Dar told Sharanya as she joined them. "Sharanya takes very good care of herself, but is working through some issues of dichotomy," she added to Jane with a quick, tight smile. Jane thought she heard a note of approval in the Kree's voice and slid her hands sheepishly into the pockets of her anorak before the dream sovereign could notice her dirty, chewed-up fingernails with the paint splatters and chipping black polish. Sharanya ran the back of her hand across her forehead. "So this is a Healing Dream? I'm not sure I've ever had one before."

"They vary greatly depending on what kind of issues you're working through," Men-Dar explained.

Jane watched Sharanya's face as Sharanya considered the realm sovereign's words. It seemed to Jane that she looked vaguely disappointed. Her graceful shoulders sagged slightly, and her mouth tightened. "So, I guess I have to make it to one side of the bridge or the other," she sighed.

Men-Dar met her eyes. "Do you? You seem in quite good balance to me."

Jane wasn't entirely sure what they were discussing, but it had a dramatic effect on Sharanya. She brightened visibly, her strong posture and warm smile returning. Though she had no idea what might have been wrong with her, it seemed incontrovertible to Jane that Sharanya was healed.

"Can you heal me, too?" she asked Men-Dar eagerly.

Men-Dar turned to Jane. "That's not how dreams work, Jane. As a sov-

ereign, I've never healed anyone—only guided them toward healing themselves." Men-Dar turned and started back across the bridge the way they'd
come. "When in doubt, remember your visualizations. Now let me take you
to Doctor Strange, as requested."

Jane turned to look at Sharanya over her shoulder. Sharanya was still smiling; she looked utterly tranquil. If visualizing peaceful walks through the
woods would help Jane feel like that, she was willing to try.

"The weirdness of dreams," Sharanya said with a playful wink. Jane pulled
her hood up as she turned back around to follow Men-Dar. She needed to get
the sun off her face—and she needed to think.

STEPHEN couldn't believe the amount of information at his fingertips. He
knew the Kree were scientifically advanced, but he hadn't given much thought
to how that might manifest in their medical record keeping. Realizing that
the patient files he was viewing were metaphysical rather than literal, he was
doubly impressed by their depth. Though it could be argued that the Kree
model of holistic health lacked a spiritual dimension, that was clearly its only
deficiency. The health of the individual had been methodically linked to the
health of the species—which, in turn, opened up into a breathtakingly interdisciplinary approach to ecological balance, stretching from the cellular to
the cosmic. It made human medical science look nascent by comparison, and
Stephen was relieved to find the occasional contradiction in their discourse.

These were particularly pronounced in the area of Inhuman genetic
manipulation. Introducing Kree DNA to proto-sentient species was intended
to guarantee either beneficial but essentially random mutations, or meticulously
designed modifications, depending on the experiment. The through-line was
a chillingly uniform acceptance of predetermination and a pervasive cultural
obsession with the deliberate generation of every conceivably useful evolutionary

niche, including environmental interfaces and sentient weapons. It became increasingly clear to Stephen that Jane was likely far more powerful than she realized, and that as lost as she seemed to feel, her life had purpose. Even though her powers fell outside his purview, Stephen felt increasingly responsible for helping her hone her gifts and find her place in the world.

He was so deeply absorbed in the material to which Men-Dar had granted him access that he didn't hear Jane and Sharanya enter with the realm sovereign. He looked up from Jane's dream health record to find her chewing on her thumbnail and watching him from under the hood of her anorak. Sharanya stood just behind her, looking calm and centered.

"I'm not really sure I can take credit for this," Sharanya admitted, referring to her earlier promise to reunite them all once they had made it into the Realm of Healing. "But here we are."

Stephen closed Jane's file. "Excellent. I've gotten some clarification on how to proceed." In their holistic expansiveness, the medical files had also partly covered the history of the Dream Dimension. Stephen had used the information to augment what he already knew. "Normally, a dream realm that has outlasted its usefulness is incorporated into a larger one. Numinous, as we've recently learned, has fought against this natural evolution, attempting to expand her influence instead. She can be thought of as a kind of cancer, growing past her initial purpose and function, and may need to be cut out of the Dream Dimension altogether."

Jane ground the toe of one sneaker into the shiny hospital floor. "You mean killed?"

"My plan is to use the energy she's amassed from the other sovereigns to restore the Pathways," he answered, getting up from the console at which he'd been studying. Men-Dar took the seat once he'd abandoned it and began logging off the console.

"By killing her," Jane insisted.

Stephen raised an eyebrow and attempted to meet her gaze. Jane averted her eyes, but was clearly still listening. "I'm hoping it won't come to that, but I'm going to need a catalyst for my regeneration spell. If she doesn't willingly surrender that excess energy, I may be forced to improvise."

Jane's focus was on the floor as she answered. "Praedivinus said it will. Come to that. Her death, I mean."

Behind Jane, Sharanya shifted uncomfortably. "He could be wrong, though, couldn't he? Surely we'll make every effort not to just...destroy inspiration."

Stephen pulled down the cuffs of his tunic, straightening his sleeves. "No matter what happens, I promise you that inspiration will not be destroyed. We're attempting to redirect a corrupt manifestation of a particular type of dream, that's all." He looked at Jane and then at Sharanya. "We're agents of Good in this encounter and, as such, will find a way to align our actions with the will of the universe."

Sharanya's eyes widened. "How do you...*know* that?"

Stephen smiled. "Because that's how magic works."

Stephen glanced at Jane, still hiding under her hood and biting her thumbnail, and could tell she wasn't convinced. He told himself he'd have time to bolster her confidence as they proceeded. Men-Dar stood up from the console, and Sharanya turned to her.

"Can it really be true that her realm has outlasted its usefulness, though?" Sharanya asked Men-Dar. "I would have guessed that people are more in need of inspiration than ever."

"I don't necessarily disagree with you," Men-Dar answered. "But her realm had been out of synch with its mission for quite some time now." Men-Dar's eyes darted to her PDA as if confirming her information. "A few epic dreams still get through, especially to those open to receiving inspirational messages, but far more of them stagnate—or, worse yet, become corrupted and are received as impetus to act out destructive, nightmarish fantasies."

"Leave Nightmare out of this! None of this is his fault!" Jane's hands had balled into fists inside her pockets, and her cheeks were flushed. Men-Dar glanced at her quizzically but then continued, directing her comments toward Sharanya.

"That very disconnect is probably what drove her to this in the first place—my guess is that she was half-mad with starvation when she started her hostile takeover of the dimension."

"Do we even know how to find her?" Sharanya asked.

Stephen turned back to Jane. "That's where you come in."

Jane startled, looking up at Stephen suspiciously. "Me?"

Stephen nodded. "You're linked with her—you unwittingly led me to her the first time around. But now I think you're strong enough to do it intentionally."

Jane shook her head, taking a step back. "I can't."

"You don't sense her presence?"

"No, that's the problem. I do. Everywhere." Jane made a gesture that encompassed the entirety of their surroundings. "*Everywhere.*"

That made sense, loath though Stephen was to admit it. The dream sovereign had absorbed multiple dream realms—physically and spiritually expanding her influence. It was the same reason directly opposing her had become dangerous...and vital. Increasingly, she *was* the Dream Dimension. "Can you find Nightmare?" he asked.

Jane swallowed and nodded. "He went back to his realm, so we'd have to go there."

"Unfortunately," Men-Dar sighed, "I'm able to help you on that score."

Stephen wasn't sure what she meant by that. "Unfortunately?"

Men-Dar gestured to them with her usual efficiency. "Follow me, please."

She led them through the hospital to a broad interior hallway surprisingly devoid of either patients or staff, and stopped just outside a set of closed double doors. The entrance was large enough for dozens of people to have passed through simultaneously had the thick automatic sliding doors not been locked. Windows were set in each door, but the transparency had been blacked out, and a high-tech electronic marquee above the doorway flashed red and scrolled a message in several languages. Stephen caught the word "Quarantine" in Taurian, Arabic, and Badoon.

"That's it for the Pathways, I take it?" Stephen asked, suddenly comprehending.

Men-Dar nodded. "I've had to cordon off the whole cafeteria. The Realm of Nightmares is butting up against us now—it's right through these doors."

Stephen regarded her gravely. "After we go through, you should evacuate this wing immediately."

Men-Dar nodded and punched a code into a cipher keypad by the doors. "It will open now when you step forward and lock again once you pass through. Good luck to all of you."

She nodded to Stephen, Sharanya, and Jane in turn and then left them standing together outside the cafeteria. Stephen turned to face Sharanya and Jane. "Ready?"

Sharanya winced. "I'm worried about the getting-separated-every-time-we-enter-a-new-realm thing. Even if I can bring us back together, Nightmare is not a place I want to spend a single moment wandering through alone."

"So keep us together," Jane said softly. She lowered her hood and then reached a hand out to Sharanya. Sharanya accepted it instantly, interlacing her fingers through Jane's. "I'll lead us through," Jane said with a confidence Stephen hadn't heard in her before. He caught himself slipping his own hands into his cloak half a second before Sharanya reached for him. In addition to being in the habit of keeping them free should he need to cast, Stephen felt his hands revealed too much about him. The whole story of his past was written in the scar tissue; a fundamental conduit to his magic lay in his palms.

"Come on, Doctor," Sharanya said patiently, continuing to hold her hand out to him. "Let's do this together."

Stephen withdrew his hand from the recesses of his cloak and took hold of Sharanya's. It was warm and stronger than he would have guessed. She smiled.

"You're going to take us through your nightmares?" Stephen asked Jane, leaning forward just enough past Sharanya to address her.

"No," Jane answered, finally meeting his eyes and holding his gaze. "Through yours."

CHAPTER XX

THE DOORS of the Realm of Healing Dream's Kree-hospital cafeteria slid open to reveal a hellscape. Stephen could see bubbling magma through cracks in the black igneous rock beneath his boots. The air was hot and acrid, the sky so dark Stephen wasn't entirely sure he was outside.

"This way," Jane urged, taking the lead. Stephen felt Sharanya squeeze his hand and followed them cautiously forward.

The volcanic plane eventually gave way to swampy quagmire, the harsh air turning humid and fetid. Spanish moss hung off mangrove and cypress so thickly that it choked out what little ambient light was left, forcing Jane to dream-weave a torch to light their way. Stephen knew several illumination spells, but was trying to keep his use of a magic to an absolute minimum. Jane stopped them suddenly, squinting through the flickering torchlight.

"I lose the trail here," Jane announced. She'd been tracking Nightmare across the landscape of his realm, convinced she could "feel" her way to his dream palace.

"That probably means we're about to step into my dreams," Stephen warned them. He somberly regarded his companions. "Ready?"

Shivering in the cold, Sharanya shook her head. "I have a question first."

Jane's torch sputtered as an icy wind blasted across the swamp. "Did Wong really stay behind to watch over my sleeping body, or is he just too smart to join you on crazy expeditions like this?"

Stephen smiled grimly. "You're catching on."

Sharanya attempted a smile but then shivered again. Stephen felt her tighten her grip on his hand and knew she was afraid. He wondered whether she was also squeezing Jane's hand.

He looked at Jane and found her staring intently into the darkness. If she was as powerful as he was coming to believe she was, she was likely to become a target in the ensuing battle. The realm sovereigns were already fighting over her mind; Stephen assumed it wouldn't be long before they began making plays for her physical form.

Seeming to sense his gaze, Jane turned to Stephen and gave a single nod. "I'm ready," she told him. "But you have to lead now. Take us through."

Stephen hesitated. It was one thing to confront your nightmares alone, but to drag others through them? The things he'd seen... There had been monsters he'd faced only because to turn one's back on such a thing was unthinkable. And some of the worst of them weren't even monsters. He'd glimpsed concepts and realities so alien that just learning about them had threatened his sanity.

Still, it seemed he had no choice but to take Jane and Sharanya with him. He returned Jane's nod, cleared his mind, and stepped into a blackness so thick the light from Jane's torch couldn't penetrate it.

He was expecting Shuma-Gorath. If the Nightmare Realm could throw any monster at him, what better than a genuine Old One—a god, a planet conqueror, a demon made up of nothing more than six enormous tentacles springing from one huge, horrific, restless eyeball? Shuma-Gorath was indirectly responsible for the death of Stephen's treasured mentor, the Ancient

One, and Stephen once had the singularly unpleasant experience of merging with the demon and then impaling himself in an effort to destroy it. He was trying not to remember the feeling of that colossal eye on his back even as he considered how to explain such a history to Jane and Sharanya.

But Shuma-Gorath wasn't there. Nothing was there but a small table, and on the table a gold ring, and in the darkness the sound of a woman sobbing. Stephen froze.

It took him a moment to remember that he was holding Sharanya's hand. Stephen let go to peer down at his left hand. His wedding band was still on his ring finger, confirming what he feared.

He was in the master bedroom of the Sanctum with its four-poster canopy bed, though she was hunched up on the floor, facing the corner, her beautiful silver hair swept up off her long, graceful neck.

"Clea, listen to me." Stephen heard himself speaking even though his lips hadn't moved. "I'm not saying nothing happened—I'm saying it didn't *mean* what you think it meant."

"I've seen her before," Sharanya whispered to Jane from where they stood together by the dresser, still holding hands. "She was with him in Erotic Dreams. I think Nightmare said she was his wife?"

Jane sighed at the floor. "If he's talking about what I think he's talking about, then my guess would be ex-wife."

"That's Clea," Stephen said tersely. "And we're still married." His attention wandered back to the wedding band on the table. "Essentially." He started toward her shuddering form. "Technically." He hesitated, then crouched down behind her. "In her dimension. She has no legal status in mine." He reached out a shaking hand to touch her shoulder. "Maybe 'estranged' is a better word."

"You don't get to decide that, Stephen." He was fairly certain that Clea was answering his statement from the past, locked in a conversation they'd already had. She started to shrug off his touch, but then couldn't seem to quite bear doing so. She looked at him over her shoulder with a tear-stained face, her voice clear though her eyes were bright with tears. "The things that happen to one of us happen to both of us."

Sharanya had inched forward, Jane still in tow, and now crouched down behind Stephen, reaching for his left hand again. Stephen let her take it reluctantly, not wanting anything to distract him from Clea. "Your actions affect me, Stephen," Clea was saying. "How can you not understand that?"

"If you'd just let me explain—" he heard himself say. He was growing increasingly confused. The conversation felt like a memory, but he knew that his concerns about infidelity had been a much more recent development. While they were still living together, he and Clea had developed their own rules, unshackling themselves from shame and convention. He couldn't think when the dream conversation might have occurred, and yet he knew precisely what she was going to ask and how he was going to answer. And he was dreading it.

"Explain, then!" she continued, as he'd known she would. "I'm trying to understand! What do you get from her that you can't get from me?"

Stephen rose, taking Sharanya and Jane up with him. He was determined not to say the words he could already hear echoing in the room like déjà vu— couldn't think why, under any circumstances, he would ever say such a thing. But Jane's attention had darted to the other side of the room, and following her gaze, Stephen saw a second version of himself, the one from the imagined past, striding toward Clea purposefully. "Don't say it," he cautioned himself, watching in frozen horror. "Please don't say it."

"I suppose it just makes me feel more human," the dream version of him said to Clea, heedless of the warning.

Jane wrinkled her nose in confusion. "Is she an Inhuman, too?"

Stephen answered quietly, his shoulders sinking. "She's from the Dark Dimension. Which is very far away."

Feeling a nauseating shift in the angle of his vision, Stephen realized he'd merged with his dream-self, just in time to watch Clea's face crumple. Sharanya made a small sound of surprise behind him as the version of him she was holding onto disappeared.

"I know we don't come from the same world, Stephen," Clea said in a quivering voice, tears sliding down her pale cheeks. They were standing back in the bedroom corner where they'd started, only she was much closer. So close he could smell her. He swallowed. It was his favorite smell in the universe. In any universe. "But I've always thought we were connected in all the ways that really mattered. I thought we made each other better. The last thing I'd ever want to do is stand between you and your humanity."

"That's not what I meant!" Stephen told the dream-Clea, panicked. He watched, stricken, as she turned away from him, crumbling back down into the posture in which he'd first found her.

He wasn't sure what changed, but realized with relief that he was no longer locked into the dialogue from the past. Free to choose his words, Stephen reached down to gently stroke Clea's hair, his voice once again calm and controlled. "I'm in the Realm of Nightmare, Clea. Can you hear me?"

He knew she wasn't truly there, not physically. But she was nearly as powerful with magic as he was, and in the past they had communicated and found each other over great distances. The presence of a dream-Clea didn't negate the possibility of speaking to the real one, and Stephen was dazed by how desperately he suddenly wanted to.

Clea stared at him, her eyes filled with love and pain. "Can I hear you? Of course not, my love. I'm gone."

The warmth of her shoulder under his palm was suddenly absent, the corner empty. She had vanished into thin air, which he tried to tell himself was a good thing. The Realm of Nightmare was no place for a reunion.

Sharanya took his hand again, speaking gently but with confidence. "You know that didn't happen, right? Not truly."

Stephen blinked at her. He was surprised to find that company in no way negated the strangling loneliness of bad dreams.

"I don't mean now—of course it isn't real now. I mean it isn't a memory, either. Dreams don't work that way." She moved closer to him, looking around the room with interest. "There may be fragments of memory in them, sometimes very vivid ones, but you're never going to see a literal, unadulterated repeat of an event that occurred in your waking life play out exactly as it happened in a dream. That kind of memory comes from a different part of your brain."

Stephen nodded curtly, realizing that he had known that intellectually, even if it had eluded him emotionally. Thinking about what Men-Dar had said about his broken heart, he realized with private embarrassment that Sharanya and Jane had just witnessed his version of an anxiety dream. He didn't know what to do about Clea—didn't even truly understand what had happened to his marriage—and somewhere in his mind, it was weighing on him more than he'd realized.

Still holding her hand, Jane was shaking her head at Sharanya in wonder.

"You still think dreams come from inside your brain? Even while you're standing here, in this place?"

Stephen noted that Sharanya was watching him as she answered Jane, her eyes tracking his gaze as he tried to figure out how to continue through the realm. "Honestly, I don't know what to think. This morning my understanding was that dreaming involved the left hemisphere using internally generated narratives to reframe episodic memories—which are notoriously unreliable even in the waking world, by the way—while moving them from the hippocampus to the cerebral cortex for long-term storage. I suppose this is somehow the spiritual dimension of that?"

Jane rolled her eyes. "Thanks for clearing that up."

Stephen interrupted with sudden but obvious impatience. He could still smell Clea in the room and was desperate to move on. "Never mind that right now. How do we get out of here?"

Jane had begun biting her thumbnail again but stopped to offer him a slight shrug. "It's your nightmare. Just keep going."

Stephen lifted his free hand to conjure a portal to take them straight to the center of the Nightmare Realm, but stopped himself. "Mundane solutions for mundane problems," he sighed. He lowered his hand and strode to the bedroom door, pulling the others behind him and yanking it open. "Let's go."

He'd only taken two steps into the hallway when he recognized the long halogen lights of New York Hospital overhead. It felt strange to travel so far back in time—was he going the wrong way? He opened his hands and peered at them. They were still scarred and trembling. Glancing over his shoulder, he saw Sharanya hurrying to catch up with him, Jane still right behind her. The Nightmare Realm wasn't making it easy for them to keep track of him, but they hadn't given up. Stephen was waiting for Sharanya and Jane to cross the small distance back to his side when a surgeon backed out of the operating room in front of him, gloved hands already wet with blood.

"Doctor Strange! Thank god! I've got a Cat One horrendoplasty in O.R. three—we're gonna lose her unless you can work your magic!"

Stephen blanched. "I don't do that anymore. The accident, remember? My hands…" He lifted his hands to show the surgeon but realized he was already scrubbed in, his hands aching and tremoring so much he had no doubt about what he'd find beneath the green surgical gloves.

"That's interesting." Sharanya had caught up to him and was looking thoughtfully over his shoulder as Jane, still holding Sharanya's hand, looked down the long hallway in the opposite direction. "Hands in dreams usually represent our connection to the people around us. I meant to ask you earlier—"

Stephen interrupted. "Car accident, many years ago. Permanent nerve damage."

Sharanya nodded as a nurse spun Stephen toward an operating table. He immediately began to sweat under the hot surgical lights. It was an intra-operative brain mapping, the patient awake but sedated, her brain already open to show multiple grade-four glioblastoma multiforme at the frontal and temporal lobes. Stephen looked at the neuroanesthesiologist, wanting to ask how they had arrived at the determination that the case was operable. Before he could speak, though, he noticed the patient's eyes on him. It was Jane. Sharanya was still standing behind him, whispering over his shoulder—suddenly dressed as a nurse.

"You feel responsible. They're making you do it. You don't want anything bad to happen to her. There's nothing you can do. They're going to blame you. It all happened so quickly. You didn't see this coming. They've backed you into a corner."

Stephen watched his hands shaking uncontrollably as he answered her. "I'm sorry if I'm responsible for making you a nurse in this scenario. I know you have a doctorate."

"What?" Sharanya was suddenly at the opposite end of the operating ta-ble, at the patient's feet, dressed as she normally was. Jane stood beside her, their hands linked. Sharanya looked down at her blouse with a frown. "You think this makes me look like a nurse?"

Stephen shook his head. "Never mind." He glanced down at the patient, who still looked like Jane.

"This is about feeling powerless," Dream-Jane said calmly.

Stephen took a deep breath behind his face mask, unwilling, even in a dream, to compromise the sterile field. "Yes, I got that."

The neuroanesthesiologist pulled down his mask, as well. It was Wong. "Do you feel powerless, Stephen?" he asked.

"You know I don't," Stephen answered.

The surgical lamp went off then, plunging Stephen into darkness. Closing his eyes, he extended his senses through the dark and immediately realized he wasn't alone.

"Wong? Is that you?"

"Yes, Stephen. I'm here."

Wong, no longer in the uniform of an anesthesiologist, lit a candle and raised it high above his head to help Stephen see. They weren't alone. Though he'd lost sight of Sharanya and Jane, the room was packed: It seemed that everyone Stephen had ever met, every person he'd ever helped—intentionally or as a byproduct of one of the many times he'd saved the world—had been crammed around the operating table. The light flickered across faces he recognized—Wanda, Monako, Lt. Bacci—but most were the faceless multitudes of humanity that were constantly saved in the course of his duties as Sorcerer Supreme. In other words, every life in existence.

As Wong passed the candle to Stephen over their heads, Stephen looked down to see that the table had vanished, and he was once again wearing his usual habiliment, the Cloak of Levitation secured around his shoulders by the Eye of Agamotto.

"Stephen?" It was Clea's voice again, although he couldn't find her face in the crowd. "I think these people need your help."

Stephen spun with the candle, still trying to find Clea, when everyone in the room began to speak at once, their voices overlapping.

"Doctor Strange?"

"…nowhere else to turn…"

"Stephen?"

"…have to help me!"

"…never been more terrified in my life…"

"…don't understand what's happening to me…"

"…have to help him!"

"Strange!"

"Someone said you might be able to help…"

"But aren't you the Sorcerer Supreme?!"

"…our last hope…"

"…have to help her!"

"…and now Earth's in grave danger!"

"…nowhere else to go…"

"Please, Doctor Strange, you have to help us!"

The crowd began to press in on him, hands reaching out to grab his cloak even as they continued crying for help. As he looked over the throng, more and more individual faces started to come into focus, but he didn't have time to linger on them. Past them, against the back walls, Stephen began to see flashes of more troubling faces: demons, aliens, monsters, and extradimensional beings.

"I'll get to all of you, I promise, but I need you to make a tight circle around me."

The creatures at the outskirts of the room became increasingly grotesque. Stephen knew the sight of them would be too much for most of the people present, likely to inspire full-blown panic if not outright insanity.

"Wong? Can you help bring them closer? Wong?"

He was trying to locate Wong again when the candle sputtered and died, the room slipping once again into total darkness. People screamed. Stephen could hear growling and slavering sounds around the edges of the crowd. He found he was no longer holding the candle and was about to activate the mystical light of the Eye of Agamotto when he heard the crackling of flames behind him. The radiant heat of fire spread across his back as he watched his own shadow extending out across the floor before him.

A horrible, familiar laugh vibrated up through Stephen's spine, and he spun around to find himself face-to-face with his greatest nemesis: the dread Dormammu, conqueror and despot of the Dark Dimension. Composed of pure mystical energy, Dormammu appeared as a demonic entity with his skull entirely composed of flames.

"Citizens of Earth!" Dormammu thundered, addressing the multitude. "Be honored! For I, Dormammu, have come to witness your annihilation! Soon your star will supernova, expanding in a blinding detonation, obliterating the inner planets of your system!"

He felt someone firmly take his hand and turned to see Sharanya, who was still successfully clasping onto Jane. "This is exactly the kind of thing I didn't want to be alone for!" Sharanya protested, clutching his hand so hard it hurt as she gaped up at Dormammu. "What is that?! Why is his head on fire?! And what does he mean by soon?!"

"That's Dormammu, and the less you know about him the better." Stephen rubbed his neck as he gazed up at his most devastatingly powerful enemy.

"But fear not!" Dormammu continued. "Your planet will survive this blast!"

"If we were seeing him outside of my nightmare, I assure you I would not be so calm," Stephen clarified. "But this, alas, is a recurring dream. And don't worry—he means five billion years from now. Time moves very differently in the Dark Dimension."

"The Dark Dimension?" Sharanya whispered. "Didn't you say that was where your wife was from?"

"Indeed I did." Stephen scanned the room for anything even remotely resembling an exit and then chin-nodded toward Dormammu. "Allow me to introduce my uncle-in-law."

"What's happening with your hands?"

Sharanya let go abruptly, as if holding his hand was hurting her. Stephen looked down to find his hands glowing with eldritch power. *Don't cast*, he reminded himself fiercely. *The Dream Dimension is still too fragile. Do not cast.*

"*Your* planet will be ripped to shreds as it spirals into the resulting white dwarf!" Dormammu concluded. He laughed again, a dissonant, rumbling sound Stephen could feel through his whole body. "Yet do not despair! For surely your Sorcerer Supreme has a plan to save you all! Who else would slave and toil as he does to defend a doomed race on a doomed rock?"

The spell energy in his hands was accumulating—Stephen was no longer sure he could control it. Finally spying an exit at the far corner of the room, he turned to tell Sharanya to follow him, but he had lost her again. Attempting to put distance between himself and his dream of Dormammu, Stephen began to struggle through the press of the crowd. Bodies blocked his progress, hands clinging to his cloak, Dormammu's voice following him as he fought through the horde.

"Ask him, doomed denizens of Earth! Ask him what his plan is! Ask Doctor Strange how he intends to save you all when your own instincts, your atmosphere, your biology, your very solar system seal your miserable fate!"

Stephen was lost in the crush of bodies, which grew increasingly skeletal and spectral as they clawed at him. Dormammu's laughter continued to shake the ground beneath him, creating a pressure Stephen could feel from the soles of his feet to the back of his teeth. It was worst in his hands, building and building—until finally it detonated. An unrestrained explosion of glaring, raw magical power—a supernova of his own making—shot out from his palms in concentric waves. As the energy swept outward, it obliterated the people around him, the operating room, even Dormammu. It scorched the ground beneath his boots and the sky above his head, leaving Stephen shuddering on his knees in a crater of dust. He stared at his hands in horror as he tried to catch his breath, astonished that they showed no signs of the power they possessed. In fact, they looked weak: pale and scarred and trembling.

Two smaller hands wrapped around his fingers suddenly, soft and steady, chipped black polish highlighting nails bitten down to the quick. Stephen looked up into Jane's hazel eyes.

"It's okay," she said, giving his fingers a quick squeeze before letting go. "We're through."

CHAPTER XXI

STEPHEN struggled to his feet, pleased to see Sharanya standing just behind Jane. He'd blasted his way out of his nightmare, but Jane had helped navigate them toward it, and Sharanya had kept the group together, as she'd promised. They were both proving to be powerful allies, moving through the Dream Dimension with increasing confidence and command.

As he strode up a barren hill in the moonlight, Stephen saw signs of civil unrest as well as invasion. Orchards to the south were full of broken branches and uprooted trees, as if giant creatures had battled through them, heedless of the damage they inflicted. To the north, a frozen tundra was muddy and red with blood. Perhaps most unsettling was the striking absence of a greeting. Stephen had never before been in Nightmare's realm for more than a handful of seconds without some kind of Horror attempting to torment or besiege him.

Stephen could sense that Sharanya was bursting with questions about the dreams they'd just moved through, but she was quiet as she followed him up the incline, as was Jane. Cresting the hill, they saw Nightmare's dream palace hulking on the other side of a deep valley just as the sounds from the battle raging below reached them.

Alexander's army was encamped behind the hill, their silver swords and golden armor flashing and gleaming in the dark as they prepared for siege. The round tents and drill formations of their meticulous camp were a small speck of order in a sea of chaos.

Between Stephen's group and Nightmare's dream palace, a frenzied battle raged. It included every monster imaginable, many still locked in combat with creatures Stephen could only assume to be Epic Nightmares—horrifying glimpses of what Numinous' rule would bring. Cthulian cephalopods wrapped their tentacles around fire-breathing snake-lizard hybrids. Giant, chest-thumping land sharks stomped their muscular legs on tiny, grotesque ghoul-monkeys, while huge zombie spiders vomited bioluminescent parasitic flukeworms all over the matted fur of screaming, sharp-clawed owlbears. Bogeymen grappled with fanged clowns, and ghostly apparitions dotted the landscape, flashing in and out of existence to scream in the faces of adversaries. The skies were teeming with winged creatures ranging from bats to manananggals. Stephen found it difficult to tell the sides apart in several instances and wondered whether even the somnavores knew anymore.

"We have to get from here to there," he told his companions, gesturing toward the palace. "And I guarantee that if there's anything in the world that scares you, it's somewhere on that field."

Jane lifted her chin as if in defiance of Stephen's statement, but Sharanya winced and looked down at her shoes. "Are we walking?" she asked.

Stephen rubbed his hands as he scanned the battlefield. "If it were safe for me to use my magic, we would fly, or teleport, or make ourselves invincible or invisible—or all of the above. But my arcana is having a negative effect on the dimension, and we can't weaken this realm without simultaneously weakening Nightmare. That wouldn't always be a concern—but at the moment, we need his help to defeat Numinous, who poses the greater risk." Sharanya and Jane exchanged a glance and then looked back at him, so Stephen continued.

"For the time being, I need to cast as infrequently as possible, and only with small, contained spells. I believe enchanted objects will be safe, as well—as long as I keep their use localized—but you two will need to make up the difference with dream-weaving."

Sharanya looked anxious. "Why can't you do it, too?"

"I could if I were dreaming right now," Stephen explained. "But I'm not. As you'll recall, I'm awake, and physically here." He turned to Jane. "You are, as well, but your Inhuman power connects you to this place in some way I don't yet fully understand. I suspect you could learn to come and go from the Dream Dimension at will, whether awake or asleep. You may even be able to dream-weave in the real world. And there's no doubt that you can do so here. So, first, we'll need a vehicle of some kind—something formidable enough to get us across."

Jane gave a single nod, and turned her back on Stephen and Sharanya to concentrate on a weedy plateau a few feet away. Stephen watched as she blew her bangs off her forehead and then waved a hand with the casualness of a practiced sorcerer. The vehicle that appeared was part tour bus and part stretch-Hummer, set upon a half-track consisting of big-rig tires in the front and tank treads in the rear. A shiny silver cowcatcher had been mounted to the front.

She met Stephen's eyes questioningly, and he gave her a nod of approval, noticing that it elicited a slight smile. She looked rather pleased with herself as she hopped into a seat in the back.

Sharanya placed a hand lightly on Strange's cloaked shoulder. "Want me to drive?" she asked softly.

Stephen smiled ruefully. It had been years since he'd had a nightmare about the car crash, but it was exactly the kind of vulnerability the realm might expose. He gave a slight nod and watched Sharanya climb into the driver's seat before settling himself into the passenger side.

Sharanya started up the rig, the entire cab vibrating as the motor rumbled to life on top of the dark hill. Though Sharanya was able to keep control, the descent was rough—bumpy and slow. The vehicle lumbered down to the base of the hill and started across the flat plane toward Nightmare's dream palace. Stephen noticed Sharanya's hands tightening around the wheel. "Okay," she said, as much to herself as to anyone else. "Here we go."

Stephen scanned the field. "Aim for the palace and just keep moving, no matter what. The good news is, you don't have to differentiate between combatants. If it gets in your way, run it over." Sharanya nodded, hunching over the steering wheel like a horse jockey.

Avoiding magic was harder than Stephen had anticipated. They took the first wave of creatures by surprise, plowing into a group of somnavores from behind, but the second knot of monsters impacted both their trajectory and their speed. Blood splattered across the windshield, obscuring their view. Sharanya clicked on the wipers, but they only streaked viscera and feathers across the glass. Squinting through the gore, Stephen could just make out the glinting of eerie, orange eyes in the dark and knew that they'd lost the element of surprise. Resistance increased as they plowed through masses of bone, blood, spikes, and scales, claws scraping against the windows as they sped on.

Sharanya activated the windshield spray nozzles, creating a rectangle of red-stained transparency. A loud bang drew everyone's eyes to the driver's side. As Sharanya corrected course, Stephen observed a burly ogre hanging off of their vehicle, attempting to muscle its way up onto the roof. Rising from his seat, he summoned the Axe of Angarruumus.

"Where are you going?" Sharanya asked anxiously.

Clutching the magical axe in one hand, Stephen opened the passenger-side door. "No matter what happens, keep going." He climbed carefully onto the vehicle's roof, reaching it just as the ogre's thick fingers found purchase. Seeing Stephen above him, the ogre glared directly into his eyes and snarled. Fighting his instinct to blast the creature with a defensive spell, Stephen smashed the emerging hand with the haft of his axe. The ogre lost his grip on the vehicle and tumbled backwards out of view.

Stephen watched him disappear into the receding darkness as the bus sped forward until he heard a cry of alarm from Sharanya. At first glance, it appeared that they were heading straight toward a wall of ice. As the back end of their vehicle broke traction and began to slide to the right, Stephen guessed that Sharanya must have panicked and hit the brakes. Had he not been wearing the Cloak of Levitation, he would have been thrown from the bus; as it was, his brief ascension afforded him a better view of the obstacle.

It wasn't a wall. It was Numinous in her giant form, directly in their path several meters ahead. She was approximately 30 feet tall, wearing a luminescent cape and sleeveless white dress that glowed in the moonlight like the ice mountain for which he'd first mistook it. Hearing the rumbling motor, she turned slowly toward them. A smile spread across her face just as Sharanya, who had been steering into the slide, corrected course and regained control of the vehicle. Dropping back onto the roof, Stephen took a wide stance, lowered his center of gravity, and wielded the axe, his cloak billowing out behind him.

"Sorcerer Supreme!" Numinous called out in a voice that rolled across the plane like thunder. "You've come to witness my greatest victory!"

As she took a step toward them, Stephen could feel the ground shudder even through the vehicle. The stride of the enormous sovereign carried her other foot ahead of them, forcing Sharanya to swerve around it.

"You needn't storm the castle for me," Numinous laughed. "I have the situation well in hand."

Stephen kept his balance until he felt the bus was close enough to the colossal dream sovereign. Numinous seemed to be stepping more deliberately into their path. Running for the front of the roof, Stephen sprang off of it.

Using the Cloak of Levitation to aid his forward momentum, he launched out ahead of the bus toward the sovereign's left thigh, heaving the axe. It caught several feet above her knee, and Stephen clung to it like a mountain climber scaling a sheer cliff face with a pickaxe, his hands stiff and aching.

Numinous shrieked in pain, giving Sharanya just enough time to drive through her legs unimpeded. Using his feet as leverage against the sovereign's thigh, Stephen wrenched out the axe and attempted to drop back down onto the bus as it passed beneath him. He hit nearly dead-center, but his feet slipped out from under him, sending him tumbling toward the rear of the vehicle. Swinging the axe out wide, he felt it bite into the metal top of the bus and caught the handle just in time to stop himself from plummeting off. Pain shot through his hands; it cost him an almost magical act of will not to let go.

"What are you doing?!" Numinous called after them. Stephen heard both anger and genuine confusion in her voice. She could not seem to fathom why anyone would oppose her. "You hurt me, Stephen! You have spilled the blood of a god!"

They were rapidly approaching the dream palace, which Stephen could now see was surrounded by a deep moat. The drawbridge was up, forming an impenetrable front door to the castle. There was nothing wide enough for the bus to cross.

"The bridge!" Sharanya shouted from the driver's seat. "What do I do?!"

Stephen had never used his cloak to levitate anything as heavy as a bus— he wasn't completely sure it could be done. But he *was* sure that his last stunt had infuriated Numinous—and she was fast in pursuit, Epic Nightmare hybrids following close behind.

"Keep going!" he shouted back.

"Nightmare is your enemy!" Numinous roared. And then, to her minions, "Stop them!"

Risking a glance over his shoulder, Stephen decided that a 50-foot drop into a dark moat was a better option than slowing down and letting Numinous' monsters overtake them. "We need something behind us to slow down our pursuers!" he shouted.

His hands were itching to cast, but he held onto the axe handle with gritted teeth, sick with pain. Less than two feet behind the bus, lightning and thunder cracked open the sky, releasing a torrent of rain at precisely the same moment that a dark, shiny puddle bubbled up from below the earth and oozed out across the field they'd just crossed.

"Rain?!" Jane cried out, exasperated.

From behind the wheel, Sharanya shouted back to her. "I thought it would help make the grass muddy. Slippery, you know, and hard to cross?"

"As slippery as the oil slick I just created? Your rain's gonna wash it all away!"

"Well, I didn't know you were doing that!"

"You knew I'd do *something*!"

Stephen climbed back onto the rooftop and yanked the axe free as they bickered. In fact, the combination of water and oil was working just fine to hamper the creatures behind the bus. Now if they could just survive the moat...

"The drawbridge is still up!" Sharanya yelled, her voice laced with panic.

"Want me to dream-weave a bridge?" Jane shouted from the back.

"Into what?" Sharanya countered. "The stone wall or the at least twelve-by-four-inch-thick bridge planks with, most likely, a portcullis behind them?"

"A what?"

"Iron gate!"

Stephen crouched on the roof of the bus and extended his senses out into the Cloak of Levitation, mingling his consciousness with it as he tried to will it to hold the entire vehicle. "Don't stop!" he shouted.

The first words to a gravity-manipulation spell were already on his lips when he saw the drawbridge start to lower. As Sharanya had predicted, it dragged an iron portcullis up as it came crashing down, dropping into place just as the bus reached the edge of the moat.

Stephen exhaled, clearing the spell, unuttered, from his head as he heard the distinct sound of rubber speeding across wooden planks, quickly followed by hoots of joy and relief from the cab. His cloak settled back down around his shoulders as the bus roared through the gates of Nightmare's dream palace.

CHAPTER XXII

FOLLOWING Strange through the palace to the throne room, Jane wondered whether the decay was the direct result of the fighting, or whether Nightmare's castle always looked decrepit. Thick marble pillars had toppled over, leaning across wide doorways at strange angles. Cracks ran up the stone walls, several of which no longer made it all the way up to the ceiling. Floor tiles were chipped and loose underfoot.

Jane reminded herself not to be afraid of the few somnavores and Horrors they passed. It appeared that in addition to taking back his palace, Nightmare had managed to cobble together what was left of his loyal forces. A room to the left of the gatehouse was crowded with demons sharpening scythes and halberds. Skeletons stood guard in one archway, following Jane with the empty sockets of their eyes as she walked between them. Just before the throne room, a beautiful naked woman stood with her back to Jane. As Jane approached, with Sharanya and Strange walking beside her, she turned to stare at them, revealing the head of a horse before racing farther into the castle ahead of them.

Nightmare himself looked even worse than his palace: gaunt and exhausted as he paced in front of his throne, his eyes dull and his expression pinched. The throne was a ghastly thing fashioned out of bones and topped with the skull of a horned creature Jane couldn't identify. A thick, black chain attached to its front leg ran to the collar of an ashen behemoth who cowered in the corner, quaking, four arms covering its giant, bald head.

The moment Strange stepped into the room, the dream sovereign turned bitterly to the sorcerer.

"Your timing is impeccable, Stephen. You'll have a front-row seat to my demise, and you won't have to so much as lift a finger."

Jane couldn't bear the undercurrent of fear in his voice. "We're here to save you!" she insisted. The demon looked surprised, as if he hadn't, until that moment, been aware of her presence there. Jane thought she saw the corners of his mouth twitch upward, a light igniting somewhere deep within his strange red eyes.

As quickly as it had brightened, his expression fell again. "You shouldn't be here, Jane. It isn't safe." He looked like he was about to say something else, but then noticed Strange staring at him and turned his attention back to his old enemy. "Numinous was already here when I arrived. Her attack has been relentless, and every time she defeats one of my minions, she turns them. My influence is shrinking by the second, and I have no doubt that her army will be within the walls in a matter of hours." He didn't say that it had already taken all the strength he had left to hold them back this long, but Jane knew it was true. Glancing at Strange, she could see that he knew it, too.

"At least you're not alone," Jane offered in an effort to be optimistic. Nightmare followed her gaze to the huge monster huddled in the corner.

"You mean Intimidāre, here? He won't be good for much of anything for quite some time yet. Punishment was necessary." His eyes narrowed menacingly, but then his expression softened. "If you're referring to the dregs of my army, I suppose it's true that I won't die alone. I don't see how our small number can defeat what's outside, though."

For his part, Strange offered a single nod before turning to face magnetic north and lifting his hands up in front of his chest. A dark-red energy began to collect between his palms. "Then you should be willing to try anything right about now," he told the demon.

Nightmare watched the sorcerer's movements with narrowed eyes. "I take it you have a plan?"

"I do."

Sharanya jumped back as Strange hurled the energy he'd summoned at the tiled floor. Jane backed up along with her. It pulsed for a moment around the sorcerer's boots and then began to slowly spread out in a growing circle. Strange locked eyes with Nightmare. "I'm going to re-establish the Pathways using a spell of regeneration, and I intend to use Numinous to do it."

Nightmare stepped back instinctively as Strange's circle expanded, and tilted his head to one side. "And you think she's going to cooperate with you?"

Strange crouched down in the center of his circle and whispered a word Jane couldn't hear while tapping the ground in front of him with one long index finger. "No." A line of glowing red energy shot out from where he'd touched the floor, burning across the sphere until it ricocheted off the opposite interior wall, creating a new diagonal line as he stood. It seemed to Jane that the magical energy was burning the floor, or perhaps the realm itself, as it careened around inside the circle, but Strange directed the spokes calmly with fluid motions of his right hand. "I think she's going to fight me."

Jane turned her attention back to Nightmare as the demon contemplated Strange's words. A slow smile broke across his face. "Stephen—that is deliciously evil!" Jane looked back down at Strange's circle. The glowing red lines inside of it had arranged themselves into the shape of a pentagram. "But how do I know it's not all a trick to use me instead?" Jane quickly glanced back up and saw that Nightmare was not asking the question in jest.

Strange straightened to his full height and looked over the shapes he'd created on the floor as he answered Nightmare. "At the moment, believe it or not, you're the lesser of two evils. But if that doesn't convince you, then understand that the pentagram will allow me to siphon Numinous' energy away the moment I have her restrained within the circle." He looked up and met Nightmare's eyes. "*You* don't have any excess energy. At the moment, you don't even have your *usual* amount of energy. All of which makes you too weak to power the restoration spell."

As Strange and Nightmare glared at each other, Numinous' voice carried over the sounds of thunder and rain outside. She sounded calmer again, once more too confident in her victory to bother with resentment. "Righteous Sorcerer Supreme! Ghastly Sovereign of the Realm of Nightmare! Come out and join me! You're both far too brave to hide from your destinies!"

Nightmare, who had looked up toward the direction of her voice, turned his attention sharply back to Strange. "How does this plan of yours work, oh Righteous One?"

"First, I'm going to go after Numinous with everything I've got."

Jane crouched carefully down outside the circle Strange had created, putting her palm out just above the red energy. Though it wasn't hot, she could distinctly smell the tiled floor burning beneath it. "But isn't magic bad for the Dream Dimension now?" she asked. "Isn't this hurting the realm?" She looked up at Strange, hoping he would hear the part she didn't say—that hurting the realm meant hurting its sovereign, too.

Nightmare flashed his teeth. "She's right. I can't endure this kind of assault in my present state."

Strange made a sweeping gesture with both hands. In response, the energy circle shimmered and then flew from the tiles of the floor to several feet above their heads, where it hovered and pulsed. Jane looked up to see small streams of sand falling from the stonework above them as the magical circle damaged the integrity of the ceiling. She shared a look of concern with Sharanya.

"It is a risk," Strange was saying. "I won't deny it. But it's also why I think this will work. Numinous believes my magic is helping her because she wants me to weaken the realms, leaving them ripe for her takeover. She isn't expecting me to turn it against her. And she's absorbed so much of the Dream Dimension now that she's made herself vulnerable to ambient damage. She isn't just a sovereign connected to a specific realm anymore—she's connected to the entire dimension. If my magic is harmful to the dimension, that means she'll be especially defenseless against it."

"As am I," Nightmare countered. "At least, in my own realm."

Strange nodded. "That's true. And you're also vulnerable to her, which she knows. This is the realm she wants now—and there's no better bait than you. This isn't the first time we've worked together, Nightmare. I know we can be an effective team when we need to be. Your realm may indeed take damage, but if the Pathway-regeneration spell works, there will be a chance to heal it. If it doesn't, or if we do nothing—"

Jane couldn't listen to another word. Her hands balled into fists at her sides as she remembered her vision of Praedivinus' pale, desiccated corpse. "You're going to lead her right here, to the seat of his power?! Knowing that she can just...absorb him?!"

"If my plan works, she'll be too weak to escape the circle. And once she's in it, she'll become weaker still as the pentagram drains her excess power."

Jane glared at the floor. "But Praedivinus said—"

"I know what Praedivinus said." Strange's voice was quiet, but he lifted his chin slightly, the very picture of self-assured confidence. "But this plan will work because Numinous won't be expecting Nightmare to take such a risk. She would never conceive of his trusting me enough to allow it." His eyes darted toward the demon. "Would *you?*"

Jane's shoulders sank. She could see by the way Nightmare met and held the sorcerer's gaze that he'd conceded the point.

They all turned toward a western window as Numinous' voice carried in clearly from outside. "Creatures of Nightmare!" Jane wrinkled her nose for a moment, confused, but then realized that Numinous was addressing the assembled army out on the field. "How fortunate you are to be here on this dark night, under this high moon! For tonight this realm is reborn! Tonight, we unite every corner of the Dream Dimension under one banner so that *all* dreams may once again influence and inspire as they were always meant to do! No longer shall we hide in the recesses of the unconscious mind! Never again will you be dismissed or forgotten in the pale light of dawn! Follow me and spark the minds of men! Follow me and touch the other side!"

There was loud cheering—followed by the sound of ladders being propped up against the walls outside.

"What can we do to help?" Sharanya asked, turning back to Strange.

The sorcerer made eye contact first with Sharanya, and then with Jane. "The two of you need to stay here and hold this room. Take care of each other, and don't let anything happen to that circle. It's integral to the Pathway-regeneration spell, and we'll be more dependent than ever on restoring the Pathways after this battle."

Jane nodded unhappily, chewing on a jagged thumbnail.

Strange continued. "The regeneration spell itself takes time, as well as a tremendous amount of energy—enough energy to destroy the realm and jeopardize the dimension as a whole should it fail to be properly channeled. Creation and destruction go hand in hand, often tipping into one another in surprising and unexpected ways." He looked up at the floating circle. "Once Numinous is bound and I start the incantation, I'll need your help to keep anyone and anything from interfering. The spell will require all my concentration."

Jane snuck a sideways glance at Nightmare and found the demon watching her. He nodded almost imperceptibly, just to her, and smiled.

CHAPTER XXIII

THE DRAWBRIDGE to Nightmare's dream palace began to drop open again. Halfway through its arc, Dreamstalker—the realm sovereign's black, bat-winged, red-eyed steed—burst from the castle entrance using the half-open drawbridge as a ramp to launch himself into the air. On his back rode the dreamscape's demon prince, his tattered cape flowing out behind him.

Doctor Strange, Sorcerer Supreme of Earth, followed closely, flying with the aid of his mystical red cloak. They had left the fortress to confront the 30-foot-tall, cyan-haired principality known as Numinous, sovereign of Epic Dreams and would-be conqueror of the Dream Dimension. In addition to being nearly omnipotent within the Dream Dimension, she had under her command the army of Alexander the Great, as well as a swelling mass of hybrid dream figments and nightmare creatures, all tainted with her zealotry. As the drawbridge touched down across the moat, having pulled the portcullis up as it fell, a small ragtag army of demons, skeletons, and other nightmarish monsters ran out to thwart the efforts to breach the castle. The drawbridge began to close the second they'd crossed it.

Nothing less than the fate of the Dream Dimension hung in the balance.

"Yes! Yes!" Numinous smiled joyfully as she spotted the two men. "Come, friends, and witness my ascension!"

Nightmare circled her head as Strange hurled a lightning bolt at her with a murmured evocation spell. It hit her right shoulder, releasing a chain of bright-blue electricity that crackled across her skin. Numinous recoiled, startled by the pain, and immediately raised her left hand to cover the injury, pulling it back sharply as the energy sizzled around her fingers.

"There is no need to fight me!" she cried, distraught. "Surrender now and merge with me so that my victory may be your own!" Residual spell energy snapping around her fingers forked upward, filling the sky with ominous blue lightning.

"Oh, Numinous," Nightmare taunted, blasting her with small orbs of sticky black energy. "Don't you know I'd only give you indigestion?"

She swatted away his attacks with an irritated sneer but was gripped in a paroxysm of pain as Strange, behind her, heaved a fireball at the small of her back.

From the air, Stephen saw the exact moment she lost her temper. She spun suddenly, her cape aflame, and swung a huge hand at him. Stephen met the move with a protective force field, further enraging her as she smashed her hand against the unyielding shield. Nightmare circled low on his steed as he threw the strongest bolts he could conjure at her knees. He was enfeebled by her assault against his realm, weak within the boundaries of a place wherein he would normally be his strongest, but determined to defeat her. Stephen saw Numinous' hands begin to glow bright blue.

"Incoming!" he shouted to Nightmare.

Numinous released a flood of incandescent energy from her palms, forcing Strange to the ground even as he braced behind his mystic shield. The terrain, already slick with blood and viscera from the ongoing battle, was starting to buckle from his increased use of magic—the moment his back touched the rain-soaked earth, the field around him began to crack, thick gray sludge welling up from the fissures. Stephen knew he was running out of time and took to the air again the moment Numinous let up.

Nightmare struck again, flinging his black energy globs at Numinous' face as he flew past her head. One hit her in the corner of her mouth, and Stephen saw her lips pull back in a furious snarl. She pivoted and backhanded Dream-stalker out of the sky, sending Nightmare hurling backwards toward his castle.

As the force of the hit carried the demon all the way through the thick stone walls of his fortress, Stephen commanded the flames at Numinous' back to rise.

She shrieked and threw off her cape, igniting a large swath of the bat-tleground as the burning garment met the oil Jane had spread across the field earlier. Numinous' armies were instantly in complete disarray. Those not caught in the conflagration hastily retreated in disorganized clusters as the huge cape lit up the dark, rain-soaked field.

While Numinous was distracted beating out the few flames that had caught at her dress, Stephen flew past the breach in the palace. Inside, he could just make out the small shape of Jane helping Nightmare up as Sharanya began to clear the debris of the shattered wall away from the area beneath his spell cir-cle. After struggling to lift a large rock with her bare arms, Sharanya employed dream-weaving, conjuring a large Indian elephant to help her haul.

The ruptured wall was not exactly how Stephen had planned to get back into the throne room, but it would have to do. He turned in midair just in time to see Numinous' enormous palm coming at him. He barely got his shield back up in time as the full force of her hand scooped him out of the sky and slammed him into the earth outside the castle.

"This wasn't how it was supposed to be, Doctor Strange!" she screamed. "Can't you see what your magic is doing to my realm?! To me?!"

Strange could see that where her hand touched his shield, her skin was blistering and burning. A huge swath of the battlefield seemed to be breaking up, leaving nothing but a gaping void behind. An entire division of Numinous' routed forces tumbled into the abyss, almost instantly blinking out of existence.

"That's a direct result of the destruction of the Pathways," Stephen informed Numinous, trying to keep her from grinding him into the muddy field. "They were the only defense this dimension had."

"*I* am this dimension's defender now." Numinous narrowed her ink-black eyes.

"You? A Defender?" Stephen scoffed. "That's funny. I haven't seen you at a single meeting."

"Now I'm going to have to kill you," Numinous said. To her credit, it sounded to Stephen as though she found the thought genuinely disappointing.

He was about to tell her that he was therefore obligated to stop her, but intoned a spell instead.

"By the virtuous Vishanti

And the powers they bestow

I sound the Bell of Ikonn

That my form should stretch and grow!"

It was agony, but Strange managed not to scream as his body shuddered and then rapidly expanded, growing until it matched Numinous' in size. The dream sovereign scrambled away from him and got quickly back up onto her feet, but Stephen was right behind her.

The new perspective was wildly disorienting, so Stephen narrowed his focus to the woman before him. Charging his hands with glowing, mystical energy, he repositioned his weight and slid his feet into an Aikido stance.

Numinous hesitated only a second before launching at him. It seemed her intent was to grab him by the throat and knock him back down onto the increasingly beleaguered terrain, but Stephen caught her outstretched arm as she charged and stepped to one side. Her momentum carried her past him, allowing Stephen to leverage her arm behind her back and drive her to one knee. Slamming his elbow into the back of her head, he directed a torrent of pure arcane force across her back before releasing her arm and stepping in front of her to reverse their positions. Though he could have held her in the lock indefinitely, he needed her to expend as much of her energy as possible while he backed her toward the palace.

Predictably infuriated, Numinous was quick to regain her footing and relaunch her attack, though the combination of pain and mystical blows had begun to weaken her: She was starting to shrink. Stephen adjusted his own stature to match—his goal wasn't to overwhelm her, but to siphon and redirect her energy.

He parried a rapid succession of blows as she came at him again before countering with a side kick, once again imbuing his limb with extra psychic energy as it made contact with the dream sovereign's form.

The kick connected, but as Stephen lowered his boot onto the ground to regain his balance, he was once again reminded of the danger his magic represented for the defenseless realm. The earth beneath his sole bunched and smeared like displaced oil paint, the colors mushing together until completely obscured by a dark-gray muck bubbling up from somewhere below. Though not normally sympathetic to the structural integrity of the Nightmare Realm, Stephen felt a pang of concern for the demon who drew his strength from it. If Nightmare was already badly injured from Numinous' last attack, the damage to his realm was going to make it almost impossible for him to heal. The good news was that the dramatic destruction of the landscape was encouraging Numinous' minions to scatter into the woods beyond the battlefield.

Knowing that the fighting couldn't continue indefinitely, Stephen redoubled his efforts. He went on the offensive, driving Numinous back toward Nightmare's palace with a series of sorcery-fueled punches and spinning kicks, each blow diminishing the sovereign further. Numinous threw her arms up defensively and began questioning the Sorcerer Supreme as he backed her across the field.

"Why, Stephen? Why do you oppose me? I wish only glory for the realm!"

"You seek to impose tyrannical rule on a place that must, by its very nature, remain open to the influence of all who pass through it. I can't allow that."

Stephen charged both his fists with pure force, lunged forward, and thrust his palms toward Numinous, sending forth a sizzling ball of energy. It struck the dream sovereign in her abdomen, the force of it sweeping her up over the ramparts and through the breach in the castle wall. Strange flew up and through the hole after her, issuing another blast to push her into the throne room. The second her body touched the tiles, Stephen landed at the head of his hovering spell circle. He raised his hands in the air and then dropped his arms, palms down. The circle he'd cast dropped from the ceiling onto the floor, entrapping Numinous in its glowing center as he swiftly turned his hands palm up and closed them into fists. The pentagram within the circle began to glow more brightly as it drew away more and more of her power.

Numinous howled in frustration the moment she became aware of her predicament. Stephen took a second to look around the room. Nightmare was in bad shape, propped up against the dais of his throne. Jane knelt beside him, trying to attend to his wounds with shaking hands. Sharanya was below the western window, standing near Nightmare's steed, which also appeared injured, and her dream-woven pachyderm, which did not. She had been working hard to clear the debris of the compromised wall from the spell circle.

Numinous raised her head, her hands flat against the floor tiles as she knelt in the center of the pentagram. "You think you can silence me?! You think you won't hear my voice again, deep within your soul? What will stir you to action? Who will see you safely through your fear? I am the fire of Prometheus! Without me there is only darkness and stagnation." The stars in her eyes seemed to glow more brightly as she turned her gaze from Strange to Nightmare. "Without me, there are only nightmares!"

Reaching out toward Nightmare, Numinous bared her teeth and curled her fingers into claws. A nebulous black emanation began to rise off of Nightmare and flow toward Numinous. Stephen started to cast the Crimson Bands of Cyttorak to bind her hands.

"No!" Jane screamed and jumped in front of Nightmare, shielding the demon with her body. Just as the Crimson Bands snapped around her wrists, Numinous sent a blast of dark-green energy hurtling toward Jane.

Stephen attempted to throw a force field over the young Inhuman. The shimmering energy of his spell glanced off of her, briefly illuminating a sparkling purple shield already in place around her. Surprised, Stephen realized that Jane had created her own defense: Like his, Numinous' energy smashed up against it and dissipated harmlessly.

With an enraged growl, Nightmare leaned out from behind Jane, using the last of his strength to hurl a shimmering black globule at Numinous. It broke across her undefended chest and throat, and thickly covered her mouth and nose. She began to convulse as Nightmare dropped back down against the tiled floor of his throne room, completely drained, but smiling.

Jane screamed, falling to her knees beside Nightmare, and Sharanya started across the room toward her, moving carefully around the outside of Stephen's spell circle. In the circle's center, Numinous struggled for breath. Stephen could feel the power ebbing away from her and knew he was running out of time. He began gathering the energy he would channel through the dream sovereign to regenerate the Pathways. Nightmare's attack had decided the issue: Stephen couldn't save Numinous.

Realizing what he was doing, Jane looked up tearfully at Stephen from across the room. "Don't! Please! This isn't right!"

Stephen looked at her sympathetically, but it was too late to stop the spell. He had to begin the incantation. He closed his eyes, pulling close the energies he'd summoned.

"In the name of the Eternal Vishanti

And the Ruby Rings of Raggadorr—"

Stephen shifted his hands into the Karana mudra, pointing his fingers toward Numinous. She continued to claw desperately at the black energy that covered her nose and mouth.

"By the icy Tendrils of Ikthalon

And the Mystic Moons of Munnopor—"

Stephen felt the energy he was channeling into the circle shift and tip, as if he were holding it in a shallow container that someone had jostled. He heard Sharanya gasp and opened his eyes. Somehow, in the few seconds he'd had his eyes closed, Jane had gotten back on her feet and taken a running leap at the circle, managing to land inside it without breaking the perimeter. Inhaling sharply, Stephen rushed to reverse the flow of the energy, pulling it back into himself in an effort to keep it from crashing over Jane. Unable to stop the spell, he held the words on the tip of his tongue as Jane went straight to Numinous and helped the struggling sovereign into a sitting position. Stephen's throat began to constrict as the spell fought to realize itself. He had to continue.

"Through this sacrificial conduit

May you catch and bind—"

"Jane, get out of there!" Sharanya was standing by Nightmare's crumpled form, shouting to Jane, but Jane ignored her, as well. "What are you doing?!"

Jane pulled the sticky substance of Nightmare's attack off Numinous' mouth, looking directly into Numinous' eyes as she answered Sharanya. "I'm being inspired."

Stephen tried to stall but could feel himself losing control of the accumulated energies. They were building and surging within him, crackling through his body as they sought release. Behind Jane, hunched over with a hand flat on her abdomen, Numinous drew long, shuddering breaths, looking stronger by the second. Stephen had a vision of losing control of the spell and hurried to act, to chase the dream from his mind before it infected his intent.

"The disparate currents of this realm,

Inviolable once entwined!"

"This is the prophecy!" Jane yelled. Stephen continued the incantation. "And it's my decision!"

"I offer up this humble shell—" Stephen stopped mid-sentence, sensing a force exerting itself on Jane's body. Numinous had reached out and grabbed the young woman's wrist. For one horrible second, Stephen thought the dream sovereign was draining energy away from Jane, but then realized that it was quite the opposite.

Jane gasped and began to glow with a silvery incandescence. There was a blast of light so bright even Stephen had to shield his eyes. When he dared to look up again, his circle had been shattered from the inside out. Standing in what had been its center, radiating with a pulsing combination of her own Inhuman power and that gifted to her by Numinous, Jane had the sovereign by the shoulders and was speaking to her, too quietly for Stephen to hear over the roar of his own swirling, chaotic restoration spell.

"I offer up this humble shell..." he said again, focusing on Numinous with the full strength of his formidable will.

"Return to your realm," Jane commanded, speaking to Numinous. "And stay there." She placed the flat of her hands gently against the sovereign's chest and seemed to give a gentle push. Numinous vanished.

Stephen stared at the space where his circle had been and then found himself meeting Jane's eyes. She looked calm again and even seemed to smile at him. "I offer up this humble shell…" he repeated with growing desperation, energy sizzling from his eyes and teeth and fingertips.

Jane walked over to Nightmare, who had struggled back up into a sitting position, and pressed a tender kiss against his forehead as he gaped up at her.

"It's okay," she told him. "This is where I belong."

The demon looked completely distraught. "Jane, no!"

Jane turned her attention to Sharanya. "I think I've been stuck between two worlds, too," she told her. "But I'm gonna stay in this one." She indicated Stephen with an incline of her head. "He has to go back, and you should go with him. It'd be nice if you visited, though. We could meet on your bridge."

She turned then, offering them both one last smile over her shoulder before walking back to where the center of Stephen's spell circle had been and turning to face him.

"Go ahead," she told him. "I know I'm the lamb. I'm the remedy. And I feel completely at peace—safe and tranquil. This is always what I was meant to do." She closed her eyes for a moment, and then opened them again, her smile widening. "I'm ready to be healed now."

Nightmare gritted his teeth and attempted unsuccessfully to get back up on to his feet. "Stephen! Stephen, I'll do it. Use me."

Stephen was quaking under the power of the unfinished spell. He met Nightmare's gaze and shook his head. The dream demon was too weak. If he tried to absorb the spell energy, it would cascade out of him and destroy the realm, which was pretty much what it was going to do anyway if Stephen couldn't direct it somewhere before his ability to hold it ran out.

The pressure building up inside of him was worse than pain—worse, even, than heartbreak. The universe was struggling toward its desired resolution, and he was standing in the way. Though he'd wholly rejected his father's faith many years before without feeling anything more troubling than contempt, the resistance he was currently exerting felt like a denial of everything to which he'd ever truly devoted himself—devotion that came not with the acquiescence of a child, but with the obligations of a grown man. In it was his affection and respect for the Ancient One, the source of his magic and determination, his very deepest assumptions and understandings of All That Was. And why? Why was he fighting it?

Because it felt wrong to him. He had doubts. The resolution of the spell, the flow of the universal, Jane's own words…he understood *what* he was meant to do—with absolute clarity—but did not understand why. It all hinged on a sacrifice he didn't feel it was his right to make. Jane was a child, an innocent. How could the universe demand such a thing of her? And why make him the instrument of its enactment—the only being, in fact, capable of seeing it through?

He thought back to Praedivinus' words about sacrifice, and to Monako's warnings. He thought about his sister, and his mother, and his father, and his brother. He thought about Clea and the Ancient One and Wong. He thought about the balance of the universe, and all that he had learned in his years of practicing sorcery.

He thought back over everything he had tried in his efforts to avoid it, but finally had to acknowledge the truth. It was a truth he had learned years ago, but it had gotten buried under the burden of responsibility as he saved the world time and again. Somehow, Jane had come to understand it, and she was reminding him.

Nightmare was shaking with anger and panic, still too weak to rise. "Harm that girl, Stephen, and I will haunt your dreams from now until the end of time!" he hissed.

Stephen met and held Jane's gaze. She continued to smile at him. "I offer up this humble shell…" she prompted, opening her hands in supplication.

Over the course of his obligations to his mantle, Stephen had outwitted gods. He'd rearranged atoms, witnessed the destruction and resurrection of galaxies, and determined the fate of entire races. But the truth...the truth was, there were some things even the Sorcerer Supreme didn't get to decide.

He took a deep breath, and told himself to accept Jane's fate. The universe continued to require his service. It could not afford his doubt.

"I offer up this humble shell

And impel it toward ascension

And proclaim its purpose to restore

Pathways through this dimension!"

For a moment, Stephen felt as if he were being pulled into a black hole, every atom in his body straining as torrents of blistering dream energy coursed out of him and rushed toward Jane. The surge of it pulled his feet up off the floor, and he was helpless to do anything other than spread his arms wide and let it leave him. When the last of it had flown to Jane, inundating her with power, he fell to one knee. Jane had been pushed two feet above the floor by the energy slamming into her, but endured the onslaught calmly. She even continued to smile as her veins began to unfurl from her body. They grew outward like vines seeking sunlight, wending into every corner of the Dream Dimension.

And then it was Jane's turn to have her atoms torn apart. She shimmered and began to fade away, her cells diffused into the atmosphere in a twinkling cloud of mist.

The last thing Stephen saw was her smile, hovering disembodied in the center of Nightmare's throne room like a demure Cheshire Cat. He was watching it fade when the space around it collapsed in on itself, then exploded outward with tremendous force, washing, just for a moment, the entire Nightmare Realm in brilliant, blinding light.

CODA

"YOU COULD create an actual office, you know. Or a high-rise or a castle, for that matter." Stephen was sitting with Sharanya under the large orange-and-white pavilion she'd set up on a dirt walking trail that wound through the new Pathways. She'd placed it under a canopy of leaves near patches of tiny blue flowers that seemed to sparkle in the dappled sunlight. The air smelled like rich soil and pine, and Sharanya smiled every time the canvas fluttered noisily in the breeze.

"I'm happy with this. Half-indoors, half-outdoors…and it makes me feel closer to Jane."

Stephen nodded, but dropped his gaze. As far as he could tell, Jane had ceased to exist in any meaningful way, but Sharanya insisted that she could feel her energy. Stephen had asked her to serve, part-time, as a kind of warden or ambassador for the Dream Dimension. His hope was that she would alert him to any future issues without speaking in riddles or jeopardizing the fate of all humanity.

"How's the rest of your work going?" he asked.

Sharanya sat forward, eager to share. "In the waking world? It's very exciting. We've been able to start working with people much earlier—delinquents as opposed to murderers—and help suppress violent behavior through dream therapy." She paused, looking around at the obvious vibrancy of the surrounding trees. "And then, of course, once they're here, I can help direct them to the most beneficial realm for whatever they're dealing with at the time."

Stephen nodded. "That sounds like a laudable integration of your new insights into your previous expertise." He moved to go, but then hesitated. "Have you had any contact with Numinous?"

Sharanya rose from her seat and met him at the entrance, then gently touched his arm as she walked with him out of the tent toward a small bridge that stretched across a green river. "I have, actually. She's much changed, Stephen. I don't think you need to worry. Perhaps because of Jane, she's become very interested in the Inhuman community and is spurring them toward heroism. I think she's doing some really good work." She watched a small flock of dream-figment birds alight on the branches of an Eastern white pine. "We're still without a replacement for Praedivinus, though, so prophecy-wise, I'm afraid we'll all be flying blind for a while."

As they stepped onto the bridge together, Stephen indicated the Eye of Agamotto. "Personally, I'm covered. And as always, I promise to keep an eye on the rest of you."

Sharanya's smile grew into a grin. She stopped halfway across the bridge. "Thank you, Doctor," she said warmly.

"You know where to find me," he answered before striding off the other end, his red cloak flapping behind him.

Exhaling, he opened his eyes. Moonlight streamed in through the Anomaly Rue, his meditation chamber hazy with incense smoke. Stephen unfurled himself from the floating lotus position he often used while meditating and moved to his lectern, where he'd left a large book open.

Wong came in, carrying a tea tray, just as Stephen had become reabsorbed in the text. His nose wrinkled involuntarily as the dank scent of valerian root reached him. Like the more floral chamomile he could also smell, it was known to help people sleep.

"You're still up," Wong noted. Not wanting to interrupt his reading, Stephen made a noncommittal humming sound without looking up from the tome before him.

"Is all well in the Dream Dimension?" Wong continued, undeterred. He set the tray down on a small Indian hardwood table.

Stephen exhaled and looked up to find Wong smiling at him placidly. Wong was usually unimpeachably respectful about Stephen's need for uninterrupted quiet, but occasionally grew stubborn about eliciting his attention. Stephen tapped a finger lightly against the line he'd been reading, effortlessly marking his place with a shimmering underscore. "It is," he answered. "I just spoke with Sharanya. She'll make an excellent ambassador."

"And Jane?" Wong asked gently. "Any sign of her?"

Stephen was quiet for a moment before answering. "Sharanya insists she can feel her energy in the Pathways, which are fully restored. But no…she no longer exists as a sentient being."

He noted a slight twitch at one corner of Wong's mouth and softened his own posture, deciding to honor the moment and open himself to the exchange. He folded his impaired hands across the pages of the open book before him. "You have questions."

Wong acknowledged Stephen's responsiveness with a slight bow of his head. "I'm just remembering the Ancient One's words," he said. "*With our great power, we must never knowingly cause harm to any.*" He met Stephen's eyes with evident worry. "Do you believe that what happened with Jane falls within that edict?"

Stephen's eyes darted back to the pages of the book on the lectern. "The spell I cast would not have been possible had it not been in service of the universe's intent."

Wong's eyes widened slightly, and he shook his head. "No, I'm sorry, I wasn't clear. I'm not worried that what you did was wrong—I have complete faith in your reading of the situation, Stephen. I'm concerned that *you* might *believe* it was wrong. That you may doubt the necessity of the steps you took to ensure our survival. And that Nightmare may attempt to use that doubt against you."

Stephen kept his eyes on the book, the words swimming on the page as he stared at them inattentively. "Thank you for your concern, Wong, but it's unnecessary."

The nightmares he'd been having were simpler than he'd anticipated, and yet they had felt strangely devastating. Was that why? Something as inconsequential as self-doubt? Since he'd returned from the Dream Dimension, he'd only closed his eyes twice, and both times Nightmare had been waiting for him, as promised.

"I've run a few permutations on Jane's possible futures," he'd said the first time, curling a sharp-nailed hand around the back of the black-leather chair in which Stephen found himself seated. "Would you like to see them?"

He'd turned on an old projector from just behind Stephen's shoulder, light hitting a screen less than 20 feet away from them. Jane's smiling face came into view—larger than life, but black and white, luminous against the screen. She was older, dressed in surgical scrubs. "Of course you would," Nightmare continued. "We'll watch together."

They watched an entire life play out for her, Jane having embarked on a career in medicine. When it was over, Nightmare started the next reel, which featured Jane having children, and then the one after that, which explored her life as an architect. The next time Stephen had fallen asleep, he'd noticed hundreds of crates full of similar reels and awoken himself with a start.

Remembering the dreams, Stephen felt his hands begin to ache and rubbed them absently. "Any messages here?" he asked Wong.

Wong stared at him for a long moment, brows knotted, and then quietly turned to the tea tray and began pouring the steaming liquid into the cup. "There's a girl upstate insisting that her closet has been invaded by a pack of Therean dog-gods, as well as an exorcism occurring tomorrow evening in Hell's Kitchen that Father Lantom was hoping you'd consult on." He passed the tea to Strange, who accepted it. "I spoke with Wanda this morning, though, and she said that everything else seems to have settled back into what passes for normal around here."

"Tell Lantom I'll be there." Stephen balanced the cup on top of the lectern and turned his face to the large, round window behind him, watching constellations drift slowly across the sky. "Would the girl still be up? We could go now."

Wong shook his head, his eyes never leaving Stephen's face. "No, Stephen, we can go in the morning. She'll be asleep now. Almost everyone on the Eastern seaboard is asleep now. Dreaming normally, thanks to you."

Stephen had already returned his gaze to his book. "I've never been a terribly good sleeper, Wong. You know that."

Wong picked a small overspill of melted white candle wax off the Vishanti altar. "I do know that. And I know that since you returned from the Dream Dimension, it's been worse."

Stephen answered without looking up from the page. "As you imagined, Nightmare was...displeased with my actions."

Wong nodded. "And yet everyone needs sleep, Stephen. Even you. Promise me you'll at least try to shut your eyes tonight? The tea should help."

"Of course." Stephen said the words automatically, hollowly, wanting to appease his friend. He read quietly until Wong left the room. It was a fascinating book—an ancient Persian necromantic grimoire. Necromancy wasn't a school of magic Stephen used often, but the book in question included one of the most powerful spells he'd ever encountered for resisting sleep.

Once the door had closed behind Wong, Stephen waved a hand over the tea cup, transforming the sleep-enhancing tea into a double shot of espresso.

Mundane solutions for mundane problems.

He threw the scalding liquid down his throat and went back to studying the spell, knowing that avoiding sleep would only be a mundane problem for the first three or four days.

After that, he'd need magic.

ACKNOWLEDGEMENTS

I owe a huge debt of gratitude to my amazing editors, Joan Hilty, Jeff Youngquist, and Sarah Brunstad, for helping me bring this story to life. Thank you, too, to all the people at Marvel who helped pull resources and check continuity for me.

I would also like to thank everyone who kept Doctor Strange alive over the years, including my own revered Ancient One, Denny O'Neil, and of course Stephen's astonishing creators, Steve Ditko and Stan Lee. Doctor Strange's original stories are as rich and mind-blowing today as when first conjured up in 1963.

I was brought to those stories in large part thanks to the brilliant essays over at Sequart written by Colin Smith—thank you, Colin, for sharing your love of Stephen so compellingly! I also owe a debt of gratitude to Michael Hoskin for so deftly helping me navigate 53 years of Strange history.

Thank you to Scott Peterson and Melissa Wiley for being my personal writer's support group and just being wonderful people I feel lucky to know.

Thank you to Mark Waid for his eternal willingness to answer truly insane questions at even crazier hours. Agamotto's got nothing on you.

Thank you to Matthew Duda for the caffeine conduit and decades of friendship, and to Alex Gombach for the tunage and introduction to magical realms.

Thank you to Beatrice for your fervent support and for the magical playlist recs. You have my eternal love and gratitude.

Thank you, Mom, for the insight into metacognitive dream research, and thank you, Dad, for the thoughtful advice on navigating violence in fiction.

Thank you to my friends and family for excusing my absences, tolerating my schedule, and accommodating my various fictional obsessions. And last but not least, thank you Arnold, David, and Griffin, for filling my life with magic, and for so graciously sharing our home with the Sorcerer Supreme.

THE
WINTER
ROOM

A Richard Jackson Book

Also by
GARY PAULSEN

The Voyage of the Frog
The Island
The Crossing
Hatchet
Sentries
Dogsong
Tracker
Dancing Carl

THE WINTER ROOM

GARY PAULSEN

ORCHARD BOOKS
A division of Franklin Watts, Inc. / New York

ORCHARD BOOKS
A division of Franklin Watts, Inc.
387 Park Avenue South
New York, NY 10016

Manufactured in the United States of America
Book design by Jeanne Abboud

10 9 8 7 6 5 4 3 2

The text of this book is set in 12/17 Meridien

Library of Congress Cataloging-in-Publication Data

Paulsen, Gary.
The winter room / Gary Paulsen.
p. cm.
"A Richard Jackson Book."
Summary: A young boy growing up on a northern Minnesota farm
describes the scenes around him and recounts his old Norwegian
uncle's tales of an almost mythological logging past.
ISBN 0-531-05839-5. —ISBN 0-531-08439-6 (lib. bdg.)
[1. Farm life—Minnesota—Fiction. 2. Minnesota—Fiction.
3. Lumber and lumbering—Fiction. 4. Norwegian Americans—Fiction.]
I. Title.
PZ7.P2843Wh   1989
[Fic]—dc19   89-42541
                                                         CIP
                                                          AC

For my father,
with great love

Contents

Tuning   1
SPRING   5
SUMMER   33
FALL   49
WINTER   59
Alida   70
Orud the Terrible   74
Crazy Alen   78
The Woodcutter   88

∾ TUNING

If books could be more, could show more, could own more, this book would have smells. . . .

It would have the smells of old farms; the sweet smell of new-mown hay as it falls off the oiled sickle blade when the horses pull the mower through the field, and the sour smell of manure steaming in a winter barn. It would have the sticky-slick smell of birth when the calves come and they suck for the first time on the rich, new milk; the dusty smell of winter hay dried and stored in the loft waiting to be dropped down to the cattle; the pungent fermented smell of the chopped corn silage when it is brought into the manger on the silage fork. This book would have the smell of new potatoes sliced and frying in light pepper on a woodstove burning dry pine, the damp smell of leather mittens steaming on the back of the stovetop, and the acrid smell of the slop bucket by the door when the lid is lifted and the potato peelings are dumped in— but it can't.

Books can't have smells.

If books could be more and own more and give more, this book would have sound. . . .

It would have the high, keening sound of the six-foot bucksaws as the men pull them back and forth through the trees to cut pine for paper pulp; the grunting-gassy sounds of the work teams snorting and slapping as they hit the harness to jerk the stumps out of the ground. It would have the chewing sounds of cows in the barn working at their cuds on a long winter's night; the solid thunking sound of the ax coming down to split stovewood, and the piercing scream of the pigs when the knife cuts their throats and they know death is at hand—but it can't.

Books can't have sound.

And finally if books could be more, give more, show more, this book would have light. . . .

Oh, it would have the soft gold light—gold

with bits of hay dust floating in it—that slips through the crack in the barn wall; the light of the Coleman lantern hissing flat-white in the kitchen; the silver-gray light of a middle winter day, the splattered, white-night light of a full moon on snow, the new light of dawn at the eastern edge of the pasture behind the cows coming in to be milked on a summer morning—but it can't.

Books can't have light.

If books could have more, give more, be more, show more, they would still need readers, who bring to them sound and smell and light and all the rest that can't be in books.

The book needs you.

G.P.

SPRING

In the spring everything is soft.

Wayne is my older brother by two years and so he thinks he knows more than I can ever know. He said Miss Halverson, who teaches eighth grade, told him spring was a time of awakening, but I think she's wrong. And Wayne is wrong too.

Or maybe it's just that Miss Halverson wants it to be that way. But she has never seen spring at our farm and if she did, if she would come out and see it, she would know it's not a time of awakening at all. Unless she means awakening of smells.

It's a time for everything to get soft. And melty. And when it all starts to melt and get soft the smells come out. In northern Minnesota where we live, the deep cold of winter keeps things from smelling. When we clean the barn and throw the manure out back it just freezes in a pile. When chickens die or sheep die or even if a cow dies it is left out back on the manure pile because like Uncle David says we're all fertilizer in the end.

Uncle David is old. So old we don't even know for sure how old he is. He says when he dies he wants to be thrown on the manure pile just like the dead animals, but he might be kidding.

The main thing is that no matter what Miss Halverson tells Wayne, in the spring everything gets soft and it's an awful mess. When the dead animals on the pile thaw out they bring early flies and that means maggots and that means stink that stops even my father, or Uncle David, or Nels when they open the back door of the barn to let the cows out.

"Shooosh," Father says when he opens the door of the barn on a spring morning to let the cows out after milking. The smell from the pile makes him sneeze.

Just outside the door the cows sink in until

their bellies are hung up in manure and slop and they have to skid and lunge to get to solid ground.

Sometimes my father and Wayne and I have to get in the muck in back of the barn and heave on the cows to help them through. There's not a part of it that can be called fun. I'm small for eleven, and the goop comes up to my crotch. When I bear down and push on some old cow's leg and she comes loose I almost always fall on my face.

That makes Wayne laugh. He's always ready to laugh when I do something dumb. And when he laughs I get mad and take after him. Then Father has to grab me by the back of my coat and hold me until I cool down—hanging there dripping manure like some old sick cat—and I can't think of any part of it that makes me come up with an awakening.

It's just soft. And stinky.

We live on a farm on the edge of a forest that reaches from our door in Minnesota all the way up to Hudson's Bay. Uncle David says the trees there are stunted and small, the people are short and round, and the polar bears have a taste for human flesh. That's how Uncle David says it when he goes into his stories. He says he's seen such things . . . but that's for later.

The farm has eighty-seven cleared acres. My father says each tree pulled to clear it was like pulling a tooth. I saw him use the team once to take out a popple stump that wasn't too big and he had the veins sticking out on the horses' necks so they looked like ropey cords before that stump let go.

The woods are tight all around the farm, come right down to the edge of it, but the fields are clean and my father says the soil is good, as good as any dirt in the world, and we get corn and oats and barley and flax and some wheat.

There are six of us in the family. My mother and father and my brother Wayne and my uncle David, who isn't really my uncle but sort of my great-uncle who is very old, and Nels, who is old like David.

We all live in a wooden house with white board siding. Downstairs are four rooms. The kitchen, which is big and has a plank table in it and a wood stove with a shiny nickel top, is my favorite. It smells all the time of fresh baked bread because Mother always has rolls rising or cooking or cooling and the smell makes my mouth water.

Next to the kitchen is a room with a table and a piano and four chairs around the table. In all my life and in all of Wayne's life, and as near as we can figure in all my parents' lives, nobody has ever sat at the table or played the old piano. Once a month, when the *Farm Gazette* comes with the pictures of Holsteins or work horses painted on the cover, my mother puts the magazine in the middle of the table in the dining room—that's what she calls it—and the magazine stays there until the next month when the new one comes. Once I asked her why. "For color and decoration," she said.

Only one time did I ever see anybody take the magazine up. Father came in of a morning after chores and picked the magazine off the table and made a comment about the cow on the cover. Mother took it from him, as if he were a kid. She put it back on the table, postioned it just so, the way she always does, and I never saw anybody move the magazine again.

Next to the room with the piano and table— we have never once dined in the room so I don't know why Mother calls it the dining room—is the winter room. Wayne says Miss Halverson showed him a picture of a house in a city and they had a room called a living room, and that's what our winter room is—the living room. But that sounds stupid to me. We live everywhere in the house, except for the room with the table and piano, so why have any one place called the living room?

We call it the winter room because we spend the winter there. In one corner is a wood stove with mica windows so you can see the flame. There are two chairs by the stove, wooden chairs with carved flowers on the back boards. They belong to Uncle David and Nels. Next to each chair is a coffee can for spitting snoose when they chew inside the house. Across from the stove is a large easy chair only a little worn, where Father sits in the winter. Next to the chair is an old horsehide couch with large, soft cushions where Mother sits and Wayne and I sometimes sit, though we usually sit on the floor in front of the stove where the heat can hit our faces and we can see the flames.

Next to the winter room is the downstairs bedroom where Mother and Father sleep on an old iron bed with a feather mattress.

Up a narrow wooden stairway there are two more rooms, built under the angle of the roof. One is for Wayne and me. We have bunk beds on one side and a board shelf on the other where Wayne keeps his baseball glove—he's going to play professional ball when he grows up and leaves the farm—and I have a box of arrowheads I've found. Most of them are small black-stone heads with razor-sharp edges that Uncle David says come from ancient times and were used for hunting birds. But one head is large, a spearhead Uncle David says, made of gray flint. I have that one in a case that used to hold an Elgin turnip pocket watch. Sometimes I take the case out from under my mattress and just look at the spearhead and think what it must have been like to hunt with it, throw it and see it hit a deer or one of the large buffalo they used to have.

The other room upstairs belongs to Uncle David and Nels. It is a little larger than our room and Wayne and I have only been in it a few times. They each have a bed, one on each side of the room back under the slant that comes down with the roof, and a small dresser with a kerosene lamp in the middle so they can blow it out from bed without having to get uncovered.

In the winter there is no heat upstairs and you don't want to get uncovered unless you have to go to the pee bucket in the hall. Even then sometimes we wrap in a quilt and take it with us.

Uncle David and Nels have quilts on their beds, all-over pattern quilts made by my grandmother when she was old. The few times I've been in the room the beds were made all neat and square. Not like ours, which look like cattle have been jumping on them.

All over the walls are calendars and pictures. On Nels' side there are pictures of work horses in harness or just standing—big ones, Belgians and Percherons with their names written below them in pretty letters. There is also an old calendar from Norway, over twenty years old, with Norwegian writing on it that I can't understand and Wayne can't either. Though he sometimes says he can. Uncle David and Nels and Dad will talk Norwegian when they don't want us to understand, but it makes Mother mad—she can't speak Norwegian either—so they don't do it much.

It's as if there is a line drawn through the middle of the room. On one side is Nels and on the other side—in almost a different world—is

David. Where Nels has horses and cows and scenery, Uncle David has pictures of farm girls holding flowers and working in gardens, calendars with girls and horses on ranches out west—all of the girls blonde and pretty and smiling. Once I asked Father why Uncle David had so many pictures of girls and he said it was because he was once married to Alida but didn't have any pictures of her. When I asked him why Nels had no pictures of girls he said it was because Nels was never married. I don't know what he meant exactly, but many questions I ask Father are answered that way, with words around the edges.

Also on Uncle David's side of the room there are books. Not just the Bible. They both have the Bible by their beds. Father says they each read one verse to the other in Norwegian before they go to sleep. But on Uncle David's side there are four other books—only I don't know what they are because the titles and the writing are all in Norwegian. I know they're thick. Big books. Sometimes Uncle David will bring one of them down and read it in the kitchen at night because that's the only room with enough light. The Coleman lantern hangs in the middle of the

room and hisses and gives off a flat light so bright
you have to squint when you come in from the
barn at night. Uncle David sits at the kitchen
table and reads silently, his lips moving, sometimes for an hour and more. Once Wayne asked
him what he was reading but he just shook his
head and didn't answer. We knew it wouldn't
do any good to ask after that. So we don't know
what's in the books.

The rest of the farm is two granaries and a
barn. The granaries are made of rough sawn
wood polished smooth by all the oats and barley
poured in and shoveled out for the stock. They
sit one on each side of the farmyard to keep the
wind from ripping through in the winter.

The barn is a large log building at the end of
the yard. It has two floors, the upstairs being the
hayloft, and is made of logs so big there aren't
trees that large anymore. The bottom logs are so
huge Wayne and I would have to link arms to
get around one of them. The logs get smaller as
the barn walls go up, because they had to be
lifted, but the corners are linked and cut with
wedge cuts so that as they settle they get tighter.

Wayne says the barn and house and granaries

were built before any of us came, even before Father's father came from the old country and died in the woods. I can't say it isn't so. Once I asked Father about it while we were waiting for hog water to heat for butchering which is the slowest of all times except Christmas Eve, waiting to fall asleep so you can get up and come down to see what's been left under the tree.

Father didn't know how old the farm was either, and when I asked Uncle David he just smiled and nodded and Nels didn't seem to hear me.

So the farm is old. Sometimes Wayne and I sit in the hayloft and wonder about the logs, about how old they are. You can see where the axes made marks when they were chopped and where the long drawknives made flat cuts when they were peeled, and in one log, near the end of the barn and down out of sight where you can barely see it, there is a name carved.

KARL, it says, in letters cut deep and so far under it had to have been done right after the tree was cut down. I asked Father and Nels and Uncle David and Mother and even Wayne, but none of them knew a Karl with a K, only several Carls that started with C. Somehow that made the name ancient. I saw Wayne sitting alone near the name touching it once with one finger and when I asked him what he was doing he just smiled.

That was the time, that spring, when Wayne and I went out in the woods near the backyard and found a large tree and carved our names in it. Wayne carved his in all large letters, using a wood chisel and a hammer, but I used a knife and didn't get mine so deep. I felt bad, until that winter Father cut the tree for pulp and sent it off to the paper mills where it would be shredded anyway. . . .

Inside the barn, the ground floor is laid out with a long aisle down the middle, where the cows are milked; on the right of that is a manger that runs the full length of the barn. The cows come in and put their heads through wooden slots called stanchions and Father or one of us goes down the line and closes them in with a locking board to hold their heads while we milk. Except in winter. In winter they stay in all the time because the deep cold is too much for them and they would die.

At the end of the manger area there is a little door cut in the wall that leads outside to a large covered pit full of silage. Silage is chopped corn and corn plants put up in the fall and fed to the cattle all winter. It is supposed to be good for them, and they love it and push against the stanchions and bellow when the small door is opened and they see Father come in with the silage fork. Uncle David says they do that because silage ferments and they get drunk on it. Either way, they eat every bit of it and lick the wood of the little silage box in front of each stanchion until the wood is shiny and as glass smooth as the salt block in the south pasture that they lick in the summer.

Across from the cows, on the other side of the barn, there is a row of calf pens. Each cow has to have a calf or it won't freshen and give milk. But the cow gives way more milk than even ten calves could drink so the calves are kept in a pen and fed milk with a bucket. The extra milk we keep for selling or drinking. There are three pens of calves and in the spring when they're born and put in the pens the barn is filled with the warm dampness of them. Uncle David calls it the best time there is, when the young come in the early spring. Sometimes he'll fill his lower lip with snoose and just stand by the pen, sucking on the tobacco and watching the calves quietly as they try to play and fall all over each other.

When the calves are brand new, they don't know how to drink out of a bucket and they run around the pen trying to suck on anything to get milk. They get each others' ears, or tails, or noses, or pieces of wood on the side of the barn. I saw one once get hold of a new kitten's tail and suck on it until the whole kitten was goobered with spit.

Wayne and I are the ones who get them to drink because our hands are smaller than the grown men's. When the milking is almost done we each take a small bucket of milk and climb into a calf pen. They're on you right away, sucking at your clothes or elbows and you have to get your fingers in their mouths and while each one is sucking on your fingers you pull your hand gently down into the warm milk and pretty soon they're sucking right at the milk and drinking it like they've known how all along. Unless they're dumb. Some of them are dumber than others and don't get it. Wayne had a calf two springs ago that never did learn, even when he got nearly big enough to be weaned. It was a sight, watching Wayne get into the pen with that huge calf. He would run over to Wayne and grab his hand and jerk it down into the bucket so he could get milk. It got so Wayne was half afraid to get into the pen and every morning when we came near to feeding calves he would start bargaining with me to take his calf.

"I'll let you read the Captain Marvel comic I got when we went to town Saturday."

"I already read it when you were sweeping the granary."

"I'll give it to you."

"I don't want to get into the pen with that calf."

"I'll give you that Captain Marvel and buy you one of those wax-teeth harmonicas when we go in with milk next Saturday. . . ."

"Nope."

I answered fast but it wasn't that easy a decision. Those orange wax teeth are something. You can play music on them for a while until you're sick of the squeaking sound they make that always causes Foursons, the dog, to cock his head sideways and look like the RCA dog on the radio in the pictures in the Sears catalog. Then you eat the wax, which has some sugar in it, and chew on it for hours and hours. And when that's done you give it to Foursons who eats it until he's sick of it and gives it to the chickens, who always follow him around hoping he'll drop something.

To be honest I thought if I held out I could maybe get a Coca Cola and a bag of peanuts to pour into it. Which I like better than the orange wax teeth.

Wayne was too tight and I didn't get any of it. He went ahead with the calf on his own even though when he climbed into the pen to feed it we all stopped our work to watch him.

On the same side of the barn as the calf pens, just at the end, is a separator room. All the milk has to have the cream taken out of it so the cream can be sold separately when we go in on Saturdays. Mother gets the cream money and egg money—and I guess all the money, come to think of it, because I saw Father turning over a check from the elevator for grain one fall, which is practically the only money we ever get. Milk and cream and egg and grain money.

The separator has a bowl on the top where we pour the milk and a crank on the side to turn it and spin the cream out. The crank is hard to turn until it gets going and then it's easy. But you have to keep turning it and turning it until all the milk's been run through, and sometimes they run it through twice.

Wayne and I have to turn the crank. He turns it one day and I turn it the next. We make marks on the wall with an old pencil stub to keep track of who's supposed to do it. We don't hate it, exactly, but like Wayne says if he had a choice between turning the separator or peeing on the weed-chopper electric fence he'd have to think about it a little and I agree with him.

Parts of it are nice, the separator. It makes a high whine, like you might have with a steam engine running; you can imagine that while you turn. And it's something to watch the cream come out one spigot, thick and rich, and the milk foam into the milk can out of the other one. It's all grass, Uncle David says, grass and corn. Wayne and I spent one whole day working out how we planted alfalfa and the cows ate it and we planted corn and the cows ate it and came into the barn and gave us milk for it which we sold to buy more alfalfa and corn seed to plant more to give them. . . .

"It's endless," Wayne said. "It just goes on and on and never ends. Like the stars and the weather."

"Unless all the cows get sick and die," I said, because I always disagree with Wayne and Wayne always disagrees with me.

"No good, Eldon," he said, shaking his head. "There's other cows and other corn and other alfalfa and other milk."

"Well, if all the cows died in all the places where there are cows it would end. Then the corn would rot and that would be the end of it."

Wayne didn't even answer. It was lame and I knew it, but it was all I could think of on short notice.

Next to the separator room is the work horses' stall. We have a team of two horses, Jim and Stacker, both geldings, so big Wayne and I have to climb their legs to help harness them. Their hooves are as large as pie plates. They stay in all winter except when they get used for hauling pulp wood on the big bobsleds or pull the stone-boat to clean the barn. Sometimes it's like they aren't real, Jim and Stacker—that's what Wayne says.

They are so big, so strong it's like they can't

be just horses. Father says they weigh close on a ton each but that doesn't mean much. It's the tallness of them. Sometimes in the barn we'll climb the stall sides and sit on the horses and talk because they are warm and gentle and somehow comfortable—like a living couch. One time we both got on Jim and sat on his rump, the two of us, and there was room to spare. It was like a huge fur table.

Come a late spring day maybe one, two years ago we went to town of a Saturday night so Father could have two beers—he always has two beers when he goes in with Mother to dance.

In the main room of the beer hall Harrin Olsen plays the accordion and does waltzes and polkas all night Saturday night. Harrin was kicked by a horse and can't talk or think much but he plays the accordion so wonderfully that people come from other towns just to hear him. And Mother and Father dance and dance. This one night he had his sleeves rolled up and clean overalls on and she was wearing a pretty flowered dress, and before you knew it everybody else had stopped to watch them twirl and twirl around the rough board floors of the beer hall. We watched till it was boring and I left to go drink a Coca Cola with peanuts in it and almost got in a fight with Evan Peterson when he tried to take my Coca Cola.

That night, in the back room, Wayne found a Zane Grey western in a dusty pile. *Guns Along the Powder River*. The cover was all in color and showed a cowboy with a roaring six-gun in each hand kind of shooting at you out of the picture. So we sat down with that book and read it and don't you know, we had to be cowboys. We asked old man Engstrom, who owns the beer hall, if we could borrow the book and he said yes so we took it home.

It didn't happen all at once. We would read a couple of pages and then we would pretend. We had some sticks we used for blazing six-guns and we would try to do whatever the cowboys in the book were doing, and that was where Wayne finally got into trouble. It was all right as long as they were just shooting each other or gallop-ing around. But we came to a scene where the hero—he was named Jed—was being held in the upstairs room in a ranch house by a gang of rustlers who were stealing cattle. Jed had set out to stop them, which he did with some pretty good shooting, but that isn't so important. What matters is that for a while they captured him and held him in the upstairs room and the bad men were downstairs. So he whistled for Black Ranger, his horse, and Black Ranger came and stood under the back upstairs window and Jed jumped out of it and landed on Black Ranger and rode away and left the rustlers. Wayne thought it was quite the fancy thing to do.

"Why, I think it would be quite the fancy thing to do." That's how he said it.

But I was thinking more of the horse and what it must be like to have somebody jump out of an upstairs window and land on your back.

A few mornings later, Father and Mother went to Orvisons' for coffee because it was too soon to plant and they wanted to visit. Nels and Uncle David were in the house in their room and Wayne motioned for me to come with him to the barn.

"I want you to hold Stacker for me," he said, whispering so Uncle David and Nels wouldn't hear upstairs. "Underneath the hayloft door . . ."

I knew without being told what Wayne was going to do and I knew it was wrong but it didn't matter. I had to see him do it. Like the time he made wings out of some sticks and two feed sacks and tried to fly off the granary roof. A fool would know it wouldn't work, but I had to see it anyway and later, when they took the cast off his arm he was even kind of proud. He claimed he'd flown, but I thought and still think he came down like a rock with some rags tied to it.

The thing with Stacker was the same. The cowboy book had been chewing at him over a week so I followed him to the barn.

"I picked Stacker because he looks most like Black Ranger," he said as we went in. "To make it look right."

"The only thing that looks the same is that Stacker is a horse and kind of brown," I said. "He's got a leg that weighs more than Black Ranger. . . ."

Last year when Mother's cousin Betty was visiting with her daughter—this three-year-old girl who I guess would be my second cousin or something—anyway when they were visiting, the little girl got away from them while they were drinking coffee and talking. Everybody was frightened that she had wandered into the hog pen and the pigs had eaten her, which Nels and

Uncle David said had happened once when they were young. But we finally found the little girl in the pasture standing under Stacker. She was right between his front legs, holding onto the long hair around his hoofs, and when he'd step forward to move to a different piece of grass to eat—those feet as big as tree stumps swinging out so carefully to miss the little girl—she just moved with him, hanging onto his legs.

When we untied him and led him out of the stall—neither one of us coming up to his nose —he was just as easy and gentle as he'd been with the little girl.

"Are you sure you want to do this?" I asked. But I really wanted to see it and that came through in my voice. Like when Wayne tried to fly.

He just nodded and when we had Stacker out in front of the barn, under the hayloft door, he lined the horse up. That took some doing because Stacker had no idea what he was supposed to be there for, standing waiting for a makebelieve cowboy to jump out of the sky onto his back, so he kept trying to move. We'd stop him just right, then he'd take a step to eat the thistles at the edge of the barn and ruin it. We went back and forth until finally Stacker seemed to get the idea and he stood.

"You hold him right here," Wayne said, "and I'll get up in the hayloft"—as if I would be the one to get in the hayloft.

He ran into the barn and I heard him thumping up the hayloft ladder and in a few seconds he opened the loft door over Stacker.

He looked down for a moment and held back. "It's pretty far. . . ."

The truth is I kind of agreed with him, but I didn't say anything. My job was to hold Stacker. Period.

Finally he shrugged. "Well, if Jed could do it . . ."

Then Wayne turned around and said back into the empty barn, "Don't worry. I'll be back with the posse," like Jed to his sidekick.

And he jumped.

I'm not sure how he figured the drop from the hayloft to Stacker. I know that when Jed did it in the book he jumped out of the window and landed perfectly in the saddle and rode away just as clean and nice as you could hope for and not a rustler knew he was leaving.

It didn't work out that way for Wayne. Of course Stacker wasn't wearing a saddle, but even if he had been, Wayne wouldn't have come anywhere close to it. Wayne had judged the distance all wrong and Stacker's front end was way out from the barn. That put his rear end directly under the hayloft opening.

Wayne hit with a sound kind of like smacking a potato with a hammer.

Chunnkks.

It must have hurt because when I looked up at his eyes all that showed were the whites, and he slowly rolled off the side of Stacker and plopped into the manure and muck on the ground and didn't move but just lay still holding himself down there making a kind of whistling sound through his nose.

Stacker is a soft and slow-moving old horse. Many times I've seen Father take a carrot and hold it in his mouth and Stacker will pluck it out without hurting a hair on Father's head. But Stacker had never had anybody jump out of a hayloft and land on his rump, and when Wayne hit him Stacker jumped forward. He moved really fast for a big horse. The jump took him into the side of the pig fence, which knocked the boards down. All the pigs—about four months old—saw the hole and went for it, which took them right across Wayne, who was still down on the ground whistling.

I couldn't help him at first because I'd been trying to hold Stacker by his halter, which was about the same as trying to hold a train. He didn't even feel me when he jumped forward. Then I looked back and saw Wayne on the ground with the little pigs running over him, holding himself and his eyes all white and the wind whistling out of his nose, and I started laughing so hard I couldn't stop. It just got worse and worse until I was hanging on the side of the hog fence and I guess I'd be hanging there still if Wayne hadn't gotten better and come after me with an old board.

He's still sore about it. All I've got to do to get his eyes glowing is look at him and say, "Don't worry. I'll be back with the posse."

SUMMER

Summer starts slow. You don't really see the work coming. One day it's spring, soft and sticky and stinking and the hard part of winter is done and you walk around looking for something to do. The next day Father is taking the plowshares to town. The soil on the back forty is rocky and dulls the cutting edge of the plow—the shares— and every year the blacksmith has to hammer them out to a sharp edge again.

Plowing is the only time Father uses the F-12. That's our tractor and it's quite a sight, with steel lug wheels and a crank start, and so ornery only Father can get it going. Even with him it's mean. Two summers ago he had the spark from the magneto too far advanced and the crank kicked back and broke his wrist. He had to wear a cast half of a summer.

Father used to use the team for plowing, riding the one-bottom plow and letting them make their own speed. But on a warm day he would have to stop and water them and let them rest at each end of the field. When he had a chance to swap two Jerseys for the tractor he did it. Mother was upset though because she liked the milk from the Jerseys better than from the Holsteins. It had more cream to it, she said, and it tasted better.

I like taking the plowshares into town with Father because I'm still young enough to go. Wayne has crossed the line now and has to work around the farm when he isn't going to school. Unless it's Saturday night in the spring, Wayne has to stay home. But I still get to climb into the old Ford truck with the cable brakes and ride with Father to town.

The blacksmith is a tall, thin man smelling of burned steel and snoose spit. We leave the plowshares there to be worked on and Father takes me to the store where I get a nickel every time and spend it on candy that costs two for a penny. It's rock-hard candy and I'm supposed to save some for Wayne. Sometimes I do, but usually I suck all of mine and some of Wayne's before I get home, and to be honest the candy is mostly why I like to come to town.

Once I asked Father why he didn't take the shares in during the winter or even spring and do it then. He said it was because the steel would forget it was sharp if it wasn't done right before early plowing. But he was smiling so I don't know about it being true and I'm afraid to ask Wayne because he would laugh at me for sounding dumb.

When the shares are heated red hot and pounded out to a new edge with the big hammer we take them home and Father bolts them onto the bottom edge of the plow to cut the soil. Then he hooks the plow to the tractor and heads for the fields.

I have to wait for Mother and walk out with her when she brings lunch to him. She takes sandwiches in a covered bucket with a quart jar full of coffee wrapped in sacking to keep it hot and two or three pieces of cake and some large pickles from last year's garden. We sit at the end of the field and wait for Father to finish his round, the tractor popping and snapping in the heat. Then he gets down and we sit in the shade to eat. Mother spreads one of the sacks from around the coffee on the ground as a tablecloth and puts out the sandwiches and cake and brushes the flies away with a hand while we eat. Father talks about how the soil is.

"She's butter," he says sometimes. "Just a little moisture this spring and she's cutting like butter. I've never seen the beat. . . ."

And when lunch is done, some days he'll let me ride on the tractor with him and watch the plow. Father says that is the best part of farming—plowing in the early summer—and I can see why he thinks it. I think the same.

The plow turns the soil, just peels it and turns it over so the bright green of the grass is folded and folded and folded under and the thick black of the soil turns up. I like to sit backward on the tractor seat and watch.

Then the seagulls come. Father says they come from large lakes to the north and maybe from Hudson's Bay which is north many hundreds of miles. He says that when he was young there were no gulls but they discovered the plowing one year and the next year they came and each year now they come.

Hundreds of them. They come to float in back of the tractor and watch, and each time the plow turns over a worm they drop down to pick it up and eat it. They float in rows and piles and heaps in the air around the tractor and plow and you would think they'd fight but they don't. No fighting. They take turns. They will hang on the air like thistledown, soft and easy, and when a worm turns up one will drop down and nail it and another will take his place, so that they seem to turn, gray and white gulls, as the soil turns over and over. It would be much prettier if they didn't poop so much.

It drops on your head and in your face and on the tractor and plow and the hot muffler on the engine. The stink burns and cuts back across the tractor seat in a thick cloud. Father says it is a rich smell, and he loves the gulls, but to me it just stinks. To Wayne it stinks. Nels and Uncle David won't say if it stinks or smells nice when I ask them. And Mother just smiles when I ask her.

Once the plowing is done, Father puts the tractor away and uses Stacker and Jim to pull the disc harrow to break the soil down still more. Then, when it is in small lumps, he drags the toothed drag with the team over it one more time and breaks it down further until it's like cake batter. That's how Father says it. He'll feel the dirt and sometimes take a pinch up and taste it and smile at me if I'm sitting on the drag or harrow with him and say, "It's smooth as cake batter."

Of course it isn't. But he's always doing that, saying things are like something else to make you think about them. Like Stacker and Jim pulling stumps when he's clearing the forty down by the swamp. That's something to see, almost to not believe—how strong they are and how they'll still let me climb their legs like trees.

Father backs them up to the stump so the doubletree—the joining bar you use on a two-horse team—is on the ground next to it. Then he wraps a short chain under the stump and hooks it to the doubletree and he says, ever so soft, "Jim. Stacker. Take it up."

They pull and their leg muscles snap and crack so hard sometimes on a warm day that the sweat sprays off those horses in a fine mist. The trace chains and doubletree creak and the stump hangs for a minute, then pop! like my old tooth in back when Mother used a string on it, pop!

that old stump comes out in a shower of dirt and Stacker and Jim lunge forward a bit with the pull before they can stop.

"Did you see their legs, boy?" Father says. "Like pistons, weren't they? Like pistons on a big engine when they snap like that . . ."

But they aren't. They're just strong meat. That's what Wayne says. But he never says it in front of Father and besides, in the summer, Wayne is working so hard there isn't time to say much of anything.

Uncle David once said it was because there was so much light in the summer.

"You work in light," he said, sitting on a cream can by the barn door, spitting in the dust so the chickens came running to see what it was. "With all the summer light it makes us work harder. In winter it gets dark earlier and the days are short enough to rest. No rest in the summer."

And sometimes Uncle David is never wrong so that might be the way of it.

I can't work all the hard ways Father and Uncle David and Nels and even Wayne work because when I was small I had a time when I couldn't quit coughing. I spit blood and was weak for what seemed forever, and now I'm supposed to take it easy until I get older. I can play hard with Wayne and it doesn't seem to bother me. But Mother and Father won't let me do the hard work like clean the barn or shovel grain or even carry wood, even though I do it when they aren't watching.

First there is plowing, then dragging and harrowing and drilling the seed: wheat, oats, barley, corn—then potatoes; and the days don't stop. Father leaves the milking to the rest of us, or I should say everybody but me, and takes Stacker and Jim out of the stalls before light. He leaves so far before light that Mother doesn't even have a chance to get breakfast for him; he just eats some cold food from supper the night before. I got up one morning and went out in my shorts with rubber boots on and watched him when he didn't see me. He talked so nice to Jim and Stacker in the dark that it was like they weren't horses but good friends.

"We got corn," he said, his voice even and steady as he hooked them to the corn planter. "Got corn to put in and we got to lay those rows so straight they be like a die, straight as a die they got to be. . . ." All the words ran together and you could hear the horses whicker to him in a kind of answer while he fastened the trace chains and raised the tongue between them to slip into the tongue ring. Then it was just the three of them as he climbed onto the planter and rode out of the yard, clucking to the team to keep them going. I thought then and still think that when he is with them working that way, Father loves those horses every bit as much as he loves Mother or Wayne or me or anything.

"Work on work on work"—that's how Uncle David says it.

When the corn is planted and comes up it has to be cultivated three or four times to make sure the weeds don't get a start. And about when the corn cultivating is done and the plants are standing alone and free of weeds it's time to do hay.

That's when the neighbors, the Ransens, come, like they do in harvest time; when they hay, we go to help them. But it's a lot of work, even with help. The hay has to be mowed, then raked into winrows and dried, then swept up with the sweeprakes and brought to the hay stackers that pull the piles of hay up and over the top again and again to make the stacks. I even get to do some work at haying time. When the hay comes up and over to fall on top of the stack, two of us—Wayne and I—have to use three-tined hay forks to smooth the hay and shape it so it sheds water down the outside of the stack. It also has to be packed, so we jump on it and bounce it down after the sweeprake teams bring in each new pile, until all the hay for winter is in stacks in the field looking like loaves of bread.

Just about when haying is done it's time to thrash. That's Father's favorite time if there's been good rain and the oats and wheat are good, and his sad time if it's been dry and the oats and wheat didn't make right.

We also thrash with the Ransens, except it's different from haying. When we hay everybody works and when the day is done we all go home to finish work at home. But when we thrash we don't go home right away. We cut the grain and use the shaulker to put it in bundles and feed it to the thrashing machine which is run by the F-12 and a long, slapping belt. Grain comes out a spout at the top and straw comes out the other end and dust, eye-dust, choke-dust, sneeze-dust, is all over the place so the men have to wear handkerchiefs over their noses just to breathe.

When we're done we wash in the water trough in back of the barn where you can also catch tadpoles if you want to put some in a jar. But instead of everybody going home, all the men and women stay and eat. There's never food like there is at thrashing. At our house Mother cooks all of a day just on pies, then all of a night, it seems, on meat and potatoes and all of the next day on all the other things there are to eat. Everybody brings something as well, and a table is made outside with planks covered with clean sheets.

I don't know how men can eat like that. Old man Ransen, who they say is close on seventy, always comes—even though he doesn't do any work except oil the thrasher now and then with an oil squirt can. That makes Uncle David mad because he thinks he should do it. Old man Ransen sets to and the gravy runs down his chin. He eats like six young men, even without teeth. I watched him last year during thrashing finish off four plates of food, half an apple pie, and close on a quart of homemade ice cream that Wayne and I had spent hours cranking. And then he looked for more.

It's something to see. Wayne and I just eat and

eat until we're close to busting and there's still so much food left the table almost creaks with it.

When the thrashing is done there's a mountain of straw out in back of the barn where the thrashing machine blows it; Wayne and I sometimes spend a whole day jumping off the barn roof onto the straw pile, even though there's the second cutting of hay to get in and the corn silage to chop. I think Father knows how much we still like to jump in the straw and just lets us have the day for it. Once I saw him and Mother watching us from the side of the granary as we jumped, and they were both laughing and looked like they wanted to jump with us. I think you could jump from the clouds and it wouldn't hurt if you landed in a straw pile. You just sink and sink and sink. . . .

Then hay again, and corn to fill the silo to feed the cattle all winter—and how hard it is. Maybe I wouldn't have known, except that last year at the end of summer I came around the end of the barn and saw Father sitting on the block of oak we use for splitting wood and killing chickens. He was just sitting looking at the ground with his hands and arms hanging down between his legs. His eyes weren't blinking and he wasn't smiling. Mother was standing in back of him rubbing his shoulders and neck, just rubbing and rubbing.

"The days are long," she said, in a kind of song like she used to sing to me when the coughing was bad and I couldn't sleep. "The days are long and the nights are short, the days are long and the nights are short. . . ."

Many times we eat supper after ten, when it is dark, the Coleman lantern hissing and nobody talking, nobody saying anything, even Wayne and me, just eating and chewing and eating until we're done and then we go up to fall in our beds for the next day.

Summer work.

You swear it will never end until one day, one hot day in September Father will head out in the morning and harness Jim and Stacker to the hayrack and look at us and say, "Pile on, we're going to the lake."

Then you know it's fall.

FALL

I hate fall.

Mother says it's her favorite time and Nels and Uncle David like it because the air starts to dry out and they don't ache so much. Father seems to walk lighter. All the grain is up and the barn is full of hay and the fields are tucked in with haystacks waiting to be used and everything is done. Almost everything.

Going to the lake starts it off better than it ends. I like that part. Three miles away over a logging road is a small lake called Jenny's Lake because a girl was supposed to have killed herself there when the man she was going to marry died in the war. I don't know which war it was, but it's supposed to be true. Wayne says her ghost

walks on the water in the dark sometimes, but he's never been there in the dark and neither have I, so there's no way to know for sure.

It's a pretty lake. Almost perfectly round with a small beach and a grassy place at one end where Father long ago—when he came there with Mother while they were courting—made a rock fireplace. In a tree at the edge of the clearing he carved their initials in a heart. They are still there, the bark grown around them so they look old and deep. Once I saw Mother go over to the tree, two, three falls ago, and put her fingers on the heart and smile and look at Father who was making a fire to cook the steaks.

We always make a fire and he lets it burn down to coals and cooks steaks on a grill. Or pork chops. Mother brings pies and potato salad and jars of raspberry drink she makes from the raspberry syrup she saves when she cans. We eat until we can't hold any more. Then Wayne and I get in the water at the beach and spend the afternoon swimming and splashing while Mother and Father and Nels and Uncle David sit on the grass and look across the lake and burp and smile and talk about silly things that don't go together. . . .

"Was a time when you couldn't move in this country," Uncle David might say. "Trees so thick you couldn't move at all. . . ."

"Sure good food," Father would answer, looking straight at Mother who would blush and blush. "For somebody so pretty. I didn't think pretty women could cook that good."

"I had a mare once," Nels might say, "that every time you slapped her she peed straight back like a bullet. Got Hans—you remember Hans, don't you, the one that got killed when the tree hit him? Got him straight in the ear and he was so mad he hit me with a peavy. . . . But he never got earaches again as long as he lived."

. . . Until it's close to evening and we eat warm apple pie and drink milk thick with cream and barely make it home in time to milk and do chores. That's how fall starts.

Not so bad a start.

But when all the grain is up and all the silage in and the hay stacked and the barn and yard cleaned it is time to kill.

And I don't like the killing part.

We have a dog named Rex that's been here longer than Wayne. He's got hair in lumps and likes to help bring the cows in, but he's so old he mostly just sits and stinks on the porch and thumps his tail if you say his name or hand him a pork-chop bone. Father says Rex stopped a bear that was chasing Mother from the garden before we were born and that's why he only has to sit on the porch and eat.

But come fall he goes crazy. It's the blood, Father says. As soon as Father walks out of the house and takes the little .22 rifle down from the old deer horns on the porch to shoot the steer, Rex gets to jumping and wheezing so hard he almost chokes.

I think he's the only one on the place that likes the killing.

It's the way of it, Father says. Something has to die so we can live. Mother nods but she doesn't come out to the barn, only when the killing is done and the skinning and cutting start.

It's one of those things I wish I didn't watch but I do. Wayne says that makes me two-faced but I can't help it. Father goes into the barn with the little rifle and holds it to the steer's head and pops it once and the steer goes down, just flumps down, and then Father cuts the throat with the curved knife and catches the blood in a large pan for mother to make blood sausage out of. I can't eat it, ever, but that's not the worst.

Then he and Uncle David and Nels use a pulley and rope to pull the steer up to the ceiling in the barn and cut the belly open, the knife sliding through it like butter, and all the guts drop down in blue coils with steam off them, but that's not the worst.

Even when Rex jumps in and starts to eat the guts and gets them all over his head, and the cats come down from the hayloft and eat at them with the funny sideways grin they have when they eat guts, and the smell makes me a little sick and I have to go outside and breathe on the sides of my tongue—that's not the worst.

The pigs are the worst.

When I was sick and couldn't play hard and coughed blood, I sometimes got hot at night, so hot I couldn't stand it and I would have dreams.

Because of the blood I coughed up I dreamt of blood. And *my* throat. And the dream has never really gone away, because sometimes I wake up even now and my eyes will be wide open and Mother will have to come in and put her hand on my head.

Blood and throats.

When Father kills a pig he doesn't shoot it like he does with a steer because he says pigs have to bleed out better.

He uses the curved knife, and the men put the pig in the same pen they used for the steer. Then they flip the pig on his back and Nels and Uncle David hold him while Father sticks the curved knife into the pig's throat. And the throat seems to jump at it, seems to pull the knife in and up in a curve to cut its big vein. And the pig screams and screams while it dies and bleeds out. The smell, the smell of the blood and the screams and the throat bleeding out is so much, so thick that I can't stand it.

There is more killing in the fall: The chickens have to be killed and canned for winter—killed with the ax so their heads lop off and the beaks open and close even though the heads aren't on the bodies and the bodies jump around and around with Rex chasing them as they splatter blood on the barn wall from their jumping— bright specks of new blood on the walls of the barn that looks like the blood I coughed up. And there's the stink of their feathers as they are dipped in hot water and plucked, Wayne and Mother and me plucking them, pulling the damp, stinking feathers out, even working close around the stump of the neck.

Then the two geese we get from Hemings every year to smoke and save for Christmas have to be killed and plucked and waxed and smoked and they stink and there is blood and blood and blood and more blood and I hate fall.

By the end of it, by the end of fall, all I know is blood and if it weren't for school to think about I couldn't stand it. I know it has to be done, and every year Mother explains it to me again, though she doesn't come to the barn when the killing happens. I can't help thinking it's wrong, though Wayne doesn't think so. Sometimes he seems to get a light in his eyes like Rex gets when Father kills. But the men don't like it, Uncle David and Nels don't like it because when Father kills the steer and it goes down and when he cuts the hog and it screams and bleeds to death, when that is done Nels and Uncle David always stand silently, take their caps off and stand silently until it is done.

And Father always turns away and spits after he has done it. Nobody says anything for a time while the animals or chickens are dying. Nothing. No sound and I hate fall.

WINTER

Wayne says there aren't any divisions in things. We had a big fight one time over whether or not there was a place between days when it wasn't the day before and it wasn't tomorrow yet. I said there were places, divisions in things so you could tell one from the next but he said no there wasn't and we set to it. By the time we were done I had a bloody nose and he had a swollen ear from where I hit him with a board and we still didn't know.

But there is a place where winter comes, a place to see it isn't fall any longer and know winter is here.

When the killing is done and the meat is up and the crops are in and the leaves have all gone to color and dropped off the trees and the gray limbs stick up like ugly fingers; when the barn is scraped clean inside and straw is laid for the first cold-weather bedding and the stock tank in back of the barn has ice on it that has to be broken in the mornings so the horses can drink; when you have to put choppers on your hands to fork hay down from the loft to the cows and the end of your nose gets cold and Rex moves into the barn to sleep and Father drains all the water out of all the radiators in the tractors and the old town truck and sometimes you suck a quick breath in the early morning that is so cold it makes your front teeth ache; when the chickens are walking around all fluffed up like white balls and the pigs burrow into the straw to sleep in the corner of their pen, and Mother goes to Hemings for the quilting bee they do each year that lasts a full day—when all that happens, fall is over.

But it still isn't winter.

When all the fall things are done there is the place between that Wayne says isn't so but is. There is something there and when we come out of the barn sometimes I can feel it. A sort of quiet. Once I stopped Wayne just as we were walking to the barn and it was getting dark and the clouds were sailing over our heads heading south and there was a north wind so you had to hold your head over into your collar to keep your ear warm; once then I stopped Wayne and asked him if he could feel it.

"Feel what?"

"Feel the place between," I said, and he looked at me and said he thought maybe I was crazy like those natives we read about in *National Geographic* who would predict weather and fall down.

But I didn't care and don't care now because I know the place is there. The place when fall is gone and winter hasn't come yet. It is a short time, in one night.

And then it snows.

First time.

You go to bed after chores and when you wake up and go downstairs and the sun starts to come up there is a new light to it, a brighter light; you look out the window and there is new snow all over everything.

First snow.

Soft and curved and white covering the yard and dirt and manure and grass and old leaves, the barns and granaries and machines out by the small tool shed, so that they don't look like buildings and machines at all but animals. White animals in the new light.

First snow.

Winter.

And winter isn't like any of the other parts of the year more than any other part isn't. Spring is close to summer, summer close to fall, but winter stands alone. That's how Uncle David says it. Back in the old country he said winter stood alone and now he says it stands alone here as well.

Winter comes in one night and of course Wayne and I look out the window in the morning and there are a million snow things to do.

After chores we take the grain shovels and slide down the river hill sitting on them, holding the handles up and trying to steer by pushing them. The first time they move kind of slow, but when the snow is packed they just fly down. We can't really steer them at all but just snort and whistle down the hill until we get so wet that Mother makes us come in and change.

Then we have to make snow forts and throw snowballs at each other. And the chickens. All fluffed and looking for a warm place to stand. If they come too close to the fort they get it, or Rex, or the cats, or anything.

. . . All the snow things to do. Father feels it too. One winter he hooked Stacker to a singletree with a rope out the back, and we stood on a piece of old tin roofing with a rope tied to it and we rode and rode, the tin so slick Stalker didn't know it was there. Big as he was the cold snapped him up and he acted like a colt, if colts can get as big as barns, just snorting and flipping his tail and making air, whipping that piece of tin and us all over the field in the snow until we were so cold and sopping that we were sticking to the tin.

Winter is all changes. Snow comes and makes it all different outside so things you see in the other times of the year are covered and gone. In back of the house there is an old elm that has a long sideways limb and one warm day some of the snow melted a bit and slipped down and then refroze so it looked like a picture of a snake we saw once in a magazine, or so Uncle David said. At night I could look out the bedroom window and see the snake hanging in the moonlight, the white snake and it seemed to move. It wasn't there in the summer or spring or fall but only in the winter. Like magic.

But finally, when the snow play is done and the barn and animals are settled in and the wood for the day finished, when our mittens are drying on the back of the kitchen stove and we have eaten the raw fried potatoes and strips of flank meat with the Watkins pepper on them and had the rhubarb sauce covered with separated cream, sitting at the kitchen table with the lantern hissing over our heads, finally when our stomachs are full Father pushes his chair away from the table and thanks Mother and God for the food and moves into the winter room. The living room.

Wayne and I have to do the dishes, and that includes washing the separator, which takes a long time, so when we get into the winter room the fire in the stove has been freshened with white oak and Mother is sitting knitting socks and mittens, and Father sits on one side of the stove and Uncle David sits on the other, with Nels next to him.

While Father has been filling the stove Mother has lighted the kerosene lamp so there is a soft yellow glow in the room. Wayne and I sit on the rug that Mother sewed out of braided rags, the colors all wrapped together in the soft light so they seem to move.

Father is working on his carving. I don't know when he started it. Maybe before I was born. But for as long as Wayne and I can remember he has been working at it every night in the winter. It will be a carving of a team of horses and a sleigh and trace chains and harnesses and reins and a man driving with a full load of pulp logs on the sleigh—all carved out of one piece of sugar-white pine he cut from a clear log many years ago. All we can see is the two horses' heads sticking out and part of one front shoulder, but Father can tell us where each thing is, pointing to where the links of chain will be and the logs and the man's head, just like he can see them even when they aren't there.

He carves quietly, his face even and somehow gentle, looking down as the small knife he uses cuts into the soft pine to peel away shavings so clear they look like honey in the yellow light from the lamp.

Wayne and I watch the fire in the stove through the mica windows in the door—all little squares—and the stove is like a friend. In the

summer it is black and large and fills the corner
of the room but now it is warm and part of us
somehow. It is tall and narrow, and on top there
is a silver ornament that looks like a big rose
upside down. Around the side there is a silver
rail that Wayne says is to put your feet on to
warm them. But one night when nobody was
looking I sneaked a spit on the rail and it snapped
and sizzled like I'd spit on the top of the stove
where it gets red, so I'm not about to stick a foot
on that rail.

Next to the stove, across from Father, sits Uncle David and right next to him sits Nels. The
two old men have straight-backed wooden
chairs and a couple of old coffee cans they use
for spitting into. They both fill their lower lip
with snoose after we eat, and they sit straight up
in the chairs, and Nels doesn't say anything except to slap his leg now and again when a story
gets good.

Every night in the winter it starts the same.
Uncle David and Nels will fill their lower lips
and Father will carve and Mother will knit and
the yellow flames will make our faces burn,
and then Uncle David will spit in the coffee can

and rub his hands on his legs and take a breath
and say:

"It was when I was young. . . ."

Then he will tell the story of Alida who was
his wife in the old country. Always it is the same.
Always he tells the story of Alida first and it is
the same story.

～ ALIDA

"It was when I was young and was thought fit only to sharpen the tools of the older men. This was wrong, wrong then and wrong now, but that is the way they did things in the old country. So each day I sat in front of the cottage and drew the stone over the axes and filed the saws until there was only new steel and the axes could shave the hair off your arm.

"It was when I was young and a day came when a girl walked by as I was sharpening tools and she was so beautiful she made my tongue stick to the roof of my mouth and I could not speak. Yellow hair she had, yellow hair like cornsilk mixed with sunlight. It was so long she had it coiled in a braid at the back of her head. And her eyes were clear blue. Ice blue. She was carrying a towel filled with loaves of bread to take to the cutters in the woods and she stopped and said good day to me and I could not answer.

"Could not answer.

"And that was Alida. She became my wife and let her hair down for me in great coils in the light from tallow candles. I could not live without her. We were married there in the old country and I put the handkerchief on my head to show I would be a good husband. I grew from sharpening tools to using an ax and a bucksaw and we planned to come to America, planned and saved. But soon Alida was with child and we had to stay and when the child came it was a wrong birth and the child died and Alida died and I died.

"I wandered into the woods along Nulsek Fjord, walked in the snow and wind and would not have come back except that my brother Nels came for me and found me and brought me with him to America to work where there was new wood to cut and woods that go to the sky. But I never remarried and never looked at another woman and my heart has never healed, and that is the story of Alida."

Uncle David always starts with the story of Alida. He has told it so often that when it comes out there aren't many stops except that his voice always hitches when he talks about Alida letting her hair down in the light from the tallow candles and I can see her so plain, so plain, and Mother always cries.

Father makes a small cough like there was something in his throat and Wayne takes a deep breath and Nels looks at the floor and doesn't move and Mother always cries and it is quiet— so quiet when he finishes the story of Alida that it seems as if time has stopped and we are all back with her and the bread in towels and Uncle David sharpening the tools of the older men.

Then Uncle David sighs and rubs his hands on his trouser leg and leans over to spit in the can and starts the second story of the night. The other stories are all different, always different night after night through the winter, so many stories I can't know them all or say them all.

But three of them I know.

Three of the stories make cuts across all the

stories the way a bucksaw cuts across wood so you can see all the rings and know how old the tree is, so you can know all about the tree.

Three are the stories like rings and show how it was that Wayne, and maybe me a little, came close to ruining it all, killing it all.

So Uncle David sits and he spits in the can and rubs his legs with hands callused so thick they look like bone or wood and he sighs and starts each one the same.

∽ ORUD THE TERRIBLE

"It was when I was young that Siggurd came to me and told me the story of Orud and the house under the sea.

"The story was from old times, when men went off in long boats and many did not come back and those who did had blood on their bodies and blood on their swords and blood in their hearts.

"Men took then, and did not give so much but took what they wanted. The man who took the most was Orud. Orud was tall and wide in the shoulder and had a helmet made of steel hammered to a point but soaked in salt until it was red, red like blood. They called him Orud the Red when they went a-viking and he was so terrible that it was said even the men in his boat feared him, and these men feared nothing.

"So it came that on one voyage they went to far shores where they had not been before. They found small houses along the shore which were not rich in gold but all had much in livestock and wool and flax and wheat, and Orud and his men went among them and took and took and killed and killed until their arms were tired with it and they had to stop.

"Orud had never taken a wife. But on this voyage in one of the houses along the sea his men found a woman of beauty and her name was Melena. Orud decided to claim her for a wife, which was his right as he was captain of the boat.

"But such was Melena's beauty, with long, red-gold hair to match the color of burnished steel and a straight back and long arms, such was her beauty that the man who found her wanted her as his own wife and claimed her, and that was his right as well.

"But Orud would not have Melena go to another man. So they fought and the other man was weaker, as all men were weaker than Orud, and the other man lost and was slain. Orud put his head on an oar to boast and would not even bury the man as his station demanded. It was an awful thing then, to kill one of your own men and not even give him a Viking funeral, but they set sail with good wind to head home. Orud tied Melena in the bow of the longboat so she could not escape.

"But she was more than beautiful. Melena was smart and strong, and she waited until the boat was entering the fjord of Orud's home village and they could hear the horns sounding, waited until all could see the boat and see her. Then she stood on the side and used her magic to release her bonds and threw herself into the water rather than be wed to Orud.

"Such was Orud's rage when she leaped that he forgot himself and jumped after her, to bring her back.

"But he forgot he was wearing armor and his sword and helmet to be welcomed with his new wife. The weight took him down into the deeps and he was not seen again.

"Except that much bad came to the village. The people had sickness and their crops died and when they tried to go a-viking to make up for it their boats sank again and again.

"It was said that Orud had found Melena and taken her to be his wife though she did not want it, and that they lived in a cottage under the sea at the mouth of the fjord but that Melena had not forgiven the village for sending the boat which carried Orud to take her. It was said she cursed the village into sickness and waste and when she looked up and saw the village send out a boat she would spread her hair up from the bottom in long strands and catch the boat and sink it in vengeance and laugh at Orud, and the wind and waves were her laughter, and that is the story of Orud and Melena and the house beneath the sea."

The night of that story we sat quietly and thought of the cottage under the water and Melena's hair streaming up to gather in the boats, and Orud's terrible rage. Then Uncle David sighed and spit again and held his hands to the stove for the warmth. Mother shook her head thinking of the horror of Orud, and Nels coughed, and Uncle David gave a little chuckle and told the story of Crazy Alen.

CRAZY ALEN

"It was when I was still young but I had come to the new country and I was cutting in the woods.

"We were cutting in a camp called Folter, on the line between two counties then. I had a way with a file so they paid me extra to sharpen the saws at night and at times during the day. Because of that I was in camp many times when the other men were out cutting and so I knew more of the story of Crazy Alen than many of them.

"Alen came years before I did, came on a boat from the old country just as I did but long ago when they had to sail. He wasn't crazy at first but cut wood better than many men and was fast. He used a bucksaw and would pull so hard he often pulled the man on the other end off his feet, and the sawdust would fly out in a plume.

"But a day came when he started to play jokes on the other men in the camp. They were not bad jokes, didn't hurt anybody, and many laughed at them and that made him do all the more. He would put pepper in their snoose or sew their stockings closed or nail a board over the hole in the outhouse.

"He was finally known for his humor and the jokes became larger until one day he waited until the foreman—he disliked the foreman then—was in the outhouse and Alen dropped a Norway pine so big you couldn't reach around it, dropped it right in front of the door so close the foreman couldn't get out. It was the best of all his jokes, dropping the tree that close to the door, and took great skill. Trees don't always drop where they are supposed to drop. Everybody thought it very funny.

"Everybody except the foreman, who saw only the danger in it. Had the tree dropped a little to the side it would have crushed the whole outhouse with the foreman inside it.

"And so it came that the foreman fired Alen

—they called him Crazy Alen by this time, because of his jokes—but Alen didn't mind. He was getting old by then and had decided to stop work and watch things for a while. He made himself a small cabin on the side of a narrow trail back in the forest.

"In the way these things work Alen and the foreman then became good friends. Part of it was that the foreman was also old and most of the rest of the crew was young; and part of it was that the foreman missed Alen's jokes and humor. He could not hire Alen back to work, because somebody might be hurt, but the foreman began to like Alen's jokes himself and one day he walked into the cabin with some honey in a bucket he'd stolen from the camp cook and a checkerboard.

"Soon he was walking back along the narrow trail once a week to play checkers and drink tea with honey and this went on through part of a winter, a spring, a summer and fall and into winter again. The two men would sit and drink tea and play checkers and speak of things they'd done when they were young, and not so young, in that small cabin in the forest.

"Of course Alen's jokes hadn't stopped. Every

time the foreman came to play checkers Alen would have a new one, a bigger joke. He would have a bucket of water over the door with a trip lever set to drop when the foreman came in. Or he would loosen the rungs in the foreman's chair so it would collapse when he sat down. Or he would put salt in his tea. Since all of these jokes were aimed at the foreman you'd think he would get mad but things were different then, different and maybe a little rough, and so men didn't mind rough jokes and the foreman didn't mind Alen.

"Nobody can know how long it would have gone on, but that winter Alen felt death coming and decided to play his best joke of all. As a young man he had been big, big and heavy. Alen stood six-and-a-half feet and weighed two hundred and seventy pounds at least in his prime and his arms were long and heavy as well. He had come in and down with age, but the frame was still there and it was a big frame.

"In the middle of that winter when it was so cold you could spit and it would bounce, when steel ax heads broke if they weren't warmed before you chopped, in that cold Alen saw his death coming.

"Nobody knew how he could have done it,

but just before he died he opened the cabin door to let the cold in and lay down on the floor on his back with his arms and legs stretched out as wide open as he could get them. And then he died.

"He died with a wide smile on his lips and his arms and legs out and his eyes staring wide open at the ceiling.

"And it was in the middle of the week and four days passed before the foreman came to play checkers. Four days with the door open Alen lay and the cold came into the room and the cold came into Alen and froze him as hard as granite. Then the foreman came and found him spread and solid on the floor.

"Alen knew these things. He knew the cabin had a small door and that the trail down through the woods was narrow and winding and he knew the foreman. He knew the foreman wouldn't be able to bring himself to break Alen's arms and legs and he knew the foreman would not dare to thaw Alen because of what would get soft with the thaw.

"He knew these things, Alen did, and he knew one more thing, knew the foreman would not leave the body. Could not leave the body.

"And so it was his greatest joke on the foreman because Alen would not fit through the door. The foreman had to use an ax to cut the door opening wider and then try to get Alen—spread and hard and smiling—get Alen down the trail. It was nearly impossible. He tried to carry Alen but he was too heavy. He tried to drag him. Finally he tried to roll him, cartwheel him, and where tree limbs were too low he used an ax to chop a way through.

"Two days and a night it took him to get Alen's body back to the camp. Two days wheeling and dragging and carrying the spread-eagled man and when he finally got to camp they put Alen in the back of a sleigh and it took two more days to get him to town and an undertaker. It was said that as the sleigh went down the road all those who saw Alen thought he was waving and they would laugh and wave back.

"And that is the story of Crazy Alen."

We sat then and listened, and Mother took a breath because she had been holding it, with one hand over her mouth, and I thought of death. Death never seemed funny to me. All I knew of it was when I had been sick and thought I would die and was afraid, or in the fall when we killed and killed. But it was impossible to think of Crazy Alen without smiling and that meant I was smiling at death, laughing at death and the picture of Alen with his arms and legs out and the foreman trying to get him down the trail.

There were many questions I wanted to ask and I knew Wayne wanted to ask some as well but we didn't. We never did. The stories were just there, not something to be questioned and opened up. Uncle David just told them and they came from him and went into us and became part of us so that his memory became our memory. But nothing about them was ever questioned.

Until he told the story that broke things.

It is strange, the way it happened, strange and kind of inside-out. It all came down to how Wayne felt about the stories. I always thought of them as just stories and didn't think they were real. I mean I know there probably aren't a man and woman living in a cottage under the sea— probably. Once Mother said the stories were not for believing so much as to be believed in.

But it was different for Wayne. I didn't know

it, but it was different. Somehow the stories had mixed in his mind so they had become a real part of his thinking, so that he believed them. And even when he knew they couldn't be— knew there couldn't be a man and woman living in a cottage under the sea—even then he wanted them to be real, wanted her hair to take the ships down, and by wanting them to be real somehow they became real in his mind. And that's how the trouble started.

There is nothing I could have done about it anyway but if I could have stopped it, stopped the hurt I saw in Uncle David's eyes, I would have given anything.

We had spent a long day splitting and carrying stove wood in because the wind had come around to the northwest and it was picking up into a storm. Father said it would blow for three or four days and drop to forty below when it stopped snowing and blowing and we wanted to be ready for it. Father split with the big double-bladed ax he kept in the ax bin in the granary, each ax so sharp you could shave the hair on your arms with it, just as Uncle David said. Wayne and I weren't allowed to use them, not even to split kindling. They were axes that used to belong to Uncle David and to Nels when they cut wood in the old days and they were something to see. All shining and silver, the two blades on each honed with a small, circular stone. I had seen Uncle David and Nels sharpening them with the stones, sitting with peaceful smiles on their faces while the stone went round and round and I thought it was the same look Mother had sometimes when she was knitting. But I had never seen Uncle David or Nels use the axes and I figured it was because they were so old now that they couldn't use them because it would hurt them somehow.

So Father split wood and I asked to help carry it and Father said yes. I felt like I must have brought in most of a cord by myself, stacking it under the overhang on the porch. When we were done, finally, I couldn't see over the pile. It covered the whole porch and I thought there was enough for two weeks before Father finally put the ax away and we went to milk and do evening chores.

That night it was my turn to crank the separator and change the buckets, and by the time we at last went to the house for supper it was so dark the lantern light from the kitchen window made all the snow in the yard seem to glow. I was so tired my brain felt filled with rags.

Mother had made a big pile of mashed potatoes with meat gravy and I made a little lake of gravy in the middle and ate around the edges until I couldn't eat any more, and then, after Wayne and I did the dishes, we went into the living room.

Father started to carve and showed us how far he'd come along since last time and Mother nodded and smiled and Nels and Uncle David filled their lower lips and talked about how the snow cover was good for the crops next year. Then they talked about work that needed doing, and I was watching the fire through the small window on the stove door and my eyes closed and I was sleeping. Or half sleeping. Just going in and out of it when I heard Uncle David start a story—and it wasn't about Alida.

～ THE
WOODCUTTER

"It was when I was young but I was old enough to have come to the new country and to the north woods and was working as a cutter.

"In the first winter we cut in the lake country and used the lakes and rivers as ice roads for the teams and sleighs. Boys too young to cut took water sleighs with tanks of water in them and soaked the grooves where the runners ran to keep them slick, and put hay in the downhill grooves to slow the loads so they wouldn't run over the teams. I tell you we moved some wood and those horses got so strong they could haul a load as big as a house down to the rivers where the logs were left on the ice to float down the rivers to the sawmills in the spring floods.

"I don't even know how much wood we cut. One camp didn't speak with another, one company didn't speak with another. We just cut and cut until there wasn't anything left. Where there had been forest so thick you couldn't see ten yards without looking at a giant Norway or white pine, you could stand on level ground and see fifteen miles and nothing higher than a stump when we were done cutting.

"It was sad and most of us wished we hadn't done it when it was finished but it was that way then just as it is now that the forest has started to grow up some again. People just cut without thinking.

"But this isn't a story about the cutting so much as it is about a man who was young then.

"There were many men who were good cutters because that was a time when all men were cutters, and there are stories about most of them. Some could use a saw this way and some could use an ax that way. There were stories of men who could cut a six-inch pine with a single swing of a double-bitted ax and other men who shaved with axes and still others who could make saws and axes sing and weep and bleed. But there was one man who they said could do all these things.

"It was said that no man could use an ax like him. The wood of the handle seemed to grow out of his hands and there was nothing he could not do. Men in the camps would stop work to watch him and this becomes important when you know that men were paid by how much they cut. To stop meant they did not receive pay.

"But he was such a wonder with an ax that they would stop. The young man would walk to a tree and swing and the chips would float off like they were made of air—chopping half the head and more deep with each blow so the tree would almost fly off the stump when he cut through.

"They said many things of him. They said he could put a match in a stump so the head was sticking up and swing the ax with his eyes closed and catch the match perfectly so that it would split and both sides would light.

"And it was true.

"They said he shaved each day with an ax and never cut himself and his cheek was as smooth as a baby's.

"And it was true.

"They said he could take a four-foot piece of cordwood and swing two axes, one in each hand, swing them into the two ends and the wood would split clean and the axes would meet in the middle.

"And it was true. . . ."

Here father caught his breath and looked up sharply and said across the stove:

"But that was you. All those things were about you. . . ."

And I felt Wayne stiffen next to me on the rug. I turned to look at him and saw he was staring at Uncle David so hard he seemed to stare a hole through him. Wayne was mad. No, more than mad, tight with it, tight with mad the way he got when Philly Hansen took him down again and again in front of the girls at school.

Hurt mad.

Mad like to burn with it—Wayne was raw mad and I could tell he wanted to say something but he didn't because we never talked during the stories.

Uncle David coughed a little and spit in the can and looked for a long time at Father and then finished the story. It was about how the young man who was the best cutter of all thought that his new life would last forever only it didn't. None of it lasted. The woods were gone and he was old, and it ended that way but I didn't hear much of it because Wayne kept staring at Uncle David. He kept stiff like wood and staring at him and I knew something was wrong but I couldn't understand what it could be.

And when the stories were done that night and we went up to our room and got under the quilts to hide from the cold, even then I didn't learn because Wayne just turned away and didn't say anything. I knew he was awake because his breathing was tight and ragged somehow. I wanted to talk to him about whatever it was but he said nothing. I tried to stay awake but the whole day of wood and work and cranking the separator and listening to the stories and the heat from the stove and the cold from the bedroom and the warmth from the stacked quilts on top came crashing down on me and I fell asleep almost before my eyes closed.

In the morning we went outside for morning chores and Wayne looked a little funny at Uncle David in the barn but he didn't seem so mad anymore and I thought whatever it was had passed.

But I was wrong, so wrong, and I would see a thing so awful I wished I had never seen it. . . .

Wayne and I have a special place in the granary in back of the oats bin. I guess it isn't very much of a place but it's close and cozy and sometimes we sit there and talk about things. It wasn't something we planned so much as it just happened when we were small and as we got older we just would find ourselves there now and again when we wanted to talk. That day Wayne looked at me and walked toward the granary. I knew he wanted to talk so I followed. It was just after chores and barely light so I left the door open because there wasn't a lantern in the granary and it was pitch dark. Even with the light coming in the door it was still pretty gray.

"He's lying," Wayne said, as soon as I came in. He was sitting on an overturned bucket by the door so I went in and squatted in the corner.

"Who's lying?"

"Uncle David. All the time he's been lying with the stories, just telling us lies."

"But they're only stories. They aren't real. They're supposed to be lies. . . ."

"It's that he put himself up as one of the

heroes—a great thing. That makes it all bragging and not just stories. Bragging makes it all a lie on a lie. How could anyone cut a match in half blindfolded? How could anyone make two axes meet in the center of a log? That's just all lies. It's all lies and he's a liar and a braggart.

"Don't you see? Father caught him at it. Uncle David told lies about himself and that makes it all lies, just lies and lies and lies."

I was surprised to see that Wayne was crying, that it hurt him, this thing of Uncle David and the stories. He was crying and he said over and over:

"Liar, liar, liar. . . ."

And that would have been bad enough but I looked up, over Wayne and there was Uncle David and I knew he had heard most of it, maybe all of it, because his eyes were full of pain; they looked like the pig's eyes just after Father cut its throat and it knew it was going to die. All pain and confused, all fall killing pain and confused Uncle David's eyes were, so hurt and ripped that it seemed he would crumble, and I could not shut Wayne up.

"Lies, all lies, and he's a liar, a liar, a liar. . . ."

I tried to make a sign, to show Wayne, but it

was too late. Uncle David turned slowly and seemed to cave in and walked away and then I told Wayne, finally I got it out, and Wayne felt bad but not as bad as I thought he should.

It was over, and Uncle David was broken and done.

That night we ate supper and it was good but tasted like wood in my mouth. I saw Wayne who usually ate like a granary dog just pick and pick at his potatoes.

After supper we went into the living room and Uncle David didn't tell a story.

Not even the story of Alida.

He sat and rubbed his face and Father talked and Mother talked and even Nels talked but there was no story, none of anything like a story. Just talk of chores and summer crops and Mother spoke a little of the neighbors who were having trouble with a sick baby, and I thought it was like fall and something had been killed.

Here, I thought, in this room a thing has died. I nearly cried and wished Wayne would be hurt for what he'd done.

And another night

And another night.

Nothing like a story—just talk and talk until

we went up to bed. I started to hate Wayne then and think he should be punished—and on the fourth or fifth day after he broke Uncle David we were in the hayloft.

Many times we went into the hayloft to fool around. It was fun to swing on the trip rope that carried the hay up into the barn when we stored it. We would swing from the little landing up under the roof near the top of the loft down on the trip rope and land in the soft hay. It was something I never got tired of because the hay would catch you, just let you sink soft and down, and it smelled nice.

But this time I was still mad at Wayne, mad and sick of him so it went bad. I made a swing and landed on his leg and he squealed a bit and before I could stop it I was on top of him beating him and crying and cursing him for what he'd done to Uncle David.

We fought around the loft and down the side of the hay, only of course he's bigger than me so it wasn't much of a fight. Pretty soon he was sitting on top of me and he gave me a clout that made my nose bleed.

I got madder then and went a little crazy but he still held me down and clamped my arms to my side while I just squirmed and I was trying to bite him when I looked up and he wasn't paying any attention.

The way we had fallen we were jammed back into the corner where the logs were crossed in together. Because the barn was very old, some of the logs had warped so there were small gaps between them. Father said if it had been a house he would have chinked it and filled the holes, but it being a barn they just ventilated the hay nice and kept it dry—like a big crib.

Wayne was looking at something through the cracks in the corner and when I saw how interested he was I forgot all about fighting.

He let me loose and I pulled up alongside of him and wiped blood off my lip and nose and looked out the crack and saw Uncle David.

In the back of the barn was a large pile of wood cut in four-foot lengths for shipment to the paper mills. Father and some other men in the neighborhood cut the wood each fall and haul it out to the railroad when the roads get frozen and slick enough for the bobsleds, and it brings in a little extra money for Christmas.

Uncle David was standing staring at the pile of wood. His arms hung down at his sides and he looked small and sad somehow and I hated Wayne again for what he'd done. I thought it would be right for me to go down to him and touch him, maybe on the hand, and lean against his leg the way I did sometimes but before I could move Uncle David turned away from the stack of wood and walked to the granary.

I thought it was over, that time when I could have touched him, but in a few seconds he came out of the granary.

He was carrying two axes. He had one in each hand, two double-bitted axes, big and shiny and sharp as razors and I knew then, I knew what he had planned and I thought no, no. I must have moved because Wayne put a hand on my arm and held a finger to his lips.

"Be still. . . ."

"But he'll hurt himself," I whispered.

Wayne didn't answer. He'd turned away and was looking out through the cracks again and I did too. I couldn't stop.

I couldn't stop though I didn't want to see it, the way I couldn't stop when they killed the pigs and chickens in the fall—I couldn't stop looking through the cracks.

Back at the woodpile Uncle David took a log

down, studied it, pushed it aside and took another one. The logs looked heavy and big, bigger
than him. He seemed so caved in and tiny, and
when he finally got the log in the right place on
the ground he had to stop and catch his breath
and I thought no, no, no I should run for Mother
or Father and have them stop him because he
should not do this and it will hurt him.

But now it was too late and I knew that, too,
knew that it would be terrible to keep him from
at least trying.

He stood to the side of the log facing it and
held the axhandles, one on each side with the
heads of the axes resting on the ground and all
of him was curved down onto the axes so they
looked like hickory crutches. He was a broken
and tired and sad old man, and there wasn't a
thing he could do, I thought, even to lift the axes:
So awful a thing, the way he stood, the axes
standing at his side, his hands on the handles
and little bits of steam coming from his breath
as he looked down at the log and I thought no.

Please no. And no matter what it would do,
no matter if Wayne tried to stop me, I was going
to run down and tell him that he didn't have to
do this, that it didn't matter.

But now he moved his head up and looked at the sky and the sun caught his face and we could see it plain, see his face in the sun. The wrinkles seemed to leave. The skin seemed to smooth as the sun covered his face.

And his hands tightened on the axhandles and the heads of the axes in the snow, the heads trembled a little and it was as if something came from the earth.

Some thing, some power passed from the earth up through the silver axheads and through the hickory handles and it started in his arms. A little movement, then the arms seemed to swell and his shoulders came up and filled and his back straightened and his whole body filled with it until he was standing straight and tall and I heard Wayne's breath come in and stop and mine did the same.

"He's young again," Wayne whispered and it was not just a whisper but more a worshiping thing, like part of a prayer, and he was right.

Uncle David stood before the log and he was young, and as we watched, as we could not turn away and we watched, the axes started to move.

Up.

They came up from the snow. The heavy axheads came up and out to the side, came up like they were floating on light air, up and up until they were over his head, one on each side, the sun catching them and splashing the silver from the heads down on him like a new light, a life light and they hung there for what seemed like hours, days, hung in the air over his head while we held our breath. And just when it seemed that all things had stopped, that nothing would or could ever happen again, just then they started down.

Down.

So slowly at first the silver heads began to swing down and then faster and faster until they were two silver curves of light, two streaks curving down and around Uncle David so fast they were just a blur coming into the ends of the log.

Thunnnnnkkk!

Such a clean sound. The silver curves went into the log clean and even and the log opened and split and the axes met exactly in the middle with a small metal sound.

"Oh . . ." Wayne whispered but he did not know he'd said it.

"Oh."

For a second, a long second, Uncle David stood

there, the axes touching in front of him and I was crying and Wayne was crying.

"We have to go down there," I said. "We have to go down there and tell him we saw it."

But Wayne held my arm and shook his head and said, "No. It was for him. All for him. Don't you see? If we go down there it will ruin it for him."

And of course he was right because Wayne is sometimes right, and I settled back down into the hay and looked out the crack again.

Uncle David stood tall for part of another second, then the power all went out of him. His shoulders and back curved down again and his arms seemed to settle on the axhandles and he became old, old and bent. He carefully laid the axes on the ground and bent for the log. He put the two split halves back up in the stack, turned so nobody would see them. Then he picked up the axes and carried them to the granary and put them away and came out, spit in the snow once and walked to the house, bent and old and tired and down.

We watched him through the crack all that time. Watched him walk until he was gone inside the house, the two of us crying, and that night when chores were done and we'd eaten a big supper we went into the living room and Uncle David told us about Alida. Then he told a tale about a man who lived in the forest who was so ugly he couldn't be seen and he sent messages of love to a girl on the wing feathers of birds and Wayne listened and I listened and I knew we would listen for always.